FROM THE PAGES OF
COMMON SENSE AND OTHER WRITINGS

That some desperate wretches should be willing to steal and enslave men by violence and murder for gain, is rather lamentable than strange. (from "African Slavery in America," page 5)

Society is produced by our wants, and government by our wickedness. (from "Common Sense," page 17)

There is another and greater distinction for which no truly natural or religious reason can be assigned, and that is the distinction of men into KINGS and SUBJECTS. Male and female are the distinctions of nature, good and bad the distinctions of Heaven; but how a race of men came into the world so exalted above the rest, and distinguished like some new species, is worth inquiring into, and whether they are the means of happiness or of misery to mankind.
(from "Common Sense," pages 22–23)

When we are planning for posterity, we ought to remember that virtue is not hereditary. (from "Common Sense," page 54)

These are the times that try men's souls.
(from "The Crisis," page 73)

Tyranny, like hell, is not easily conquered; yet we have this consolation with us, that the harder the conflict, the more glorious the triumph. What we obtain too cheap, we esteem too lightly: it is dearness only that gives every thing its value.
(from "The Crisis," page 73)

Every child born into the world must be considered as deriving its existence from God. The world is as new to him as it was to the first man that existed, and his natural right in it is of the same kind.

(from "Rights of Man," page 128)

When it is laid down as a maxim, that *a King can do no wrong*, it places him in a state of similar security with that of ideots and persons insane, and responsibility is out of the question with respect to himself.   (from "Rights of Man," page 164)

All national institutions of churches, whether Jewish, Christian, or Turkish, appear to me no other than human inventions set up to terrify and enslave mankind, and monopolize power and profit.

(from "The Age of Reason," page 258)

When authors and critics talk of the sublime, they see not how nearly it borders on the ridiculous.

(from "The Age of Reason," page 319)

The present state of civilization is as odious as it is unjust. It is absolutely the opposite of what it should be, and it is necessary that a revolution should be made in it. The contrast of affluence and wretchedness continually meeting and offending the eye, is like dead and living bodies chained together.

(from "Agrarian Justice," page 339)

As laws may be bad as well as good, an empire of laws may be the best of all governments or the worst of all tyrannies.

(from "Letters to American Citizens," page 352)

COMMON SENSE AND OTHER WRITINGS

THOMAS PAINE

With an Introduction and Notes
by Joyce Appleby

GEORGE STADE

CONSULTING EDITORIAL DIRECTOR

NEW YORK

B
BARNES & NOBLE CLASSICS
NEW YORK

Published by Barnes & Noble Books
122 Fifth Avenue
New York, NY 10011

www.barnesandnoble.com/classics

The works in this volume were originally published from 1775 to 1803.

Published in 2005 by Barnes & Noble Classics with new Introduction, Notes,
Biography, Chronology, Inspired By, Comments & Questions,
and For Further Reading.

Introduction, Notes, and For Further Reading
Copyright © 2005 by Joyce Appleby.

Note on Frances Thomas Paine, The World of
Thomas Paine and His Writings, Inspired by Thomas Paine
and His Writings, and Comments & Questions
Copyright © 2005 by Barnes & Noble, Inc.

Common Sense and Other Writings
ISBN-10: 1-59308-209-6
ISBN-13: 978-1-59308-209-3
LC Control Number 2005922117

Produced and published in conjunction with:
Fine Creative Media, Inc.
322 Eighth Avenue
New York, NY 10001

Michael J. Fine, President and Publisher

Printed in the United States of America

QM

1   3   5   7   9   10   8   6   4   2

FIRST PRINTING

THOMAS PAINE

Thomas Paine was born in the village of Thetford in Norfolk, England, on January 29, 1737, the son of Joseph Pain, a Quaker who made stays for women's corsets, and Frances Cocke, the daughter of a lawyer. Tom attended the village grammar school, where he showed an early talent for poetry, mathematics, and the natural sciences. At age thirteen he was put to work as an apprentice to his father. Upon the outbreak of the Seven Years War with France in 1756, he ran off to sea, enlisting as a crewman on a privateer; his father stopped him from boarding that ship, but he served as a crewman on another for six months, returning to England in August 1757. While in London he pursued his interest in natural science, attending lectures at the Royal Society.

Paine returned to staymaking, first in Dover, then, in 1759, setting up his own business in Sandwich, Kent. Subsequently he secured a position as an excise officer in Lincolnshire, collecting taxes from merchants and smugglers, but was discharged in 1765. He returned to staymaking again briefly, then in 1766 took a teaching position in London for a few months. In May of that year he was readmitted into the Excise Service and in early 1768 was appointed as an excise officer at Lewes, Sussex, where he remained for the next six years. He found his political voice as a representative for his fellow excise officers in their petition to Parliament for better wages, writing *The Case of the Officers of Excise* (1772); he spent several months in London distributing copies of his pamphlet, to no avail. During his time there he was admitted into a distinguished circle of intellectuals and political thinkers that included English historian Edward Gibbon and Benjamin Franklin, America's colonial agent for Pennsylvania.

In 1774 Paine was again dismissed from the excise service. At age thirty-seven, he had failed at every enterprise and was virtually penniless. At Franklin's urging, and with his letter of recommendation, Paine immigrated to Philadelphia in the fall of 1774. Arriving in the thick of political tumult, he found work as an editor at the *Pennsylvania Magazine* and wrote articles condemning British tyranny. Impassioned by the revolutionary zeal around him and the outbreak of war, Paine published *Common Sense* in January 1776 to enormous popularity. The pamphlet's clear and powerful argument for American independence from Great Britain sounded the revolutionary call as the voice of the common citizen. He followed with the first of his *American Crisis Papers* (1776–1783). "These are the times that try men's souls," he began, in an address so inspiring that General George Washington had it read to his troops. But Paine was not merely a propagandist; his articles were brilliantly reasoned, and he gained the ear of the Revolutionary leadership. A prolific writer, he published influential essays on political theory, the war effort, foreign affairs, taxes, and monetary policy. His influence grew as the war progressed, and he was rewarded upon victory with secretarial posts in the new government.

In 1787 Paine traveled to Europe, sometimes acting as an unofficial envoy of the American government. The bloody outbreak of the French Revolution in 1789 shocked the monarchy and many progressive reformers in Britain, but Paine vigorously defended it. In 1791 he published the first part of *Rights of Man* (the second appeared in 1792), articulating the political necessity of the revolution in France and calling for the English to establish a constitutional democracy. The pamphlet was wildly successful; in response, in May 1792 the English government charged Paine with seditious libel and issued a warrant for his arrest. Before his case came to trial Paine left for France, never to return to England, where he was tried and convicted of treason in absentia.

Paine was made an honorary delegate to the National Convention and helped frame a new French constitution. He did not escape the Reign of Terror led by Maximilien Robespierre; in 1793 Paine was arrested as an enemy of France and sentenced to death. Shortly before his imprisonment, he finished writing the first part of *The Age of Reason* (1794), an essay attacking organized religion and the Bible. He spent ten months in prison until James Monroe, the American minister to France, secured his release in late 1794. Seriously ill, he stayed at Monroe's home to recuperate and finished writing the second part of *The Age of Reason* (1796).

Paine remained in France for seven more years, fearing arrest or seizure should he attempt a return to England or America. In 1797 he published his last major work, *Agrarian Justice*, and for the next few years attempted to advise Napoleon Bonaparte. But life abroad had become less and less tenable, and when Paine's old friend Thomas Jefferson, newly elected president of the United States, offered him safe passage on an American warship, he returned to his adopted country in 1802.

But America had changed since he had left in 1787. Political partisanship was rife. And Paine found that through a number of his radical views—his attack on religion with *The Age of Reason*, in particular—he had alienated many of his former friends. *Common Sense* and the climate in which it had been written seemed all but forgotten. Without family or many close friends and in poor health, he spent his remaining years in New York City and at his farm in New Rochelle, continuing his polemical writing nonetheless. Thomas Paine died on June 8, 1809.

TABLE OF CONTENTS

THE WORLD OF THOMAS PAINE
AND HIS WRITINGS

1737   Thomas Paine is born in the English village of Thetford, in Norfolk, on January 29, to Joseph Pain, a Quaker staymaker, and Frances Cocke.

1743   Thomas Jefferson, third president of the United States, is born.

1748   Charles-Louis de Montesquieu publishes *The Spirit of Laws*, advocating government with separation of powers.

1750   Joseph Pain takes Tom out of grammar school, employing him in his staymaking shop in Thetford.

1756   The Seven Years War between England and France breaks out. Tom runs away from home, enlisting for work on a privateer, but his father prevents him from boarding ship.

1757   Paine lives in London working as a staymaker. He attends lectures on science and mathematics. He joins the crew of another privateer, the *King of Prussia*, disembarking in August of that year.

1759   Paine sets up a modest staymaking business in Sandwich, Kent. In September he marries his first wife, Mary Lambert, a maid. Voltaire's *Candide* is published.

1760   Mary Lambert dies. Paine studies in preparation for a post as an excise officer.

1764   Paine begins work as the tax collector for the town of Alford, in Lincolnshire, but continues his study of science.

1765   Fired from his position as tax collector, Paine works again as a staymaker.

1766   In London, Paine takes a job teaching English. The British Parliament repeals the Stamp Act, relieving tensions with the American colonies.

1767   Paine applies to be readmitted to the Excise Service.

1768   Paine is commissioned as tax collector for the village of
        Lewes, Sussex. He joins a political debating club, where he
        gains a reputation for acute reasoning and obstinate opin-
        ions.

1771   In a marriage of convenience, he weds Elizabeth Ollive, the
        daughter of his deceased landlord, inheriting the manage-
        ment duties of her father's shop.

1772   While petitioning Parliament on behalf of his fellow excise
        men, Paine writes and prints his first pamphlet, *The Case of
        the Officers of Excise*. Through his friend George Scott, a
        mathematician, Paine joins an intellectual crowd in London
        that includes Edward Gibbon, Samuel Johnson, and Ben-
        jamin Franklin.

1773   The Boston Tea Party takes place in Boston, Massachusetts.

1774   The 1772 petition fails, and Paine is dismissed again from his
        position as an excise officer. He is impoverished, and his
        goods are auctioned. In June Paine separates from his wife,
        Elizabeth. In November he emigrates from Britain to the
        American colonies, arriving on November 30 with an intro-
        duction from Benjamin Franklin. The First Continental
        Congress meets in Philadelphia. Paine writes "Dialogue Be-
        tween General Wolfe and General Gage in a Wood Near
        Boston" for the local newspaper.

1775   In March Paine publishes "African Slavery in America," an
        article denouncing the hypocrisy of the American slave
        trade. In April the American Revolution begins at the Bat-
        tle of Lexington. In October Paine publishes *A Serious
        Thought*, in which he predicts American independence from
        Britain.

1776   On January 10 Paine publishes *Common Sense* as an anony-
        mous fifty-page pamphlet that denounces the British
        monarch and monarchy in general. Its popularity is enor-
        mous; more than 150,000 copies are printed. Adam Smith
        publishes *The Wealth of Nations*. The Second Continental
        Congress signs the Declaration of Independence. George
        Washington commands the Continental Army. Paine volun-
        teers for the army, working as a secretary to General Nathanael
        Greene. Following a string of defeats by the British, Paine re-

turns to Philadelphia, where he writes the first of his *American Crisis Papers*.

1777 As Paine continues writing the *Crisis Papers*, his influence with the leaders of the Revolution grows.

1778 Paine is appointed secretary to the Committee for Foreign Affairs and continues the *Crisis Papers*. France allies with America, thanks to the efforts of Benjamin Franklin.

1779 Amid controversy over his attacks on war profiteers, Paine resigns from his post as secretary to the Committee for Foreign Affairs and is appointed clerk to the Pennsylvania Assembly.

1780 Paine works toward the creation of a bank to finance the war effort. He continues the *Crisis Papers* and is awarded an honorary degree from the University of Pennsylvania. He publishes a pamphlet, *Public Good*.

1781 The leader of British forces, General Charles Cornwallis, surrenders to General George Washington, ending military conflict.

1782 The new government enlists Paine as a propagandist, agitating for the Articles of Confederation. He publishes essays 10, 11, and 12 of the *Crisis Papers*.

1783 The Treaty of Paris formally ends the war. Paine petitions the new government for a pension. He writes *A Supernumerary Crisis*.

1785 Paine is granted $3,000 by Congress in recognition of his service to the nation.

1787 Paine travels to Europe.

1788 In England, Paine secures a patent for an iron bridge design. He corresponds with Edmund Burke. The Marquis de Lafayette drafts "Declaration of the Rights of Man and the Citizen."

1789 The United States Constitution, ratified in 1788, takes effect. The French Revolution begins at the Bastille in Paris.

1791 In England, Paine publishes the first part of *Rights of Man*, in part a response to Edmund Burke's *Reflections on the Revolution in France* (1790). The treatise is banned, yet more than 200,000 copies are sold in England alone.

1792 Fleeing charges of treason, Paine goes to France. The second part of *Rights of Man* is published. Paine is made an honorary French citizen and a delegate to the National Convention.

1793   The Reign of Terror begins in France. Paine is declared an enemy of France and is arrested by Maximilien Robespierre.

1794   Robespierre is executed, ending the Reign of Terror. Paine publishes *The Age of Reason* to great controversy. James Monroe, the newly appointed American minister to France, secures Paine's release from prison.

1795   The essay "Dissertations on First Principles of Government" is published.

1796   The second part of *The Age of Reason* is published. Paine's influence with the American leadership wanes following articles attacking Washington and America.

1797   Paine's last major treatise, *Agrarian Justice*, is published.

1799   George Washington dies.

1802   Paine returns to America. He publishes open letters attacking the Federalist government.

1803   The American government purchases the Louisiana Territory from France. Paine divides his time between New York City and his farm in New Rochelle. His health begins a long decline.

1809   Thomas Paine dies on June 8.

INTRODUCTION

Thomas Paine, one of America's most illustrious immigrants, arrived in Philadelphia at the end of 1774 with high hopes, no money, and a letter of introduction from Benjamin Franklin. Like many who had already decamped from Great Britain to the colonies, Paine left behind him a record of failure with frequent job switches, multiple bankruptcies, and two marriages ending in death and separation. At age thirty-seven, he was an obscure figure, no different in his outward aspect from the hundreds of men and women who sailed into Philadelphia every year. But Paine brought with him powerful talents and a forceful personality. Quickly he secured a writing job and gained access to the liveliest political circles in the colonies' preeminent city. The publication of *Common Sense* (1776) fourteen months later turned him into a celebrity. During the next two decades, Paine inspired his admirers and vexed his critics with the publication of *Rights of Man* (1791–1792), *The Age of Reason* (1794), and *Agrarian Justice* (1797).

The port city where Paine disembarked had far fewer people than London, but it radiated prosperity. Within the previous two decades a building boom had doubled the number of houses. It abounded with petty enterprises, wide open to all comers with a dynamism not to be found in all of Great Britain. The presence of enslaved men and women shocked Paine, but the numerous servants, day laborers, and apprentices signaled to him the success of this busy hub in Britain's far-flung commerce. The English Quaker leader and founder of the Pennsylvania colony William Penn had laid out his green country town in a grid pattern situated between the Schuykill and Delaware Rivers. A century of sustained development had filled in the space with wharves, warehouses, and workshops where artisans, their family members, and servants crowded into the upper floors. New town houses attested to the wealth of some merchants and crown officials who distinguished themselves from others with their elegant dress, handsome carriages, and liveried servants. Yet political participation had broadened widely in the 1750s and '60s. And if Benjamin Franklin's career can serve as a gauge, ambition had few checks when mixed with determination, talent, and the capacity for hard work.

The self-made man who moved smartly from apprentice to journeyman to master and possibly beyond to become an entrepreneur, like Franklin, held up a model for Paine. The animation and intelligence he exuded undoubtedly account for the fact that Franklin, then in England serving as a colonial agent, gave Paine a letter of introduction to his son-in-law, in which he wrote that Paine was "an ingenious worthy young man" suitable for employment as "a clerk or school teacher."[1] Franklin and Paine, both sons of artisans and apprenticed in their early teens, had many things in common: a keen interest in the new science, zeal to work for the betterment of society, and a fine writing style. Yet they differed in one striking characteristic: Franklin strove to fit into the social order, while Paine raged at its injustices. Franklin had arrived in Philadelphia from Boston a generation earlier and had worked tirelessly to find a niche for himself as a printer and shopkeeper. Franklin was an assiduous self-improver who acquired the personal habits that would appeal to others, particularly his social superiors. He too brought letters of introduction that he used to cultivate patrons. His only challenge to the inherited, serried ranks that organized families in the Anglo-American world was to outshine everyone else in knowledge, enterprise, and political connections.

The contrast only became more apparent as time passed. Paine failed in business. He did not establish a family, and he remained indifferent to the refined tastes that conferred respectability. He was as voracious a reader as Franklin, self-taught as well in natural philosophy, mathematics, and mechanics, but the driving spirits of Franklin and Paine pointed them in opposite directions. Paine had none of Franklin's equanimity. Perhaps there was a time when he would have gladly fit in, but the hardships he encountered as a corsetmaker, seaman, collector of the excise, and sometime tutor predisposed him to rage at the privileges and preferential treatment accorded the great men he saw all around him in England. Paine galvanized his considerable talents to tear down the walls that the upper class had raised against ordinary persons. One might have expected the self-made man of the New World to become the agent for radical change, but it was the outcast from the Old World who saw in his adopted home the chance "to build the world anew."

Paine was a persuasive speaker and vigorous debater. These qualities, always in short supply, had gained him entrance into reform circles in England. How much more in demand were these traits in the colonies, where even the most prominent men and women knew themselves to be cut off from the sophisticated tastes of Europe. One can imagine him, with his quick wit, describing the conversations he partook of in London. Franklin once gave vent to the provincial's sense of deprivation when he wrote that of all the things he loved about England, "I envy it most its people." "Why should that petty island," he asked, "which compared to America, is but like a stepping-stone in a brook, scarce enough of it above water to keep one's shoes dry; why, I say, should that little island enjoy in almost every neighborhood, more sensible, virtuous, and elegant Minds, than we can collect in ranging two leagues of our vast Forest?"[2]

Mingling a bit with the "sensible, virtuous, and elegant minds" of Great Britain had given Paine a chance to test through conversation the ideas he gleaned from his readings. Men and women were still grappling with the implications of the revolutionary concept of nature propounded by Sir Isaac Newton, in which cause and effect trumped royal will, religious authority, and popular superstitions. During his youth, Paine had saved all the money he could from his meager income to pay for books, scientific equipment, and entrance fees to scientific lectures. For him, Newton's brilliance had greatly enhanced the reputation of all human reasoning. Paine crafted reason into a potent weapon to wield against those who insisted that men were too weak to govern themselves, making it likely that the world would continue as it always had. The new science led thinkers to question the assumptions of conservatives. Far from distinct areas, science and politics were inextricably bound up together in Paine's mind, the former offering hope for reforming the latter.

When talk turned to politics in English taverns and parlors, the much-vaunted British constitution often came up. England's Glorious Revolution of 1688 had led to a constitutional monarchy and a government respectful of the rights of Englishmen, with the king-in-Parliament as the sovereign. French intellectuals, chafing at the arbitrary rule of their kings, carried away from visits to England profound respect for the freedom of speech and protection from arbitrary arrest there. Signs in front of royal palaces—"trespassers will be prosecuted"—captured the difference between a king under the law and an absolute monarch. In England suspected criminals were prosecuted, not thrown into prison without a trial.

European admiration for England's balanced government of king, nobles, and commons (that is, commoners) complicated matters for opponents of the British government like Paine. They took a much more jaundiced view of the English institutions they were forced to cope with in practice rather than discuss in theory. Aristocratic privileges and restricted access to votes and offices gave the lie to the ideal of commoners' participation. The fourteenth-century distribution of seats in Parliament, which still prevailed in Paine's day, gave seats to empty spaces—the "rotten boroughs," that is, election districts with few inhabitants—while leaving populous new manufacturing cities without representation. All these things rankled with Paine, who viewed England's government as corrupt and unjust. He did not arrive in the American colonies as an informal ambassador of the mother country, but rather as a bitter critic, as the next few months would reveal.

Paine's religious background played a part in shaping his radical sensibilities. His mother belonged to the established Church of England, but he was reared with the Quaker convictions of his father's family.[3] Influence is always an elusive force in a person's life, but there seems little doubt that the Society of Friends' recent proscription of slavery readied him to become slavery's ardent opponent in America. One in six Philadelphia households contained at least one slave. Franklin owned four of the city's some 1,500 slaves.[4] Within a year Paine joined the Pennsylvania Antislavery Society and wrote "African Slavery in America" (1775) which appeared in the *Pennsylvania Journal and the Weekly Advertiser*, excoriating those who participated in the "savage practice . . . contrary to the light of nature, to every principle of Justice and Humanity, and even good policy" (p. 5). Always quick to get to the point, Paine may have been the first person publicly to advocate emancipation. In his journal article, he was particularly effective in dismissing claims of biblical support for slavery. After becoming the new editor of the *Pennsylvania Magazine*, he wrote about the treatment of Indians and women. All the arguments over rights and abuses he had been carrying on for two decades now became the subjects of essays. A man with many arrows in his quiver, Paine also composed humorous verses, scientific treatises, and a ballad for the journal. In a matter of months he had honed his straightforward, lucid, and cogent prose. The epigrams, metaphors, and barbs that peppered his essays seem to have come naturally.

Paine's first publication, a plea to Parliament for salary raises for the underpaid excise men—*The Case of the Officers of Excise* (1772)— only got him sacked, but "African Slavery in America" led in five years to an invitation to compose the preamble to an act providing for the gradual abolition of slavery. In 1780 Pennsylvania passed a landmark piece of legislation, the world's first abolition law, and Paine had the satisfaction of reading it aloud to the Pennsylvania Assembly in his capacity as clerk. Other northern states followed suit, and by 1801 slavery had been put on the course toward extinction in that part of America. The Mason-Dixon Line, the boundary that a team of surveyors laid between Pennsylvania and Maryland, now demarked something even more portentous: the division between free and slave labor in the United States.

Paine's reputation over the course of two centuries has stressed the impact of *Common Sense* on America. Less attention has been paid to how colonial society affected Paine. Exhilarated by the absence of noblemen whose conspicuous opulence and haughty manners vivified for him the unjust hierarchies in England, Paine felt immediately at home in America. The wealthy in Philadelphia were but pale imitations of the English aristocracy. Indeed he became the friend of many of them. Here no group had a monopoly of places of honor and power, as Franklin's career had demonstrated. Paine loved the free exchanges in daily life, the easy mingling of men and women on the city's streets. He even found a different kind of cosmopolitanism to boast about in this provincial outpost: the integration of diverse ethnic groups in Pennsylvania. An inadvertent tolerance had sprung up that showed that people might live in peace despite the enmities fostered by patriotic bombast and religious zeal. Americans were cosmopolitan because they had surmounted local prejudices. They regarded people from different nations as their countrymen and ignored neighborhoods, towns, and counties, he noted, as "distinctions too limited for Continental minds" (p. 34). And of course Paine's success in finding a position of responsibility and an outlet for his writings could only have enhanced his enthusiasm for his new country.

No more propitious moment for a Thomas Paine to arrive in British North America could be imagined than the end of 1774. The colonies had been resisting the British government's new measures for regulating its empire for more than eight years. They had opposed new taxes and changes in admiralty law, as well as new restrictions on their trade. They had recoiled at invasions of their legislative prerogatives, but all to no avail. British reactions to their protests had demonstrated to colonial leaders that they had neither the power nor influence to budge king or Parliament. While they inveighed in vain for "no taxation without representation," the rights of Englishmen that they had so long extolled began to seem hollow. British officials appeared determined to retract the informal autonomy the colonies had long enjoyed in the interest of making the empire run better—better, that was, for the mother country.

In the year before Paine's arrival, a group of Bostonians had stealthily boarded three British ships laded with tea and thrown the cargo into the harbor to protest the detested tax on tea. Great Britain retaliated with punitive laws, closing the port of Boston, proscribing town meetings in Massachusetts, and ordering the billeting of British soldiers in colonial homes. In September 1774 delegates from every colony except Georgia arrived in Philadelphia for what they called the Continental Congress, a rather startling appellation coming from twelve sparsely settled colonies located between the Appalachian Mountains and the Atlantic Ocean. Despite divisions of opinion, the delegates managed to agree to boycott all trade with Great Britain as a way of insisting on their rights under "the principles of the English constitution." An order for all colonies to form militias of citizen soldiers signaled their seriousness. In response, George III declared that the colonies were in a state of rebellion.

Like a metal filing drawn to a magnet, Paine found the places where Philadelphians gathered to debate the issue of the colonies' relations with Great Britain. There he heard the array of positions circulating during these tense months. He learned of the deep pride most colonists felt for their British citizenship. Local officials regularly took oaths of loyalty to the king and were loath to break them. And the status of Americans as colonists made many timid in the face of the grandeur, might, and legitimacy of the British crown. All of this was anathema to Paine, for whom familiarity with the English King and his grandees had bred contempt.[5]

In the ensuing year, Great Britain beefed up its military position in the colonies, sending instructions to the new governor to disarm the Massachusetts militia and arrest the leaders of the resistance movement. From these orders came the "shot heard round the world" (the phrase is from Ralph Waldo Emerson's 1837 poem "The Concord Hymn"), when minutemen stood their ground before the British redcoats at Lexington in April 1775. But even with this spilling of blood, many colonists recoiled from using force and pledged their devotion to Great Britain. As loyalists, they stepped up their campaign to isolate the radicals—they argued that more resistance would only bring down the ferocious wrath of Great Britain. Loyalists and patriots continued to argue while the Second Continental Congress meeting in May 1775 began actually to govern the colonies.

Common Sense, with its defiant call for independence, electrified readers when it appeared in January 1776. Its incredible success can best be understood in the context of the excruciating indecision that had gripped the colonists. While there were radical leaders prepared to push for independence—for instance, Samuel and John Adams— too many men and women were apprehensive, not just about the dangers of a struggle for independence, but about the rightness of such a move. The British officials had a closed case from their point of view. The rights of Englishmen were protected by Parliament, and Parliament had rejected the Americans' interpretation of their place in the empire. *Common Sense* ministered to the deep longing for clarity in those who had lived in a high state of unresolved agitation for more than a decade.

Paine was not a profound thinker. He was more a vector for the radical theorizing about the origins of government that Thomas

Hobbes and John Locke began in the seventeenth century. In Paine's day these heady ideas had bounced back to England from French *philosophes* like Montesquieu, Voltaire, and Rousseau, who were wrestling with the problems of monarchical absolutism. European thinkers in the eighteenth century also wrote eloquently about how to reform penal codes, abolish slavery, and eradicate privilege. Paine had taken this all in, mixed it with his rage at the way English institutions thwarted the ambitions of ordinary men, and discovered in the American struggle "the cause of all mankind" (p. 13).

Paine stirred readers with the pungent prose of a Speaker's Corner incendiary. He blended righteous indignation and grandiosity, even going so far as to implicate providence in the cause by suggesting that the "Reformation was preceded by the discovery of America: As if the Almighty graciously meant to open a sanctuary to the persecuted" (p. 35). He elevated the decisions of a group of provincials on the remote side of the Atlantic to enduring fame: "'Tis not the concern of a day, a year, or an age; posterity are virtually involved in the contest, and will be more or less affected even to the end of time, by the proceedings now" (p. 31).

An instant best-seller, *Common Sense* cut through the language of deference with the scalpel of analysis. Paine revealed the practicality of supporting American independence. He also provided a moral justification for armed resistance by linking American independence to progressive forces at loose in the world—or at least Western Europe! Effective without being orderly, *Common Sense* exudes a haste that heightens the urgency of his appeal. One can imagine Paine coming home from the tavern after an evening of contentious debates on the merits of independence and furiously writing down answers to the arguments he had just heard. When he could contain them no longer, he poured his points into his pamphlet: Monarchy is without biblical warrant; the English monarchy, in particular, has failed the colonies; the very idea of monarchy goes against nature and common sense; commerce in foodstuffs had created a self-sufficient colonial economy; details for building a constitution and navy prove their viability; and finally, the present precious moment for seizing independence is fast disappearing.

Read carefully, *Common Sense* also yields a running attack on the unexamined assumptions of classical republican thought that many

American leaders had imbibed from writings of the English opposition. In this political scheme it was assumed that government was difficult to establish and maintain, and that Britain's special balance of the one, the few, and the many in the shared power of its king, lords, and commons miraculously guaranteed freedom while maintaining order. Fearful of change, classical republicans harked back to a purer time when men—gentlemen like themselves—put the good of the whole before their individual interests. Adhering to the kinds of philosophies that take their inspiration from a previous, golden era, classical republican thinkers lamented the declension of recent times and hoped to check further corruption by rallying the country's leaders to the standard of civic virtue.

Paine dismissed the whole classical republican edifice with his stunning opening lines: "Some writers have so confounded society with government, as to leave little or no distinction between them; whereas they are not only different, but have different origins." "Society," he went on to explain, "is produced by our wants, and government by our wickedness; the former promotes our happiness *possitively* by uniting our affections, the latter *negatively* by restraining our vices" (p. 17). Paine then demonstrated that the English constitutional balance was unnecessarily complicated, and outmoded to boot, its sole utility being that of befuddling disenfranchised subjects of the king. The source of discord in society was not human nature, Paine argued, but the oppression from those given social privileges: "Male and female are the distinctions of nature, good and bad the distinctions of Heaven" (p. 22). The English constitution was "noble for the dark and slavish times in which it was erected" (p. 19). And with this pithy comment he dispatched kings and nobles to the dustbin of history.

The eighteenth-century concept of nature does heavy-duty service in Paine's frontal attack on the English monarchy and its philosophical underpinning in *Common Sense* and all subsequent writings. Paine announced that he had drawn his "idea of the form of government from a principle in nature which no art can overturn, viz. that the more simple any thing is, the less liable it is to be disordered" (p. 19). Indeed, nature comes in to support most of the assertions Paine made in *Common Sense*. Of independence, he wrote, "the simple voice of nature and reason will say, 'tis right" (p. 19). And he offered the shrewd advice that he "who takes nature for his guide, is not easily beaten out of his argument."[6] He offered nature as a contrast to the artifices that had given kings and lords their unwarranted power and intimidating prestige.

Nature had become the handmaiden of most eighteenth-century reformers who contrasted its regularity, simplicity, and beneficence with the Byzantine qualities of their archaic institutions. They drew on a succession of philosophers of nature from Newton through the Scottish economist Adam Smith, who at this time was preparing for publication his *Inquiry into the Nature and Causes of the Wealth of Nations*. In this mighty synthesis, Smith drew together a century of theorizing about the commercial system. With trade generating new levels of wealth, observers began speculating about the dynamics behind this novel system of enterprises and exchanges. Gradually they recast the economy as a natural system working invisibly to produce harmony among buyers and sellers instead of being a hodgepodge of commercial transactions, necessarily subject to political direction.

The reconceptualization of the economy as a natural, unregulated system of exchanges greatly influenced Paine. He saw commerce as an alternative to war in getting people what they wanted. He described it as "a pacific system, operating to cordialise mankind" (p. 233). Self-interest, formerly viewed as a tool of the devil, figured benignly throughout *Common Sense* as a prompter to good reasoning. His opening lines drew a contrast between society, with its voluntary cooperation prompted by mutual interests, and government, with its coercive power used for the benefit of the king and his courtiers. For those living in a hierarchical society where there was much fawning over patrons, self-interest also breathed a spirit of honesty, for when people followed their interest, there was no hint of hypocrisy. Ironically, royal revenue from this ebullient economy that Paine so admired had given the king the money to secure compliant members of Parliament—the corruption that so rankled him.

American readers were undoubtedly more interested in reading what Paine had to say about their situation than his musings about social theory. More than 150,000 copies of *Common Sense* sold within a year at a time when the number of readers in the colonies could not have exceeded 700,000. Editions quickly appeared in London, Edinburgh, Paris, and Copenhagen.[7] Those who were illiterate could listen to Paine's rhetoric read aloud to them in private parlors and public gatherings. Soon everyone was quoting such phrases as "the Continental belt is too loosely buckled" (p. 61) or descriptions of William the Conqueror as "a French bastard landing with an armed Banditti" (p. 27). American colonies, Paine wryly commented, will thrive as long as "eating is the custom of Europe" (p. 32). Although *Common Sense* was published anonymously as "written by an Englishman," readers quickly identified the author as Paine.

An elixir to the spirits of the pro-independence faction, *Common Sense* reached a much larger audience than the pamphlets that had been flowing from colonial presses since the passage of the Stamp Act in 1765. Paine's simple syntax was easy to understand, and his exhilarating bravado was contagious. When he referred to George III as "the Royal Brute of Great Britain," making "a havoc of mankind," readers could hyperventilate over such a seditious statement (p. 44). Judging from contemporary correspondence and diary entries, Paine was responsible for convincing many colonists that independence was not only the best choice, but one that would put them on the side of the angels. As he was to do many times again, Paine had taken ideas out of gentlemen's conversations and pushed them into the public arena for all to talk about.

After Congress declared independence in July 1776, Paine enlisted in a Pennsylvania military outfit, serving as aide-de-camp to General Nathanael Greene. Witness to the disastrous early months of the war, when New York fell and the Continental army fled across New Jersey, Paine took up his pen again to write about the so-called American crisis. Beginning with the famous opening, "These are the times that try men's souls," the dozen or so pieces that constitute *The American Crisis Papers* extended Paine's commentary from 1776 to 1783, when the Treaty of Paris between Great Britain and the United States granted the latter independence. Although Paine's unflagging service won gratitude and respect from Revolutionary leaders, particularly George Washington, his life began to acquire some of the ragged edges it had had in England. Always in debt, he got by with government stipends and awards, a mark of his carelessness with money as well as a generosity that drained his pocket. Paine gave freely to the causes he believed in, donating all of his earnings at one point to the Continental army. He had argued strongly for an international copyright, but he rarely received any royalties from his works, best-sellers that they were. In the aftermath of the war he secured some stipends, and Washington successfully spearheaded an effort to secure a 300-acre estate near New Rochelle, New York, confiscated from a British loyalist, to which Paine would return many years later.

Paine went back to his love of science and mechanics. He designed an innovative 400-foot single-span iron bridge and continued to write in response to postwar issues. Yet Paine was a true revolutionary; peace made him restless. In 1787 he left the United States with a 13-foot model of his bridge, going first to France and then to England, where eventually his bridge was built. Most gratifying to Paine was that his reputation preceded him. He brought back to his birthplace the cachet of both prophet and victor. Many English political figures had reacted with hostility to all things associated with their former colonies, but others had cheered the Americans in their struggle. Edmund Burke, the great Whig leader in Parliament, had judged the Americans right. He cultivated Paine as an expert on the terra incognita of the new United States. Paine did not forget his American friends either. He visited with Thomas Jefferson, who was then serving as minister to France, and corresponded with Washington, Franklin, and Samuel Adams, among others.

As early as 1782 Paine had predicted that the example of the United States would influence the French and English and eventually resonate around the world. He had an acute awareness of the asymmetry of power and of the arbitrariness of actual social arrangements that lay buried, like a land mine, slightly beneath the surface of daily life. His prediction did not take long to come true. While British radicals talked about reform, a fiscal crisis in France actually forced the king, Louis XVI, to convene an unprecedented assembly, followed by the first convocation of the Estates General in more than a century. Backing the American Revolution had broken the royal bank; fixing it created an opening for those who had been inveighing against the government for decades. A series of dramatic events ensued, starting with the fall of the Bastille, the formidable royal prison in the heart of Paris. The great French Revolution had begun and would continue in various permutations until Napoleon Bonaparte came to power a decade later.

With that mine actually exploding, Paine rushed back to France, where he consorted, through Jefferson's connections, with the leaders of the Girondin party—the marquis de Lafayette, the marquis de Condorcet, and Jacques Brissot. Both Lafayette and Brissot had actually been to the United States, and Condorcet had written about it. They were even called *américanistes* because of their opposition to the French *anglomanes* who wanted to copy the British constitution. During these heady days the members of the National Assembly abolished feudal privileges and pressed the king to accept their drastic changes. Lafayette, who was then riding high as the aristocratic champion of radical reform, presented Paine with the key to the Bastille, symbol of oppression, with the request that he forward it to General Washington.

As French leaders drafted the "Declaration of the Rights of Man and the Citizen" (adopted by the National Assembly 1789), their English counterparts recoiled from what they considered dangerous social engineering. Burke especially dreaded any linkage of what was going on in France with possible changes in England. He had reacted strongly to those who earlier had seized on the centenary of the Glorious Revolution to assert the right of the English nation to reform its institutions. Although Burke had supported the American cause, he was actually conservative. At least, the opening events in the French Revolution brought out a deeply conservative side in him. He discerned in rationality an acid that would burn right through the layers of respect and loyalty that he considered the glue holding society together. He hated appeals to the Newtonian nature of consistency and transparency that radicals on both sides of the Atlantic made. Having enjoyed a safe seat in Parliament since 1766, Burke also saw the beauty in Britain's peculiar political traditions.

The thought of seemingly sane men abandoning their time-honored institutions for such chimeras as "liberty, equality, and fraternity" compelled Burke to sound the alarm with his *Reflections on*

the Revolution in France (1790). In a sustained attack on the theories
spawned by the Enlightenment, Burke lectured his readers on true
constitutional principles of kingship in Britain, the true meaning of
the rights of men, and the true principle of social stability. Nothing
if not supremely confident of his understanding of political realities
and the history that produced them, Burke must be credited with
recognizing the difficulties of replacing existing institutions with
innovative ones, a reality that often escaped Paine. In his denuncia-
tion of the rash theories circulating through Europe in his *Reflections on the Revolution in France*, Burke paused long enough to
compose an apotheosis to the beauty of Queen Marie Antoinette.
In an unprecedented invasion of the royal space, a mob had hustled
her from her chambers at Versailles in the summer of 1789, a fact
that Burke reported under the rubric "the outrages against the royal
family, aristocracy, and the clergy."[8]

Burke's tome seemed a worse outrage to Paine, who had re-
sponded as both prophet and patron to the French people's assertion of their rights against the absolutism of the monarchy that
Louis XIV—Louis XVI's great-great-great-grandfather—had
perfected. Many took up their pens to respond to Burke, including Mary Wollstonecraft, whose *Vindication of the Rights of Man*
(her *Vindication of the Rights of Woman* came later) was a public
letter to Burke. Paine caused the greatest stir with *Rights of Man*.
In this, his largest and most important work, he elaborated on the
principles he had introduced in *Common Sense*. Paine was elated
by exactly what horrified Burke—the possibility that the British
might follow the French and discard their ancient institutions.
Precedent reigned supreme with Burke; only arrangements that
had stood the test of time deserved respect. Challenged by criticism of a restricted suffrage, English leaders had conjured up the
idea that those who couldn't vote had given their "tacit agree-
ment" to the laws. It was exactly this ingenious concept that the
Americans had rejected.

The lever Paine chose to upend Burke's position was the irra-
tionality of allowing one generation to make political arrangements in perpetuity, leaving the living tied to the compromises of
their ancestors. Having challenged this assumption, Paine proceeded to detail the rights men carried with them naturally—their

capacity to speak out, believe, think. And yet, it was exactly this competency that the entire edifice of conventional assumptions expressed in literature, laws, and popular entertainment had denied ordinary men and women. Paine viewed France's repudiation of the privileges of the aristocracy and the clergy as evidence of its "regenerating itself from slavery" (p. 136). He described the English as left with customs dating back to William the Conqueror. He could never resist the chance to correct someone's historical facts, and Burke, as a beneficiary of the corrupt system of parliamentary representation that Paine hated, was an especially appealing target.

Rights of Man rambled through political theory, American precedents, English history, and the provisions of the new French constitution. Paine celebrated the French for their success in lifting the dead hand of the past that had been pressing upon their shoulders. He constantly urged the disenfranchised among his readers to insist upon popular sovereignty, universal suffrage, and a truly representative government. It was exactly this proposition, that the English nation had the right to create its own constitution, that so frightened Burke and other conservatives.

Building on Adam Smith's idea of an invisible hand guiding the private acts of men and women to unintended, but beneficent, consequences, Paine in *Rights of Man* dwelt on the natural sociability of human beings that rendered them cooperative. Yearning for much, men and women worked together so they could better serve their needs and wants.

Paine also chided Burke for his indifference to the victims of the *Ancien Régime* (a term used in reference to France under the Bourbon monarchy), like the men who had been languishing in the Bastille before its fall. This attack gave him the opening for addressing Burke's adoring remarks about the Queen. "He is not affected by the reality of distress," Paine noted, because "He pities the plumage, but forgets the dying bird." "His hero or his heroine must be a tragedy-victim expiring in show," he continued, "and not the real prisoner of misery, sliding into death in the silence of a dungeon" (p. 117).

Paine's hope that *Rights of Man* would stir British leaders to respond positively to events in France was quickly dashed. Since

Paine had failed to take the measure of the political nation, he reached out to a new audience among the disenfranchised, using his royalties to print cheap copies of *Rights of Man* that various radical clubs quickly distributed throughout Great Britain. The artisans, storekeepers, and white-collar workers in England were overjoyed by Paine's assertions of their political capacity. They memorized his rhetorical zingers. They delighted in his descriptions of the shenanigans that their "superiors" engaged in to keep them from their legitimate role in the polity. The French, he told them in his "Address and Declaration of the Friends of Universal Peace and Liberty" (1791), "laid the axe to the root of tyranny" and erected their new government "on the sacred hereditary rights of man." They should do the same, Paine urged.

Events in France lured Paine back to where his friends held power. When King Louis XVI attempted to flee the country rather than preside over a constitutional monarchy, Paine and others began to call for a republic. In the midst of this turmoil Burke published a reply to Paine's *Rights of Man* that drew Paine back to London to compose a second part. Not content with advocating the expansion of the suffrage and rationalizing parliamentary representation in England, Paine laid out in the second part of *Rights of Man* an array of radical goals like universal public education, pensions for the aged, state relief for the unemployed, and a graduated income tax.

This time the British government was ready. While various political groups, again with help from Paine's royalties, distributed 100,000 copies of Paine's new work throughout the country, the government charged Paine with seditious libel. With characteristic bravado, Paine wrote, "If, to expose the fraud and imposition of monarchy, and every species of hereditary government—to lessen the oppression of taxes—to propose plans for the education of helpless infancy, and the comfortable support of the aged and distressed . . . and to break the chains of political superstition, and raise degraded man to his proper rank; if these things be libelous, let me live the life of a libeller, and let the name of LIBELLER be engraved on my tomb!"[9] But he returned to France.

In his summary of the case against Paine, the British attorney general played perfectly the role Paine cast for British officials when he described Paine's audience as the ignorant, credulous, and desperate. To inoculate themselves against this affront of stirring up ordinary people, the British government distributed 2 million copies of a cheap tract from Evangelical philanthropist Hannah More urging people to honor the king and fear God.[10] Meanwhile, back in the United States, the French Revolution had brought out the conservatism in many Revolutionary leaders. Under the banner of the Federalists, the men in the first Washington administration rejected any comparison of their revolution with what was going on in France. They turned against Paine. John Quincy Adams, whose father, John Adams, was George Washington's vice president from 1789 to 1797, answered Paine's *Rights of Man* in a series of anonymous essays, signed "Publicola," in a Boston newspaper.

Just as France had its *américanistes* and *anglomanes* when they were writing their first constitution, so did politically aware Americans divide between "Anglomen" and "Gallomen" after France executed the royal family and turned itself into a republic.[11] From 1793 until the 1800 election of Thomas Jefferson, events conspired to embroil Americans in the most fundamental questions about government. Critics of the Washington administration bemoaned its pro-British policies, while the Federalists castigated the French and their American followers. The key issue became how important government was to the maintenance of order. Conservatives claimed that ordinary men were too unruly to handle too much freedom. After all, if they had been so tractable through the ages, why was history replete with tales of riots and rebellions, mayhem and anarchy? Paine's answer was ingenious. People were naturally self-regulating if given a chance to cultivate their reason and independence through the exercise of free choice. It was government, with its abusive control, that was responsible for this record of discord.

The British prosecution of Paine turned him into a hero in Paris. He was elected to a seat in the National Convention, the latest legislative embodiment of the French nation. But events swept Paine's French associates onto the wrong side of history. The Jacobins rose to power and dispatched their opponents to the guillotine during the Reign of Terror (1793–1794). The Jacobins also arrested Paine as an enemy alien; France and England were now at war. Just before entering Luxembourg Prison, Paine gave his friend Joel Barlow, an American poet, the manuscript for *The Age of Reason*, yet one more outraged and outrageous attack on the status quo.

Paine spent ten months incarcerated before James Monroe, the new American minister to France and an ardent supporter of the French Revolution, rescued him. Seriously ill at the time of his release, Paine convalesced in Monroe's home, where he completed the second part of *The Age of Reason*.

Perhaps more than any other of his writings, *The Age of Reason* resonates today because the issues of revelation, human divinity, and the contradictory claims of the world's religions that Paine addressed are still being debated. He started off his tract on religion flying his colors: "My own mind is my own church" (p. 258). From that declaration, Paine plowed into the thicket of biblical exegesis. He blithely compared the gospels with Greek mythology because both involved divinities visiting the earth. Revelation, he argued, could happen only to the person to whom God was revealed. For all others, the account was mere hearsay. Perhaps the most radical aspect of his discourse on his faith was the jaunty way he wrote about beliefs that most of his contemporaries considered sacred. Declaring himself a Deist, Paine acknowledged the existence of God and of an afterlife. The evidence of a creator was the creation of the world itself, he believed. The argument for the existence of God from design had been talked about for a long time, but Paine, with his usual flair, reached a larger audience with his promotion of this religious position. What Paine took on faith was the orderliness of nature and the existence of a divine design. Introducing people to this creation-centered religion was, for Paine, another way of unshackling them from the outworn ideas that restricted their God-given potential to develop freely.

Paine maintained that moribund ideas acted like chains binding the imagination of his contemporaries. As his many writings attest, he knew the Bible thoroughly. Along with Shakespeare's plays, the Bible represented the one literary resource that all the people knew. It was read aloud every Sunday. What he had come to detest was the literal interpretation of the Bible used by conservatives to repel reform and instill the fear of change in credulous people. Leaders, in

Paine's view, should be fighting superstition, not pandering to people's fears. Education, not indoctrination, would erase their ignorance and timidity in tandem. Like most Enlightenment reformers, Paine was more anticlerical than antireligious. He abhorred established religions that operated as a monopoly of religious truths. Equally, he rejected the claims of all religions, relishing the observation that their pretensions—whether about Jesus, Muhammad, or Moses—were contradictory.

Paine stayed on in France for the next seven years, fearing arrest if he went to England or seizure on the high seas were he to attempt to return to the United States. He maintained his position of respect, even presenting various plans to Napoleon Bonaparte, who had come to power following the successive downfalls of the Girondists, Jacobins, and the Directory. In 1797 Paine published *Agrarian Justice*, his last major work. Emblazoned on the title page was the proposition that every person at age twenty-one should receive fifteen pounds sterling "to enable HIM or HER to begin the World!" (p. 323). A radical proposition, Paine's scheme was integral to his critique of private property within. In the beginning the world was "*the common property of the human race*," he announced (p. 332), an assertion that John Locke had popularized in the seventeenth century. People who improved property added greatly to the wealth and comforts of modern society, but they should, Paine argued, pay a ground rent, since that property originally belonged to all. It was from the revenues of this rent that Paine projected financing his gift to those passing into adulthood.

What *The Age of Reason* was to religious fidelity, *Agrarian Justice* was to political and economic orthodoxy. Paine's goal was to eliminate existing inequalities in wealth and make the interests of all people converge with those of the nation. Here his peculiar blend of liberal and democratic convictions appears most salient. He believed in economic freedom and limited government. He was no socialist, but his indignation about poverty compelled him to devise ways to invest everyone with some stake in society. Always ahead of his time, he went on in *Agrarian Justice* to propose social insurance for the aged and public welfare programs financed through progressive taxation. To demonstrate the reasonableness of these proposals, he detailed with typical brio the historical trajectory of civilization from the equal state within Indian tribes to the egregious social distances of contemporary society.

An invitation from the newly elected Jefferson offering Paine passage on an American warship proved decisive. In 1802 Paine sailed back to an America quite different from the one he had left fourteen years earlier. Both Washington and Franklin were now dead. Partisan warfare between the Federalists and their Democratic-Republican opponents had replaced the cooperation among the patriot leaders during the Revolution. Jefferson's election had been accompanied by a campaign filled with vituperation. Publication of *The Age of Reason*, which Paine had dedicated to the citizens of the United States, had wrecked his reputation, especially among the Federalists. The *New England Palladium* greeted news of Paine's return by characterizing him as "that lying, drunken, brutal infidel who enjoyed the opportunity of basking and wallowing in the confusion, devastation, bloodshed, rapine, and murder, in which his soul delights." A century later Theodore Roosevelt called Paine "that filthy little atheist."[12]

The Federalists convinced themselves that the success of the Jeffersonians was ephemeral and that people would come to their senses soon. Paine's radicalism, they believed, was out of step with the sentiments of the American people, many of whom had been swept up in the religious revivals that were changing the spiritual complexion of the United States. Attacking Paine was one way of getting at Jefferson, who was associated with him in the public mind. And they were probably right, but somehow Jefferson remained popular while Paine remained controversial. Ever the polemicist, Paine plunged into politics with his year-long series *To the Citizens of the United States*, in which he excoriated the Federalists' betrayal of what he and the Jeffersonians considered the true principles of the American Revolution.

Far from backing away from the sentiments in *The Age of Reason*, he carried on a running war with his critics in published letters that continued his examination of biblical prophecies and introduced new themes like the use of dreams in the New Testament. With one of his best-known proselytes, Elihu Palmer, a free-thinking former Presbyterian clergyman and fellow Deist, Paine founded a theistic church in New York City. Palmer's journal, *The Prospect; or, View of the Moral World*, offered Paine an outlet for his never-ending stream of commentary and polemics. He also found a new friend in inventor Robert Fulton, who shared Paine's love of mechanics, science, Deism, and democracy with almost equal fervor.

Paine was useful to the Federalists as a brush for painting Jefferson as an infidel, but America was essential to Paine. Upon his return, he hailed the United States as "the country of my heart, and the place of my political and literary birth" (p. 367). True enough, but there was more. The success of ordinary men and women establishing a society with protected rights, open opportunity, widespread property ownership, religious freedom, and no political privileges or social distinctions was all the proof Paine needed to hammer home the truth that the future would be different. More than anyone else, Paine made America "the cause of all mankind" and used its example to show how to make good on the Enlightenment promise that people born with a capacity for benign self-direction could work out their own destinies and bring into existence a world that reflected the fulfillment of desire rather than a compromise with despair.

Paine had been ill several years before his death in 1809. He was buried on his farm in New Rochelle. Having seen his ideas ignite people all over the world, he lived long enough to taste the bitterness of a younger generation's indifference to his prescriptions. Paine wanted his remains to rest in his adopted country, but another English radical, William Cobbett, had a different scheme. Cobbett had lived in the United States when the Federalists were vilifying Paine and had himself promoted their views in his *Peter Porcupine* essays. Returning to England, Cobbett became a convert to Paine's reforms. He turned his acerbic wit on those who still blocked their adoption twenty-five years after Paine had proposed them. In 1819 Cobbett came back to the United States and, in homage to Paine, dug up his bones for repatriation. Those were Cobbett's intentions, but somewhere along the line the bones got lost.[13]

This was not a fitting tribute to Paine, but an impulse that demonstrates the powerful attachments he had generated among those who were committed to change. And his relevance continued.

In 1821, when Latin America was on the cusp of its great colonial revolutions, an edition of *Common Sense* appeared in Lima. And today, with this new edition of his writings, Paine has moved into the twenty-first century. His fame will persist because his passion for human rights never flagged, and his expression of that passion has proved enduringly contagious. Joel Barlow hit the mark when he said that Paine's writings were "his best life."[14]

***

Joyce Appleby, Professor Emerita at the University of California, Los Angeles, has followed the trajectory of American nation-building in her *Capitalism and a New Social Order: The Republican Vision of the 1790s* (1978), *Inheriting the Revolution: The First Generation of Americans* (2000), *Thomas Jefferson* (2003), and *A Restless Past: History and the American Public* (2004). Past president of the Organization of American Historians, the American Historical Association, and the Society for the History of the Early Republic, she has thought deeply about the complex relationship of the American public with the country's professional historians. Her research on the seventeenth and eighteenth centuries in England, France, and America has focused on the impact of an expanding world market on the way people understood and talked about their society. A revolution in social theory accompanied a revolution in economic activity, according to Appleby, exemplified here in the writings of Thomas Paine.

Notes to the Introduction

1. Philip S. Foner, *The Complete Writings of Thomas Paine*, 2 vols., New York, Citadel Press, 1945, p. xi.
2. Franklin to Mary Stevenson, Philadelphia, March 25, 1763.
3. Peach, *Selections*, p. xi.
4. Gary B. Nash, *First City: Philadelphia and the Forging of Historical Memory*, Philadelphia, University of Pennsylvania Press, 2002, pp. 53–54.
5. Eric Foner, *Tom Paine and Revolutionary America*, New York, Oxford University Press, 1976.
6. Philip Foner, Appendix to *Common Sense* in *The Complete Writings of Thomas Paine*, p. 116.
7. David Powell, *Tom Paine: The Greatest Exile*, London, Croom Helm, 1985, p. 11.
8. Edmund Burke, *Reflections on the Revolution in France*, edited by Thomas H. D. Mahoney, New York, Liberal Arts Press, 1955, pp. 81–83.

9. *Letter Addressed to the Addressers, on the Late Proclamation*, London, 1792, p. 12.

10. Mark Philp, *Paine*, Oxford and New York, Oxford University Press, 1989, pp. 116–118.

11. Joyce Appleby, *Capitalism and a New Social Order: The Republican Vision of the 1790s*, New York, New York University Press, 1984, pp. 59–60.

12. Powell, *Tom Paine*, preface.

13. Michael Foot and Isaac Kramnick, eds., *Thomas Paine Reader*, Harmondsworth, UK, and New York, Penguin Books, 1987, p. 29.

14. Powell, *Tom Paine*, p. 11.

COMMON SENSE AND
OTHER WRITINGS

PUBLISHER'S NOTE

We have elected to preserve Thomas Paine's often erractic typography, regardless of whether it agress with modern usage or even itself (e.g. "Great-Britain" vs. "Great Britain," "controuling" vs. "controlling"), as we feel it best represents the mercurial energy so essential to this storied agitator.

AFRICAN SLAVERY IN AMERICA

[1775]

African Slavery in America.

To Americans.

That some desperate wretches should be willing to steal and enslave men by violence and murder for gain, is rather lamentable than strange. But that many civilized, nay, christianized people should approve, and be concerned in the savage practice, is surprising; and still persist, though it has been so often proved contrary to the light of nature, to every principle of Justice and Humanity, and even good policy, by a succession of eminent men,* and several late publications.

Our Traders in MEN (*an unnatural commodity!*) must know the wickedness of that SLAVE-TRADE, if they attend to reasoning, or the dictates of their own hearts; and such as shun and stiffle all these, wilfully sacrifice Conscience, and the character of integrity to that golden Idol.

The Managers of that Trade themselves, and others, testify, that many of these African nations inhabit fertile countries, are industrious farmers, enjoy plenty, and lived quietly, averse to war, before the Europeans debauched them with liquors, and bribing them against one another; and that these inoffensive people are brought into slavery, by stealing them, tempting Kings to sell subjects, which they can have no right to do, and hiring one tribe to war against another, in order to catch prisoners. By such wicked and inhuman ways the English are said to enslave towards one hundred thousand yearly; of which thirty thousand are supposed to die by barbarous treatment in the first year; besides all that are slain in the unnatural wars excited to take them. So much innocent blood have the Managers and

---

*Dr. Ames, Baxter, Durham, [John] Locke, Carmichael, [Francis] Hutcheson, Montesquieu, and Blackstone, Wallace, etc., etc. Bishop of Gloucester [Author's note].

5

Supporters of this inhuman Trade to answer for to the common Lord of all!

Many of these were not prisoners of war, and redeemed from savage conquerors, as some plead; and they who were such prisoners, the English, who promote the war for that very end, are the guilty authors of their being so; and if they were redeemed, as is alleged, they would owe nothing to the redeemer but what he paid for them.

They show as little Reason as Conscience who put the matter by with saying—"Men, in some cases, are lawfully made Slaves, and why may not these?" So men, in some cases, are lawfully put to death, deprived of their goods, without their consent; may any man, therefore, be treated so, without any conviction of desert? Nor is this plea mended by adding—"They are set forth to us as slaves, and we buy them without farther inquiry, let the sellers see to it." Such men may as well join with a known band of robbers, buy their ill-got goods, and help on the trade; ignorance is no more pleadable in one case than the other; the sellers plainly own how they obtain them. But none can lawfully buy without evidence that they are not concurring with Men-Stealers; and as the true owner has a right to reclaim his goods that were stolen, and sold; so the slave, who is proper owner of his freedom, has a right to reclaim it, however often sold.

Most shocking of all is alledging the Sacred Scriptures to favour this wicked practice. One would have thought none but infidel cavillers would endeavour to make them appear contrary to the plain dictates of natural light, and Conscience, in a matter of common Justice and Humanity; which they cannot be. Such worthy men, as referred to before, judged otherways; MR. BAXTER* declared, *the Slave-Traders should be called Devils, rather than Christians; and that it is a heinous crime to buy them.* But some say, "the practice was permitted to the Jews." To which may be replied,

1. The example of the Jews, in many things, may not be imitated by us; they had not only orders to cut off several nations altogether, but if they were obliged to war with others, and conquered them, to

---

*Richard Baxter, seventeenth-century English nonconformist minister.

cut off every male; they were suffered to use polygamy and divorces, and other things utterly unlawful to us under clearer light.

2. The plea is, in a great measure, false; they had no permission to catch and enslave people who never injured them.

3. Such arguments ill become us, *since the time of reformation came*, under Gospel light. All distinctions of nations, and privileges of one above others, are ceased; Christians are taught to *account all men their neighbours; and love their neighbours as themselves; and do to all men as they would be done by; to do good to all men; and Man-stealing is ranked with enormous crimes.* Is the barbarous enslaving our inoffensive neighbours, and treating them like wild beasts subdued by force, reconcilable with all these *Divine precepts?* Is this doing to them as we would desire they should do to us? If they could carry off and enslave some thousands of us, would we think it just?—One would almost wish they could for once; it might convince more than Reason, or the Bible.

As much in vain, perhaps, will they search ancient history for examples of the modern Slave-Trade. Too many nations enslaved the prisoners they took in war. But to go to nations with whom there is no war, who have no way provoked, without farther design of conquest, purely to catch inoffensive people, like wild beasts, for slaves, is an hight of outrage against Humanity and Justice, that seems left by Heathen nations to be practised by pretended Christians. How shameful are all attempts to colour and excuse it!

As these people are not convicted of forfeiting freedom, they have still a natural, perfect right to it; and the Governments whenever they come should, in justice set them free, and punish those who hold them in slavery.

So monstrous is the making and keeping them slaves at all, abstracted from the barbarous usage they suffer, and the many evils attending the practice; as selling husbands away from wives, children from parents, and from each other, in violation of sacred and natural ties; and opening the way for adulteries, incests, and many shocking consequences, for all of which the guilty Masters must answer to the final Judge.

If the slavery of the parents be unjust, much more is their children's; if the parents were justly slaves, yet the children are born free; this is the natural, perfect right of all mankind; they are nothing but a just recompense to those who bring them up: And as much less is commonly spent on them than others, they have a right, in justice, to be proportionably sooner free.

Certainly one may, with as much reason and decency, plead for murder, robbery, lewdness, and barbarity, as for this practice: They are not more contrary to the natural dictates of Conscience, and feelings of Humanity; nay, they are all comprehended in it.

But the chief design of this paper is not to disprove it, which many have sufficiently done; but to entreat Americans to consider.

1. With what consistency, or decency they complain so loudly of attempts to enslave them, while they hold so many hundred thousands in slavery; and annually enslave many thousands more, without any pretence of authority, or claim upon them?

2. How just, how suitable to our crime is the punishment with which Providence threatens us? We have enslaved multitudes, and shed much innocent blood in doing it; and now are threatened with the same. And while other evils are confessed, and bewailed, why not this especially, and publicly; than which no other vice, if all others, has brought so much guilt on the land?

3. Whether, then, all ought not immediately to discontinue and renounce it, with grief and abhorrence? Should not every society bear testimony against it, and account obstinate persisters in it bad men, enemies to their country, and exclude them from fellowship; as they often do for much lesser faults?

4. The great Question may be—What should be done with those who are enslaved already? To turn the old and infirm free, would be injustice and cruelty; they who enjoyed the labours of their better days should keep, and treat them humanely. As to the rest, let prudent men, with the assistance of legislatures, determine what is practicable for masters, and best for them. Perhaps some could give them lands upon reasonable rent, some, employing them in their labour still, might give them some reasonable allowances for it; so as all may have some property, and fruits of their labours at their own disposal, and be encouraged to industry; the family may live together, and enjoy the natural satisfaction of exercising relative affections and duties, with civil protection, and other advantages, like fellow men. Perhaps they might sometime form useful barrier settlements on the frontiers. Thus they may become interested in the

public welfare, and assist in promoting it; instead of being dangerous, as now they are, should any enemy promise them a better condition.

5. The past treatment of Africans must naturally fill them with
abhorrence of Christians; lead them to think our religion would
make them more inhuman savages, if they embraced it; thus the
gain of that trade has been pursued in opposition to the Redeemer's
cause, and the happiness of men: Are we not, therefore, bound in
duty to him and to them to repair these injuries, as far as possible,
by taking some proper measures to instruct, not only the slaves here,
but the Africans in their own countries? Primitive Christians
laboured always to spread their *Divine Religion;* and this is equally
our duty while there is an Heathen nation: But what singular obligations are we under to these injured people!

These are the sentiments of

JUSTICE AND HUMANITY.

COMMON SENSE

[1776]

INTRODUCTION.

PERPHAPS THE SENTIMENTS CONTAINED in the following pages, are not *yet* sufficiently fashionable to procure them general Favor; a long Habit of not thinking a Thing *wrong*, gives it a superficial appearance of being *right*, and raises at first a formidable outcry in defence of Custom. But the Tumult soon subsides. Time makes more Converts than Reason.

As a long and violent abuse of power is generally the means of calling the right of it in question, (and in matters too which might never have been thought of, had not the sufferers been aggravated into the inquiry,) and as the King of England hath undertaken in his *own right*, to support the Parliament in what he calls *Theirs*, and as the good People of this Country are grievously oppressed by the Combination, they have an undoubted privilege to enquire into the Pretensions of both, and equally to reject the Usurpation of *either*.

In the following Sheets, the Author hath studiously avoided every thing which is personal among ourselves. Compliments as well as censure to individuals make no part thereof. The wise and the worthy need not the triumph of a Pamphlet; and those whose sentiments are injudicious or unfriendly will cease of themselves, unless too much pains is bestowed upon their conversions.

The cause of America is in a great measure the cause of all mankind. Many circumstances have, and will arise, which are not local, but universal, and through which the principles of all lovers of mankind are affected, and in the event of which their affections are interested. The laying a country desolate with fire and sword, declaring war against the natural rights of all mankind, and extirpating the defenders thereof from the face of the earth, is the concern of every man to whom nature hath given the power of feeling; of which class, regardless of party censure, is

THE AUTHOR.

P. S. *(Postscript to Preface in the third edition.)* The Publication of this new Edition hath been delayed, with a view of taking notice (had it been necessary) of any attempt to refute the Doctrine of Independence: As no answer hath yet appeared, it is now presumed that none will, the time needful for getting such a Performance ready for the Public being considerably past.

Who the Author of this Production is, is wholly unnecessary to the Public, as the Object for Attention is the *Doctrine itself*, not the *Man*. Yet it may not be unnecessary to say, That he is unconnected with any party, and under no sort of Influence, public or private, but the influence of reason and principle.

PHILADELPHIA, FEBRUARY 14, 1776.

COMMON SENSE;

ADDRESSED TO THE

INHABITANTS OF AMERICA,

ON THE FOLLOWING
INTERESTING SUBJECTS:

I. Of the Origin and Design of Government in general, with concise Remarks on the English Constitution.
II. Of Monarchy and Hereditary Succession.
III. Thoughts on the present State of American Affairs.
IV. Of the present ability of America, with some miscellaneous Reflections.

A NEW EDITION, with several Additions in the Body of the Work. To which is Added an APPENDIX; together with an Address to the People called QUAKERS.

Man knows no Master save creating HEAVEN,
Or those whom choice and common Good ordain.

THOMSON.

COMMON SENSE.

On the Origin and Design of Government in General, with Concise Remarks on the English Constitution.

SOME WRITERS HAVE SO confounded society with government, as to leave little or no distinction between them; whereas they are not only different, but have different origins. Society is produced by our wants, and government by our wickedness; the former promotes our happiness *positively* by uniting our affections, the latter *negatively* by restraining our vices. The one encourages intercourse, the other creates distinctions. The first is a patron, the last a punisher.

Society in every state is a blessing, but Government, even in its best state, is but a necessary evil; in its worst state an intolerable one: for when we suffer, or are exposed to the same miseries *by a Government*, which we might expect in a country *without Government*, our calamity is heightened by reflecting that we furnish the means by which we suffer. Government, like dress, is the badge of lost innocence; the palaces of kings are built upon the ruins of the bowers of paradise. For were the impulses of conscience clear, uniform and irresistibly obeyed, man would need no other law-giver; but that not being the case, he finds it necessary to surrender up a part of his property to furnish means for the protection of the rest; and this he is induced to do by the same prudence which in every other case advises him, out of two evils to choose the least. Wherefore, security being the true design and end of government, it unanswerably follows that whatever form thereof appears most likely to ensure it to us, with the least expence and greatest benefit, is preferable to all others.

In order to gain a clear and just idea of the design and end of government, let us suppose a small number of persons settled in some sequestered part of the earth, unconnected with the rest; they will then represent the first peopling of any country, or of the world. In this state of natural liberty, society will be their first thought. A thousand motives will excite them thereto; the strength of one man is so unequal to his wants, and his mind so unfitted for perpetual solitude, that he is soon obliged to seek assistance and relief of another, who in his turn requires the same. Four or five united would be able to raise a tolerable dwelling in the midst of a wilderness, but one man might labour out the common period of life without accomplishing any thing; when he had felled his timber he could not remove it, nor erect it after it was removed; hunger in the mean time would urge him to quit his work, and every different want would call him a different way. Disease, nay even misfortune, would be death; for though neither might be mortal, yet either would disable him from living, and reduce him to a state in which he might rather be said to perish than to die.

Thus necessity, like a gravitating power, would soon form our newly arrived emigrants into society, the reciprocal blessings of which would supercede, and render the obligations of law and government unnecessary while they remained perfectly just to each other; but as nothing but Heaven is impregnable to vice, it will unavoidably happen that in proportion as they surmount the first difficulties of emigration, which bound them together in a common cause, they will begin to relax in their duty and attachment to each other: and this remissness will point out the necessity of establishing some form of government to supply the defect of moral virtue.

Some convenient tree will afford them a State House, under the branches of which the whole Colony may assemble to deliberate on public matters. It is more than probable that their first laws will have the title only of Regulations and be enforced by no other penalty than public disesteem. In this first parliament every man by natural right will have a seat.

But as the Colony encreases, the public concerns will encrease likewise, and the distance at which the members may be separated, will render it too inconvenient for all of them to meet on every occasion as at first, when their number was small, their habitations near, and the public concerns few and trifling. This will point out the convenience of their consenting to leave the legislative part to be managed by a select number chosen from the whole body, who are supposed to have the same concerns at stake which those have who appointed them, and who will act in the same manner as the whole body would act were they present. If the colony continue encreasing, it will become necessary to augment the number of representatives, and that the interest of every part of the colony may be attended to, it will be found best to divide the whole into convenient parts, each part sending its proper number: and that the *elected* might never form to themselves an interest separate from the *electors*, prudence will point out the propriety of having elections often: because as the *elected* might by that means return and mix again with the general body of the *electors* in a few months, their fidelity to the public will be secured by the prudent reflection of not making a rod for themselves. And as this frequent interchange will establish a common interest with every part of the community, they will mutually and naturally support each other, and on this, (not on the unmeaning name of king,) depends the *strength of government, and the happiness of the governed.*

Here then is the origin and rise of government; namely, a mode rendered necessary by the inability of moral virtue to govern the world; here too is the design and end of government, viz. Freedom and security. And however our eyes may be dazzled with show, or our ears deceived by sound; however prejudice may warp our wills, or interest darken our understanding, the simple voice of nature and reason will say, 'tis right.

I draw my idea of the form of government from a principle in nature which no art can overturn, viz. that the more simple any thing is, the less liable it is to be disordered, and the easier repaired when disordered; and with this maxim in view I offer a few remarks on the so much boasted constitution of England. That it was noble for the dark and slavish times in which it was erected, is granted. When the world was overrun with tyranny the least remove therefrom was a glorious rescue. But that it is imperfect, subject to convulsions, and incapable of producing what it seems to promise, is easily demonstrated.

Absolute governments, (tho' the disgrace of human nature) have this advantage with them, they are simple; if the people suffer, they know the head from which their suffering springs; know likewise the remedy; and are not bewildered by a variety of causes and cures.

But the constitution of England is so exceedingly complex, that the nation may suffer for years together without being able to discover in which part the fault lies; some will say in one and some in another, and every political physician will advise a different medicine.

I know it is difficult to get over local or long standing prejudices, yet if we will suffer ourselves to examine the component parts of the English constitution, we shall find them to be the base remains of two ancient tyrannies, compounded with some new Republican materials.

First.—The remains of Monarchical tyranny in the person of the King.

Secondly.—The remains of Aristocratical tyranny in the persons of the Peers.

Thirdly.—The new Republican materials, in the persons of the Commons, on whose virtue depends the freedom of England.

The two first, by being hereditary, are independant of the People; wherefore in a *constitutional sense* they contribute nothing towards the freedom of the State.

To say that the constitution of England is an *union* of three powers, reciprocally *checking* each other, is farcical; either the words have no meaning, or they are flat contradictions.

To say that the Commons is a check upon the King, presupposes two things.

First.—That the King is not to be trusted without being looked after; or in other words, that a thirst for absolute power is the natural disease of monarchy.

Secondly.—That the Commons, by being appointed for that purpose, are either wiser or more worthy of confidence than the Crown.

But as the same constitution which gives the Commons a power to check the King by withholding the supplies, gives afterwards the King a power to check the Commons, by empowering him to reject their other bills; it again supposes that the King is wiser than those whom it has already supposed to be wiser than him. A mere absurdity!

There is something exceedingly ridiculous in the composition of Monarchy; it first excludes a man from the means of information, yet empowers him to act in cases where the highest judgment is required. The state of a king shuts him from the World, yet the business of a king requires him to know it thoroughly; wherefore the different parts, by unnaturally opposing and destroying each other, prove the whole character to be absurd and useless.

Some writers have explained the English constitution thus: the King, say they, is one, the people another; the Peers are a house in behalf of the King, the commons in behalf of the people; but this hath all the distinctions of a house divided against itself; and though the expressions be pleasantly arranged, yet when examined they appear idle and ambiguous; and it will always happen, that the nicest construction that words are capable of, when applied to the description of something which either cannot exist, or is too incomprehensible to be within the compass of description, will be words of sound only, and though they may amuse the ear, they cannot inform the mind: for this explanation includes a previous question, viz. *how came the king by a power which the people are afraid to trust, and always obliged to check?* Such a power could not be the gift of a wise people, neither can any power, *which needs checking*, be from God; yet the provision which the constitution makes supposes such a power to exist.

But the provision is unequal to the task; the means either cannot or will not accomplish the end, and the whole affair is a *Felo de se*:* for as the greater weight will always carry up the less, and as all the wheels of a machine are put in motion by one, it only remains to know which power in the constitution has the most weight, for that will govern: and tho' the others, or a part of them, may clog, or, as the phrase is, check the rapidity of its motion, yet so long as they cannot stop it, their endeavours will be ineffectual: The first moving power will at last have its way, and what it wants in speed is supplied by time.

That the crown is this overbearing part in the English constitution needs not be mentioned, and that it derives its whole consequence merely from being the giver of places and pensions is self-evident; wherefore, though we have been wise enough to shut and lock a door against absolute Monarchy, we at the same time have been foolish enough to put the Crown in possession of the key.

---

*Self-murderer.

The prejudice of Englishmen, in favour of their own government, by King, Lords and Commons, arises as much or more from national pride than reason. Individuals are undoubtedly safer in England than in some other countries: but the will of the king is as much the law of the land in Britain as in France, with this difference, that instead of proceeding directly from his mouth, it is handed to the people under the formidable shape of an act of parliament. For the fate of Charles the First hath only made kings more subtle—not more just.

Wherefore, laying aside all national pride and prejudice in favour of modes and forms, the plain truth is that *it is wholly owing to the constitution of the people, and not to the constitution of the government* that the crown is not as oppressive in England as in Turkey.

An inquiry into the *constitutional errors* in the English form of government, is at this time highly necessary; for as we are never in a proper condition of doing justice to others, while we continue under the influence of some leading partiality, so neither are we capable of doing it to ourselves while we remain fettered by any obstinate prejudice. And as a man who is attached to a prostitute is unfitted to choose or judge of a wife, so any prepossession in favour of a rotten constitution of government will disable us from discerning a good one.

Of Monarchy and Hereditary Succession. pp. 22-30

Mankind being originally equals in the order of creation, the equality could only be destroyed by some subsequent circumstance: the distinctions of rich and poor may in a great measure be accounted for, and that without having recourse to the harsh ill-sounding names of oppression and avarice. Oppression is often the *consequence*, but seldom or never the *means* of riches; and tho' avarice will preserve a man from being necessitously poor, it generally makes him too timorous to be wealthy.

But there is another and greater distinction for which no truly natural or religious reason can be assigned, and that is the distinction of men into KINGS and SUBJECTS. Male and female are the distinctions of nature, good and bad the distinctions of Heaven; but how a race of men came into the world so exalted above the rest, and distinguished like some new species, is worth inquiring into, and whether they are the means of happiness or of misery to mankind.

In the early ages of the world, according to the scripture chronology there were no kings; the consequence of which was, there were no wars; it is the pride of kings which throws mankind into confusion. Holland, without a king hath enjoyed more peace for this last century than any of the monarchical governments in Europe. Antiquity favours the same remark; for the quiet and rural lives of the first Patriarchs have a happy something in them, which vanishes when we come to the history of Jewish royalty.

Government by kings was first introduced into the world by the Heathens, from whom the children of Israel copied the custom. It was the most prosperous invention the Devil ever set on foot for the promotion of idolatry. The Heathens paid divine honours to their deceased kings, and the Christian World hath improved on the plan by doing the same to their living ones. How impious is the title of sacred Majesty applied to a worm, who in the midst of his splendor is crumbling into dust!

As the exalting one man so greatly above the rest cannot be justified on the equal rights of nature, so neither can it be defended on the authority of scripture; for the will of the Almighty as declared by Gideon, and the prophet Samuel,* expressly disapproves of government by Kings. All anti-monarchical parts of scripture, have been very smoothly glossed over in monarchical governments, but they undoubtedly merit the attention of countries which have their governments yet to form. *Render unto Cesar the things which are Cesar's,* is the scripture doctrine of courts, yet it is no support of monarchical government, for the Jews at that time were without a king, and in a state of vassalage to the Romans.

Near three thousand years passed away, from the Mosaic account of the creation, till the Jews under a national delusion requested a king. Till then their form of government (except in extraordinary cases where the Almighty interposed) was a kind of Republic, administered by a judge and the elders of the tribes. Kings they had none, and it was held sinful to acknowledge any being under that

---

*Gideon was a great military leader of the Old Testament; Samuel was the first great Hebrew prophet.

title but the Lord of Hosts. And when a man seriously reflects on the idolatrous homage which is paid to the persons of kings, he need not wonder that the Almighty, ever jealous of his honour, should disapprove a form of government which so impiously invades the prerogative of Heaven.

Monarchy is ranked in scripture as one of the sins of the Jews, for which a curse in reserve is denounced against them. The history of that transaction is worth attending to.

The children of Israel being oppressed by the Midianites, Gideon marched against them with a small army, and victory thro' the divine interposition decided in his favour. The Jews, elate with success, and attributing it to the generalship of Gideon, proposed making him a king, saying, *Rule thou over us, thou and thy son, and thy son's son.* Here was temptation in its fullest extent; not a kingdom only, but an hereditary one; but Gideon in the piety of his soul replied, *I will not rule over you, neither shall my son rule over you.* THE LORD SHALL RULE OVER YOU. Words need not be more explicit; Gideon doth not decline the honour, but denieth their right to give it; neither doth he compliment them with invented declarations of his thanks, but in the positive stile of a prophet charges them with disaffection to their proper Sovereign, the King of Heaven.

About one hundred and thirty years after this, they fell again into the same error. The hankering which the Jews had for the idolatrous customs of the Heathens, is something exceedingly unaccountable; but so it was, that laying hold of the misconduct of Samuel's two sons, who were intrusted with some secular concerns, they came in an abrupt and clamorous manner to Samuel, saying, *Behold thou art old, and thy sons walk not in thy ways, now make us a king to judge us like all the other nations.* And here we cannot but observe that their motives were bad, viz. that they might be *like* unto other nations, i. e. the Heathens, whereas their true glory lay in being as much *unlike* them as possible. *But the thing displeased Samuel when they said, give us a King to judge us; and Samuel prayed unto the Lord, and the Lord said unto Samuel, hearken unto the voice of the people in all that they say unto thee, for they have not rejected thee, but they have rejected me,* THAT I SHOULD NOT REIGN OVER THEM. *According to all the works which they have done since the day that I brought them up out of Egypt even unto this day, wherewith they have forsaken me, and served* *other Gods: so do they also unto thee. Now therefore hearken unto their voice, howbeit, protest solemnly unto them and show them the manner of the King that shall reign over them,* i. e. not of any particular King, but the general manner of the Kings of the earth whom Israel was so eagerly copying after. And notwithstanding the great distance of time and difference of manners, the character is still in fashion. *And Samuel told all the words of the Lord unto the people, that asked of him a King. And he said, This shall be the manner of the King that shall reign over you. He will take your sons and appoint them for himself for his chariots and to be his horsemen, and some shall run before his chariots* (this description agrees with the present mode of impressing men) *and he will appoint him captains over thousands and captains over fifties, will set them to ear his ground and to reap his harvest, and to make his instruments of war, and instruments of his chariots. And he will take your daughters to be confectionaries, and to be cooks, and to be bakers* (this describes the expense and luxury as well as the oppression of Kings) *and he will take your fields and your vineyards, and your olive yards, even the best of them, and give them to his servants. And he will take the tenth of your seed, and of your vineyards, and give them to his officers and to his servants* (by which we see that bribery, corruption, and favouritism, are the standing vices of Kings) *and he will take the tenth of your men servants, and your maid servants, and your goodliest young men, and your asses, and put them to his work: and he will take the tenth of your sheep, and ye shall be his servants, and ye shall cry out in that day because of your king which ye shall have chosen,* AND THE LORD WILL NOT HEAR YOU IN THAT DAY. This accounts for the continuation of Monarchy; neither do the characters of the few good kings which have lived since, either sanctify the title, or blot out the sinfulness of the origin; the high encomium given of David* takes no notice of him *officially as a King,* but only as a *Man* after God's own heart. *Nevertheless the people refused to obey the voice of Samuel, and they said, Nay but we will have a king over us, that we may be like all the nations, and that our king may judge us, and go out before us and fight our battles.* Samuel continued to reason with them but to no purpose; he set before them their ingratitude, but all would not

---

*Biblical king of Judah and Israel.

avail; and seeing them fully bent on their folly, he cried out, *I will call unto the Lord, and he shall send thunder and rain* (which was then a punishment, being in the time of wheat harvest) *that ye may perceive and see that your wickedness is great which ye have done in the sight of the Lord,* IN ASKING YOU A KING. *So Samuel called unto the Lord, and the Lord sent thunder and rain that day, and all the people greatly feared the Lord and Samuel. And all the people said unto Samuel, Pray for thy servants unto the Lord thy God that we die not, for* WE HAVE ADDED UNTO OUR SINS THIS EVIL, TO ASK A KING. These portions of scripture are direct and positive. They admit of no equivocal construction. That the Almighty hath here entered his protest against monarchical government is true, or the scripture is false. And a man hath good reason to believe that there is as much of kingcraft as priestcraft in withholding the scripture from the public in popish countries. For monarchy in every instance is the popery of government.

To the evil of monarchy we have added that of hereditary succession; and as the first is a degradation and lessening of ourselves, so the second, claimed as a matter of right, is an insult and imposition on posterity. For all men being originally equals, no one by birth could have a right to set up his own family in perpetual preference to all others for ever, and tho' himself might deserve some decent degree of honours of his cotemporaries, yet his descendants might be far too unworthy to inherit them. One of the strongest natural proofs of the folly of hereditary right in Kings, is that nature disapproves it, otherwise she would not so frequently turn it into ridicule, by giving mankind an *Ass for a Lion*.

Secondly, as no man at first could possess any other public honors than were bestowed upon him, so the givers of those honors could have no power to give away the right of posterity, and though they might say "We choose you for our head," they could not without manifest injustice to their children say "that your children and your children's children shall reign over ours forever." Because such an unwise, unjust, unnatural compact might (perhaps) in the next succession put them under the government of a rogue or a fool. Most wise men in their private sentiments have ever treated hereditary right with contempt; yet it is one of those evils which when once established is not easily removed: many submit from fear, others from superstition, and the more powerful part shares with the king the plunder of the rest.

This is supposing the present race of kings in the world to have had an honorable origin: whereas it is more than probable, that, could we take off the dark covering of antiquity and trace them to their first rise, we should find the first of them nothing better than the principal ruffian of some restless gang, whose savage manners or pre-eminence in subtilty obtained him the title of chief among plunderers: and who by increasing in power and extending his depredations, overawed the quiet and defenceless to purchase their safety by frequent contributions. Yet his electors could have no idea of giving hereditary right to his descendants, because such a perpetual exclusion of themselves was incompatible with the free and unrestrained principles they professed to live by. Wherefore, hereditary succession in the early ages of monarchy could not take place as a matter of claim, but as something casual or complemental; but as few or no records were extant in those days, and traditionary history stuff'd with fables, it was very easy, after the lapse of a few generations, to trump up some superstitious tale conveniently timed, Mahomet-like, to cram hereditary right down the throats of the vulgar. Perhaps the disorders which threatened, or seemed to threaten, on the decease of a leader and the choice of a new one (for elections among ruffians could not be very orderly) induced many at first to favour hereditary pretensions; by which means it happened, as it hath happened since, that what at first was submitted to as a convenience was afterwards claimed as a right.

England since the conquest hath known some few good monarchs, but groaned beneath a much larger number of bad ones: yet no man in his senses can say that their claim under William the Conqueror* is a very honourable one. A French bastard landing with an armed Banditti and establishing himself king of England against the consent of the natives, is in plain terms a very paltry rascally original. It certainly hath no divinity in it. However it is needless to spend much time in exposing the folly of hereditary right; if there are any so weak as to believe it, let them promiscuously wor-

---

*French Norman leader who conquered England in 1066.

ship the Ass and the Lion, and welcome. I shall neither copy their humility, nor disturb their devotion.

Yet I should be glad to ask how they suppose kings came at first? The question admits but of three answers, viz. either by lot, by election, or by usurpation. If the first king was taken by lot, it establishes a precedent for the next, which excludes hereditary succession. Saul was by lot, yet the succession was not hereditary, neither does it appear from that transaction that there was any intention it ever should. If the first king of any country was by election, that likewise establishes a precedent for the next; for to say, that the right of all future generations is taken away, by the act of the first electors, in their choice not only of a king but of a family of kings for ever, hath no parallel in or out of scripture but the doctrine of original sin, which supposes the free will of all men lost in Adam; and from such comparison, and it will admit of no other, hereditary succession can derive no glory. For as in Adam all sinned, and as in the first electors all men obeyed; as in the one all mankind were subjected to Satan, and in the other to sovereignty; as our innocence was lost in the first, and our authority in the last; and as both disable us from re-assuming some former state and privilege, it unanswerably follows that original sin and hereditary succession are parallels. Dishonourable rank! inglorious connection! yet the most subtle sophist cannot produce a juster simile.

As to usurpation, no man will be so hardy as to defend it; and that William the Conqueror was an usurper is a fact not to be contradicted. The plain truth is, that the antiquity of English monarchy will not bear looking into.

But it is not so much the absurdity as the evil of hereditary succession which concerns mankind. Did it ensure a race of good and wise men it would have the seal of divine authority, but as it opens a door to the *foolish*, the *wicked*, and the *improper*, it hath in it the nature of oppression. Men who look upon themselves born to reign, and others to obey, soon grow insolent. Selected from the rest of mankind, their minds are early poisoned by importance; and the world they act in differs so materially from the world at large, that they have but little opportunity of knowing its true interests, and when they succeed to the government are frequently the most ignorant and unfit of any throughout the dominions.

Another evil which attends hereditary succession is, that the throne is subject to be possessed by a minor at any age; all which time the regency acting under the cover of a king have every opportunity and inducement to betray their trust. The same national misfortune happens when a king worn out with age and infirmity enters the last stage of human weakness. In both these cases the public becomes a prey to every miscreant who can tamper successfully with the follies either of age or infancy.

The most plausible plea which hath ever been offered in favor of hereditary succession is, that it preserves a nation from civil wars; and were this true, it would be weighty; whereas it is the most barefaced falsity ever imposed upon mankind. The whole history of England disowns the fact. Thirty kings and two minors have reigned in that distracted kingdom since the conquest, in which time there has been (including the revolution) no less than eight civil wars and nineteen Rebellions. Wherefore instead of making for peace, it makes against it, and destroys the very foundation it seems to stand upon.

The contest for monarchy and succession, between the houses of York and Lancaster,* laid England in a scene of blood for many years. Twelve pitched battles besides skirmishes and sieges were fought between Henry and Edward. Twice was Henry prisoner to Edward, who in his turn was prisoner to Henry. And so uncertain is the fate of war and the temper of a nation, when nothing but personal matters are the ground of a quarrel, that Henry was taken in triumph from a prison to a palace, and Edward obliged to fly from a palace to a foreign land; yet, as sudden transitions of temper are seldom lasting, Henry in his turn was driven from the throne, and Edward re-called to succeed him. The parliament always following the strongest side.

This contest began in the reign of Henry the Sixth, and was not entirely extinguished till Henry the Seventh, in whom the families were united. Including a period of 67 years, viz. from 1422 to 1489.

In short, monarchy and succession have laid (not this or that kingdom only) but the world in blood and ashes. 'Tis a form of gov-

---

*Noble families struggling for control of the English throne in the so-called Wars of the Roses (1455–1487).

ernment which the word of God bears testimony against, and blood will attend it.

If we enquire into the business of a King, we shall find that in some countries they may have none; and after sauntering away their lives without pleasure to themselves or advantage to the nation, withdraw from the scene, and leave their successors to tread the same idle round. In absolute monarchies the whole weight of business civil and military lies on the King; the children of Israel in their request for a king urged this plea, "that he may judge us, and go out before us and fight our battles." But in countries where he is neither a Judge nor a General, as in England, a man would be puzzled to know what *is* his business.

The nearer any government approaches to a Republic, the less business there is for a King. It is somewhat difficult to find a proper name for the government of England. Sir William Meredith calls it a Republic; but in its present state it is unworthy of the name, because the corrupt influence of the Crown, by having all the places in its disposal, hath so effectually swallowed up the power, and eaten out the virtue of the House of Commons (the Republican part in the constitution) that the government of England is nearly as monarchical as that of France or Spain. Men fall out with names without understanding them. For 'tis the Republican and not the Monarchical part of the constitution of England which Englishmen glory in, viz. the liberty of choosing an House of Commons from out of their own body—and it is easy to see that when Republican virtues fails, slavery ensues. Why is the constitution of England sickly, but because monarchy hath poisoned the Republic; the Crown hath engrossed the Commons.

In England a King hath little more to do than to make war and give away places; which, in plain terms, is to empoverish the nation and set it together by the ears. A pretty business indeed for a man to be allowed eight hundred thousand sterling a year for, and worshipped into the bargain! Of more worth is one honest man to society, and in the sight of God, than all the crowned ruffians that ever lived.

Thoughts on the Present State of American Affairs.

In the following pages I offer nothing more than simple facts, plain arguments, and common sense: and have no other preliminaries to settle with the reader, than that he will divest himself of prejudice and prepossession, and suffer his reason and his feelings to determine for themselves: that he will put on, or rather that he will not put off, the true character of a man, and generously enlarge his views beyond the present day.

Volumes have been written on the subject of the struggle between England and America. Men of all ranks have embarked in the controversy, from different motives, and with various designs; but all have been ineffectual, and the period of debate is closed. Arms as the last resource decide the contest; the appeal was the choice of the King, and the Continent has accepted the challenge.

It hath been reported of the late Mr. Pelham* (who tho' an able minister was not without his faults) that on his being attacked in the House of Commons on the score that his measures were only of a temporary kind, replied, "*they will last my time.*" Should a thought so fatal and unmanly possess the Colonies in the present contest, the name of ancestors will be remembered by future generations with detestation.

The Sun never shined on a cause of greater worth. 'Tis not the affair of a City, a County, a Province, or a Kingdom; but of a Continent—of at least one eighth part of the habitable Globe. 'Tis not the concern of a day, a year, or an age; posterity are virtually involved in the contest, and will be more or less affected even to the end of time, by the proceedings now. Now is the seed-time of Continental union, faith and honour. The least fracture now will be like a name engraved with the point of a pin on the tender rind of a young oak; the wound would enlarge with the tree, and posterity read it in full grown characters.

By referring the matter from argument to arms, a new æra for politics is struck—a new method of thinking hath arisen. All plans, proposals, &c. prior to the nineteenth of April, *i. e.* to the commencement of hostilities, are like the almanacks of the last year;

---

*Henry Pelham, prime minister of England from 1743 to 1754.

which tho' proper then, are superceded and useless now. Whatever was advanced by the advocates on either side of the question then, terminated in one and the same point, viz. a union with Great Britain; the only difference between the parties was the method of effecting it; the one proposing force, the other friendship; but it hath so far happened that the first hath failed, and the second hath withdrawn her influence.

As much hath been said of the advantages of reconciliation, which, like an agreeable dream, hath passed away and left us as we were, it is but right that we should examine the contrary side of the argument, and enquire into some of the many material injuries which these Colonies sustain, and always will sustain, by being connected with and dependant on Great-Britain. To examine that connection and dependance, on the principles of nature and common sense, to see what we have to trust to, if separated, and what we are to expect, if dependant.

I have heard it asserted by some, that as America has flourished under her former connection with Great-Britain, the same connection is necessary towards her future happiness, and will always have the same effect. Nothing can be more fallacious than this kind of argument. We may as well assert that because a child has thrived upon milk, that it is never to have meat, or that the first twenty years of our lives is to become a precedent for the next twenty. But even this is admitting more than is true; for I answer roundly, that America would have flourished as much, and probably much more, had no European power taken any notice of her. The commerce by which she hath enriched herself are the necessaries of life, and will always have a market while eating is the custom of Europe.

But she has protected us, say some. That she hath engrossed us is true, and defended the Continent at our expense as well as her own, is admitted; and she would have defended Turkey from the same motive, *viz.* for the sake of trade and dominion.

Alas! we have been long led away by ancient prejudices and made large sacrifices to superstition. We have boasted the protection of Great Britain, without considering, that her motive was *interest* not *attachment;* and that she did not protect us from *our enemies* on *our account;* but from *her enemies* on *her own account,* from those who had no quarrel with us on any *other account,* and who will always be our enemies on the *same account*. Let Britain waive her pretensions to the Continent, or the Continent throw off the dependance, and we should be at peace with France and Spain, were they at war with Britain. The miseries of Hanover* last war ought to warn us against connections.

It hath lately been asserted in parliament, that the Colonies have no relation to each other but through the Parent Country, *i. e.* that Pennsylvania and the Jerseys, and so on for the rest, are sister Colonies by the way of England; this is certainly a very roundabout way of proving relationship, but it is the nearest and only true way of proving enmity (or enemyship, if I may so call it.) France and Spain never were, nor perhaps ever will be, our enemies as *Americans*, but as our being the *subjects of Great Britain.*

But Britain is the parent country, say some. Then the more shame upon her conduct. Even brutes do not devour their young, nor savages make war upon their families; Wherefore, the assertion, if true, turns to her reproach; but it happens not to be true, or only partly so, and the phrase *parent* or *mother country* hath been jesuitically adopted by the King and his parasites, with a low papistical design of gaining an unfair bias on the credulous weakness of our minds. Europe, and not England, is the parent country of America. This new World hath been the asylum for the persecuted lovers of civil and religious liberty from *every part* of Europe. Hither have they fled, not from the tender embraces of the mother, but from the cruelty of the monster; and it is so far true of England, that the same tyranny which drove the first emigrants from home, pursues their descendants still.

In this extensive quarter of the globe, we forget the narrow limits of three hundred and sixty miles (the extent of England) and carry our friendship on a larger scale; we claim brotherhood with every European Christian, and triumph in the generosity of the sentiment.

It is pleasant to observe by what regular gradations we surmount the force of local prejudices, as we enlarge our acquaintance with the World. A man born in any town in England divided into parishes,

---

*Electorate in Germany whose ruling family provided kings of England starting with George I in 1714.

will naturally associate most with his fellow parishioners (because their interests in many cases will be common) and distinguish him by the name of *neighbour;* if he meet him but a few miles from home, he drops the narrow idea of a street, and salutes him by the name of *townsman;* if he travel out of the county and meet him in any other, he forgets the minor divisions of street and town, and calls him *countryman, i. e. countyman:* but if in their foreign excursions they should associate in France, or any other part of *Europe*, their local remembrance would be enlarged into that of *Englishmen*. And by a just parity of reasoning, all Europeans meeting in America, or any other quarter of the globe, are *countrymen;* for England, Holland, Germany, or Sweden, when compared with the whole, stand in the same places on the larger scale, which the divisions of street, town, and county do on the smaller ones; Distinctions too limited for Continental minds. Not one third of the inhabitants, even of this province, [Pennsylvania], are of English descent. Wherefore, I reprobate the phrase of Parent or Mother Country applied to England only, as being false, selfish, narrow and ungenerous.

But, admitting that we were all of English descent, what does it amount to? Nothing. Britain, being now an open enemy, extinguishes every other name and title: and to say that reconciliation is our duty, is truly farcical. The first king of England, of the present line (William the Conqueror) was a Frenchman, and half the peers of England are descendants from the same country; wherefore, by the same method of reasoning, England ought to be governed by France.

Much hath been said of the united strength of Britain and the Colonies, that in conjunction they might bid defiance to the world: But this is mere presumption; the fate of war is uncertain, neither do the expressions mean any thing; for this continent would never suffer itself to be drained of inhabitants, to support the British arms in either Asia, Africa, or Europe.

Besides, what have we to do with setting the world at defiance? Our plan is commerce, and that, well attended to, will secure us the peace and friendship of all Europe; because it is the interest of all Europe to have America a free port. Her trade will always be a protection, and her barrenness of gold and silver secure her from invaders.

I challenge the warmest advocate for reconciliation to show a single advantage that this continent can reap by being connected with Great Britain. I repeat the challenge; not a single advantage is derived. Our corn will fetch its price in any market in Europe, and our imported goods must be paid for buy them where we will.

But the injuries and disadvantages which we sustain by that connection, are without number; and our duty to mankind at large, as well as to ourselves, instruct us to renounce the alliance: because, any submission to, or dependance on, Great Britain, tends directly to involve this Continent in European wars and quarrels, and set us at variance with nations who would otherwise seek our friendship, and against whom we have neither anger nor complaint. As Europe is our market for trade, we ought to form no partial connection with any part of it. It is the true interest of America to steer clear of European contentions, which she never can do, while, by her dependance on Britain, she is made the make-weight in the scale of British politics.

Europe is too thickly planted with Kingdoms to be long at peace, and whenever a war breaks out between England and any foreign power, the trade of America goes to ruin, *because of her connection with Britain.* The next war may not turn out like the last, and should it not, the advocates for reconciliation now will be wishing for separation then, because neutrality in that case would be a safer convoy than a man of war. Every thing that is right or reasonable pleads for separation. The blood of the slain, the weeping voice of nature cries, 'TIS TIME TO PART. Even the distance at which the Almighty hath placed England and America is a strong and natural proof that the authority of the one over the other, was never the design of Heaven. The time likewise at which the Continent was discovered, adds weight to the argument, and the manner in which it was peopled, encreases the force of it. The Reformation was preceded by the discovery of America: As if the Almighty graciously meant to open a sanctuary to the persecuted in future years, when home should afford neither friendship nor safety.

The authority of Great Britain over this continent, is a form of government, which sooner or later must have an end: And a serious mind can draw no true pleasure by looking forward, under the painful and positive conviction that what he calls "the present con-stitution" is merely temporary. As parents, we can have no joy, knowing that this government is not sufficiently lasting to ensure any thing which we may bequeath to posterity: And by a plain method of argument, as we are running the next generation into debt, we ought to do the work of it, otherwise we use them meanly and pitifully. In order to discover the line of our duty rightly, we should take our children in our hand, and fix our station a few years farther into life; that eminence will present a prospect which a few present fears and prejudices conceal from our sight.

Though I would carefully avoid giving unnecessary offence, yet I am inclined to believe, that all those who espouse the doctrine of reconciliation, may be included within the following descriptions.

Interested men, who are not to be trusted, weak men who *cannot* see, prejudiced men who will not see, and a certain set of moderate men who think better of the European world than it deserves; and this last class, by an ill-judged deliberation, will be the cause of more calamities to this Continent than all the other three.

It is the good fortune of many to live distant from the scene of present sorrow; the evil is not sufficiently brought to their doors to make them feel the precariousness with which all American prop-erty is possessed. But let our imaginations transport us a few mo-ments to Boston;* that seat of wretchedness will teach us wisdom, and instruct us for ever to renounce a power in whom we can have no trust. The inhabitants of that unfortunate city who but a few months ago were in ease and affluence, have now no other alterna-tive than to stay and starve, or turn out to beg. Endangered by the fire of their friends if they continue within the city, and plundered by the soldiery if they leave it, in their present situation they are prisoners without the hope of redemption, and in a general attack for their relief they would be exposed to the fury of both armies.

Men of passive tempers look somewhat lightly over the offences of Great Britain, and, still hoping for the best, are apt to call out, *Come, come, we shall be friends again for all this.* But examine the pas-

---

*Eastern Massachusetts city then suffering from the closing of its port by Great Britain in 1774.

sions and feelings of mankind: bring the doctrine of reconciliation to the touchstone of nature, and then tell me whether you can hereafter love, honour, and faithfully serve the power that hath carried fire and sword into your land? If you cannot do all these, then are you only deceiving yourselves, and by your delay bringing ruin upon posterity. Your future connection with Britain, whom you can neither love nor honour, will be forced and unnatural, and being formed only on the plan of present convenience, will in a little time fall into a relapse more wretched than the first. But if you say, you can still pass the violations over, then I ask, hath your house been burnt? Hath your property been destroyed before your face? Are your wife and children destitute of a bed to lie on, or bread to live on? Have you lost a parent or a child by their hands, and yourself the ruined and wretched survivor? If you have not, then are you not a judge of those who have. But if you have, and can still shake hands with the murderers, then are you unworthy the name of husband, father, friend, or lover, and whatever may be your rank or title in life, you have the heart of a coward, and the spirit of a sycophant.

This is not inflaming or exaggerating matters, but trying them by those feelings and affections which nature justifies, and without which we should be incapable of discharging the social duties of life, or enjoying the felicities of it. I mean not to exhibit horror for the purpose of provoking revenge, but to awaken us from fatal and unmanly slumbers, that we may pursue determinately some fixed object. 'Tis not in the power of Britain or of Europe to conquer America, if she doth not conquer herself by delay and timidity. The present winter is worth an age if rightly employed, but if lost or neglected the whole Continent will partake of the misfortune; and there is no punishment which that man doth not deserve, be he who, or what, or where he will, that may be the means of sacrificing a season so precious and useful.

'Tis repugnant to reason, to the universal order of things, to all examples from former ages, to suppose that this Continent can long remain subject to any external power. The most sanguine in Britain doth not think so. The utmost stretch of human wisdom cannot, at this time, compass a plan, short of separation, which can promise the continent even a year's security. Reconciliation is *now* a fallacious dream. Nature hath deserted the connection, and art cannot

supply her place. For, as Milton wisely expresses, "never can true rec-
oncilement grow where wounds of deadly hate have pierced so
deep."

Every quiet method for peace hath been ineffectual. Our prayers
have been rejected with disdain; and hath tended to convince us that
nothing flatters vanity or confirms obstinacy in Kings more than repeated petitioning—and nothing hath contributed more than that
very measure to make the Kings of Europe absolute. Witness Den-
mark and Sweden. Wherefore, since nothing but blows will do, for
God's sake let us come to a final separation, and not leave the next
generation to be cutting throats under the violated unmeaning
names of parent and child.

To say they will never attempt it again is idle and visionary; we
thought so at the repeal of the stamp act, yet a year or two unde-
ceived us; as well may we suppose that nations which have been
once defeated will never renew the quarrel.

As to government matters, 'tis not in the power of Britain to do
this continent justice: the business of it will soon be too weighty and
intricate to be managed with any tolerable degree of convenience, by
a power so distant from us, and so very ignorant of us; for if they
cannot conquer us, they cannot govern us. To be always running
three or four thousand miles with a tale or a petition, waiting four
or five months for an answer, which, when obtained, requires five or
six more to explain it in, will in a few years be looked upon as folly
and childishness. There was a time when it was proper, and there is
a proper time for it to cease.

Small islands not capable of protecting themselves are the proper
objects for government to take under their care; but there is something absurd, in supposing a Continent to be perpetually governed
by an island. In no instance hath nature made the satellite larger
than its primary planet; and as England and America, with respect
to each other, reverse the common order of nature, it is evident that
they belong to different systems. England to Europe: America to
itself.

I am not induced by motives of pride, party, or resentment to espouse the doctrine of separation and independence; I am clearly,
positively, and conscientiously persuaded that it is the true interest
of this Continent to be so; that every thing short of *that* is mere

patchwork, that it can afford no lasting felicity,—that it is leaving the sword to our children, and shrinking back at a time when a little more, a little further, would have rendered this Continent the glory of the earth.

As Britain hath not manifested the least inclination towards a compromise, we may be assured that no terms can be obtained worthy the acceptance of the Continent, or any ways equal to the expence of blood and treasure we have been already put to.

The object contended for, ought always to bear some just proportion to the expense. The removal of North, or the whole detestable junto, is a matter unworthy the millions we have expended. A temporary stoppage of trade was an inconvenience, which would have sufficiently ballanced the repeal of all the acts complained of, had such repeals been obtained; but if the whole Continent must take up arms, if every man must be a soldier, 'tis scarcely worth our while to fight against a contemptible ministry only. Dearly, dearly do we pay for the repeal of the acts, if that is all we fight for; for, in a just estimation 'tis as great a folly to pay a Bunker-hill price* for law as for land. As I have always considered the independancy of this continent, as an event which sooner or later must arrive, so from the late rapid progress of the Continent to maturity, the event cannot be far off. Wherefore, on the breaking out of hostilities, it was not worth the while to have disputed a matter which time would have finally redressed, unless we meant to be in earnest: otherwise it is like wasting an estate on a suit at law, to regulate the trespasses of a tenant whose lease is just expiring. No man was a warmer wisher for a reconciliation than myself, before the fatal nineteenth of April, 1775, but the moment the event of that day was made known, I rejected the hardened, sullen-tempered Pharaoh of England for ever; and disdain the wretch, that with the pretended title of FATHER OF HIS PEOPLE can unfeelingly hear of their slaughter, and composedly sleep with their blood upon his soul.

But admitting that matters were now made up, what would be the event? I answer, the ruin of the Continent. And that for several reasons.

---

*Reference to losses in the Battle of Bunker Hill (1775).

First. The powers of governing still remaining in the hands of the King, he will have a negative over the whole legislation of this Continent. And as he hath shown himself such an inveterate enemy to liberty, and discovered such a thirst for arbitrary power, is he, or is he not, a proper person to say to these colonies, *You shall make no laws but what I please!*? And is there any inhabitant of America so ignorant as not to know, that according to what is called the *present constitution*, this Continent can make no laws but what the king gives leave to; and is there any man so unwise as not to see, that (considering what has happened) he will suffer no law to be made here but such as suits *his* purpose? We may be as effectually enslaved by the want of laws in America, as by submitting to laws made for us in England. After matters are made up (as it is called) can there be any doubt, but the whole power of the crown will be exerted to keep this continent as low and humble as possible? Instead of going forward we shall go backward, or be perpetually quarrelling, or ridiculously petitioning. We are already greater than the King wishes us to be, and will he not hereafter endeavor to make us less? To bring the matter to one point, Is the power who is jealous of our prosperity, a proper power to govern us? Whoever says *No*, to this question, is an Independant for independency means no more than this, whether we shall make our own laws, or, whether the King, the greatest enemy this continent hath, or can have, shall tell us *there shall be no laws but such as I like.*

But the King, you will say, has a negative in England; the people there can make no laws without his consent. In point of right and good order, it is something very ridiculous that a youth of twenty-one (which hath often happened) shall say to several millions of people older and wiser than himself, "I forbid this or that act of yours to be law." But in this place I decline this sort of reply, though I will never cease to expose the absurdity of it, and only answer that England being the King's residence, and America not so, makes quite another case. The King's negative here is ten times more dangerous and fatal than it can be in England; for there he will scarcely refuse his consent to a bill for putting England into as strong a state of defense as possible, and in America he would never suffer such a bill to be passed.

America is only a secondary object in the system of British politics. England consults the good of this country no further than it answers her own purpose. Wherefore, her own interest leads her to suppress the growth of ours in every case which doth not promote her advantage, or in the least interferes with it. A pretty state we should soon be in under such a second hand government, considering what has happened! Men do not change from enemies to friends by the alteration of a name: And in order to show that reconciliation now is a dangerous doctrine, I affirm, *that it would be policy in the King at this time to repeal the acts, for the sake of reinstating himself in the government of the provinces;* In order that HE MAY ACCOMPLISH BY CRAFT AND SUBTLETY, IN THE LONG RUN, WHAT HE CANNOT DO BY FORCE AND VIOLENCE IN THE SHORT ONE. Reconciliation and ruin are nearly related.

Secondly. That as even the best terms which we can expect to obtain can amount to no more than a temporary expedient, or a kind of government by guardianship, which can last no longer than till the Colonies come of age, so the general face and state of things in the interim will be unsettled and unpromising. Emigrants of property will not choose to come to a country whose form of government hangs but by a thread, and who is every day tottering on the brink of commotion and disturbance; and numbers of the present inhabitants would lay hold of the interval to dispose of their effects, and quit the Continent.

But the most powerful of all arguments is, that nothing but independance, *i. e.* a Continental form of government, can keep the peace of the Continent and preserve it inviolate from civil wars. I dread the event of a reconciliation with Britain now, as it is more than probable that it will be followed by a revolt some where or other, the consequences of which may be far more fatal than all the malice of Britain.

Thousands are already ruined by British barbarity; (thousands more will probably suffer the same fate.) Those men have other feelings than us who have nothing suffered. All they now possess is liberty; what they before enjoyed is sacrificed to its service, and having nothing more to lose they disdain submission. Besides, the general temper of the Colonies, towards a British government will be like that of a youth who is nearly out of his time; they will care very little about her: And a government which cannot preserve the peace is no government at all, and in that case we pay our money for nothing; and pray what is it that Britain can do, whose power will be wholly on paper, should a civil tumult break out the very day after reconciliation? I have heard some men say, many of whom I believe spoke without thinking, that they dreaded an independance, fearing that it would produce civil wars: It is but seldom that our first thoughts are truly correct, and that is the case here; for there is ten times more to dread from a patched up connection than from independance. I make the sufferer's case my own, and I protest, that were I driven from house and home, my property destroyed, and my circumstances ruined, that as a man, sensible of injuries, I could never relish the doctrine of reconciliation, or consider myself bound thereby.

The Colonies have manifested such a spirit of good order and obedience to Continental government, as is sufficient to make every reasonable person easy and happy on that head. No man can assign the least pretence for his fears, on any other grounds, than such as are truly childish and ridiculous, viz., that one colony will be striving for superiority over another.

Where there are no distinctions there can be no superiority; perfect equality affords no temptation. The Republics of Europe are all (and we may say always) in peace. Holland and Switzerland are without wars, foreign or domestic: Monarchical governments, it is true, are never long at rest: the crown itself is a temptation to enterprising ruffians at home; and that degree of pride and insolence ever attendant on regal authority, swells into a rupture with foreign powers in instances where a republican government, by being formed on more natural principles, would negociate the mistake.

If there is any true cause of fear respecting independance, it is because no plan is yet laid down. Men do not see their way out. Wherefore, as an opening into that business I offer the following hints; at the same time modestly affirming, that I have no other opinion of them myself, than that they may be the means of giving rise to something better. Could the straggling thoughts of individuals be collected, they would frequently form materials for wise and able men to improve into useful matter.

Let the assemblies be annual, with a president only. The representation more equal, their business wholly domestic, and subject to the authority of a Continental Congress.

Let each Colony be divided into six, eight, or ten, convenient districts, each district to send a proper number of Delegates to Congress, so that each Colony send at least thirty. The whole number in Congress will be at least 390. Each congress to sit and to choose a President by the following method. When the Delegates are met, let a Colony be taken from the whole thirteen Colonies by lot, after which let the Congress choose (by ballot) a president from out of the Delegates of that Province. In the next Congress, let a Colony be taken by lot from twelve only, omitting that Colony from which the president was taken in the former Congress, and so proceeding on till the whole thirteen shall have had their proper rotation. And in order that nothing may pass into a law but what is satisfactorily just, not less than three fifths of the Congress to be called a majority. He that will promote discord, under a government so equally formed as this, would have joined Lucifer in his revolt.

But as there is a peculiar delicacy from whom, or in what manner, this business must first arise, and as it seems most agreeable and consistent that it should come from some intermediate body between the governed and the governors, that is, between the Congress and the People, let a Continental Conference be held in the following manner, and for the following purpose,

A Committee of twenty six members of congress, *viz*. Two for each Colony. Two Members from each House of Assembly, or Provincial Convention; and five Representatives of the people at large, to be chosen in the capital city or town of each Province, for, and in behalf of the whole Province, by as many qualified voters as shall think proper to attend from all parts of the Province for that purpose; or, if more convenient, the Representatives may be chosen in two or three of the most populous parts thereof. In this conference, thus assembled, will be united the two grand principles of business, *knowledge* and *power*. The Members of Congress, Assemblies, or Conventions, by having had experience in national concerns, will be able and useful counsellors, and the whole, being impowered by the people, will have a truly legal authority.

The conferring members being met, let their business be to frame a Continental Charter, or Charter of the United Colonies; (answering to what is called the Magna Charta of England) fixing the number and manner of choosing Members of Congress, Members of Assembly, with their date of sitting; and drawing the line of business and jurisdiction between them: Always remembering, that our strength is Continental, not Provincial. Securing freedom and property to all men, and above all things, the free exercise of religion, according to the dictates of conscience; with such other matter as it is necessary for a charter to contain. Immediately after which, the said conference to dissolve, and the bodies which shall be chosen conformable to the said charter, to be the Legislators and Governors of this Continent for the time being: Whose peace and happiness, may GOD preserve. AMEN.

Should any body of men be hereafter delegated for this or some similar purpose, I offer them the following extracts from that wise observer on Governments, Dragonetti. "The science," says he, "of the Politician consists in fixing the true point of happiness and freedom. Those men would deserve the gratitude of ages, who should discover a mode of government that contained the greatest sum of individual happiness, with the least national expense." (Dragonetti on "Virtues and Reward.")

But where, say some, is the King of America? I'll tell you, friend, he reigns above, and doth not make havoc of mankind like the Royal Brute of Great Britain. Yet that we may not appear to be defective even in earthly honours, let a day be solemnly set apart for proclaiming the Charter; let it be brought forth placed on the Divine Law, the Word of God; let a crown be placed thereon, by which the world may know, that so far as we approve of monarchy, that in America the law is king. For as in absolute governments the King is law, so in free countries the law ought to be king; and there ought to be no other. But lest any ill use should afterwards arise, let the Crown at the conclusion of the ceremony be demolished, and scattered among the people whose right it is.

A government of our own is our natural right: and when a man seriously reflects on the precariousness of human affairs, he will become convinced, that it is infinitely wiser and safer, to form a constitution of our own in a cool deliberate manner, while we have it in our power, than to trust such an interesting event to time and chance. If we omit it now, some Massanello* may hereafter arise, who, laying hold of popular disquietudes, may collect together the desperate and the discontented, and by assuming to themselves the powers of government, finally sweep away the liberties of the Continent like a deluge. Should the government of America return again into the hands of Britain, the tottering situation of things will be a temptation for some desperate adventurer to try his fortune; and in such a case, what relief can Britain give? Ere she could hear the news, the fatal business might be done; and ourselves suffering like the wretched Britons under the oppression of the Conqueror. Ye that oppose independance now, ye know not what ye do: ye are opening a door to eternal tyranny, by keeping vacant the seat of government. There are thousands and tens of thousands, who would think it glorious to expel from the Continent, that barbarous and hellish power, which hath stirred up the Indians and the Negroes to destroy us; the cruelty hath a double guilt, it is dealing brutally by us, and treacherously by them.

To talk of friendship with those in whom our reason forbids us to have faith, and our affections wounded thro' a thousand pores instruct us to detest, is madness and folly. Every day wears out the little remains of kindred between us and them; and can there be any reason to hope, that as the relationship expires, the affection will encrease, or that we shall agree better when we have ten times more and greater concerns to quarrel over than ever?

Ye that tell us of harmony and reconciliation, can ye restore to us the time that is past? Can ye give to prostitution its former innocence? neither can ye reconcile Britain and America. The last cord now is broken, the people of England are presenting addresses against us. There are injuries which nature cannot forgive; she would cease to be nature if she did. As well can the lover forgive the ravisher of his mistress, as the Continent forgive the murders of Britain. The Almighty hath implanted in us these unextinguishable

*Thomas Anello, otherwise Massanello, a fisherman of Naples, who after spiriting up his countrymen in the public market place, against the oppression of the Spaniards, to whom the place was then subject, prompted them to revolt, and in the space of a day became King [Author's note].

feelings for good and wise purposes. They are the Guardians of his Image in our hearts. They distinguish us from the herd of common animals. The social compact would dissolve, and justice be extirpated from the earth, or have only a casual existence were we callous to the touches of affection. The robber and the murderer would often escape unpunished, did not the injuries which our tempers sustain, provoke us into justice.

O! ye that love mankind! Ye that dare oppose not only the tyranny but the tyrant, stand forth! Every spot of the old world is overrun with oppression. Freedom hath been hunted round the Globe. Asia and Africa have long expelled her. Europe regards her like a stranger, and England hath given her warning to depart. O! receive the fugitive, and prepare in time an asylum for mankind.

Of the Present Ability of America: *With Some Miscellaneous Reflections.*

I have never met with a man, either in England or America, who hath not confessed his opinion, that a separation between the countries would take place one time or other: And there is no instance in which we have shown less judgment, than in endeavoring to describe, what we call, the ripeness or fitness of the Continent for independance.

As all men allow the measure, and vary only in their opinion of the time, let us, in order to remove mistakes, take a general survey of things, and endeavor if possible to find out the *very* time. But I need not go far, the inquiry ceases at once, for the *time hath found us.* The general concurrence, the glorious union of all things, proves the fact.

'Tis not in numbers but in unity that our great strength lies: yet our present numbers are sufficient to repel the force of all the world. The Continent hath at this time the largest body of armed and disciplined men of any power under Heaven: and is just arrived at that pitch of strength, in which no single colony is able to support itself, and the whole, when united, is able to do any thing. Our land force is more than sufficient, and as to Naval affairs, we cannot be insensible that Britain would never suffer an American man of war to be built, while the Continent remained in her hands. Wherefore, we should be no forwarder an hundred years hence in that branch than we are now; but the truth is, we should be less so, because the timber of the Country is every day diminishing, and that which will remain at last, will be far off or difficult to procure.

Were the Continent crowded with inhabitants, her sufferings under the present circumstances would be intolerable. The more seaport-towns we had, the more should we have both to defend and to lose. Our present numbers are so happily proportioned to our wants, that no man need be idle. The diminution of trade affords an army, and the necessities of an army create a new trade.

Debts we have none: and whatever we may contract on this account will serve as a glorious memento of our virtue. Can we but leave posterity with a settled form of government, an independant constitution of its own, the purchase at any price will be cheap. But to expend millions for the sake of getting a few vile acts repealed, and routing the present ministry only, is unworthy the charge, and is using posterity with the utmost cruelty; because it is leaving them the great work to do, and a debt upon their backs from which they derive no advantage. Such a thought 's unworthy a man of honour, and is the true characteristic of a narrow heart and a pidling politician.

The debt we may contract doth not deserve our regard if the work be but accomplished. No nation ought to be without a debt. A national debt is a national bond; and when it bears no interest, is in no case a grievance. Britain is oppressed with a debt of upwards of one hundred and forty millions sterling, for which she pays upwards of four millions interest. And as a compensation for her debt, she has a large navy; America is without a debt, and without a navy; yet for the twentieth part of the English national debt, could have a navy as large again. The navy of England is not worth at this time more than three millions and a half sterling.

The first and second editions of this pamphlet were published without the following calculations which are now given as a proof that the above estimation of the navy is a just one. See Entic's "Naval History," Intro., p. 56.

The charge of building a ship of each rate, and furnishing her with masts, yards, sails, and rigging, together with a proportion of eight months boatswain's and carpenter's sea-stores, as calculated by Mr. Burchett, Secretary to the navy.

For a ship of 100 guns,	.	.	35,553*l.*
90	.	.	29,886
80	.	.	23,638
70	.	.	17,785
60	.	.	14,197
50	.	.	10,606
40	.	.	7,558
30	.	.	5,846
20	.	.	3,710

And hence it is easy to sum up the value, or cost, rather, of the whole British navy, which, in the year 1757, when it was at its greatest glory, consisted of the following ships and guns.

Ships.		Guns.		Cost of one.		Cost of all.
6	.	100	.	55,553*l.*	.	213,318*l.*
12	.	90	.	29,886	.	358,632
12	.	80	.	23,638	.	283,656
43	.	70	.	17,785	.	764,755
35	.	60	.	14,197	.	496,895
40	.	50	.	10,605	.	424,240
45	.	40	.	7,558	.	340,110
58	.	20	.	3,710	.	215,180
85 Sloops, bombs, and fireships, one with another, at				2,000	.	170,000

Cost,	3,266,786*l.*
Remains for guns,	233,214
Total,	3,500,000*l.*

No country on the globe is so happily situated, or so internally capable of raising a fleet as America. Tar, timber, iron, and cordage are her natural produce. We need go abroad for nothing. Whereas the Dutch, who make large profits by hiring out their ships of war to the Spaniards and Portugese, are obliged to import most of the materials they use. We ought to view the building a fleet as an article of commerce, it being the natural manufactory of this country. 'Tis the best money we can lay out. A navy when finished is worth more than it cost: And is that nice point in national policy, in which commerce and protection are united. Let us build; if we want them not, we can sell; and by that means replace our paper currency with ready gold and silver.

In point of manning a fleet, people in general run into great errors; it is not necessary that one fourth part should be sailors. The Terrible privateer, captain Death, stood the hottest engagement of any ship last war, yet had not twenty sailors on board; though her complement of men was upwards of two hundred. A few able and social sailors will soon instruct a sufficient number of active landsmen in the common work of a ship. Wherefore we never can be more capable of beginning on maritime matters than now, while our timber is standing, our fisheries blocked up, and our sailors and shipwrights out of employ. Men of war, of seventy and eighty guns, were built forty years ago in New England, and why not the same now? Ship building is America's greatest pride, and in which she will, in time, excel the whole world. The great empires of the east are mostly inland, and consequently excluded from the possibility of rivalling her. Africa is in a state of barbarism; and no power in Europe, hath either such an extent of coast, or such an internal supply of materials. Where nature hath given the one, she hath withheld the other; to America only hath she been liberal to both. The vast empire of Russia is almost shut out from the sea; wherefore her boundless forests, her tar, iron, and cordage are only articles of commerce.

In point of safety, ought we to be without a fleet? We are not the little people now, which we were sixty years ago; at that time we might have trusted our property in the streets, or fields rather, and slept securely without locks or bolts to our doors and windows. The case is now altered, and our methods of defence ought to improve with our encrease of property. A common pirate, twelve months ago, might have come up the Delaware, and laid the city of Philadelphia under contribution for what sum he pleased; and the same might have happened to other places. Nay, any daring fellow, in a brig of fourteen or sixteen guns, might have robbed the whole Continent, and carried off half a million of money. These are circumstances which demand our attention, and point out the necessity of naval protection.

Some perhaps will say, that after we have made it up with Britain, she will protect us. Can they be so unwise as to mean, that she will keep a navy in our Harbours for that purpose? Common sense will tell us, that the power which hath endeavoured to subdue us, is of all others, the most improper to defend us. Conquest may be effected under the pretence of friendship; and ourselves, after a long and brave resistance, be at last cheated into slavery. And if her ships are not to be admitted into our harbours, I would ask, how is she to protect us? A navy three or four thousand miles off can be of little use, and on sudden emergencies, none at all. Wherefore if we must hereafter protect ourselves, why not do it for ourselves? Why do it for another?

The English list of ships of war, is long and formidable, but not a tenth part of them are at any one time fit for service, numbers of them are not in being; yet their names are pompously continued in the list, if only a plank be left of the ship: and not a fifth part of such as are fit for service, can be spared on any one station at one time. The East and West Indies, Mediterranean, Africa, and other parts, over which Britain extends her claim, make large demands upon her navy. From a mixture of prejudice and inattention, we have contracted a false notion respecting the navy of England, and have talked as if we should have the whole of it to encounter at once, and, for that reason, supposed that we must have one as large; which not being instantly practicable, has been made use of by a set of disguised Tories to discourage our beginning thereon. Nothing can be further from truth than this; for if America had only a twentieth part of the naval force of Britain, she would be by far an over-match for her; because, as we neither have, nor claim any foreign dominion, our whole force would be employed on our own coast, where we should, in the long run, have two to one the advantage of those who had three or four thousand miles to sail over, before they could attack us, and the same distance to return in order to refit and recruit. And although Britain, by her fleet, hath a check over our trade to Europe, we have as large a one over her trade to the West Indies, which, by laying in the neighborhood of the Continent, lies entirely at its mercy.

Some method might be fallen on to keep up a naval force in time of peace, if we should not judge it necessary to support a constant navy. If premiums were to be given to Merchants to build and employ in their service, ships mounted with twenty, thirty, forty, or fifty guns, (the premiums to be in proportion to the loss of bulk to the merchant,) fifty or sixty of those ships, with a few guardships on constant duty, would keep up a sufficient navy, and that without burdening ourselves with the evil so loudly complained of in England, of suffering their fleet in time of peace to lie rotting in the docks. To unite the sinews of commerce and defence is sound policy; for when our strength and our riches play into each other's hand, we need fear no external enemy.

In almost every article of defence we abound. Hemp flourishes even to rankness, so that we need not want cordage. Our iron is superior to that of other countries. Our small arms equal to any in the world. Cannon we can cast at pleasure. Saltpetre and gunpowder we are every day producing. Our knowledge is hourly improving. Resolution is our inherent character, and courage hath never yet forsaken us. Wherefore, what is it that we want? Why is it that we hesitate? From Britain we can expect nothing but ruin. If she is once admitted to the government of America again, this Continent will not be worth living in. Jealousies will be always arising; insurrections will be constantly happening; and who will go forth to quell them? Who will venture his life to reduce his own countrymen to a foreign obedience? The difference between Pennsylvania and Connecticut, respecting some unlocated lands, shows the insignificance of a British government, and fully proves that nothing but Continental authority can regulate Continental matters.

Another reason why the present time is preferable to all others, is, that the fewer our numbers are, the more land there is yet unoccupied, which, instead of being lavished by the king on his worthless dependants, may be hereafter applied, not only to the discharge of the present debt, but to the constant support of government. No nation under Heaven hath such an advantage as this.

The infant state of the Colonies, as it is called, so far from being against, is an argument in favour of independance. We are sufficiently numerous, and were we more so we might be less united. 'Tis a matter worthy of observation, that the more a country is peopled, the smaller their armies are. In military numbers, the ancients far exceeded the moderns: and the reason is evident, for trade being the consequence of population, men became too much absorbed thereby to attend to any thing else. Commerce diminishes the spirit both of patriotism and military defence. And history sufficiently informs us, that the bravest achievements were always accomplished in the non-age of a nation. With the increase of commerce England hath lost its spirit. The city of London, notwithstanding its numbers, submits to continued insults with the patience of a coward. The more men have to lose, the less willing are they to venture. The rich are in general slaves to fear, and submit to courtly power with the trembling duplicity of a spaniel.

Youth is the seed-time of good habits as well in nations as in individuals. It might be difficult, if not impossible, to form the Continent into one Government half a century hence. The vast variety of interests, occasioned by an increase of trade and population, would create confusion. Colony would be against Colony. Each being able would scorn each other's assistance: and while the proud and foolish gloried in their little distinctions, the wise would lament that the union had not been formed before. Wherefore the present time is the true time for establishing it. The intimacy which is contracted in infancy, and the friendship which is formed in misfortune, are of all others the most lasting and unalterable. Our present union is marked with both these characters: we are young, and we have been distressed, but our concord hath withstood our troubles, and fixes a memorable æra for posterity to glory in.

The present time, likewise, is that peculiar time which never happens to a nation but once, viz. the time of forming itself into a government. Most nations have let slip the opportunity, and by that means have been compelled to receive laws from their conquerors, instead of making laws for themselves. First, they had a king, and then a form of government; whereas the articles or charter of government should be formed first, and men delegated to execute them afterwards: but from the errors of other nations let us learn wisdom, and lay hold of the present opportunity—*to begin government at the right end*.

When William the Conqueror subdued England, he gave them law at the point of the sword; and, until we consent that the seat of government in America be legally and authoritatively occupied, we shall be in danger of having it filled by some fortunate ruffian, who may treat us in the same manner, and then, where will be our freedom? where our property?

As to religion, I hold it to be the indispensable duty of government to protect all conscientious professors thereof, and I know of no other business which government hath to do therewith. Let a man throw aside that narrowness of soul, that selfishness of principle, which the niggards of all professions are so unwilling to part with, and he will be at once delivered of his fears on that head. Suspicion is the companion of mean souls, and the bane of all good society. For myself, I fully and conscientiously believe, that it is the will of the Almighty that there should be a diversity of religious opinions among us. It affords a larger field for our Christian kindness: were we all of one way of thinking, our religious dispositions would want matter for probation; and on this liberal principle I look on the various denominations among us, to be like children of the same family, differing only in what is called their Christian names.

In page [44] I threw out a few thoughts on the propriety of a Continental Charter (for I only presume to offer hints, not plans) and in this place, I take the liberty of re-mentioning the subject, by observing, that a charter is to be understood as a bond of solemn obligation, which the whole enters into, to support the right of every separate part, whether of religion, professional freedom, or property. A firm bargain and a right reckoning make long friends.

I have heretofore likewise mentioned the necessity of a large and equal representation; and there is no political matter which more deserves our attention. A small number of electors, or a small number of representatives, are equally dangerous. But if the number of the representatives be not only small, but unequal, the danger is encreased. As an instance of this, I mention the following; when the petition of the associators was before the House of Assembly of Pennsylvania, twenty-eight members only were present; all the Bucks county members, being eight, voted against it, and had seven of the Chester members done the same, this whole province had been governed by two counties only; and this danger it is always exposed to. The unwarrantable stretch likewise, which that house made in their last sitting, to gain an undue authority over the Delegates of that Province, ought to warn the people at large, how they trust power out of their own hands. A set of instructions for their Delegates were put together, which in point of sense and business would have dishonoured a school-boy, and after being approved by a few, a very few, without doors, were carried into the house, and there passed *in behalf of the whole Colony;* whereas, did the whole colony know with what ill will that house had entered on some necessary public measures, they would not hesitate a moment to think them unworthy of such a trust.

Immediate necessity makes many things convenient, which if continued would grow into oppressions. Expedience and right are different things. When the calamities of America required a consultation, there was no method so ready, or at that time so proper, as to appoint persons from the several houses of Assembly for that purpose; and the wisdom with which they have proceeded hath preserved this Continent from ruin. But as it is more than probable that we shall never be without a CONGRESS, every well wisher to good order must own that the mode for choosing members of that body, deserves consideration. And I put it as a question to those who make a study of mankind, whether representation and election is not too great a power for one and the same body of men to possess? When we are planning for posterity, we ought to remember that virtue is not hereditary.

It is from our enemies that we often gain excellent maxims, and are frequently surprised into reason by their mistakes. Mr. Cornwall (one of the Lords of the Treasury) treated the petition of the New York Assembly with contempt, because *that* house, he said, consisted but of twenty-six members, which trifling number, he argued, could not with decency be put for the whole. We thank him for his involuntary honesty.*

TO CONCLUDE, however strange it may appear to some, or however unwilling they may be to think so, matters not, but many strong and striking reasons may be given to show, that nothing can settle our affairs so expeditiously as an open and determined declaration for independance. Some of which are,

First—It is the custom of Nations, when any two are at war, for some other powers, not engaged in the quarrel, to step in as media-

---

*Those who would fully understand of what great consequence a large and equal representation is to a state, should read Burgh's *Political Disquisitions* [Author's note].

tors, and bring about the preliminaries of a peace: But while America calls herself the subject of Great Britain, no power, however well disposed she may be, can offer her mediation. Wherefore, in our present state we may quarrel on for ever.

Secondly—It is unreasonable to suppose, that France or Spain will give us any kind of assistance, if we mean only to make use of that assistance for the purpose of repairing the breach, and strengthening the connection between Britain and America; because, those powers would be sufferers by the consequences.

Thirdly—While we profess ourselves the subjects of Britain, we must, in the eyes of foreign nations, be considered as Rebels. The precedent is somewhat dangerous to their peace, for men to be in arms under the name of subjects: we, on the spot, can solve the paradox; but to unite resistance and subjection, requires an idea much too refined for common understanding.

Fourthly—Were a manifesto to be published, and despatched to foreign Courts, setting forth the miseries we have endured, and the peaceful methods which we have ineffectually used for redress; declaring at the same time, that not being able any longer to live happily or safely under the cruel disposition of the British Court, we had been driven to the necessity of breaking off all connections with her; at the same time, assuring all such Courts of our peaceable disposition towards them, and of our desire of entering into trade with them: such a memorial would produce more good effects to this Continent, than if a ship were freighted with petitions to Britain.

Under our present denomination of British subjects, we can neither be received nor heard abroad: the custom of all Courts is against us, and will be so, until by an independance we take rank with other nations.

These proceedings may at first seem strange and difficult, but like all other steps which we have already passed over, will in a little time become familiar and agreeable: and until an independance is declared, the Continent will feel itself like a man who continues putting off some unpleasant business from day to day, yet knows it must be done, hates to set about it, wishes it over, and is continually haunted with the thoughts of its necessity.

Appendix.

Since the publication of the first edition of this pamphlet, or rather, on the same day on which it came out, the —'s Speech made its appearance in this city. Had the spirit of prophecy directed the birth of this production, it could not have brought it forth, at a more seasonable juncture, or a more necessary time. The bloody mindedness of the one, shew the necessity of pursuing the doctrine of the other. Men read by way of revenge. And the speech instead of terrifying, prepared a way for the manly principles of Independance.

Ceremony, and even, silence, from whatever motive they may arise, have a hurtful tendency, when they give the least degree of countenance to base and wicked performances; wherefore, if this maxim be admitted, it naturally follows, that the —'s speech, as being a piece of finished villainy, deserved, and still deserves, a general execration both by the Congress and the people. Yet as the domestic tranquility of a nation, depends greatly on the *chastity* of what may properly be called NATIONAL MATTERS, it is often better, to pass some things over in silent disdain, than to make use of such new methods of dislike, as might introduce the least innovation, on that guardian of our peace and safety. And perhaps, it is chiefly owing to this prudent delicacy, that the —'s Speech, hath not before now, suffered a public execution. The Speech if it may be called one, is nothing better than a wilful audacious libel against the truth, the common good, and the existence of mankind; and is a formal and pompous method of offering up human sacrifices to the pride of tyrants. But this general massacre of mankind, is one of the privileges, and the certain consequences of K—s; for as nature knows them *not*, they know *not her*, and although they are beings of our *own* creating, they know not *us*, and are become the gods of their creators. The speech hath one good quality, which is, that it is not calculated to deceive, neither can we, even if we would, be deceived

by it. Brutality and tyranny appear on the face of it. It leaves us at
no loss: And every line convinces, even in the moment of reading,
that He, who hunts the woods for prey, the naked and untutored Indian, is less a Savage than the — of B—.

Sir J—n D—e, the putative father of a whining jesuitical piece,
fallaciously called, '*The Address of the people of* ENGLAND *to the inhabitants of* AMERICA,' hath, perhaps from a vain supposition, that
the people *here* were to be frightened at the pomp and description
of a king, given, (though very unwisely on his part) the real character of the present one: 'But,' says this writer, 'if you are inclined to
pay compliments to an administration, which we do not complain
of,' (meaning the Marquis of Rockingham's at the repeal of the
Stamp Act) 'it is very unfair in you to withhold them from that
prince, *by whose* NOD ALONE *they were permitted to do any thing.*' this
is toryism with a witness! Here is idolatry even without a mask: And
he who can calmly hear, and digest such doctrine, hath forfeited his
claim to rationality—an apostate from the order of manhood; and
ought to be considered—as one, who hath, not only given up the
proper dignity of a man, but sunk himself beneath the rank of animals, and contemptibly crawl through the world like a worm.

However, it matters very little now, what the—of E— either says
or does; he hath wickedly broken through every moral and human
obligation, trampled nature and conscience beneath his feet; and by
a steady and constitutional spirit of insolence and cruelty, procured
for himself an universal hatred. It is *now* the interest of America to
provide for herself. She hath already a large and young family, whom
it is more her duty to take care of, than to be granting away her
property, to support a power who is become a reproach to the names
of men and christians—YE, whose office it is to watch over the
morals of a nation, of whatsoever sect or denomination ye are of, as
well as ye, who are more immediately the guardians of the public
liberty, if ye wish to preserve your native country uncontaminated by
European corruption, ye must in secret wish a separation—But
leaving the moral part to private reflection, I shall chiefly confine
my farther remarks to the following heads.

First. That it is the interest of America to be separated from
Britain.

Secondly. Which is the easiest and most practicable plan, REC-ONCILIATION or INDEPENDANCE? with some occasional remarks.

In support of the first, I could, if I judged it proper, produce the opinion of some of the ablest and most experienced men on this continent; and whose sentiments, on that head, are not yet publickly known. It is in reality a self-evident position: For no nation in a state of foreign dependance, limited in its commerce, and cramped and fettered in its legislative powers, can ever arrive at any material em-inence. America doth not yet know what opulence is; and although the progress which she hath made stands unparalleled in the history of other nations, it is but childhood, compared with what she would be capable of arriving at, had she, as she ought to have, the legisla-tive powers in her own hands. England is, at this time, proudly cov-eting what would do her no good, were she to accomplish it; and the Continent hesitating on a matter, which will be her final ruin if neglected. It is the commerce and not the conquest of America, by which England is to be benefited, and that would in a great mea-sure continue, were the countries as independant of each other as France and Spain; because in many articles, neither can go to a bet-ter market. But it is the independance of this country on Britain or any other, which is now the main and only object worthy of con-tention, and which, like all other truths discovered by necessity, will appear clearer and stronger every day.

First. Because it will come to that one time or other.

Secondly. Because the longer it is delayed the harder it will be to accomplish.

I have frequently amused myself both in public and private com-panies, with silently remarking the spacious errors of those who speak without reflecting. And among the many which I have heard, the following seems the most general, viz. that had this rupture hap-pened forty or fifty years hence, instead of *now*, the Continent would have been more able to have shaken off the dependance. To which I reply, that our military ability *at this time*, arises from the ex-perience gained in the last war, and which in forty or fifty years time, would have been totally extinct. The Continent, would not, by that time, have had a General, or even a military officer left; and we, or those who may succeed us, would have been as ignorant of mar-tial matters as the ancient Indians: And this single position, closely

attended to, will unanswerably prove, that the present time is preferable to all others: The argument turns thus—at the conclusion of
the last war, we had experience, but wanted numbers; and forty or
fifty years hence, we should have numbers, without experience;
wherefore, the proper point of time, must be some particular point
between the two extremes, in which a sufficiency of the former remains, and a proper increase of the latter is obtained: And that point
of time is the present time.

The reader will pardon this digression, as it does not properly
come under the head I first set out with, and to which I again return by the following position, viz.

Should affairs be patched up with Britain, and she to remain the
governing and sovereign power of America, (which as matters are
now circumstanced, is giving up the point entirely) we shall deprive
ourselves of the very means of sinking the debt we have or may contract. The value of the back lands which some of the provinces are
clandestinely deprived of, by the unjust extention of the limits of
Canada, valued only at five pounds sterling per hundred acres,
amount to upwards of twenty-five millions, Pennsylvania currency;
and the quit-rents at one penny sterling per acre, to two millions
yearly.

It is by the sale of those lands that the debt may be sunk, without burthen to any, and the quit-rent reserved thereon, will always
lessen, and in time, will wholly support the yearly expence of government. It matters not how long the debt is in paying, so that the
lands when sold be applied to the discharge of it, and for the execution of which, the Congress for the time being, will be the continental trustees.

I proceed now to the second head, viz. Which is the earliest and
most practicable plan, RECONCILIATION or INDEPENDANCE? with
some occasional remarks.

He who takes nature for his guide is not easily beaten out of his
argment, and on that ground, I answer *generally*—*That* INDEPEN-
DANCE *being a* SINGLE SIMPLE LINE, *contained within ourselves; and
reconciliation, a matter exceedingly perplexed and complicated, and in
which, a treacherous capricious court is to interfere, gives the answer
without a doubt.*

The present state of America is truly alarming to every man who is capable of reflexion. Without law, without government, without any other mode of power than what is founded on, and granted by courtesy. Held together by an unexampled concurrence of sentiment, which is nevertheless subject to change, and which every secret enemy is endeavouring to dissolve. Our present condition, is, Legislation without law; wisdom without a plan; a constitution without a name; and, what is strangely astonishing, perfect Independance contending for Dependance. The instance is without a precedent; the case never existed before; and who can tell what may be the event? The property of no man is secure in the present unbraced system of things. The mind of the multitude is left at random, and feeling no fixed object before them, they pursue such as fancy or opinion starts. Nothing is criminal; there is no such thing as treason; wherefore, every one thinks himself at liberty to act as he pleases. The Tories dared not to have assembled offensively, had they known that their lives, by that act were forfeited to the laws of the state. A line of distinction should be drawn, between English soldiers taken in battle, and inhabitants of America taken in arms. The first are prisoners, but the latter traitors. The one forfeits his liberty the other his head.

Notwithstanding our wisdom, there is a visible feebleness in some of our proceedings which gives encouragement to dissentions. The Continental belt is too loosely buckled. And if something is not done in time, it will be too late to do any thing, and we shall fall into a state, in which, neither *reconciliation* nor *independance* will be practicable. The — and his worthless adherents are got at their old game of dividing the Continent, and there are not wanting among us, Printers, who will be busy spreading specious falsehoods. The artful and hypocritical letter which appeared a few months ago in two of the New-York papers, and likewise in two others, is an evidence that there are men who want either judgement or honesty.

It is easy getting into holes and corners and talking of reconciliation: But do such men seriously consider, how difficult the task is, and how dangerous it may prove, should the Continent divide thereon. Do they take within their view, all the various orders of men whose situation and circumstances, as well as their own, are to be considered therein. Do they put themselves in the place of the sufferer whose *all* is *already* gone, and of the soldier, who hath quitted *all* for the defence of his country. If their ill-judged moderation be suited to their own private situations *only*, regardless of others, the event will convince them, that 'they are reckoning without their Host.'

Put us, says some, on the footing we were on in sixty-three: To which I answer, the request is not *now* in the power of Britain to comply with, neither will she propose it; but if it were, and even should be granted, I ask, as a reasonable question, By what means is such a corrupt and faithless court to be kept to its engagements? Another parliament, nay, even the present, may hereafter repeal the obligation, on the pretence of its being violently obtained, or unwisely granted; and in that case, Where is our redress?—No going to law with nations; cannon are the barristers of crowns; and the sword, not of justice, but of war, decides the suit. To be on the footing of sixty-three, it is not sufficient, that the laws only be put on the same state, but, that our circumstances, likewise, be put on the same state; our burnt and destroyed towns repaired or built up, our private losses made good, our public debts (contracted for defence) discharged; otherwise, we shall be millions worse than we were at that enviable period. Such a request had it been complied with a year ago, would have won the heart and soul of the Continent—but now it is too late, 'The Rubicon is passed.'

Besides the taking up arms, merely to enforce the repeal of a pecuniary law, seems as unwarrantable by the divine law, and as repugnant to human feelings, as the taking up arms to enforce obedience thereto. The object, on either side, doth not justify the ways and means; for the lives of men are too valuable to be cast away on such trifles. It is the violence which is done and threatened to our persons; the destruction of our property by an armed force; the invasion of our country by fire and sword, which conscientiously qualifies the use of arms: And the instant, in which such a mode of defence became necessary, all subjection to Britain ought to have ceased; and the independancy of America should have been considered, as dating its æra from, and published by, *the first musket that was fired against her*. This line is a line of consistency; neither drawn by caprice, nor extended by ambition; but produced by a chain of events, of which the colonies were not the authors.

I shall conclude these remarks, with the following timely and well intended hints, We ought to reflect, that there are three different ways by which an independancy may hereafter be effected; and that *one* of those *three*, will one day or other, be the fate of America, viz. By the legal voice of the people in Congress; by a military power; or by a mob: It may not always happen that our soldiers are citizens, and the multitude a body of reasonable men; virtue, as I have already remarked, is not hereditary, neither is it perpetual. Should an independancy be brought about by the first of those means, we have every opportunity and every encouragement before us, to form the noblest, purest constitution on the face of the earth. We have it in our power to begin the world over again. A situation, similar to the present, hath not happened since the days of Noah until now. The birth-day of a new world is at hand, and a race of men perhaps as numerous as all Europe contains, are to receive their portion of freedom from the event of a few months. The Reflexion is awful—and in this point of view, How trifling, how ridiculous, do the little, paltry cavellings, of a few weak or interested men appear, when weighed against the business of a world.

Should we neglect the present favorable and inviting period, and an independance be hereafter effected by any other means, we must charge the consequence to ourselves, or to those rather, whose narrow and prejudiced souls, are habitually opposing the measure, without either inquiring or reflecting. There are reasons to be given in support of Independance, which men should rather privately think of, than be publicly told of. We ought not now to be debating whether we shall be independant or not, but, anxious to accomplish it on a firm, secure, and honorable basis, and uneasy rather that it is not yet began upon. Every day convinces us of its necessity. Even the Tories (if such beings yet remain among us) should, of all men, be the most solicitous to promote it; for, as the appointment of committees at first, protected them from popular rage, so, a wise and well established form of government, will be the only certain means of continuing it securely to them. *Wherefore*, if they have not virtue enough to be WHIGS, they ought to have prudence enough to wish for Independance.

In short, Independance is the only BOND that can tye and keep us together. We shall then see our object, and our ears will be legally shut against the schemes of an intriguing, as well as a cruel enemy.

We shall then too, be on a proper footing, to treat with Britain; for there is reason to conclude, that the pride of that court, will be less hurt by treating with the American states for terms of peace, than with those, whom she denominates, 'rebellious subjects,' for terms of accommodation. It is our delaying it that encourages her to hope for conquest, and our backwardness tends only to prolong the war. As we have, without any good effect therefrom, with-held our trade to obtain a redress of our grievances, let us *now* try the alternative, by *independantly* redressing them ourselves, and then offering to open the trade. The mercantile and reasonable part of England will be still with us; because, peace *with* trade, is preferable to war *without* it. And if this offer be not accepted, other courts may be applied to.

On these grounds I rest the matter. And as no offer hath yet been made to refute the doctrine contained in the former editions of this pamphlet, it is a negative proof, that either the doctrine cannot be refuted, or, that the party in favour of it are too numerous to be opposed. WHEREFORE, instead of gazing at each other with suspicious or doubtful curiosity, let each of us, hold out to his neighbour the hearty hand of friendship, and unite in drawing a line, which, like an act of oblivion, shall bury in forgetfulness every former dissention. Let the names of Whig and Tory be extinct; and let none other be heard among us, than those of *a good citizen, an open and resolute friend, and a virtuous supporter of the* RIGHTS *of* MANKIND *and of the* FREE AND INDEPENDANT STATES OF AMERICA.

*   *   *   *

To the Representatives of the Religious Society of the People called Quakers, or to so many of them as were concerned in publishing a late piece, entitled 'The Ancient Testimony and Principles of the people called Quakers renewed, with respect to the King and Government, and Touching the Commotions now prevailing in these and other parts of America, addressed to the people in general.'

The Writer of this, is one of those few, who never dishonors religion either by ridiculing, or cavilling at any denomination whatsoever. To God, and not to man, are all men accountable on the score of religion. Wherefore, this epistle is not so properly addressed to you as a religious, but as a political body, dabbling in matters, which the professed Quietude of your Principles instruct you not to meddle with.

As you have, without a proper authority for so doing, put yourselves in the place of the whole body of the Quakers, so, the writer of this, in order to be on an equal rank with yourselves, is under the necessity, of putting himself in the place of all those who approve the very writings and principles, against which your testimony is directed: And he hath chosen their singular situation, in order that you might discover in him, that presumption of character which you cannot see in yourselves. For neither he nor you have any claim or title to *Political Representation.*

When men have departed from the right way, it is no wonder that they stumble and fall. And it is evident from the manner in which ye have managed your testimony, that politics, (as a religious body of men) is not your proper Walk; for however well adapted it might appear to you, it is, nevertheless, a jumble of good and bad put unwisely together, and the conclusion drawn therefrom, both unnatural and unjust.

The two first pages, (and the whole doth not make four) we give you credit for, and expect the same civility from you, because the love and desire of peace is not confined to Quakerism, it is the *natural*, as well as the religious wish of all denominations of men. And on this ground, as men labouring to establish an Independant Constitution of our own, do we exceed all others in our hope, end, and aim. *Our plan is peace for ever.* We are tired of contention with Britain, and can see no real end to it but in a final separation. We act consistently, because for the sake of introducing an endless and uninterrupted peace, do we bear the evils and burthens of the present day. We are endeavouring, and will steadily continue to endeavor, to separate and dissolve a connexion which hath already filled our land with blood; and which, while the name of it remains, will be the fatal cause of future mischiefs to both countries.

We fight neither for revenge nor conquest; neither from pride nor passion; we are not insulting the world with our fleets and armies, nor ravaging the globe for plunder. Beneath the shade of our own vines are we attacked; in our own houses, and on our own lands, is the violence committed against us. We view our enemies in the characters of Highwaymen and Housebreakers, and having no defence for ourselves in the civil law, are obliged to punish them by the military one, and apply the sword, in the very case, where you have before now, applied the halter.—Perhaps we feel for the ruined and insulted sufferers in all and every part of the continent, and with a degree of tenderness which hath not yet made its way into some of your bosoms. But be ye sure that ye mistake not the cause and ground of your Testimony. Call not coldness of soul, religion; nor put the *Bigot* in the place of the *Christian*.

O ye partial ministers of your own acknowledged principles. If the bearing arms be sinful, the first going to war must be more so, by all the difference between wilful attack and unavoidable defence. Wherefore, if ye really preach from conscience, and mean not to make a political hobby-horse of your religion, convince the world thereof, by proclaiming your doctrine to our enemies, *for they likewise bear* ARMS. Give us proof of your sincerity by publishing it at St. James's, to the commanders in chief at Boston, to the Admirals and Captains who are piratically ravaging our coasts, and to all the murdering miscreants who are acting in authority under HIM whom ye profess to serve. Had ye the honest soul of *Barclay** ye would preach repentance to *your* king; Ye would tell the Royal—his sins, and warn him of eternal ruin. Ye would not spend your partial invectives against the injured and the insulted only, but like faithful ministers, would cry aloud and *spare none*. Say not that ye are persecuted, neither endeavour to make us the authors of that reproach, which, ye are bringing upon yourselves; for we testify unto all men, that we do not complain against you because ye are *Quakers*, but because ye pretend to *be* and are NOT Quakers.

---

*'Thou hast tasted of prosperity and adversity; thou knowest what it is to be banished thy native country, to be over-ruled as well as to rule, and set upon the throne; and being *oppressed* thou hast reason to know now *hateful* the *oppressor* is both to God and man: If after all these warnings and advertisements, thou dost not turn unto the Lord with all thy heart, but forget him who remembered thee in thy distress, and give up thyself to follow lust and vanity, surely great will be thy condemnation.—Against which snare, as well as the temptation of those who may or do feed thee, and prompt thee to evil, the most excellent and prevalent remedy will be, to apply thyself to that light of Christ which shineth in thy conscience and which neither can, nor will flatter thee, nor suffer thee to be at ease in thy sins.' *Barclay's Address to Charles II* [Author's note].

Alas! it seems by the particular tendency of some part of your testimony, and other parts of your conduct, as if all sin was reduced to, and comprehended in *the act of bearing arms*, and that by the *people only*. Ye appear to us, to have mistaken party for conscience, because the general tenor of your actions wants uniformity: And it is exceedingly difficult to us to give credit to many of your pretended scruples; because we see them made by the same men, who, in the very instant that they are exclaiming against the mammon of this world, are nevertheless, hunting after it with a step as steady as Time, and an appetite as keen as Death.

The quotation which ye have made from Proverbs, in the third page of your testimony, that, 'when a man's ways please the Lord, he maketh even his enemies to be at peace with him'; is very unwisely chosen on your part; because it amounts to a proof, that the king's ways (whom ye are so desirous of supporting) do *not* please the Lord, otherwise, his reign would be in peace.

I now proceed to the latter part of your testimony, and that, for which all the foregoing seems only an introduction, viz.

'It hath ever been our judgment and principle, since we were 'called to profess the light of Christ Jesus, manifested in our con- 'sciences unto this day, that the setting up and putting down kings 'and governments, is God's peculiar prerogative; for causes best 'known to himself: And that it is not our business to have any hand 'or contrivance therein; nor to be busy bodies above our station, 'much less to plot and contrive the ruin, or overturn any of them, but 'to pray for the king, and safety of our nation, and good of all men: 'That we may live a peaceable and quiet life, in all goodliness and 'honesty; *under the government which God is pleased to set over us.*'— If these are *really* your principles why do ye not abide by them? Why do ye not leave that, which ye call God's Work, to be managed by himself? These very principles instruct you to wait with patience and humility, for the event of all public measures, and to receive *that event* as the divine will towards you. *Wherefore*, what occasion is there for your *political testimony* if you fully believe what it contains? And the very publishing it proves, that either, ye do not believe what ye profess, or have not virtue enough to practise what ye believe.

The principles of Quakerism have a direct tendency to make a man the quiet and inoffensive subject of any, and every government *which is set over him.* And if the setting up and putting down of kings and governments is God's peculiar prerogative, he most certainly will not be robbed thereof by us; wherefore, the principle itself leads you to approve of every thing, which ever happened, or may happen to kings as being his work, OLIVER CROMWELL thanks you.— CHARLES, then, died not by the hands of man; and should the present Proud Imitator of him, come to the same untimely end, the writers and publishers of the testimony, are bound by the doctrine it contains, to applaud the fact. Kings are not taken away by miracles, neither are changes in governments brought about by any other means than such as are common and human; and such as we are now using. Even the dispersing of the Jews, though foretold by our Saviour, was effected by arms. Wherefore, as ye refuse to be the means on one side, ye ought not to be meddlers on the other; but to wait the issue in silence; and unless you can produce divine authority, to prove, that the Almighty who hath created and placed this *new* world, at the greatest distance it could possibly stand, east and west, from every part of the old, doth, nevertheless, disapprove of its being independant of the corrupt and abandoned court of B—n, unless I say, ye can show this, how can ye, on the ground of your principles, justify the exciting and stirring up of the people 'firmly to 'unite in the *abhorrence* of all such *writings,* and *measures,* as evidence 'a desire and design to break off the *happy* connexion we have hith-'erto enjoyed, with the kingdom of Great-Britain, and our just and 'necessary subordination to the king, and those who are lawfully 'placed in authority under him.' What a slap in the face is here! the men, who, in the very paragraph before, have quietly and passively resigned up the ordering, altering, and disposal of kings and governments, into the hands of God, are now recalling their principles, and putting in for a share of the business. Is it possible, that the conclusion, which is here justly quoted, can any ways follow from the doctrine laid down? The inconsistency is too glaring not to be seen; the absurdity too great not to be laughed at; and such as could only have been made by those, whose understandings were darkened by the narrow and crabby spirit of a despairing political party; for ye are not to be considered as the whole body of the Quakers but only as a factional and fractional part thereof.

Here ends the examination of your testimony; (which I call upon no man to abhor, as ye have done, but only to read and judge of fairly;) to which I subjoin the following remark; 'That the setting up and putting down of kings,' most certainly mean, the making him a king, who is yet not so, and the making him no king who is already one. And pray what hath this to do in the present case? We neither mean to *set up* nor to *put down*, neither to *make* nor to *unmake*, but to have nothing to *do* with them. Wherefore, your testimony in whatever light it is viewed serves only to dishonour your judgment, and for many other reasons had better have been let alone than published.

First. Because it tends to the decrease and reproach of all religion whatever, and is of the utmost danger to society, to make it a party in political disputes.

Secondly. Because it exhibits a body of men, numbers of whom disavow the publishing political testimonies, as being concerned therein and approvers thereof.

Thirdly. Because it hath a tendency to undo that continental harmony and friendship which yourselves by your late liberal and charitable donations hath lent a hand to establish; and the preservation of which, is of the utmost consequence to us all.

And here without anger or resentment I bid you farewell. Sincerely wishing, that as men and christians, ye may always fully and uninterruptedly enjoy every civil and religious right; and be, in your turn, the means of securing it to others; but that the example which ye have unwisely set, of mingling religion with politics, *may be disavowed and reprabated by every inhabitant of* AMERICA.

FINIS

THE AMERICAN CRISIS PAPERS

Nos. 1, 10, and 13
[1776–1783]

The Crisis.

No. 1.

THESE ARE THE TIMES that try men's souls. The summer soldier and the sunshine patriot will, in this crisis, shrink from the service of their country; but he that stands it *now*, deserves the love and thanks of man and woman. Tyranny, like hell, is not easily conquered; yet we have this consolation with us, that the harder the conflict, the more glorious the triumph. What we obtain too cheap, we esteem too lightly: it is dearness only that gives every thing its value. Heaven knows how to put a proper price upon its goods; and it would be strange indeed if so celestial an article as FREEDOM should not be highly rated. Britain, with an army to enforce her tyranny, has declared that she has a right (*not only to* TAX) but "to BIND *us in* ALL CASES WHATSOEVER," and if being *bound in that manner*, is not slavery, then is there not such a thing as slavery upon earth. Even the expression is impious; for so unlimited a power can belong only to God.

Whether the independence of the continent was declared too soon, or delayed too long, I will not now enter into as an argument; my own simple opinion is, that had it been eight months earlier, it would have been much better. We did not make a proper use of last winter, neither could we, while we were in a dependant state. However, the fault, if it were one, was all our own*; we have none to blame but ourselves. But no great deal is lost yet. All that Howe† has been doing for this month past, is rather a ravage than a conquest,

---

*The present winter is worth an age, if rightly employed; but, if lost or neglected, the whole continent will partake of the evil; and there is no punishment that man does not deserve, be he who, or what, or where he will, that may be the means of sacrificing a season so precious and useful.—[Author's note]—a citation from his "Common Sense."

†Sir William Howe (1729–1814), commander of British troops in America until 1778.

which the spirit of the Jerseys, a year ago, would have quickly re-
pulsed, and which time and a little resolution will soon recover.

I have as little superstition in me as any man living, but my secret
opinion has ever been, and still is, that God Almighty will not give up
a people to military destruction, or leave them unsupportedly to perish, who have so earnestly and so repeatedly sought to avoid the
calamities of war, by every decent method which wisdom could invent.
Neither have I so much of the infidel in me, as to suppose that He has
relinquished the government of the world, and given us up to the care
of devils; and as I do not, I cannot see on what grounds the king of
Britain can look up to heaven for help against us: a common murderer,
a highwayman, or a house-breaker, has as good a pretence as he.

'Tis surprising to see how rapidly a panic will sometimes run
through a country. All nations and ages have been subject to them:
Britain has trembled like an ague at the report of a French fleet of flat
bottomed boats; and in the fourteenth [fifteenth] century the whole
English army, after ravaging the kingdom of France, was driven back
like men petrified with fear; and this brave exploit was performed by
a few broken forces collected and headed by a woman, Joan of Arc.
Would that heaven might inspire some Jersey maid to spirit up her
countrymen, and save her fair fellow sufferers from ravage and rav-
ishment! Yet panics, in some cases, have their uses; they produce as
much good as hurt. Their duration is always short; the mind soon
grows through them, and acquires a firmer habit than before. But
their peculiar advantage is, that they are the touchstones of sincerity
and hypocrisy, and bring things and men to light, which might otherwise have lain forever undiscovered. In fact, they have the same effect on secret traitors, which an imaginary apparition would have
upon a private murderer. They sift out the hidden thoughts of man,
and hold them up in public to the world. Many a disguised Tory has
lately shown his head, that shall penitentially solemnize with curses
the day on which Howe arrived upon the Delaware.

As I was with the troops at Fort Lee, and marched with them to
the edge of Pennsylvania, I am well acquainted with many circumstances, which those who live at a distance know but little or nothing of. Our situation there was exceedingly cramped, the place being
a narrow neck of land between the North River and the Hackensack.
Our force was inconsiderable, being not one fourth so great as Howe

could bring against us. We had no army at hand to have relieved the garrison, had we shut ourselves up and stood on our defence. Our ammunition, light artillery, and the best part of our stores, had been removed, on the apprehension that Howe would endeavor to penetrate the Jerseys, in which case fort Lee could be of no use to us; for it must occur to every thinking man, whether in the army or not, that these kind of field forts are only for temporary purposes, and last in use no longer than the enemy directs his force against the particular object, which such forts are raised to defend. Such was our situation and condition at fort Lee on the morning of the 20th of November, when an officer arrived with information that the enemy with 200 boats had landed about seven miles above: Major General [Nathaniel] Green, who commanded the garrison, immediately ordered them under arms, and sent express to General Washington at the town of Hackensack, distant by the way of the ferry = six miles. Our first object was to secure the bridge over the Hackensack, which laid up the river between the enemy and us, about six miles from us, and three from them. General Washington arrived in about three quarters of an hour, and marched at the head of the troops towards the bridge, which place I expected we should have a brush for; however, they did not choose to dispute it with us, and the greatest part of our troops went over the bridge, the rest over the ferry, except some which passed at a mill on a small creek, between the bridge and the ferry, and made their way through some marshy grounds up to the town of Hackensack, and there passed the river. We brought off as much baggage as the wagons could contain, the rest was lost. The simple object was to bring off the garrison, and march them on till they could be strengthened by the Jersey or Pennsylvania militia, so as to be enabled to make a stand. We staid four days at Newark, collected our out-posts with some of the Jersey militia, and marched out twice to meet the enemy, on being informed that they were advancing, though our numbers were greatly inferior to theirs. Howe, in my little opinion, committed a great error in generalship in not throwing a body of forces off from Staten Island through Amboy, by which means he might have seized all our stores at Brunswick, and intercepted our march into Pennsylvania; but if we believe the power of hell to be limited, we must likewise believe that their agents are under some providential controul.

I shall not now attempt to give all the particulars of our retreat to the Delaware; suffice it for the present to say, that both officers and men, though greatly harassed and fatigued, frequently without rest, covering, or provision, the inevitable consequences of a long retreat, bore it with a manly and martial spirit. All their wishes centred in one, which was, that the country would turn out and help them to drive the enemy back. Voltaire has remarked that king William never appeared to full advantage but in difficulties and in action; the same remark may be made on General Washington, for the character fits him. There is a natural firmness in some minds which cannot be unlocked by trifles, but which, when unlocked, discovers a cabinet of fortitude; and I reckon it among those kind of public blessings, which we do not immediately see, that God hath blessed him with uninterrupted health, and given him a mind that can even flourish upon care.

I shall conclude this paper with some miscellaneous remarks on the state of our affairs; and shall begin with asking the following question, Why is it that the enemy have left the New-England provinces, and made these middle ones the seat of war? The answer is easy: New-England is not infested with tories, and we are. I have been tender in raising the cry against these men, and used numberless arguments to show them their danger, but it will not do to sacrifice a world either to their folly or their baseness. The period is now arrived, in which either they or we must change our sentiments, or one or both must fall. And what is a tory? Good God! what is he? I should not be afraid to go with a hundred whigs against a thousand tories, were they to attempt to get into arms. Every tory is a coward; for servile, slavish, self-interested fear is the foundation of toryism; and a man under such influence, though he may be cruel, never can be brave.

But, before the line of irrecoverable separation be drawn between us, let us reason the matter together: Your conduct is an invitation to the enemy, yet not one in a thousand of you has heart enough to join him. Howe is as much deceived by you as the American cause is injured by you. He expects you will all take up arms, and flock to his standard, with muskets on your shoulders. Your opinions are of no use to him, unless you support him personally, for 'tis soldiers, and not tories, that he wants.

I once felt all that kind of anger, which a man ought to feel, against the mean principles that are held by the tories: a noted one, who kept a tavern at Amboy, was standing at his door, with as pretty a child in his hand, about eight or nine years old, as I ever saw, and after speaking his mind as freely as he thought was prudent, finished with this un-fatherly expression, "*Well! give me peace in my day.*" Not a man lives on the continent but fully believes that a separation must some time or other finally take place, and a generous parent should have said, "*If there must be trouble, let it be in my day, that my child may have peace;*" and this single reflection, well applied, is sufficient to awaken every man to duty. Not a place upon earth might be so happy as America. Her situation is remote from all the wrangling world, and she has nothing to do but to trade with them. A man can distinguish himself between temper and principle, and I am as confident, as I am that God governs the world, that America will never be happy till she gets clear of foreign dominion. Wars, without ceasing, will break out till that period arrives, and the continent must in the end be conqueror; for though the flame of liberty may sometimes cease to shine, the coal can never expire.

America did not, nor does not want force; but she wanted a proper application of that force. Wisdom is not the purchase of a day, and it is no wonder that we should err at the first setting off. From an excess of tenderness, we were unwilling to raise an army, and trusted our cause to the temporary defence of a well-meaning militia. A summer's experience has now taught us better; yet with those troops, while they were collected, we were able to set bounds to the progress of the enemy, and, thank God! they are again assembling. I always considered militia as the best troops in the world for a sudden exertion, but they will not do for a long campaign. Howe, it is probable, will make an attempt on this city; should he fail on this side the Delaware, he is ruined: if he succeeds, our cause is not ruined. He stakes all on his side against a part on ours; admitting he succeeds, the consequence will be, that armies from both ends of the continent will march to assist their suffering friends in the middle states; for he cannot go everywhere, it is impossible. I consider Howe as the greatest enemy the tories have; he is bringing a war into their country, which, had it not been for him and partly for themselves, they had been clear of. Should he now be expelled, I wish with all the devotion of a Christian, that the names of whig and tory may never more be mentioned; but should the tories give him encouragement to come, or assistance if he come, I as sincerely wish that our next year's arms may expel them from the continent, and the congress appropriate their possessions to the relief of those who have suffered in well-doing. A single successful battle next year will settle the whole. America could carry on a two years war by the confiscation of the property of disaffected persons, and be made happy by their expulsion. Say not that this is revenge, call it rather the soft resentment of a suffering people, who, having no object in view but the *good* of *all*, have staked their *own all* upon a seemingly doubtful event. Yet it is folly to argue against determined hardness; eloquence may strike the ear, and the language of sorrow draw forth the tear of compassion, but nothing can reach the heart that is steeled with prejudice.

Quitting this class of men, I turn with the warm ardor of a friend to those who have nobly stood, and are yet determined to stand the matter out: I call not upon a few, but upon all: not on *this* state or *that* state, but on *every* state: up and help us; lay your shoulders to the wheel; better have too much force than too little, when so great an object is at stake. Let it be told to the future world, that in the depth of winter, when nothing but hope and virtue could survive, that the city and the country, alarmed at one common danger, came forth to meet and to repulse it. Say not that thousands are gone, turn out your tens of thousands; throw not the burden of the day upon Providence, but "*show your faith by your works,*" that God may bless you. It matters not where you live, or what rank of life you hold, the evil or the blessing will reach you all. The far and the near, the home counties and the back, the rich and the poor, will suffer or rejoice alike. The heart that feels not now, is dead: the blood of his children will curse his cowardice, who shrinks back at a time when a little might have saved the whole, and made *them* happy. I love the man that can smile in trouble, that can gather strength from distress, and grow brave by reflection. 'Tis the business of little minds to shrink; but he whose heart is firm, and whose conscience approves his conduct, will pursue his principles unto death. My own line of reasoning is to myself as straight and clear as a ray of light. Not all the treasures of the world so far as I believe, could have induced me to support an offensive war, for I think it murder; but if a thief breaks into my house, burns and destroys my property, and kills or threatens to kill me, or those that are in it, and to "*bind me in all cases* *whatsoever"** to his absolute will, am I to suffer it? What signifies it to me, whether he who does it is a king or a common man; my countryman or not my countryman; whether it be done by an individual villain, or an army of them? If we reason to the root of things we shall find no difference; neither can any just cause be assigned why we should punish in the one case and pardon in the other. Let them call me rebel, and welcome, I feel no concern from it; but I should suffer the misery of devils, were I to make a whore of my soul by swearing allegiance to one whose character is that of a sottish, stupid, stubborn, worthless, brutish man. I conceive likewise a horrid idea in receiving mercy from a being, who at the last day shall be shrieking to the rocks and mountains to cover him, and fleeing with terror from the orphan, the widow, and the slain of America.

There are cases which cannot be overdone by language, and this is one. There are persons, too, who see not the full extent of the evil which threatens them; they solace themselves with hopes that the enemy, if he succeed, will be merciful. It is the madness of folly, to expect mercy from those who have refused to do justice; and even mercy, where conquest is the object, is only a trick of war; the cunning of the fox is as murderous as the violence of the wolf, and we ought to guard equally against both. Howe's first object is, partly by threats and partly by promises, to terrify or seduce the people to deliver up their arms and receive mercy. The ministry recommended the same plan to Gage,† and this is what the tories call making their peace, *"a peace which passeth all understanding"* indeed! A peace which would be the immediate forerunner of a worse ruin than any we have yet thought of. Ye men of Pennsylvania, do reason upon these things! Were the back counties to give up their arms, they would fall an easy prey to the Indians, who are all armed: this perhaps is what some tories would not be sorry for. Were the home counties to deliver up their arms, they would be exposed to the resentment of the back counties, who would then have it in their power to chastise their defection at pleasure. And were any one state to give up its arms, *that* state must be garrisoned by all Howe's army of Britons

---

*Line from Parliament's Declaratory Act of 1766 asserting authority over the American colonies.
†Thomas Gage (1721–1787), last royal governor of Massachusetts.

and Hessians to preserve it from the anger of the rest. Mutual fear is the principal link in the chain of mutual love, and woe be to that state that breaks the compact. Howe is mercifully inviting you to barbarous destruction, and men must be either rogues or fools that will not see it. I dwell not upon the vapours of imagination: I bring reason to your ears, and, in language as plain as A, B, C, hold up truth to your eyes.

I thank God, that I fear not. I see no real cause for fear. I know our situation well, and can see the way out of it. While our army was collected, Howe dared not risk a battle; and it is no credit to him that he decamped from the White Plains, and waited a mean opportunity to ravage the defenceless Jerseys; but it is great credit to us, that, with a handful of men, we sustained an orderly retreat for near an hundred miles, brought off our ammunition, all our field pieces, the greatest part of our stores, and had four rivers to pass. None can say that our retreat was precipitate, for we were near three weeks in performing it, that the country might have time to come in. Twice we marched back to meet the enemy, and remained out till dark. The sign of fear was not seen in our camp, and had not some of the cowardly and disaffected inhabitants spread false alarms through the country, the Jerseys had never been ravaged. Once more we are again collected and collecting; our new army at both ends of the continent is recruiting fast, and we shall be able to open the next campaign with sixty thousand men, well armed and clothed. This is our situation, and who will may know it. By perseverance and fortitude we have the prospect of a glorious issue; by cowardice and submission, the sad choice of a variety of evils—a ravaged country—a depopulated city—habitations without safety, and slavery without hope—our homes turned into barracks and bawdy-houses for Hessians, and a future race to provide for, whose fathers we shall doubt of. Look on this picture and weep over it! and if there yet remains one thoughtless wretch who believes it not, let him suffer it unlamented.

COMMON SENSE.

December 23, 1776.

THE CRISIS.

No. 10.
On the King of England's Speech.

OF ALL THE INNOCENT passions which actuate the human mind there is none more universally prevalent than curiosity. It reaches all mankind, and in matters which concern us, or concern us not, it alike provokes in us a desire to know them.

Although the situation of America, superior to every effort to enslave her, and daily rising to importance and opulence, hath placed her above the region of anxiety, it has still left her within the circle of curiosity; and her fancy to see the speech of a man who had proudly threatened to bring her to his feet, was visibly marked with that tranquil confidence which cared nothing about its contents. It was inquired after with a smile, read with a laugh, and dismissed with disdain.

But, as justice is due, even to an enemy, it is right to say, that the speech is as well managed as the embarrassed condition of their affairs could well admit of; and though hardly a line of it is true, except the mournful story of Cornwallis,* it may serve to amuse the deluded commons and people of England, for whom it was calculated.

"The war," says the speech, "is still unhappily prolonged by that restless ambition which first excited our enemies to commence it, and which still continues to disappoint my earnest wishes and diligent exertions to restore the public tranquillity."

How easy it is to abuse truth and language, when men, by habit-

---

*Charles Cornwallis (1735–1805), English general who surrendered in October 1781 to George Washington at Yorktown, in the last major battle of the American Revolution.

ual wickedness, have learned to set justice at defiance. That the very man who began the war, who with the most sullen insolence refused to answer, and even to hear the humblest of all petitions, who hath encouraged his officers and his army in the most savage cruelties, and the most scandalous plunderings, who hath stirred up the Indians on one side, and the negroes on the other, and invoked every aid of hell in his behalf, should now, with an affected air of pity, turn the tables from himself, and charge to another the wickedness that, is his own, can only be equalled by the baseness of the heart that spoke it.

To be nobly wrong is more manly than to be meanly right, is an expression I once used on a former occasion, and it is equally applicable now. We feel something like respect for consistency even in error. We lament the virtue that is debauched into a vice, but the vice that affects a virtue becomes the more detestable: and amongst the various assumptions of character, which hypocrisy has taught, and men have practised, there is none that raises a higher relish of disgust, than to see disappointed inveteracy twisting itself, by the most visible falsehoods, into an appearance of piety which it has no pretensions to.

> "But I should not," continues the speech, "answer the trust committed to the sovereign of a *free people*, nor make a suitable return to my subjects for their constant, zealous, and affectionate attachment to my person, family and government, if I consented to sacrifice, either to my own desire of peace, or to their temporary ease and relief, *those essential rights and permanent interests*, upon the maintenance and preservation of which, the future strength and security of this country must principally depend."

That the man whose ignorance and obstinacy first involved and still continues the nation in the most hopeless and expensive of all wars, should now meanly flatter them with the name of a *free people*, and make a merit of his crime, under the disguise of their essential rights and permanent interests, is something which disgraces even the character of perverseness. Is he afraid they will send him to Hanover, or what does he fear? Why is the sycophant thus added to the hypocrite, and the man who pretends to govern, sunk into the humble and submissive memorialist?

What those essential rights and permanent interests are, on which the future strength and security of England must principally *depend*, are not so much as alluded to. They are words which impress nothing but the ear, and are calculated only for the sound.

But if they have any reference to America, then do they amount to the disgraceful confession, that England, who once assumed to be her protectress, has now become her *dependant*. The British king and ministry are constantly holding up the vast importance which America is of to England, in order to allure the nation to carry on the war: now, whatever ground there is for this idea, it ought to have operated as a reason for not beginning it; and, therefore, they support their present measures to their own disgrace, because the arguments which they now use, are a direct reflection on their former policy.

"The favorable appearance of affairs," continues the speech, "in the East Indies, and the safe arrival of the numerous commercial fleets of my kingdom, must have given you satisfaction."

That things are not *quite* so bad every where as in America may be some cause of consolation, but can be none for triumph. One broken leg is better than two, but still it is not a source of joy: and let the appearance of affairs in the East Indies be ever so favorable, they are nevertheless worse than at first, without a prospect of their ever being better. But the mournful story of Cornwallis was yet to be told, and it was necessary to give it the softest introduction possible.

"But in the course of this year," continues the speech, "my assiduous endeavors to guard the extensive dominions of my crown have not been attended with success equal to the justice and uprightness of my views."—What justice and uprightness there was in beginning a war with America, the world will judge of, and the unequalled barbarity with which it has been conducted, is not to be worn from the memory by the cant of snivelling hypocrisy.

"And it is with *great concern* that I inform you that the events of war have been very unfortunate to my arms in Virginia, having ended in the loss of my forces in that province."—And *our* great concern is that they are not all served in the same manner.

"No endeavors have been wanting on my part," says the speech, "to extinguish that spirit of rebellion which our enemies have found means to foment and maintain in the colonies; and to restore to my *deluded subjects* in America that happy and prosperous condition which they formerly derived from a due obedience to the laws."

The expression of *deluded subjects* is become so hacknied and contemptible, and the more so when we see them making prisoners of whole armies at a time, that the pride of not being laughed at would induce a man of common sense to leave it off. But the most offensive falsehood in the paragraph is the attributing the prosperity of America to a wrong cause. It was the unremitted industry of the settlers and their descendants, the hard labor and toil of persevering fortitude, that were the true causes of the prosperity of America. The former tyranny of England served to people it, and the virtue of the adventurers to improve it. Ask the man, who, with his axe, hath cleared a way in the wilderness, and now possesses an estate, what made him rich, and he will tell you the labor of his hands, the sweat of his brow, and the blessing of heaven. Let Britain but leave America to herself and she asks no more. She has risen into greatness without the knowledge and against the will of England, and has a right to the unmolested enjoyment of her own created wealth.

"I will order," says the speech, "the estimates of the ensuing year to be laid before you. I rely on your wisdom and public spirit for such supplies as the circumstances of our affairs shall be found to require. Among the many ill consequences which attend the continuation of the present war, I most sincerely regret the additional burdens which it must unavoidably bring upon my faithful subjects."

It is strange that a nation must run through such a labyrinth of trouble, and expend such a mass of wealth to gain the wisdom which an hour's reflection might have taught. The final superiority of America over every attempt that an island might make to conquer her, was as naturally marked in the constitution of things, as the future ability of a giant over a dwarf is delineated in his features while an infant. How far providence, to accomplish purposes which no human wisdom could foresee, permitted such extraordinary errors, is still a secret in the womb of time, and must remain so till futurity shall give it birth.

"In the prosecution of this great and important contest," says the speech, "in which we are engaged, I retain a firm confidence in the *protection of divine providence*, and a perfect conviction in the justice of my cause, and I have no doubt, but, that by the concurrence and support of my parliament, by the valour of my fleets and armies, and by a vigorous, animated, and united exertion of the faculties and resources of my people, I shall be enabled to restore the blessings of a safe and honorable peace to all my dominions."

The king of England is one of the readiest believers in the world. In the beginning of the contest he passed an act to put America out of the protection of the crown of England, and though providence, for seven years together, hath put him out of *her* protection, still the man has no doubt. Like Pharaoh on the edge of the Red sea, he sees not the plunge he is making, and precipitately drives across the flood that is closing over his head.

I think it is a reasonable supposition, that this part of the speech was composed before the arrival of the news of the capture of Cornwallis: for it certainly has no relation to their condition at the time it was spoken. But, be this as it may, it is nothing to us. Our line is fixed. Our lot is cast; and America, the child of fate, is arriving at maturity. We have nothing to do but by a spirited and quick exertion, to stand prepared for war or peace. Too great to yield, and too noble to insult; superior to misfortune, and generous in success, let us untaintedly preserve the character which we have gained, and show to future ages an example of unequalled magnanimity. There is something in the cause and consequence of America that has drawn on her the attention of all mankind. The world has seen her brave. Her love of liberty; her ardour in supporting it; the justice of her claims, and the constancy of her fortitude have won her the esteem of Europe, and attached to her interest the first power in that country.

Her situation now is such, that to whatever point, past, present or to come, she casts her eyes, new matter rises to convince her that she is right. In her conduct towards her enemy, no reproachful sentiment lurks in secret. No sense of injustice is left upon the mind. Untainted with ambition, and a stranger to revenge, her progress hath been marked by providence, and she, in every stage of the conflict, has blest her with success.

But let not America wrap herself up in delusive hope and suppose the business done. The least remissness in preparation, the least relaxation in execution, will only serve to prolong the war, and increase expenses. If our enemies can draw consolation from misfortune, and exert themselves upon despair, how much more ought we, who are to win a continent by the conquest, and have already an earnest of success?

Having, in the preceding part, made my remarks on the several matters which the speech contains, I shall now make my remarks on what it does not contain.

There is not a syllable in it respecting alliances. Either the injustice of Britain is too glaring, or her condition too desperate, or both, for any neighboring power to come to her support. In the beginning of the contest, when she had only America to contend with, she hired assistance from Hesse, and other smaller states of Germany, and for nearly three years did America, young, raw, undisciplined and unprovided, stand against the power of Britain, aided by twenty thousand foreign troops, and made a complete conquest of one entire army. The remembrance of those things ought to inspire us with confidence and greatness of mind, and carry us through every remaining difficulty with content and cheerfulness. What are the little sufferings of the present day, compared with the hardships that are past? There was a time, when we had neither house nor home in safety; when every hour was the hour of alarm and danger; when the mind, tortured with anxiety, knew no repose, and every thing, but hope and fortitude, was bidding us farewell.

It is of use to look back upon these things; to call to mind the times of trouble and the scenes of complicated anguish that are past and gone. Then every expense was cheap, compared with the dread of conquest and the misery of submission. We did not stand debating upon trifles, or contending about the necessary and unavoidable charges of defence. Every one bore his lot of suffering, and looked forward to happier days, and scenes of rest.

Perhaps one of the greatest dangers which any country can be exposed to, arises from a kind of trifling which sometimes steals upon the mind, when it supposes the danger past; and this unsafe situation marks at this time the peculiar crisis of America. What would she once have given to have known that her condition at this day should be what it now is? And yet we do not seem to place a proper value upon it, nor vigorously pursue the necessary measures to secure it. We know that we cannot be defended, nor yet defend ourselves, without trouble and expense. We have no right to expect it; neither ought we to look for it. We are a people, who, in our situation, differ from all the world. We form one common floor of public good, and, whatever is our charge, it is paid for our own interest and upon our own account.

Misfortune and experience have now taught us system and method; and the arrangements for carrying on the war are reduced to rule and order. The quotas of the several states are ascertained, and I intend in a future publication to show what they are, and the necessity as well as the advantages of vigorously providing for them. . . .

COMMON SENSE.

PHILADELPHIA, MARCH 5, 1782.

THE CRISIS.

No. 13.

Thoughts on the Peace, and the Probable Advantages Thereof.

"THE TIMES THAT TRIED men's souls,"* are over—and the greatest and completest revolution the world ever knew, gloriously and happily accomplished.

But to pass from the extremes of danger to safety—from the tumult of war to the tranquillity of peace, though sweet in contemplation, requires a gradual composure of the senses to receive it. Even calmness has the power of stunning, when it opens too instantly upon us. The long and raging hurricane that should cease in a moment, would leave us in a state rather of wonder than enjoyment; and some moments of recollection must pass, before we could be capable of tasting the felicity of repose. There are but few instances, in which the mind is fitted for sudden transitions: it takes in its pleasures by reflection and comparison and those must have time to act, before the relish for new scenes is complete.

In the present case—the mighty magnitude of the object—the various uncertainties of fate it has undergone—the numerous and complicated dangers we have suffered or escaped—the eminence we now stand on, and the vast prospect before us, must all conspire to impress us with contemplation.

To see it in our power to make a world happy—to teach mankind the art of being so—to exhibit, on the theatre of the universe a character hitherto unknown—and to have, as it were, a new creation intrusted to our hands, are honors that command reflection, and can neither be too highly estimated, nor too gratefully received.

---

*"These are the times that try men's souls," The Crisis No. 1. published December, 1776 [Author's note].

In this pause then of recollection—while the storm is ceasing, and the long agitated mind vibrating to a rest, let us look back on the scenes we have passed, and learn from experience what is yet to be done.

Never, I say, had a country so many openings to happiness as this. Her setting out in life, like the rising of a fair morning, was unclouded and promising. Her cause was good. Her principles just and liberal. Her temper serene and firm. Her conduct regulated by the nicest steps, and everything about her wore the mark of honour. It is not every country (perhaps there is not another in the world) that can boast so fair an origin. Even the first settlement of America corresponds with the character of the revolution. Rome, once the proud mistress of the universe, was originally a band of ruffians. Plunder and rapine made her rich, and her oppression of millions made her great. But America need never be ashamed to tell her birth, nor relate the stages by which she rose to empire.

The remembrance, then, of what is past, if it operates rightly, must inspire her with the most laudable of all ambition, that of adding to the fair fame she began with. The world has seen her great in adversity; struggling, without a thought of yielding, beneath accumulated difficulties, bravely, nay proudly, encountering distress, and rising in resolution as the storm increased. All this is justly due to her, for her fortitude has merited the character. Let, then, the world see that she can bear prosperity: and that her honest virtue in time of peace, is equal to the bravest virtue in time of war.

She is now descending to the scenes of quiet and domestic life. Not beneath the cypress shade of disappointment, but to enjoy in her own land, and under her own vine, the sweet of her labours, and the reward of her toil.—In this situation, may she never forget that a fair national reputation is of as much importance as independence. That it possesses a charm that wins upon the world, and makes even enemies civil. That it gives a dignity which is often superior to power, and commands reverence where pomp and splendour fail.

It would be a circumstance ever to be lamented and never to be forgotten, were a single blot, from any cause whatever, suffered to fall on a revolution, which to the end of time must be an honour to the age that accomplished it: and which has contributed more to enlighten the world, and diffuse a spirit of freedom and liberality among mankind, than any human event (if this may be called one) that ever preceded it.

It is not among the least of the calamities of a long continued war, that it unhinges the mind from those nice sensations which at other times appear so amiable. The continual spectacle of wo blunts the finer feelings, and the necessity of bearing with the sight, renders it familiar. In like manner, are many of the moral obligations of society weakened, till the custom of acting by necessity becomes an apology, where it is truly a crime. Yet let but a nation conceive rightly of its character, and it will be chastely just in protecting it. None ever began with a fairer than America and none can be under a greater obligation to preserve it.

The debt which America has contracted, compared with the cause she has gained, and the advantages to flow from it, ought scarcely to be mentioned. She has it in her choice to do, and to live as happily as she pleases. The world is in her hands. She has no foreign power to monopolize her commerce, perplex her legislation, or control her prosperity. The struggle is over, which must one day have happened, and, perhaps, never could have happened at a better time.* And instead of a domineering master, she has gained an

---

*That the revolution began at the exact period of time best fitted to the purpose, is sufficiently proved by the event.—But the great hinge on which the whole machine turned, is the *Union of the States:* and this union was naturally produced by the inability of any one state to support itself against any foreign enemy without the assistance of the rest.

Had the states severally been less able than they were when the war began, their united strength would not have been equal to the undertaking, and they must in all human probability have failed.—And, on the other hand, had they severally been more able, they might not have seen, or, what is more, might not have felt, the necessity of uniting: and, either by attempting to stand alone or in small confederacies, would have been separately conquered.

Now, as we cannot see a time (and many years must pass away before it can arrive) when the strength of any one state, or several united, can be equal to the whole of the present United States, and as we have seen the extreme difficulty of collectively prosecuting the war to a successful issue, and preserving our national importance in the world, therefore, from the experience we have had, and the knowledge we have gained, we must, unless we make a waste of wisdom, be strongly impressed with the advantage, as well as the necessity of strengthening that happy union which had been our salvation, and without which we should have been a ruined people.

While I was writing this note, I cast my eye on the pamphlet, Common Sense, from which I shall make an extract, as it exactly applies to the case. It is as follows:

ally whose exemplary greatness, and universal liberality, have ex-
torted a confession even from her enemies.

With the blessings of peace, independence, and an universal
commerce, the states, individually and collectively, will have leisure
and opportunity to regulate and establish their domestic concerns,
and to put it beyond the power of calumny to throw the least reflection on their honor. Character is much easier kept than recovered, and that man, if any such there be, who, from sinister views, or
littleness of soul, lends unseen his hand to injure it, contrives a
wound it will never be in his power to heal.

As we have established an inheritance for posterity, let that inheritance descend, with every mark of an honourable conveyance.
The little it will cost, compared with the worth of the states, the
greatness of the object, and the value of the national character, will
be a profitable exchange.

But that which must more forcibly strike a thoughtful, penetrating
mind, and which includes and renders easy all inferior concerns, is the
UNION OF THE STATES. On this our great national character depends.
It is this which must give us importance abroad and security at home.
It is through this only that we are, or can be, nationally known in the
world; it is the flag of the United States which renders our ships and
commerce safe on the seas, or in a foreign port. Our Mediterranean
passes must be obtained under the same style. All our treaties, whether
of alliance, peace, or commerce, are formed under the sovereignty of
the United States, and Europe knows us by no other name or title.

"I have never met with a man, either in England or America, who hath not confessed it as his opinion that a separation between the countries would take place one
time or other; and there is no instance in which we have shown less judgment, than
in endeavoring to describe what we call the ripeness or fitness of the continent for
independence.

"As all men allow the measure, and differ only in their opinion of the time, let
us, in order to remove mistakes, take a general survey of things, and endeavour, if
possible, to find out the *very time*. But we need not to go far, the inquiry ceases at
once, for, *the time has found us*. The general concurrence, the glorious union of all
things prove the fact.

"It is not in numbers, but in a union, that our great strength lies. The continent
is just arrived at that pitch of strength, in which no single colony is able to support
itself, and the whole, when united, can accomplish the matter; and either more or
less than this, might be fatal in its effects." [Author's note].

The division of the empire into states is for our own convenience, but abroad this distinction ceases. The affairs of each state are local. They can go no further than to itself. And were the whole worth of even the richest of them expended in revenue, it would not be sufficient to support sovereignty against a foreign attack. In short, we have no other national sovereignty than as United States. It would even be fatal for us if we had—too expensive to be maintained, and impossible to be supported. Individuals, or individual states, may call themselves what they please; but the world, and especially the world of enemies, is not to be held in awe by the whistling of a name. Sovereignty must have power to protect all the parts that compose and constitute it: and as UNITED STATES we are equal to the importance of the title, but otherwise we are not. Our union, well and wisely regulated and cemented, is the cheapest way of being great—the easiest way of being powerful, and the happiest invention in government which the circumstances of America can admit of.— Because it collects from each state, that which, by being inadequate, can be of no use to it, and forms an aggregate that serves for all.

The states of Holland are an unfortunate instance of the effects of individual sovereignty. Their disjointed condition exposes them to numerous intrigues, losses, calamities, and enemies; and the almost impossibility of bringing their measures to a decision, and that decision into execution, is to them, and would be to us, a source of endless misfortune.

It is with confederated states as with individuals in society; something must be yielded up to make the whole secure. In this view of things we gain by what we give, and draw an annual interest greater than the capital.—I ever feel myself hurt when I hear the union, that great palladium of our liberty and safety, the least irreverently spoken of. It is the most sacred thing in the constitution of America, and that which every man should be most proud and tender of. Our citizenship in the United States is our national character. Our citizenship in any particular state is only our local distinction. By the latter we are known at home, by the former to the world. Our great title is AMERICANS—our inferior one varies with the place.

So far as my endeavours could go, they have all been directed to conciliate the affections, unite the interests, and draw and keep the mind of the country together; and the better to assist in this foundation work of the revolution, I have avoided all places of profit or office, either in the state I live in, or in the United States; kept myself at a distance from all parties and party connexions, and even disregarded all private and inferior concerns: and when we take into view the great work which we have gone through, and feel, as we ought to feel, the just importance of it, we shall then see, that the little wranglings and indecent contentions of personal parley, are as dishonourable to our characters, as they are injurious to our repose.

It was the cause of America that made me an author. The force with which it struck my mind, and the dangerous condition the country appeared to me in, by courting an impossible and an unnatural reconciliation with those who were determined to reduce her, instead of striking out into the only line that could cement and save her, A DECLARATION OF INDEPENDENCE, made it impossible for me, feeling as I did, to be silent: and if, in the course of more than seven years, I have rendered her any service, I have likewise added something to the reputation of literature, by freely and disinterestedly employing it in the great cause of mankind, and showing that there may be genius without prostitution.

Independence always appeared to me practicable and probable, provided the sentiment of the country could be formed and held to the object: and there is no instance in the world, where a people so extended, and wedded to former habits of thinking, and under such a variety of circumstances, were so instantly and effectually pervaded, by a turn in politics, as in the case of independence; and who supported their opinion, undiminished, through such a succession of good and ill fortune, till they crowned it with success.

But as the scenes of war are closed, and every man preparing for home and happier times, I therefore take my leave of the subject. I have most sincerely followed it from beginning to end, and through all its turns and windings: and whatever country I may hereafter be in, I shall always feel an honest pride at the part I have taken and acted, and a gratitude to nature and providence for putting it in my power to be of some use to mankind.

COMMON SENSE.

PHILADELPHIA, APRIL 19, 1783.

RIGHTS OF MAN

It really begins on p. 183

(selections)

Part the First [1791]
Part the Second [1792]

RIGHTS OF MAN

[Part the First]

BEING AN ANSWER TO MR. BURKE'S ATTACK ON THE FRENCH
REVOLUTION

BY

THOMAS PAINE

SECRETARY FOR FOREIGN AFFAIRS TO CONGRESS IN THE
AMERICAN WAR, AND
AUTHOR OF THE WORKS ENTITLED "COMMON SENSE" AND "A LETTER TO THE ABBÉ RAYNAL"

GEORGE WASHINGTON,

PRESIDENT OF THE UNITED STATES OF AMERICA.

SIR,—

I present you a small treatise in defence of those principles of freedom which your exemplary virtue hath so eminently contributed to establish. That the Rights of Man may become as universal as your benevolence can wish, and that you may enjoy the happiness of seeing the New World regenerate the Old, is the prayer of

SIR,

Your much obliged, and

Obedient humble Servant,

THOMAS PAINE.

Preface to the English Edition.

FROM THE PART MR. Burke took in the American Revolution, it was natural that I should consider him a friend to mankind; and as our acquaintance commenced on that ground, it would have been more agreeable to me to have had cause to continue in that opinion than to change it.

At the time Mr. Burke made his violent speech last winter in the English Parliament against the French Revolution and the National Assembly, I was in Paris, and had written to him but a short time before to inform him how prosperously matters were going on. Soon after this I saw his advertisement of the Pamphlet he intended to publish: As the attack was to be made in a language but little studied, and less understood in France, and as everything suffers by translation, I promised some of the friends of the Revolution in that country that whenever Mr. Burke's Pamphlet came forth, I would answer it. This appeared to me the more necessary to be done, when I saw the flagrant misrepresentations which Mr. Burke's Pamphlet contains; and that while it is an outrageous abuse on the French Revolution, and the principles of Liberty, it is an imposition on the rest of the world.

I am the more astonished and disappointed at this conduct in Mr. Burke, as (from the circumstances I am going to mention) I had formed other expectations.

I had seen enough of the miseries of war, to wish it might never more have existence in the world, and that some other mode might be found out to settle the differences that should occasionally arise in the neighbourhood of nations. This certainly might be done if Courts were disposed to set honestly about it, or if countries were enlightened enough not to be made the dupes of Courts. The people of America had been bred up in the same prejudices against France, which at that time characterised the people of England; but experience and an acquaintance with the French Nation have most

effectually shown to the Americans the falsehood of those prejudices; and I do not believe that a more cordial and confidential
intercourse exists between any two countries than between America
and France.

When I came to France, in the spring of 1787, the Archbishop of
Thoulouse was then Minister, and at that time highly esteemed. I
became much acquainted with the private Secretary of that Minister, a man of an enlarged benevolent heart; and found, that his sentiments and my own perfectly agreed with respect to the madness of
war, and the wretched impolicy of two nations, like England and
France, continually worrying each other, to no other end than that
of a mutual increase of burdens and taxes. That I might be assured
I had not misunderstood him, nor he me, I put the substance of our
opinions into writing and sent it to him; subjoining a request, that
if I should see among the people of England, any disposition to
cultivate a better understanding between the two nations than had
hitherto prevailed, how far I might be authorised to say that the
same disposition prevailed on the part of France? He answered me
by letter in the most unreserved manner, and that not for himself
only, but for the Minister, with whose knowledge the letter was declared to be written.

I put this letter into the hands of Mr. Burke almost three years
ago, and left it with him, where it still remains; hoping, and at the
same time naturally expecting, from the opinion I had conceived of
him, that he would find some opportunity of making good use of it,
for the purpose of removing those errors and prejudices which two
neighbouring nations, from the want of knowing each other, had
entertained, to the injury of both.

When the French Revolution broke out, it certainly afforded to
Mr. Burke an opportunity of doing some good, had he been disposed to it; instead of which, no sooner did he see the old prejudices
wearing away, than he immediately began sowing the seeds of a new
inveteracy, as if he were afraid that England and France would cease
to be enemies. That there are men in all countries who get their
living by war, and by keeping up the quarrels of Nations, is as shocking as it is true; but when those who are concerned in the government of a country, make it their study to sow discord and cultivate
prejudices between Nations, it becomes the more unpardonable.

With respect to a paragraph in this work alluding to Mr. Burke's having a pension, the report has been some time in circulation, at least two months; and as a person is often the last to hear what concerns him the most to know, I have mentioned it, that Mr. Burke may have an opportunity of contradicting the rumour, if he thinks proper.

THOMAS PAINE.

PREFACE TO THE FRENCH EDITION.

THE ASTONISHMENT WHICH THE French Revolution has caused throughout Europe should be considered from two different points of view: first as it affects foreign peoples, secondly as it affects their governments.

The cause of the French people is that of all Europe, or rather of the whole world; but the governments of all those countries are by no means favorable to it. It is important that we should never lose sight of this distinction. We must not confuse the peoples with their governments; especially not the English people with its government.

The government of England is no friend to the revolution of France. Of this we have sufficient proofs in the thanks given by that weak and witless person, the Elector of Hanover, sometimes called the King of England, to Mr. Burke for the insults heaped on it in his book, and in the malevolent comments of the English Minister, Mr. Pitt, in his speeches in Parliament.

In spite of the professions of sincerest friendship found in the official correspondence of the English government with that of France, its conduct gives the lie to all its declarations, and shows us clearly that it is not a court to be trusted, but an insane court, plunging in all the quarrels and intrigues of Europe, in quest of a war to satisfy its folly and countenance its extravagance.

The English nation, on the contrary, is very favorably disposed towards the French Revolution, and to the progress of liberty in the whole world; and this feeling will become more general in England as the intrigues and artifices of its government are better known, and the principles of the revolution better understood. The French should know that most English newspapers are directly in the pay of government, or, if indirectly connected with it, always under its orders; and that those papers constantly distort and attack the revolution in France in order to deceive the nation. But, as it is impossible long to prevent the prevalence of truth, the daily falsehoods of those papers no longer have the desired effect.

To be convinced that the voice of truth has been stifled in England, the world needs only to be told that the government regards and prosecutes as a libel that which it should protect.* This outrage on morality is called *law*, and judges are found wicked enough to inflict penalties on truth.

The English government presents, just now, a curious phenomenon. Seeing that the French and English nations are getting rid of the prejudices and false notions formerly entertained against each other, and which have cost them so much money, that government seems to be placarding its need of a foe; for unless it finds one somewhere, no pretext exists for the enormous revenue and taxation now deemed necessary.

Therefore it seeks in Russia the enemy it has lost in France, and appears to say to the universe, or to say to itself: "If nobody will be so kind as to become my foe, I shall need no more fleets nor armies, and shall be forced to reduce my taxes. The American war enabled me to double the taxes; the Dutch business to add more; the Nootka humbug gave me a pretext for raising three millions sterling more; but unless I can make an enemy of Russia the harvest from wars will end. I was the first to incite Turk against Russian, and now I hope to reap a fresh crop of taxes."

If the miseries of war, and the flood of evils it spreads over a country, did not check all inclination to mirth, and turn laughter into grief, the frantic conduct of the government of England would only excite ridicule. But it is impossible to banish from one's mind the images of suffering which the contemplation of such vicious policy presents. To reason with governments, as they have existed for ages, is to argue with brutes. It is only from the nations themselves that reforms can be expected. There ought not now to exist any doubt that the peoples of France, England, and America, enlightened and enlightening each other, shall henceforth be able, not merely to give the world an example of good government, but by their united influence enforce its practice.

---

*The main and uniform maxim of the judges is, the greater the truth the greater the libel [Author's note].

Rights of Man.

Among the incivilities by which nations or individuals provoke and irritate each other, Mr. Burke's pamphlet on the French Revolution is an extraordinary instance. Neither the People of France, nor the National Assembly, were troubling themselves about the affairs of England, or the English Parliament; and that Mr. Burke should commence an unprovoked attack upon them, both in Parliament and in public, is a conduct that cannot be pardoned on the score of manners, nor justified on that of policy.

There is scarcely an epithet of abuse to be found in the English language, with which Mr. Burke has not loaded the French Nation and the National Assembly. Everything which rancour, prejudice, ignorance or knowledge could suggest, is poured forth in the copious fury of near four hundred pages. In the strain and on the plan Mr. Burke was writing, he might have written on to as many thousands. When the tongue or the pen is let loose in a phrenzy of passion, it is the man, and not the subject, that becomes exhausted.

Hitherto Mr. Burke has been mistaken and disappointed in the opinions he had formed of the affairs of France; but such is the ingenuity of his hope, or the malignancy of his despair, that it furnishes him with new pretences to go on. There was a time when it was impossible to make Mr. Burke believe there would be any Revolution in France. His opinion then was, that the French had neither spirit to undertake it nor fortitude to support it; and now that there is one, he seeks an escape by condemning it.

Not sufficiently content with abusing the National Assembly, a great part of his work is taken up with abusing Dr. Price* (one of the best-hearted men that lives) and the two societies in England

---

*Richard Price (1723–1791), Unitarian minister, moral philosopher, and political activist.

known by the name of the Revolution Society and the Society for Constitutional Information.

Dr. Price had preached a sermon on the 4th of November, 1789, being the anniversary of what is called in England the Revolution, which took place 1688. Mr. Burke, speaking of this sermon, says: "The political Divine proceeds dogmatically to assert, that by the principles of the Revolution, the people of England have acquired three fundamental rights.

1. To choose our own governors.
2. To cashier them for misconduct.
3. To frame a government for ourselves."

Dr. Price does not say that the right to do these things exists in this or in that person, or in this or in that description of persons, but that it exists in the *whole;* that it is a right resident in the nation. Mr. Burke, on the contrary, denies that such a right exists in the nation, either in whole or in part, or that it exists anywhere; and, what is still more strange and marvellous, he says: "that the people of England utterly disclaim such a right, and that they will resist the practical assertion of it with their lives and fortunes." That men should take up arms and spend their lives and fortunes, *not* to maintain their rights, but to maintain they have *not* rights, is an entirely new species of discovery, and suited to the paradoxical genius of Mr. Burke.

The method which Mr. Burke takes to prove that the people of England have no such rights, and that such rights do not now exist in the nation, either in whole or in part, or anywhere at all, is of the same marvellous and monstrous kind with what he has already said; for his arguments are that the persons, or the generation of persons, in whom they did exist, are dead, and with them the right is dead also. To prove this, he quotes a declaration made by Parliament about a hundred years ago, to William and Mary, in these words: "The Lords Spiritual and Temporal, and Commons, do, in the name of the people aforesaid" (meaning the people of England then living) "most humbly and faithfully *submit* themselves, their *heirs* and *posterities*, for EVER." He quotes a clause of another Act of Parliament made in the same reign, the terms of which he says, "bind us" (meaning the people of their day), "our *heirs* and our *posterity*, to *them*, their *heirs* and *posterity*, to the end of time."

Mr. Burke conceives his point sufficiently established by producing those clauses, which he enforces by saying that they exclude the right of the nation for *ever*. And not yet content with making such declarations, repeated over and over again, he farther says, "that if the people of England possessed such a right before the Revolution" (which he acknowledges to have been the case, not only in England, but throughout Europe, at an early period), "yet that the *English Nation* did, at the time of the Revolution, most solemnly renounce and abdicate it, for themselves, and for *all their posterity, for ever.*"

As Mr. Burke occasionally applies the poison drawn from his horrid principles, not only to the English nation, but to the French Revolution and the National Assembly, and charges that august, illuminated and illuminating body of men with the epithet of *usurpers*, I shall, *sans cérémonie*, place another system of principles in opposition to his.

The English Parliament of 1688 did a certain thing, which, for themselves and their constituents, they had a right to do, and which it appeared right should be done. But, in addition to this right, which they possessed by delegation, *they set up another right by assumption*, that of binding and controlling posterity to the end of time. The case, therefore, divides itself into two parts; the right which they possessed by delegation, and the right which they set up by assumption. The first is admitted; but with respect to the second, I reply—

There never did, there never will, and there never can, exist a Parliament, or any description of men, or any generation of men, in any country, possessed of the right or the power of binding and controuling posterity to the "*end of time*," or of commanding for ever how the world shall be governed, or who shall govern it; and therefore all such clauses, acts or declarations by which the makers of them attempt to do what they have neither the right nor the power to do, nor the power to execute, are in themselves null and void. Every age and generation must be as free to act for itself *in all cases* as the age and generations which preceded it. The vanity and presumption of governing beyond the grave is the most ridiculous and insolent of all tyrannies. Man has no property in man; neither has any generation a property in the generations which are to follow. The Parliament or the people of 1688, or of any other period, had no more right to dispose of the people of the present day, or to bind or to control them *in any shape whatever*, than the parliament or the people of the present day have to dispose of, bind or control those who are to live a hundred or a thousand years hence. Every generation is, and must be, competent to all the purposes which its occasions require. It is the living, and not the dead, that are to be accommodated. When man ceases to be, his power and his wants cease with him; and having no longer any participation in the concerns of this world, he has no longer any authority in directing who shall be its governors, or how its government shall be organised, or how administered.

I am not contending for nor against any form of government, nor for nor against any party, here or elsewhere. That which a whole nation chooses to do it has a right to do. Mr. Burke says, No. Where, then, does the right exist? I am contending for the rights of the *living*, and against their being willed away and controuled and contracted for by the manuscript assumed authority of the dead, and Mr. Burke is contending for the authority of the dead over the rights and freedom of the living. There was a time when kings disposed of their crowns by will upon their death-beds, and consigned the people, like beasts of the field, to whatever successor they appointed. This is now so exploded as scarcely to be remembered, and so monstrous as hardly to be believed. But the Parliamentary clauses upon which Mr. Burke builds his political church are of the same nature.

The laws of every country must be analogous to some common principle. In England no parent or master, nor all the authority of Parliament, omnipotent as it has called itself, can bind or control the personal freedom even of an individual beyond the age of twenty-one years. On what ground of right, then, could the Parliament of 1688, or any other Parliament, bind all posterity for ever?

Those who have quitted the world, and those who have not yet arrived at it, are as remote from each other as the utmost stretch of mortal imagination can conceive. What possible obligation, then, can exist between them—what rule or principle can be laid down that of two nonentities, the one out of existence and the other not in, and who never can meet in this world, the one should controul the other to the end of time?

In England it is said that money cannot be taken out of the pockets of the people without their consent. But who authorised, or who could authorise, the Parliament of 1688 to control and take away the freedom of posterity (who were not in existence to give or to withhold their consent), and limit and confine their right of acting in certain cases for ever?

A greater absurdity cannot present itself to the understanding of man than what Mr. Burke offers to his readers. He tells them, and he tells the world to come, that a certain body of men who existed a hundred years ago made a law, and that there does not exist in the nation, nor ever will, nor ever can, a power to alter it. Under how many subtilties or absurdities has the divine right to govern been imposed on the credulity of mankind? Mr. Burke has discovered a new one, and he has shortened his journey to Rome by appealing to the power of this infallible Parliament of former days, and he produces what it has done as of divine authority, for that power must certainly be more than human which no human power to the end of time can alter.

But Mr. Burke has done some service—not to his cause, but to his country—by bringing those clauses into public view. They serve to demonstrate how necessary it is at all times to watch against the attempted encroachment of power, and to prevent its running to excess. It is somewhat extraordinary that the offence for which James II. was expelled, that of setting up power by *assumption*, should be re-acted, under another shape and form, by the Parliament that expelled him. It shews that the Rights of Man were but imperfectly understood at the Revolution, for certain it is that the right which that Parliament set up by *assumption* (for by the delegation it had not, and could not have it, because none could give it) over the persons and freedom of posterity for ever was of the same tyrannical unfounded kind which James attempted to set up over the Parliament and the nation, and for which he was expelled. The only difference is (for in principle they differ not) that the one was an usurper over the living, and the other over the unborn; and as the one has no better authority to stand upon than the other, both of them must be equally null and void, and of no effect.

From what, or from whence, does Mr. Burke prove the right of any human power to bind posterity for ever? He has produced his clauses, but he must produce also his proofs that such a right existed, and shew how it existed. If it ever existed it must now exist, for whatever appertains to the nature of man cannot be annihilated by man. It is the nature of man to die, and he will continue to die as long as he continues to be born. But Mr. Burke has set up a sort of political Adam, in whom all posterity are bound for ever. He must, therefore, prove that his Adam possessed such a power, or such a right.

The weaker any cord is, the less will it bear to be stretched, and the worse is the policy to stretch it, unless it is intended to break it. Had anyone proposed the overthrow of Mr. Burke's positions, he would have proceeded as Mr. Burke has done. He would have magnified the authorities, on purpose to have called the *right* of them into question; and the instant the question of right was started, the authorities must have been given up.

It requires but a very small glance of thought to perceive that altho' laws made in one generation often continue in force through succeeding generations, yet they continue to derive their force from the consent of the living. A law not repealed continues in force, not because it *cannot* be repealed, but because it is *not* repealed; and the non-repealing passes for consent.

But Mr. Burke's clauses have not even this qualification in their favor. They become null, by attempting to become immortal. The nature of them precludes consent. They destroy the right which they *might* have, by grounding it on a right which they *cannot* have. Immortal power is not a human right, and therefore cannot be a right of Parliament. The Parliament of 1688 might as well have passed an act to have authorised themselves to live for ever, as to make their authority live for ever. All, therefore, that can be said of those clauses is that they are a formality of words, of as much import as if those who used them had addressed a congratulation to themselves, and in the oriental style of antiquity had said: O Parliament, live for ever!

The circumstances of the world are continually changing, and the opinions of men change also; and as government is for the living, and not for the dead, it is the living only that has any right in it.

That which may be thought right and found convenient in one age may be thought wrong and found inconvenient in another. In such cases, who is to decide, the living or the dead?

As almost one hundred pages of Mr. Burke's book are employed upon these clauses, it will consequently follow that if the clauses themselves, so far as they set up an *assumed usurped* dominion over posterity for ever, are unauthoritative, and in their nature null and void; that all his voluminous inferences, and declamation drawn therefrom, or founded thereon, are null and void also; and on this ground I rest the matter.

We now come more particularly to the affairs of France. Mr. Burke's book has the appearance of being written as instruction to the French nation; but if I may permit myself the use of an extravagant metaphor, suited to the extravagance of the case, it is darkness attempting to illuminate light.

While I am writing this there are accidentally before me some proposals for a declaration of rights by the Marquis de la Fayette (I ask his pardon for using his former address, and do it only for distinction's sake) to the National Assembly, on the 11th of July, 1789, three days before the taking of the Bastille, and I cannot but remark with astonishment how opposite the sources are from which that gentleman and Mr. Burke draw their principles. Instead of referring to musty records and mouldy parchments to prove that the rights of the living are lost, "renounced and abdicated for ever," by those who are now no more, as Mr. Burke has done, M. de la Fayette applies to the living world, and emphatically says: "Call to mind the sentiments which nature has engraved on the heart of every citizen, and which take a new force when they are solemnly recognised by all:— For a nation to love liberty, it is sufficient that she knows it; and to be free, it is sufficient that she wills it." How dry, barren, and obscure is the source from which Mr. Burke labors! and how ineffectual, though gay with flowers, are all his declamation and his arguments compared with these clear, concise, and soul-animating sentiments! Few and short as they are, they lead on to a vast field of generous and manly thinking, and do not finish, like Mr. Burke's periods, with music in the ear, and nothing in the heart.

As I have introduced M. de la Fayette, I will take the liberty of adding an anecdote respecting his farewel address to the Congress of America in 1783, and which occurred fresh to my mind, when I saw Mr. Burke's thundering attack on the French Revolution. M. de la Fayette went to America at the early period of the war, and continued a volunteer in her service to the end. His conduct through the whole of that enterprise is one of the most extraordinary that is to be found in the history of a young man, scarcely twenty years of age. Situated in a country that was like the lap of sensual pleasure, and with the means of enjoying it, how few are there to be found who would exchange such a scene for the woods and wildernesses of America, and pass the flowery years of youth in unprofitable danger and hardship! but such is the fact. When the war ended, and he was on the point of taking his final departure, he presented himself to Congress, and contemplating in his affectionate farewel the Revolution he had seen, expressed himself in these words: "May this great monument raised to liberty serve as a lesson to the oppressor, and an example to the oppressed!" When this address came to the hands of Dr. Franklin, who was then in France, he applied to Count Vergennes* to have it inserted in the French Gazette, but never could obtain his consent. The fact was that Count Vergennes was an aristocratical despot at home, and dreaded the example of the American Revolution in France, as certain other persons now dread the example of the French Revolution in England, and Mr. Burke's tribute of fear (for in this light his book must be considered) runs parallel with Count Vergennes' refusal. But to return more particularly to his work.

"We have seen," says Mr. Burke, "the French rebel against a mild and lawful monarch, with more fury, outrage, and insult, than any people has been known to rise against the most illegal usurper, or the most sanguinary tyrant." This is one among a thousand other instances, in which Mr. Burke shows that he is ignorant of the springs and principles of the French Revolution.

It was not against Louis XVIth but against the despotic principles of the Government, that the nation revolted. These principles

---

*Charles Gravier, comte de Vergennes (1717–1787), minister of foreign affairs under Louis XVI; Vergennes signed, with Benjamin Franklin, France's alliance with the Americans in the American Revolution, and later assisted in negotiating the Treaty of Paris (1783).

had not their origin in him, but in the original establishment, many centuries back: and they were become too deeply rooted to be removed, and the Augean stables of parasites and plunderers too abominably filthy to be cleansed by anything short of a complete and universal Revolution. When it becomes necessary to do anything, the whole heart and soul should go into the measure, or not attempt it. That crisis was then arrived, and there remained no choice but to act with determined vigor, or not to act at all. The king was known to be the friend of the nation, and this circumstance was favorable to the enterprise. Perhaps no man bred up in the style of an absolute king, ever possessed a heart so little disposed to the exercise of that species of power as the present King of France. But the principles of the Government itself still remained the same. The Monarch and the Monarchy were distinct and separate things; and it was against the established despotism of the latter, and not against the person or principles of the former, that the revolt commenced, and the Revolution has been carried.

Mr. Burke does not attend to the distinction between men and principles, and, therefore, he does not see that a revolt may take place against the despotism of the latter, while there lies no charge of despotism against the former.

The natural moderation of Louis XVIth contributed nothing to alter the hereditary despotism of the monarchy. All the tyrannies of former reigns, acted under that hereditary despotism, were still liable to be revived in the hands of a successor. It was not the respite of a reign that would satisfy France, enlightened as she was then become. A casual discontinuance of the *practice* of despotism, is not a discontinuance of its *principles:* the former depends on the virtue of the individual who is in immediate possession of the power; the latter, on the virtue and fortitude of the nation. In the case of Charles Ist and James IInd of England, the revolt was against the personal despotism of the men; whereas in France, it was against the hereditary despotism of the established Government. But men who can consign over the rights of posterity for ever on the authority of a mouldy parchment, like Mr. Burke, are not qualified to judge of this Revolution. It takes in a field too vast for their views to explore, and proceeds with a mightiness of reason they cannot keep pace with.

But there are many points of view in which this Revolution may be considered. When despotism has established itself for ages in a country, as in France, it is not in the person of the king only that it resides. It has the appearance of being so in show, and in nominal authority; but it is not so in practice and in fact. It has its standard everywhere. Every office and department has its despotism, founded upon custom and usage. Every place has its Bastille,* and every Bastille its despot. The original hereditary despotism resident in the person of the king, divides and sub-divides itself into a thousand shapes and forms, till at last the whole of it is acted by deputation. This was the case in France; and against this species of despotism, proceeding on through an endless labyrinth of office till the source of it is scarcely perceptible, there is no mode of redress. It strength-ens itself by assuming the appearance of duty, and tyrannises under the pretence of obeying.

When a man reflects on the condition which France was in from the nature of her government, he will see other causes for revolt than those which immediately connect themselves with the person or character of Louis XVI. There were, if I may so express it, a thou-sand despotisms to be reformed in France, which had grown up under the hereditary despotism of the monarchy, and became so rooted as to be in a great measure independent of it. Between the Monarchy, the Parliament, and the Church there was a *rivalship* of despotism; besides the feudal despotism operating locally, and the ministerial despotism operating everywhere. But Mr. Burke, by con-sidering the king as the only possible object of a revolt, speaks as if France was a village, in which everything that passed must be known to its commanding officer, and no oppression could be acted but what he could immediately controul. Mr. Burke might have been in the Bastille his whole life, as well under Louis XVI. as Louis XIV., and neither the one nor the other have known that such a man as Burke existed. The despotic principles of the government were the same in both reigns, though the dispositions of the men were as re-mote as tyranny and benevolence.

What Mr. Burke considers as a reproach to the French Revolu-

---

*Famous royal prison (now demolished) in the center of Paris and despised symbol of absolutism; a crowd seized it on July 14, 1789, in the early months of the French Revolution.

tion (that of bringing it forward under a reign more mild than the preceding ones) is one of its highest honors. The Revolutions that have taken place in other European countries, have been excited by personal hatred. The rage was against the man, and he became the victim. But, in the instance of France we see a Revolution generated in the rational contemplation of the Rights of Man, and distinguishing from the beginning between persons and principles.

But Mr. Burke appears to have no idea of principles when he is contemplating Governments. "Ten years ago," says he, "I could have felicitated France on her having a Government, without inquiring what the nature of that Government was, or how it was administered." Is this the language of a rational man? Is it the language of a heart feeling as it ought to feel for the rights and happiness of the human race? On this ground, Mr. Burke must compliment all the Governments in the world, while the victims, who suffer under them, whether sold into slavery, or tortured out of existence, are wholly forgotten. It is power, and not principles, that Mr. Burke venerates; and under this abominable depravity he is disqualified to judge between them. Thus much for his opinion as to the occasions of the French Revolution. I now proceed to other considerations.

I know a place in America called Point-no-Point, because as you proceed along the shore, gay and flowery as Mr. Burke's language, it continually recedes and presents itself at a distance before you; but when you have got as far as you can go, there is no point at all. Just thus it is with Mr. Burke's three hundred and sixty-six pages. It is therefore difficult to reply to him. But as the points he wishes to establish may be inferred from what he abuses, it is in his paradoxes that we must look for his arguments.

As to the tragic paintings by which Mr. Burke has outraged his own imagination, and seeks to work upon that of his readers, they are very well calculated for theatrical representation, where facts are manufactured for the sake of show, and accommodated to produce, through the weakness of sympathy, a weeping effect. But Mr. Burke should recollect that he is writing history, and not *plays*, and that his readers will expect truth, and not the spouting rant of high-toned exclamation.

When we see a man dramatically lamenting in a publication intended to be believed that "*The age of chivalry!* that *The glory of*

Europe is extinguished for ever! that *The unbought grace of life* (if any-one knows what it is), *the cheap defence of nations, the nurse of manly sentiment and heroic enterprise is gone!*" and all this because the Quixot age of chivalry nonsense is gone, what opinion can we form of his judgment, or what regard can we pay to his facts? In the rhapsody of his imagination he has discovered a world of wind mills, and his sorrows are that there are no Quixots to attack them. But if the age of aristocracy, like that of chivalry, should fall (and they had originally some connection) Mr. Burke, the trumpeter of the Order, may continue his parody to the end, and finish with exclaiming: "*Othello's occupation's gone!*"

Notwithstanding Mr. Burke's horrid paintings, when the French Revolution is compared with the Revolutions of other countries, the astonishment will be that it is marked with so few sacrifices; but this astonishment will cease when we reflect that *principles*, and not *persons*, were the meditated objects of destruction. The mind of the nation was acted upon by a higher stimulus than what the consideration of persons could inspire, and sought a higher conquest than could be produced by the downfal of an enemy. Among the few who fell there do not appear to be any that were intentionally singled out. They all of them had their fate in the circumstances of the moment, and were not pursued with that long, cold-blooded unabated revenge which pursued the unfortunate Scotch in the affair of 1745.

Through the whole of Mr. Burke's book I do not observe that the Bastille is mentioned more than once, and that with a kind of implication as if he were sorry it was pulled down, and wished it were built up again. "We have rebuilt Newgate," says he, "and tenanted the mansion; and we have prisons almost as strong as the Bastille for those who dare to libel the queens of France."* As to what a mad-

---

*Since writing the above, two other places occur in Mr. Burke's pamphlet in which the name of the Bastille is mentioned, but in the same manner. In the one he introduces it in a sort of obscure question, and asks: "Will any ministers who now serve such a king, with but a decent appearance of respect, cordially obey the orders of those whom but the other day, *in his name*, they had committed to the Bastille?" In the other the taking it is mentioned as implying criminality in the French guards, who assisted in demolishing it. "They have not," says he, "forgot the taking the king's castles at Paris." This is Mr. Burke, who pretends to write on constitutional freedom [Author's note].

man like the person called Lord G[eorge] G[ordon] might say, and to whom Newgate is rather a bedlam than a prison, it is unworthy a rational consideration. It was a madman that libelled, and that is sufficient apology; and it afforded an opportunity for confining him, which was the thing that was wished for. But certain it is that Mr. Burke, who does not call himself a madman (whatever other people may do), has libelled in the most unprovoked manner, and in the grossest style of the most vulgar abuse, the whole representative authority of France, and yet Mr. Burke takes his seat in the British House of Commons! From his violence and his grief, his silence on some points and his excess on others, it is difficult not to believe that Mr. Burke is sorry, extremely sorry, that arbitrary power, the power of the Pope and the Bastille, are pulled down.

Not one glance of compassion, not one commiserating reflexion that I can find throughout his book, has he bestowed on those who lingered out the most wretched of lives, a life without hope in the most miserable of prisons. It is painful to behold a man employing his talents to corrupt himself. Nature has been kinder to Mr. Burke than he is to her. He is not affected by the reality of distress touching his heart, but by the showy resemblance of it striking his imagination. He pities the plumage, but forgets the dying bird. Accustomed to kiss the aristocratical hand that hath purloined him from himself, he degenerates into a composition of art, and the genuine soul of nature forsakes him. His hero or his heroine must be a tragedy-victim expiring in show, and not the real prisoner of misery, sliding into death in the silence of a dungeon.

As Mr. Burke has passed over the whole transaction of the Bastille (and his silence is nothing in his favor), and has entertained his readers with reflections on supposed facts distorted into real falsehoods, I will give, since he has not, some account of the circumstances which preceded that transaction. They will serve to shew that less mischief could scarcely have accompanied such an event when considered with the treacherous and hostile aggravations of the enemies of the Revolution.

The mind can hardly picture to itself a more tremendous scene than what the city of Paris exhibited at the time of taking the Bastille, and for two days before and after, nor perceive the possibility of its quieting so soon. At a distance this transaction has appeared only as an act of heroism standing on itself, and the close political connection it had with the Revolution is lost in the brilliancy of the achievement. But we are to consider it as the strength of the parties brought man to man, and contending for the issue. The Bastille was to be either the prize or the prison of the assailants. The downfall of it included the idea of the downfall of despotism, and this compounded image was become as figurative united as Bunyan's Doubting Castle and Giant Despair.*

The National Assembly, before and at the time of taking the Bastille, was sitting at Versailles, twelve miles distant from Paris. About a week before the rising of the Parisians, and their taking the Bastille, it was discovered that a plot was forming, at the head of which was the Count d'Artois, the king's youngest brother, for demolishing the National Assembly, seizing its members, and thereby crushing, by a *coup de main*, all hopes and prospects of forming a free government. For the sake of humanity, as well as freedom, it is well this plan did not succeed. Examples are not wanting to show how dreadfully vindictive and cruel are all old governments, when they are successful against what they call a revolt.

This plan must have been some time in contemplation; because, in order to carry it into execution, it was necessary to collect a large military force round Paris, and cut off the communication between that city and the National Assembly at Versailles. The troops destined for this service were chiefly the foreign troops in the pay of France, and who, for this particular purpose, were drawn from the distant provinces where they were then stationed. When they were collected to the amount of between twenty-five and thirty thousand, it was judged time to put the plan into execution. The ministry who were then in office, and who were friendly to the Revolution, were instantly dismissed and a new ministry formed of those who had concerted the project, among whom was Count de Broglio,† and to his share was given the command of those troops. The character of this man as described to me in a letter which I

---

*References to *The Pilgrim's Progress*, a prose allegory by the English writer and preacher John Bunyan (1628–1688); it was published in two parts, in 1678 and 1684.

†Victor Claude, prince de Broglie (1757–1794), president of the Constituent Assembly (1791) and adjutant general of the French Revolutionary army.

communicated to Mr. Burke before he began to write his book, and from an authority which Mr. Burke well knows was good, was that of "a high-flying aristocrat, cool, and capable of every mischief."

While these matters were agitating the National Assembly stood in the most perilous and critical situation that a body of men can be supposed to act in. They were the devoted victims, and they knew it. They had the hearts and wishes of their country on their side, but military authority they had none. The guards of Broglio surrounded the hall where the Assembly sat, ready, at the word of command, to seize their persons, as had been done the year before to the Parliament of Paris. Had the National Assembly deserted their trust, or had they exhibited signs of weakness or fear, their enemies had been encouraged and their country depressed. When the situation they stood in, the cause they were engaged in, and the crisis then ready to burst, which should determine their personal and political fate and that of their country, and probably of Europe, are taken into one view, none but a heart callous with prejudice or corrupted by dependence can avoid interesting itself in their success.

The Archbishop of Vienne was at this time President of the National Assembly—a person too old to undergo the scene that a few days or a few hours might bring forth. A man of more activity and bolder fortitude was necessary, and the National Assembly chose (under the form of a Vice-President, for the Presidency still resided in the Archbishop) M. de la Fayette; and this is the only instance of a Vice-President being chosen. It was at the moment that this storm was pending (July 11th) that a declaration of rights was brought forward by M. de la Fayette, and is the same which is alluded to in p. [111.] It was hastily drawn up, and makes only a part of the more extensive declaration of rights agreed upon and adopted afterwards by the National Assembly. The particular reason for bringing it forward at this moment (M. de la Fayette has since informed me) was that, if the National Assembly should fall in the threatened destruction that then surrounded it, some trace of its principles might have the chance of surviving the wreck.

Everything now was drawing to a crisis. The event was freedom or slavery. On one side, an army of nearly thirty thousand men; on the other, an unarmed body of citizens—for the citizens of Paris, on whom the National Assembly must then immediately depend, were as unarmed and as undisciplined as the citizens of London are now. The French guards had given strong symptoms of their being attached to the national cause; but their numbers were small, not a tenth part of the force that Broglio commanded, and their officers were in the interest of Broglio.

Matters being now ripe for execution, the new ministry made their appearance in office. The reader will carry in his mind that the Bastille was taken the 14th July; the point of time I am now speaking of is the 12th. Immediately on the news of the change of ministry reaching Paris, in the afternoon, all the playhouses and places of entertainment, shops and houses, were shut up. The change of ministry was considered as the prelude of hostilities, and the opinion was rightly founded.

The foreign troops began to advance towards the city. The Prince de Lambesc, who commanded a body of German cavalry, approached by the Place of Louis XV., which connects itself with some of the streets. In his march, he insulted and struck an old man with a sword. The French are remarkable for their respect to old age; and the insolence with which it appeared to be done, uniting with the general fermentation they were in, produced a powerful effect, and a cry of "To arms! to arms!" spread itself in a moment over the city.

Arms they had none, nor scarcely anyone who knew the use of them; but desperate resolution, when every hope is at stake, supplies, for a while, the want of arms. Near where the Prince de Lambesc was drawn up, were large piles of stones collected for building the new bridge, and with these the people attacked the cavalry. A party of French guards upon hearing the firing, rushed from their quarters and joined the people; and night coming on, the cavalry retreated.

The streets of Paris, being narrow, are favorable for defence, and the loftiness of the houses, consisting of many stories, from which great annoyance might be given, secured them against nocturnal enterprises; and the night was spent in providing themselves with every sort of weapon they could make or procure: guns, swords, blacksmiths' hammers, carpenters' axes, iron crows, pikes, halberts, pitchforks, spits, clubs, etc., etc. The incredible numbers in which they assembled the next morning, and the still more incredible resolution they exhibited, embarrassed and astonished their enemies.

Little did the new ministry expect such a salute. Accustomed to slavery themselves, they had no idea that liberty was capable of such inspiration, or that a body of unarmed citizens would dare to face the military force of thirty thousand men. Every moment of this day was employed in collecting arms, concerting plans, and arranging themselves into the best order which such an instantaneous movement could afford. Broglio continued lying round the city, but made no further advances this day, and the succeeding night passed with as much tranquility as such a scene could possibly produce.

But defence only was not the object of the citizens. They had a cause at stake, on which depended their freedom or their slavery. They every moment expected an attack, or to hear of one made on the National Assembly; and in such a situation, the most prompt measures are sometimes the best. The object that now presented itself was the Bastille; and the *éclat* of carrying such a fortress in the face of such an army, could not fail to strike terror into the new ministry, who had scarcely yet had time to meet. By some intercepted correspondence this morning, it was discovered that the Mayor of Paris, M. Deffleseslles, who appeared to be in the interest of the citizens, was betraying them; and from this discovery, there remained no doubt that Broglio would reinforce the Bastille the ensuing evening. It was therefore necessary to attack it that day; but before this could be done, it was first necessary to procure a better supply of arms than they were then possessed of.

There was, adjoining to the city a large magazine of arms deposited at the Hospital of the Invalids, which the citizens summoned to surrender; and as the place was neither defensible, nor attempted much defence, they soon succeeded. Thus supplied, they marched to attack the Bastille; a vast mixed multitude of all ages, and of all degrees, armed with all sorts of weapons. Imagination would fail in describing to itself the appearance of such a procession, and of the anxiety of the events which a few hours or a few minutes might produce. What plans the ministry were forming, were as unknown to the people within the city, as what the citizens were doing was unknown to the ministry; and what movements Broglio might make for the support or relief of the place, were to the citizens equally as unknown. All was mystery and hazard.

That the Bastille was attacked with an enthusiasm of heroism, such only as the highest animation of liberty could inspire, and carried in the space of a few hours, is an event which the world is fully possessed of. I am not undertaking the detail of the attack, but bringing into view the conspiracy against the nation which provoked it, and which fell with the Bastille. The prison to which the new ministry were dooming the National Assembly, in addition to its being the high altar and castle of despotism, became the proper object to begin with. This enterprise broke up the new ministry, who began now to fly from the ruin they had prepared for others. The troops of Broglio dispersed, and himself fled also.

Mr. Burke has spoken a great deal about plots, but he has never once spoken of this plot against the National Assembly, and the liberties of the nation; and that he might not, he has passed over all the circumstances that might throw it in his way. The exiles who have fled from France, whose case he so much interests himself in, and from whom he has had his lesson, fled in consequence of the miscarriage of this plot. No plot was formed against them; they were plotting against others; and those who fell, met, not unjustly, the punishment they were preparing to execute. But will Mr. Burke say, that if this plot, contrived with the subtilty of an ambuscade, had succeeded, the successful party would have restrained their wrath so soon? Let the history of all governments answer the question.

Whom has the National Assembly brought to the scaffold? None. They were themselves the devoted victims of this plot, and they have not retaliated; why, then, are they charged with revenge they have not acted? In the tremendous breaking forth of a whole people, in which all degrees, tempers and characters are confounded, delivering themselves, by a miracle of exertion, from the destruction meditated against them, is it to be expected that nothing will happen? When men are sore with the sense of oppressions, and menaced with the prospects of new ones, is the calmness of philosophy or the palsy of insensibility to be looked for? Mr. Burke exclaims against outrage; yet the greatest is that which himself has committed. His book is a volume of outrage, not apologised for by the impulse of a moment, but cherished through a space of ten months; yet Mr. Burke had no provocation—no life, no interest, at stake.

More of the citizens fell in this struggle than of their opponents:

but four or five persons were seized by the populace, and instantly put to death; the Governor of the Bastille, and the Mayor of Paris, who was detected in the act of betraying them; and afterwards Foulon, one of the new ministry, and Berthier, his son-in-law, who had accepted the office of intendant of Paris. Their heads were struck upon spikes, and carried about the city; and it is upon this mode of punishment that Mr. Burke builds a great part of his tragic scene. Let us therefore examine how men came by the idea of punishing in this manner.

They learn it from the governments they live under; and retaliate the punishments they have been accustomed to behold. The heads stuck upon spikes, which remained for years upon Temple Bar, differed nothing in the horror of the scene from those carried about upon spikes at Paris; yet this was done by the English Government. It may perhaps be said that it signifies nothing to a man what is done to him after he is dead; but it signifies much to the living; it either tortures their feelings or hardens their hearts, and in either case it instructs them how to punish when power falls into their hands.

Lay then the axe to the root, and teach governments humanity. It is their sanguinary punishments which corrupt mankind. In England the punishment in certain cases is by *hanging, drawing* and *quartering;* the heart of the sufferer is cut out and held up to the view of the populace. In France, under the former Government, the punishments were not less barbarous. Who does not remember the execution of Damien, torn to pieces by horses? The effect of those cruel spectacles exhibited to the populace is to destroy tenderness or excite revenge; and by the base and false idea of governing men by terror, instead of reason, they become precedents. It is over the lowest class of mankind that government by terror is intended to operate, and it is on them that it operates to the worst effect. They have sense enough to feel they are the objects aimed at; and they inflict in their turn the examples of terror they have been instructed to practise.

There is in all European countries a large class of people of that description, which in England is called the "*mob.*" Of this class were those who committed the burnings and devastations in London in 1780, and of this class were those who carried the heads on iron spikes in Paris. Foulon and Berthier were taken up in the country, and sent to Paris, to undergo their examination at the Hotel de Ville; for the National Assembly, immediately on the new ministry coming into office, passed a decree, which they communicated to the King and Cabinet, that they (the National Assembly) would hold the ministry, of which Foulon was one, responsible for the measures they were advising and pursuing; but the mob, incensed at the appearance of Foulon and Berthier, tore them from their con-ductors before they were carried to the Hotel de Ville, and executed them on the spot. Why then does Mr. Burke charge outrages of this kind on a whole people? As well may he charge the riots and out-rages of 1780 on all the people of London, or those in Ireland on all his countrymen.

But everything we see or hear offensive to our feelings and derogatory to the human character should lead to other reflections than those of reproach. Even the beings who commit them have some claim to our consideration. How then is it that such vast classes of mankind as are distinguished by the appellation of the vul-gar, or the ignorant mob, are so numerous in all old countries? The instant we ask ourselves this question, reflection feels an answer. They rise, as an unavoidable consequence, out of the ill construction of all old governments in Europe, England included with the rest. It is by distortedly exalting some men, that others are distortedly debased, till the whole is out of nature. A vast mass of mankind are degradedly thrown into the back-ground of the human picture, to bring forward, with greater glare, the puppet-show of state and aris-tocracy. In the commencement of a revolution, those men are rather the followers of the *camp* than of the *standard* of liberty, and have yet to be instructed how to reverence it.

I give to Mr. Burke all his theatrical exaggerations for facts, and I then ask him if they do not establish the certainty of what I here lay down? Admitting them to be true, they show the necessity of the French Revolution, as much as any one thing he could have as-serted. These outrages were not the effect of the principles of the Revolution, but of the degraded mind that existed before the Revo-lution, and which the Revolution is calculated to reform. Place them then to their proper cause, and take the reproach of them to your own side.

It is the honour of the National Assembly and the city of Paris that, during such a tremendous scene of arms and confusion, beyond the controul of all authority, they have been able, by the influence of example and exhortation, to restrain so much. Never were more pains taken to instruct and enlighten mankind, and to make them see that their interest consisted in their virtue, and not in their revenge, than have been displayed in the Revolution of France. I now proceed to make some remarks on Mr. Burke's account of the expedition to Versailles, October the 5th and 6th.

I can consider Mr. Burke's book in scarcely any other light than a dramatic performance; and he must, I think, have considered it in the same light himself, by the poetical liberties he has taken of omitting some facts, distorting others, and making the whole machinery bend to produce a stage effect. Of this kind is his account of the expedition to Versailles. He begins this account by omitting the only facts which as causes are known to be true; everything beyond these is conjecture, even in Paris; and he then works up a tale accommodated to his own passions and prejudices.

It is to be observed throughout Mr. Burke's book that he never speaks of plots *against* the Revolution; and it is from those plots that all the mischiefs have arisen. It suits his purpose to exhibit the consequences without their causes. It is one of the arts of the drama to do so. If the crimes of men were exhibited with their sufferings, stage effect would sometimes be lost, and the audience would be inclined to approve where it was intended they should commiserate.

After all the investigations that have been made into this intricate affair (the expedition to Versailles), it still remains enveloped in all that kind of mystery which ever accompanies events produced more from a concurrence of awkward circumstances than from fixed design. While the characters of men are forming, as is always the case in revolutions, there is a reciprocal suspicion, and a disposition to misinterpret each other; and even parties directly opposite in principle will sometimes concur in pushing forward the same movement with very different views, and with the hopes of its producing very different consequences. A great deal of this may be discovered in this embarrassed affair, and yet the issue of the whole was what nobody had in view.

The only things certainly known are that considerable uneasiness was at this time excited at Paris by the delay of the King in not sanctioning and forwarding the decrees of the National Assembly, particularly that of the *Declaration of the Rights of Man*, and the decrees of the *fourth of August*, which contained the foundation principles on which the constitution was to be erected. The kindest, and perhaps the fairest conjecture upon this matter is, that some of the ministers intended to make remarks and observations upon certain parts of them before they were finally sanctioned and sent to the provinces; but be this as it may, the enemies of the Revolution derived hope from the delay, and the friends of the Revolution uneasiness. . . .

Before anything can be reasoned upon to a conclusion, certain facts, principles, or data, to reason from, must be established, admitted, or denied. Mr. Burke with his usual outrage, abused the *Declaration of the Rights of Man*, published by the National Assembly of France, as the basis on which the constitution of France is built. This he calls "paltry and blurred sheets of paper about the rights of man." Does Mr. Burke mean to deny that *man* has any rights? If he does, then he must mean that there are no such things as rights anywhere, and that he has none himself; for who is there in the world but man? But if Mr. Burke means to admit that man has rights, the question then will be: What are those rights, and how man came by them originally?

The error of those who reason by precedents drawn from antiquity, respecting the rights of man, is that they do not go far enough into antiquity. They do not go the whole way. They stop in some of the intermediate stages of an hundred or a thousand years, and produce what was then done, as a rule for the present day. This is no authority at all. If we travel still farther into antiquity, we shall find a direct contrary opinion and practice prevailing; and if antiquity is to be authority, a thousand such authorities may be produced, successively contradicting each other; but if we proceed on, we shall at last come out right; we shall come to the time when man came from the hand of his Makers. What was he then? Man. Man was his high and only title, and a higher cannot be given him. But of titles I shall speak hereafter.

We are now got at the origin of man, and at the origin of his rights. As to the manner in which the world has been governed from that day to this, it is no farther any concern of ours than to make a proper use of the errors or the improvements which the history of it presents. Those who lived a hundred or a thousand years ago, were then moderns, as we are now. They had *their* ancients, and those ancients had others, and we also shall be ancients, in our turn. If the mere name of antiquity is to govern in the affairs of life, the people who are to live an hundred or a thousand years hence, may as well take us for a precedent, as we make a precedent of those who lived an hundred or a thousand years ago. The fact is, that portions of antiquity, by proving everything, establish nothing. It is authority against authority all the way, till we come to the divine origin of the rights of man at the creation. Here our enquiries find a resting-place, and our reason finds a home. If a dispute about the rights of man had arisen at the distance of an hundred years from the creation, it is to this source of authority they must have referred, and it is to this same source of authority that we must now refer.

Though I mean not to touch upon any sectarian principle of religion, yet it may be worth observing, that the genealogy of Christ is traced to Adam. Why then not trace the rights of man to the creation of man? I will answer the question. Because there have been upstart governments, thrusting themselves between, and presumptuously working to *un-make* man.

If any generation of men ever possessed the right of dictating the mode by which the world should be governed for ever, it was the first generation that existed; and if that generation did it not, no succeeding generation can show any authority for doing it, nor can set any up. The illuminating and divine principle of the equal rights of man (for it has its origin from the Maker of man) relates, not only to the living individuals, but to generations of men succeeding each other. Every generation is equal in rights to generations which preceded it, by the same rule that every individual is born equal in rights with his contemporary.

Every history of the creation, and every traditionary account, whether from the lettered or unlettered world, however they may vary in their opinion or belief of certain particulars, all agree in establishing one point, *the unity of man;* by which I mean that men are all of *one degree,* and consequently that all men are born equal, and with equal natural right, in the same manner as if posterity had been continued by *creation* instead of *generation*, the latter being the only mode by which the former is carried forward; and consequently every child born into the world must be considered as deriving its existence from God. The world is as new to him as it was to the first man that existed, and his natural right in it is of the same kind.

The Mosaic account of the creation, whether taken as divine authority or merely historical, is full to this point, *the unity or equality of man*. The expression admits of no controversy. "And God said, Let us make man in our own image. In the image of God created he him; male and female created he them." The distinction of sexes is pointed out, but no other distinction is even implied. If this be not divine authority, it is at least historical authority, and shews that the equality of man, so far from being a modern doctrine, is the oldest upon record.

It is also to be observed that all the religions known in the world are founded, so far as they relate to man, on the *unity of man*, as being all of one degree. Whether in heaven or in hell, or in whatever state man may be supposed to exist hereafter, the good and the bad are the only distinctions. Nay, even the laws of governments are obliged to slide into this principle, by making degrees to consist in crimes and not in persons.

It is one of the greatest of all truths, and of the highest advantage to cultivate. By considering man in this light, and by instructing him to consider himself in this light, it places him in a close connection with all his duties, whether to his Creator or to the creation, of which he is a part; and it is only when he forgets his origin, or, to use a more fashionable phrase, his *birth and family*, that he becomes dissolute. It is not among the least of the evils of the present existing governments in all parts of Europe that man, considered as man, is thrown back to a vast distance from his Maker, and the artificial chasm filled up with a succession of barriers, or sort of turnpike gates, through which he has to pass. I will quote Mr. Burke's catalogue of barriers that he has set up between man and his Maker. Putting himself in the character of a herald, he says: "We fear God—we look with *awe* to kings—with affection to Parliaments—with duty to magistrates—with reverence to priests, and with respect to nobility." Mr. Burke has forgotten to put in "*chivalry*." He has also forgotten to put in Peter.

The duty of man is not a wilderness of turnpike gates, through which he is to pass by tickets from one to the other. It is plain and simple, and consists but of two points. His duty to God, which every man must feel; and with respect to his neighbor, to do as he would be done by. If those to whom power is delegated do well, they will be respected: if not, they will be despised; and with regard to those to whom no power is delegated, but who assume it, the rational world can know nothing of them.

Hitherto we have spoken only (and that but in part) of the natural rights of man. We have now to consider the civil rights of man, and to show how the one originates from the other. Man did not enter into society to become worse than he was before, nor to have fewer rights than he had before, but to have those rights better secured. His natural rights are the foundation of all his civil rights. But in order to pursue this distinction with more precision, it will be necessary to mark the different qualities of natural and civil rights.

A few words will explain this. Natural rights are those which appertain to man in right of his existence. Of this kind are all the intellectual rights, or rights of the mind, and also all those rights of acting as an individual for his own comfort and happiness, which are not injurious to the natural rights of others. Civil rights are those which appertain to man in right of his being a member of society. Every civil right has for its foundation some natural right pre-existing in the individual, but to the enjoyment of which his individual power is not, in all cases, sufficiently competent. Of this kind are all those which relate to security and protection.

From this short review it will be easy to distinguish between that class of natural rights which man retains after entering into society and those which he throws into the common stock as a member of society.

The natural rights which he retains are all those in which the *power* to execute is as perfect in the individual as the right itself. Among this class, as is before mentioned, are all the intellectual rights, or rights of the mind; consequently religion is one of those rights. The natural rights which are not retained, are all those in which, though the right is perfect in the individual, the power to execute them is defective. They answer not his purpose. A man, by natural right, has a right to judge in his own cause; and so far as the right of the mind is concerned, he never surrenders it. But what availeth it him to judge, if he has not power to redress? He therefore deposits this right in the common stock of society, and takes the arm of society, of which he is a part, in preference and in addition to his own. Society *grants* him nothing. Every man is a proprietor in society, and draws on the capital as a matter of right.

From these premises two or three certain conclusions will follow:

First, That every civil right grows out of a natural right; or, in other words, is a natural right exchanged.

Secondly, That civil power properly considered as such is made up of the aggregate of that class of the natural rights of man, which becomes defective in the individual in point of power, and answers not his purpose, but when collected to a focus becomes competent to the purpose of every one.

Thirdly, That the power produced from the aggregate of natural rights, imperfect in power in the individual, cannot be applied to invade the natural rights which are retained in the individual, and in which the power to execute is as perfect as the right itself.

We have now, in a few words, traced man from a natural individual to a member of society, and shewn, or endeavoured to shew, the quality of the natural rights retained, and of those which are exchanged for civil rights. Let us now apply these principles to governments.

In casting our eyes over the world, it is extremely easy to distinguish the governments which have arisen out of society, or out of the social compact, from those which have not; but to place this in a clearer light than what a single glance may afford, it will be proper to take a review of the several sources from which governments have arisen and on which they have been founded.

They may be all comprehended under three heads. First, Superstition. Secondly, Power. Thirdly, the common interest of society and the common rights of man.

The first was a government of priestcraft, the second of conquerors, and the third of reason.

When a set of artful men pretended, through the medium of oracles, to hold intercourse with the Deity, as familiarly as they now march up the back-stairs in European courts, the world was completely under the government of superstition. The oracles were consulted, and whatever they were made to say became the law; and this sort of government lasted as long as this sort of superstition lasted.

After these a race of conquerors arose, whose government, like that of William the Conqueror, was founded in power, and the sword assumed the name of a sceptre. Governments thus established last as long as the power to support them lasts; but that they might avail themselves of every engine in their favor, they united fraud to force, and set up an idol which they called *Divine Right*, and which, in imitation of the Pope, who affects to be spiritual and temporal, and in contradiction to the Founder of the Christian religion, twisted itself afterwards into an idol of another shape, called *Church and State*. The key of St. Peter and the key of the Treasury became quartered on one another, and the wondering cheated multitude worshipped the invention.

When I contemplate the natural dignity of man, when I feel (for Nature has not been kind enough to me to blunt my feelings) for the honour and happiness of its character, I become irritated at the attempt to govern mankind by force and fraud, as if they were all knaves and fools, and can scarcely avoid disgust at those who are thus imposed upon.

We have now to review the governments which arise out of society, in contradistinction to those which arose out of superstition and conquest.

It has been thought a considerable advance towards establishing the principles of Freedom to say that Government is a compact between those who govern and those who are governed; but this cannot be true, because it is putting the effect before the cause; for as man must have existed before governments existed, there necessarily was a time when governments did not exist, and consequently there could originally exist no governors to form such a compact with.

The fact therefore must be that the *individuals themselves*, each in his own personal and sovereign right, *entered into a compact with each other* to produce a government: and this is the only mode in which governments have a right to arise, and the only principle on which they have a right to exist.

To possess ourselves of a clear idea of what government is, or ought to be, we must trace it to its origin. In doing this we shall easily discover that governments must have arisen either *out* of the people or *over* the people. Mr. Burke has made no distinction. He investigates nothing to its source, and therefore he confounds everything; but he has signified his intention of undertaking, at some future opportunity, a comparison between the constitution of England and France. As he thus renders it a subject of controversy by throwing the gauntlet, I take him upon his own ground. It is in high challenges that high truths have the right of appearing; and I accept it with the more readiness because it affords me, at the same time, an opportunity of pursuing the subject with respect to governments arising out of society.

But it will be first necessary to define what is meant by a *Constitution*. It is not sufficient that we adopt the word; we must fix also a standard signification to it.

A constitution is not a thing in name only, but in fact. It has not an ideal, but a real existence; and wherever it cannot be produced in a visible form, there is none. A constitution is a thing *antecedent* to a government, and a government is only the creature of a constitution. The constitution of a country is not the act of its government, but of the people constituting its government. It is the body of elements, to which you can refer, and quote article by article; and which contains the principles on which the government shall be established, the manner in which it shall be organised, the powers it shall have, the mode of elections, the duration of Parliaments, or by what other name such bodies may be called; the powers which the executive part of the government shall have; and in fine, everything that relates to the complete organization of a civil government, and the principles on which it shall act, and by which it shall be bound. A constitution, therefore, is to a government what the laws made afterwards by that government are to a court of judicature. The court of judicature does not make the laws, neither can it alter them; it only acts in conformity to the laws made: and the government is in like manner governed by the constitution.

Can, then, Mr. Burke produce the English Constitution? If he cannot, we may fairly conclude that though it has been so much talked about, no such thing as a constitution exists, or ever did exist, and consequently that the people have yet a constitution to form.

Mr. Burke will not, I presume, deny the position I have already advanced—namely, that governments arise either *out* of the people or *over* the people. The English Government is one of those which arose out of a conquest, and not out of society, and consequently it arose over the people; and though it has been much modified from the opportunity of circumstances since the time of William the Conqueror, the country has never yet regenerated itself, and is therefore without a constitution.

I readily perceive the reason why Mr. Burke declined going into the comparison between the English and French constitutions, because he could not but perceive, when he sat down to the task, that no such a thing as a constitution existed on his side the question. His book is certainly bulky enough to have contained all he could say on this subject, and it would have been the best manner in which people could have judged of their separate merits. Why then has he declined the only thing that was worth while to write upon? It was the strongest ground he could take, if the advantages were on his side, but the weakest if they were not; and his declining to take it is either a sign that he could not possess it or could not maintain it.

Mr. Burke said, in a speech last winter in Parliament, "that when the National Assembly first met in three Orders (the Tiers Etats, the Clergy, and the Noblesse), France had then a good constitution." This shews, among numerous other instances, that Mr. Burke does not understand what a constitution is. The persons so met were not a *constitution*, but a *convention*, to make a constitution.

The present National Assembly of France is, strictly speaking, the personal social compact. The members of it are the delegates of the nation in its *original* character; future assemblies will be the delegates of the nation in its *organised* character. The authority of the present Assembly is different from what the authority of future Assemblies will be. The authority of the present one is to form a constitution; the authority of future assemblies will be to legislate according to the principles and forms prescribed in that constitution; and if experience should hereafter shew that alterations, amendments, or additions are necessary, the constitution will point out the mode by which such things shall be done, and not leave it to the discretionary power of the future government.

A government on the principles on which constitutional governments arising out of society are established, cannot have the right of altering itself. If it had, it would be arbitrary. It might make itself what it pleased; and wherever such a right is set up, it shows there is no constitution. The act by which the English Parliament empowered itself to sit seven years, shows there is no constitution in England. It might, by the same self-authority, have sat any great number of years, or for life. The bill which the present Mr. Pitt brought into Parliament some years ago, to reform Parliament, was on the same erroneous principle. The right of reform is in the nation in its original character, and the constitutional method would be by a general convention elected for the purpose. There is, moreover, a paradox in the idea of vitiated bodies reforming themselves.

From these preliminaries I proceed to draw some comparisons. I have already spoken of the declaration of rights; and as I mean to be as concise as possible, I shall proceed to other parts of the French Constitution.

The constitution of France says, that every man who pays a tax of sixty sous *per annum* (2s. 6d. English) is an elector. What article will Mr. Burke place against this? Can anything be more limited, and at the same time more capricious, than the qualification of electors is in England? Limited—because not one man in an hundred (I speak much within compass) is admitted to vote. Capricious— because the lowest character that can be supposed to exist, and who has not so much as the visible means of an honest livelihood, is an elector in some places: while in other places, the man who pays very large taxes, and has a known fair character, and the farmer who rents to the amount of three or four hundred pounds a year, with a property on that farm to three or four times that amount, is not admitted to be an elector. Everything is out of nature, as Mr. Burke says on another occasion, in this strange chaos, and all sorts of follies are blended with all sorts of crimes. William the Conqueror and his descendants parcelled out the country in this manner, and bribed some parts of it by what they call charters to hold the other parts of it the better subjected to their will. This is the reason why so many of those charters abound in Cornwall; the people were averse to the Government established at the Conquest, and the towns were garrisoned and bribed to enslave the country. All the old charters are the badges of this conquest, and it is from this source that the capriciousness of election arises.

The French Constitution says, that the number of representatives for any place shall be in a ratio to the number of taxable inhabitants or electors. What article will Mr. Burke place against this? The county of York, which contains nearly a million of souls, sends two county members; and so does the county of Rutland, which contains not an hundredth part of that number. The old town of Sarum, which contains not three houses, sends two members; and the town of Manchester, which contains upward of sixty thousand souls, is not admitted to send any. Is there any principle in these things? It is admitted that all this is altered, but there is much to be done yet, before we have a fair representation of the people. Is there anything by which you can trace the marks of freedom, or discover those of wisdom? No wonder then Mr. Burke has declined the comparison, and endeavored to lead his readers from the point by a wild, unsystematical display of paradoxical rhapsodies.

The French Constitution says that the National Assembly shall be elected every two years. What article will Mr. Burke place against this? Why, that the nation has no right at all in the case; that the government is perfectly arbitrary with respect to this point; and he can quote for his authority the precedent of a former Parliament.

The French Constitution says there shall be no game laws, that the farmer on whose lands wild game shall be found (for it is by the produce of his lands they are fed) shall have a right to what he can take; that there shall be no monopolies of any kind—that all trades shall be free and every man free to follow any occupation by which he can procure an honest livelihood, and in any place, town, or city throughout the nation. What will Mr. Burke say to this? In England, game is made the property of those at whose expense it is not fed; and with respect to monopolies, the country is cut up into monopolies. Every chartered town is an aristocratical monopoly in itself, and the qualification of electors proceeds out of those chartered monopolies. Is this freedom? Is this what Mr. Burke means by a constitution?

In these chartered monopolies, a man coming from another part of the country is hunted from them as if he were a foreign enemy. An Englishman is not free of his own country; every one of those places presents a barrier in his way, and tells him he is not a freeman—that he has no rights. Within these monopolies are other monopolies. In a city, such for instance as Bath, which contains between twenty and thirty thousand inhabitants, the right of electing representatives to Parliament is monopolised by about thirty-one persons. And within these monopolies are still others. A man even of the same town, whose parents were not in circumstances to give him an occupation, is debarred, in many cases, from the natural right of acquiring one, be his genius or industry what it may.

Are these things examples to hold out to a country regenerating itself from slavery, like France? Certainly they are not, and certain am I, that when the people of England come to reflect upon them they will, like France, annihilate those badges of ancient oppression, those traces of a conquered nation. Had Mr. Burke possessed talents similar to the author of "On the Wealth of Nations," he would have comprehended all the parts which enter into, and, by assemblage, form a constitution. He would have reasoned from minutiæ to magnitude. It is not from his prejudices only, but from the disorderly cast of his genius, that he is unfitted for the subject he writes upon. Even his genius is without a constitution. It is a genius at random, and not a genius, constituted. But he must say something. He has therefore mounted in the air like a balloon, to draw the eyes of the multitude from the ground they stand upon.

Much is to be learned from the French Constitution. Conquest and tyranny transplanted themselves with William the Conqueror from Normandy into England, and the country is yet disfigured with the marks. May, then, the example of all France contribute to regenerate the freedom which a province of it destroyed!

The French Constitution says that to preserve the national representation from being corrupt no member of the National Assembly shall be an officer of the government, a placeman or a pensioner. What will Mr. Burke place against this? I will whisper his answer; *Loaves and Fishes.* Ah! this government of loaves and fishes has more mischief in it than people have yet reflected on. The National Assembly has made the discovery, and it holds out the example to the world. Had governments agreed to quarrel on purpose to fleece their countries by taxes, they could not have succeeded better than they have done.

Everything in the English government appears to me the reverse of what it ought to be, and of what it is said to be. The Parliament, imperfectly and capriciously elected as it is, is nevertheless *supposed* to hold the national purse in *trust* for the nation; but in the manner in which an English Parliament is constructed it is like a man being both mortgagor and mortgagee, and in the case of misapplication of trust it is the criminal sitting in judgment upon himself. If those who vote the supplies are the same persons who receive the supplies when voted, and are to account for the expenditure of those supplies to those who voted them, it is *themselves accountable to themselves*, and the Comedy of Errors concludes with the pantomime of *Hush*. Neither the Ministerial party nor the Opposition will touch upon this case. The national purse is the common hack which each mounts upon. It is like what the country people call "Ride and tie— you ride a little way, and then I."* They order these things better in France.

The French Constitution says that the right of war and peace is in the nation. Where else should it reside but in those who are to pay the expense?

In England this right is said to reside in a *metaphor* shown at the Tower for sixpence or a shilling a piece: so are the lions; and it would be a step nearer to reason to say it resided in them, for any inanimate metaphor is no more than a hat or a cap. We can all see the absurdity of worshipping Aaron's molten calf, or Nebuchadnezzar's golden image; but why do men continue to practise themselves the absurdities they despise in others?

It may with reason be said that in the manner the English nation is represented it signifies not where the right resides, whether in the Crown or in the Parliament. War is the common harvest of all those who participate in the division and expenditure of public money, in all countries. It is the art of *conquering at home;* the object of it is an increase of revenue; and as revenue cannot be increased without taxes, a pretence must be made for expenditure. In reviewing the history of the English Government, its wars and its taxes, a by-

---

*It is a practice in some parts of the country, when two travellers have but one horse, which, like the national purse, will not carry double, that the one mounts and rides two or three miles ahead, and then ties the horse to a gate and walks on. When the second traveller arrives he takes the horse, rides on, and passes his companion a mile or two, and ties again, and so on—*Ride and tie* [Author's note].

stander, not blinded by prejudice nor warped by interest, would declare that taxes were not raised to carry on wars, but that wars were raised to carry on taxes.

Mr. Burke, as a member of the House of Commons, is a part of the English Government; and though he professes himself an enemy to war, he abuses the French Constitution, which seeks to explode it. He holds up the English Government as a model, in all its parts, to France; but he should first know the remarks which the French make upon it. They contend in favor of their own, that the portion of liberty enjoyed in England is just enough to enslave a country more productively than by despotism, and that as the real object of all despotism is revenue, a government so formed obtains more than it could do either by direct despotism, or in a full state of freedom, and is, therefore on the ground of interest, opposed to both. They account also for the readiness which always appears in such governments for engaging in wars by remarking on the different motives which produced them. In despotic governments wars are the effect of pride; but in those governments in which they become the means of taxation, they acquire thereby a more permanent promptitude.

The French Constitution, therefore, to provide against both these evils, has taken away the power of declaring war from kings and ministers, and placed the right where the expence must fall.

When the question of the right of war and peace was agitating in the National Assembly, the people of England appeared to be much interested in the event, and highly to applaud the decision. As a principle it applies as much to one country as another. William the Conqueror, *as a conqueror*, held this power of war and peace in himself, and his descendants have ever since claimed it under him as a right.

Although Mr. Burke has asserted the right of the Parliament at the Revolution to bind and controul the nation and posterity for *ever*, he denies at the same time that the Parliament or the nation had any right to alter what he calls the succession of the crown in anything but in part, or by a sort of modification. By his taking this ground he throws the case back to the *Norman Conquest*, and by thus running a line of succession springing from William the Conqueror to the present day, he makes it necessary to enquire who and what

William the Conqueror was, and where he came from, and into the origin, history and nature of what are called prerogatives. Everything must have had a beginning, and the fog of time and antiquity should be penetrated to discover it. Let, then, Mr. Burke bring forward his William of Normandy, for it is to this origin that his argument goes. It also unfortunately happens, in running this line of succession, that another line parallel thereto presents itself, which is that if the succession runs in the line of the conquest, the nation runs in the line of being conquered, and it ought to rescue itself from this reproach. . . .

MISCELLANEOUS CHAPTER.

TO PREVENT INTERRUPTING THE argument in the preceding part of this work, or the narrative that follows it, I reserved some observations to be thrown together in a Miscellaneous Chapter; by which variety might not be censured for confusion. Mr. Burke's book is *all* Miscellany. His intention was to make an attack on the French Revolution; but instead of proceeding with an orderly arrangement, he has stormed it with a mob of ideas tumbling over and destroying one another.

But this confusion and contradiction in Mr. Burke's Book is easily accounted for.—When a man in a wrong cause attempts to steer his course by anything else than some polar truth or principle, he is sure to be lost. It is beyond the compass of his capacity to keep all the parts of an argument together, and make them unite in one issue, by any other means than having this guide always in view. Neither memory nor invention will supply the want of it. The former fails him, and the latter betrays him.

Notwithstanding the nonsense, for it deserves no better name, that Mr. Burke has asserted about hereditary rights, and hereditary succession, and that a Nation has not a right to form a Government of itself; it happened to fall in his way to give some account of what Government is. "*Government*," says he, "*is a contrivance of human wisdom.*"

Admitting that government is a contrivance of human *wisdom*, it must necessarily follow, that hereditary succession, and hereditary rights (as they are called), can make no part of it, because it is impossible to make wisdom hereditary; and on the other hand, *that* cannot be a wise contrivance, which in its operation may commit the government of a nation to the wisdom of an idiot. The ground which Mr. Burke now takes is fatal to every part of his cause. The argument changes from hereditary rights to hereditary wisdom; and the question is, Who is the wisest man? He must now shew that every one in the line of hereditary succession was a Solomon, or his title is not good to be a king. What a stroke has Mr. Burke now made! To use a sailor's phrase, he has *swabbed the deck*, and scarcely left a name legible in the list of Kings; and he has mowed down and thinned the House of Peers, with a scythe as formidable as Death and Time.

But Mr. Burke appears to have been aware of this retort; and he has taken care to guard against it, by making government to be not only a *contrivance* of human wisdom, but a *monopoly* of wisdom. He puts the nation as fools on one side, and places his government of wisdom, all wise men of Gotham, on the other side; and he then proclaims, and says that "*Men have a* RIGHT *that their* WANTS *should be provided for by this wisdom.*" Having thus made proclamation, he next proceeds to explain to them what their *wants* are, and also what their *rights* are. In this he has succeeded dextrously, for he makes their wants to be a *want* of wisdom; but as this is cold comfort, he then informs them, that they have a *right* (not to any of the wisdom) but to be governed by it; and in order to impress them with a solemn reverence for this monopoly-government of wisdom, and of its vast capacity for all purposes, possible or impossible, right or wrong, he proceeds with astrological mysterious importance, to tell to them its powers in these words: "The rights of men in government are their advantages; and these are often in balance between differences of good; and in compromises sometimes between *good* and *evil*, and sometimes between *evil* and *evil*. Political reason is a *computing principle;* adding—subtracting—multiplying—and dividing, morally and not metaphysically or mathematically, true moral denominations."

As the wondering audience, whom Mr. Burke supposes himself talking to, may not understand all this learned jargon, I will undertake to be its interpreter. The meaning, then, good people, of all this, is: *That government is governed by no principle whatever, that it can make evil good, or good evil, just as it pleases. In short, that government is arbitrary power.*

But there are some things which Mr. Burke has forgotten. *First,* he has not shewn where the wisdom originally came from: and *secondly,* he has not shewn by what authority it first began to act. In the manner he introduces the matter, it is either government stealing wisdom, or wisdom stealing government. It is without an origin, and its powers without authority. In short, it is usurpation.

Whether it be from a sense of shame, or from a consciousness of some radical defect in a government necessary to be kept out of sight, or from both, or from any other cause, I undertake not to determine, but so it is, that a monarchical reasoner never traces government to its source, or from its source. It is one of the *shibboleths* by which he may be known. A thousand years hence, those who shall live in America or France, will look back with contemplative pride on the origin of their government, and say, *This was the work of our glorious ancestors!* But what can a monarchical talker say? What has he to exult in? Alas he has nothing. A certain something forbids him to look back to a beginning, lest some robber, or some Robin Hood, should rise from the long obscurity of time and say, *I am the origin*. Hard as Mr. Burke labored at the Regency Bill and Hereditary Succession two years ago, and much as he dived for precedents, he still had not boldness enough to bring up William of Normandy, and say, *There is the head of the list! there is the fountain of honor!* the son of a prostitute, and the plunderer of the English nation.

The opinions of men with respect to government are changing fast in all countries. The Revolutions of America and France have thrown a beam of light over the world, which reaches into man. The enormous expense of governments has provoked people to think, by making them feel; and when once the veil begins to rend, it admits not of repair. Ignorance is of a peculiar nature: once dispelled, it is impossible to re-establish it. It is not originally a thing of itself, but is only the absence of knowledge; and though man may be *kept* ignorant, he cannot be *made* ignorant. The mind, in discovering truth, acts in the same manner as it acts through the eye in discovering objects; when once any object has been seen, it is impossible to put the mind back to the same condition it was in before it saw it. Those who talk of a counter-revolution in France, show how little they understand of man. There does not exist in the compass of language an arrangement of words to express so much as the means of effecting a counter-revolution. The means must be an obliteration of knowledge; and it has never yet been discovered how to make man *unknow* his knowledge, or *unthink* his thoughts.

Mr. Burke is laboring in vain to stop the progress of knowledge; and it comes with the worse grace from him, as there is a certain transaction known in the city which renders him suspected of being a pensioner in a fictitious name. This may account for some strange doctrine he has advanced in his book, which though he points it at the Revolution Society, is effectually directed against the whole nation.

"The King of England," says he, "holds *his* crown (for it does not belong to the Nation, according to Mr. Burke) in *contempt* of the choice of the Revolution Society, who have not a single vote for a king among them either *individually* or *collectively;* and his Majesty's heirs each in their time and order, will come to the Crown *with the same contempt* of their choice, with which his Majesty has succeeded to that which he now wears."

As to who is King in England or elsewhere, or whether there is any King at all, or whether the people choose a Cherokee chief, or a Hessian hussar for a King, it is not a matter that I trouble myself about—be that to themselves; but with respect to the doctrine, so far as it relates to the Rights of Men and Nations, it is as abominable as anything ever uttered in the most enslaved country under heaven. Whether it sounds worse to my ear, by not being accustomed to hear such despotism, than what it does to another person, I am not so well a judge of; but of its abominable principle I am at no loss to judge.

It is not the Revolution Society that Mr. Burke means; it is the Nation, as well in its *original* as in its *representative* character; and he has taken care to make himself understood, by saying that they have not a vote either *collectively* or *individually*. The Revolution Society is composed of citizens of all denominations, and of members of both the Houses of Parliament; and consequently, if there is not a right to a vote in any of the characters, there can be no right to any either in the nation or in its Parliament. This ought to be a caution to every country how to import foreign families to be kings. It is somewhat curious to observe, that although the people of England had been in the habit of talking about kings, it is always a Foreign House of Kings; hating Foreigners yet governed by them.—It is now the House of Brunswick, one of the petty tribes of Germany.

It has hitherto been the practice of the English Parliaments to regulate what was called the succession (taking it for granted that the Nation then continued to accord to the form of annexing a monarchical branch of its government; for without this the Parliament could not have had authority to have sent either to Holland or to Hanover, or to impose a king upon the nation against its will.) And this must be the utmost limit to which Parliament can go upon this case; but the right of the Nation goes to the *whole* case, because it has the right of changing its *whole* form of government. The right of a Parliament is only a right in trust, a right by delegation, and that but from a very small part of the Nation; and one of its Houses has not even this. But the right of the Nation is an original right, as universal as taxation. The nation is the paymaster of everything, and everything must conform to its general will.

I remember taking notice of a speech in what is called the English House of Peers, by the then Earl of Shelburne, and I think it was at the time he was Minister, which is applicable to this case. I do not directly charge my memory with every particular; but the words and the purport, as nearly as I remember, were these: "*That the form of a Government was a matter wholly at the will of the Nation at all times, that if it chose a monarchical form, it had a right to have it so; and if it afterwards chose to be a Republic, it had a right to be a Republic, and to say to a King, 'We have no longer any occasion for you.'*"

When Mr. Burke says that "His Majesty's heirs and successors, each in their time and order, will come to the crown with the *same contempt* of their choice with which His Majesty had succeeded to that he wears," it is saying too much even to the humblest individual in the country; part of whose daily labor goes towards making up the million sterling a-year, which the country gives the person it styles a king. Government with insolence is despotism; but when contempt is added it becomes worse; and to pay for contempt is the excess of slavery. This species of government comes from Germany; and reminds me of what one of the Brunswick soldiers told me, who was taken prisoner by the Americans in the late war: "Ah!" said he, "America is a fine free country, it is worth the people's fighting for; I know the difference by knowing my own: in my country, if the prince says eat straw, we eat straw." God help that country, thought I, be it England or elsewhere, whose liberties are to be protected by German principles of government, and Princes of Brunswick!

As Mr. Burke sometimes speaks of England, sometimes of France, and sometimes of the world, and of government in general, it is difficult to answer his book without apparently meeting him on the same ground. Although principles of Government are general subjects, it is next to impossible, in many cases, to separate them from the idea of place and circumstance, and the more so when circumstances are put for arguments, which is frequently the case with Mr. Burke.

In the former part of his book, addressing himself to the people of France, he says: "No experience has taught us (meaning the English), that in any other course or method than that of a *hereditary crown*, can our liberties be regularly perpetuated and preserved sacred as our *hereditary right.*" I ask Mr. Burke, who is to take them away? M. de la Fayette, in speaking to France, says: *"For a Nation to be free, it is sufficient that she wills it."* But Mr. Burke represents England as wanting capacity to take care of itself, and that its liberties must be taken care of by a King holding it in "contempt." If England is sunk to this, it is preparing itself to eat straw, as in Hanover, or in Brunswick. But besides the folly of the declaration, it happens that the facts are all against Mr. Burke. It was by the government *being hereditary*, that the liberties of the people were endangered. Charles I. and James II. are instances of this truth; yet neither of them went so far as to hold the Nation in contempt.

As it is sometimes of advantage to the people of one country to hear what those of other countries have to say respecting it, it is possible that the people of France may learn something from Mr. Burke's book, and that the people of England may also learn something from the answers it will occasion. When Nations fall out about freedom, a wide field of debate is opened. The argument commences with the rights of war, without its evils, and as knowledge is the object contended for, the party that sustains the defeat obtains the prize.

Mr. Burke talks about what he calls an hereditary crown, as if it were some production of Nature; or as if, like Time, it had a power to operate, not only independently, but in spite of man; or as if it were a thing or a subject universally consented to. Alas! it has none of those properties, but is the reverse of them all. It is a thing in imagination, the propriety of which is more than doubted, and the legality of which in a few years will be denied.

But, to arrange this matter in a clearer view than what general expression can convey, it will be necessary to state the distinct heads under which (what is called) an hereditary crown, or more properly speaking, an hereditary succession to the Government of a Nation, can be considered; which are,

First, The right of a particular Family to establish itself.

Secondly, The right of a Nation to establish a particular Family.

With respect to the *first* of these heads, that of a Family establishing itself with hereditary powers on its own authority, and independent of the consent of a Nation, all men will concur in calling it despotism; and it would be trespassing on their understanding to attempt to prove it.

But the *second* head, that of a Nation establishing a particular Family with *hereditary powers*, does not present itself as despotism on the first reflexion; but if men will permit a second reflexion to take place, and carry that reflexion forward but one remove out of their own persons to that of their offspring, they will then see that hereditary succession becomes in its consequences the same despotism to others, which they reprobated for themselves. It operates to preclude the consent of the succeeding generations; and the preclusion of consent is despotism. When the person who at any time shall be in possession of a Government, or those who stand in succession to him, shall say to a Nation, I hold this power in "contempt" of you, it signifies not on what authority he pretends to say it. It is no relief, but an aggravation to a person in slavery, to reflect that he was sold by his parent; and as that which heightens the criminality of an act cannot be produced to prove the legality of it, hereditary succession cannot be established as a legal thing.

In order to arrive at a more perfect decision on this head, it will be proper to consider the generation which undertakes to establish a Family with *hereditary powers*, apart and separate from the generations which are to follow; and also to consider the character in which the first generation acts with respect to succeeding generations.

The generation which first selects a person, and puts him at the head of its Government, either with the title of King, or any other distinction, acts on its *own choice*, be it wise or foolish, as a free agent for itself. The person so set up is not hereditary, but selected and appointed; and the generation who sets him up, does not live under a hereditary government, but under a government of its own choice and establishment. Were the generation who sets him up, and the person so set up, to live for ever, it never could become hereditary succession; and of consequence hereditary succession can only follow on the death of the first parties.

As, therefore, hereditary succession is out of the question with respect to the *first* generation, we have now to consider the character in which *that* generation acts with respect to the commencing generation, and to all succeeding ones.

It assumes a character, to which it has neither right nor title. It changes itself from a *Legislator* to a *Testator*, and effects to make its Will, which is to have operation after the demise of the makers, to bequeath the Government; and it not only attempts to bequeath, but to establish on the succeeding generation, a new and different form of Government under which itself lived. Itself, as already observed, lived not under a hereditary Government but under a Government of its own choice and establishment; and it now attempts, by virtue of a will and testament (and which it has not authority to make), to take from the commencing generation, and all future ones, the rights and free agency by which itself acted.

But, exclusive of the right which any generation has to act collectively as a testator, the objects to which it applies itself in this case, are not within the compass of any law, or of any will or testament.

The rights of men in society, are neither devisable or transferable, nor annihilable, but are descendable only, and it is not in the power of any generation to intercept finally, and cut off the descent. If the present generation, or any other, are disposed to be slaves, it does not lessen the right of the succeeding generation to be free. Wrongs cannot have a legal descent. When Mr. Burke attempts to maintain that the *English nation did at the Revolution of 1688, most solemnly renounce and abdicate their rights for themselves, and for all their posterity forever*, he speaks a language that merits not reply, and which can only excite contempt for his prostitute principles, or pity for his ignorance.

In whatever light hereditary succession, as growing out of the will and testament of some former generation, presents itself, it is an absurdity. A cannot make a will to take from B the property of B, and give it to C; yet this is the manner in which (what is called) hereditary succession by law operates. A certain former generation made a will, to take away the rights of the commencing generation, and all future ones, and convey those rights to a third person, who afterwards comes forward, and tells them, in Mr. Burke's language, that they have *no rights*, that their rights are already bequeathed to him and that he will govern in *contempt* of them. From such principles, and such ignorance, good Lord deliver the world!

But, after all, what is this metaphor called a crown, or rather what is monarchy? Is it a thing, or is it a name, or is it a fraud? Is it a "contrivance of human wisdom," or of human craft to obtain money from a nation under specious pretences? Is it a thing necessary to a nation? If it is, in what does that necessity consist, what service does it perform, what is its business, and what are its merits? Does the virtue consist in the metaphor, or in the man? Doth the goldsmith that makes the crown, make the virtue also? Doth it operate like Fortunatus's wishing-cap, or Harlequin's wooden sword? Doth it make a man a conjurer? In fine, what is it? It appears to be something going much out of fashion, falling into ridicule, and rejected in some countries, both as unnecessary and expensive. In America it is considered as an absurdity; and in France it has so far declined, that the goodness of the man, and the respect for his personal character, are the only things that preserve the appearance of its existence.

If government be what Mr. Burke describes it, "a contrivance of human wisdom," I might ask him, if wisdom was at such a low ebb in England, that it was become necessary to import it from Holland and from Hanover? But I will do the country the justice to say, that was not the case; and even if it was, it mistook the cargo. The wisdom of every country, when properly exerted, is sufficient for all its purposes; and there could exist no more real occasion in England to have sent for a Dutch Stadtholder, or a German Elector, than there was in America to have done a similar thing. If a country does not understand its own affairs, how is a foreigner to understand them, who knows neither its laws, its manners, nor its language? If there existed a man so transcendently wise above all others, that his wisdom was necessary to instruct a nation, some reason might be offered for monarchy; but when we cast our eyes about a country, and observe how every part understands its own affairs; and when we look around the world, and see that of all men in it, the race of kings are the most insignificant in capacity, our reason cannot fail to ask us—What are those men kept for?

If there is anything in monarchy which we people of America do not understand, I wish Mr. Burke would be so kind as to inform us. I see in America, a government extending over a country ten times as large as England, and conducted with regularity, for a fortieth part of the expense which Government costs in England. If I ask a man in America if he wants a King, he retorts, and asks me if I take him for an ideot? How is it that this difference happens? are we more or less wise than others? I see in America the generality of people living in a style of plenty unknown in monarchical countries; and I see that the principle of its government, which is that of the *equal Rights of Man*, is making a rapid progress in the world.

If monarchy is a useless thing, why is it kept up anywhere? and if a necessary thing, how can it be dispensed with? That *civil government* is necessary, all civilised nations will agree; but civil government is republican government. All that part of the government of England which begins with the office of constable, and proceeds through the department of magistrate, quarter-sessions, and general assize, including trial by jury, is republican government. Nothing of monarchy appears in any part of it, except in the name which William the Conqueror imposed upon the English, that of obliging them to call him "Their Sovereign Lord the King."

It is easy to conceive that a band of interested men, such as Placemen, Pensioners, Lords of the bed-chamber, Lords of the kitchen, Lords of the necessary-house, and the Lord knows what besides, can find as many reasons for monarchy as their salaries, paid at the expence of the country, amount to; but if I ask the farmer, the manufacturer, the merchant, the tradesman, and down through all the occupations of life to the common laborer, what service monarchy is to him? he can give me no answer. If I ask him what monarchy is, he believes it is something like a sinecure.

Notwithstanding the taxes of England amount to almost seventeen millions a year, said to be for the expences of Government, it is still evident that the sense of the Nation is left to govern itself, and does govern itself, by magistrates and juries, almost at its own charge, on republican principles, exclusive of the expence of taxes. The salaries of the judges are almost the only charge that is paid out of the revenue. Considering that all the internal government is executed by the people, the taxes of England ought to be the lightest of any nation in Europe; instead of which, they are the contrary. As this cannot be accounted for on the score of civil government, the subject necessarily extends itself to the monarchical part.

When the people of England sent for George the First (and it would puzzle a wiser man than Mr. Burke to discover for what he could be wanted, or what service he could render), they ought at least to have conditioned for the abandonment of Hanover. Besides the endless German intrigues that must follow from a German Elector being King of England, there is a natural impossibility of uniting in the same person the principles of Freedom and the principles of Despotism, or as it is usually called in England Arbitrary Power. A German Elector is in his electorate a despot; how then could it be expected that he should be attached to principles of liberty in one country, while his interest in another was to be supported by despotism? The union cannot exist; and it might easily have been foreseen that German Electors would make German Kings, or in Mr. Burke's words, would assume government with "contempt." The English have been in the habit of considering a King of England only in the character in which he appears to them; whereas the same person, while the connection lasts, has a home-seat in another country, the interest of which is different to their own, and the principles of the governments in opposition to each other. To such a person England will appear as a town-residence, and the Electorate as the estate. The English may wish, as I believe they do, success to the principles of liberty in France, or in Germany; but a German Elector trembles for the fate of despotism in his electorate; and the Duchy of Mecklenburgh, where the present Queen's family governs, is under the same wretched state of arbitrary power, and the people in slavish vassalage.

There never was a time when it became the English to watch continental intrigues more circumspectly than at the present moment, and to distinguish the politics of the Electorate from the politics of the Nation. The Revolution of France has entirely changed the ground with respect to England and France, as nations; but the German despots, with Prussia at their head, are combining against liberty; and the fondness of Mr. Pitt for office, and the interest which all his family connections have obtained, do not give sufficient security against this intrigue.

As everything which passes in the world becomes matter for history, I will now quit this subject, and take a concise review of the state of parties and politics in England, as Mr. Burke has done in France.

Whether the present reign commenced with contempt, I leave to Mr. Burke: certain, however, it is, that it had strongly that appearance. The animosity of the English nation, it is very well remembered, ran high; and, had the true principles of Liberty been as well understood then as they now promise to be, it is probable the Nation would not have patiently submitted to so much. George the First and Second were sensible of a rival in the remains of the Stuarts; and as they could not but consider themselves as standing on their good behaviour, they had prudence to keep their German principles of government to themselves; but as the Stuart family wore away, the prudence became less necessary.

The contest between rights, and what were called prerogatives, continued to heat the nation till some time after the conclusion of the American War, when all at once it fell a calm—Execration exchanged itself for applause, and Court popularity sprung up like a mushroom in a night.

To account for this sudden transition, it is proper to observe that there are two distinct species of popularity; the one excited by merit, and the other by resentment. As the Nation had formed itself into two parties, and each was extolling the merits of its parliamentary champions for and against prerogative, nothing could operate to give a more general shock than an immediate coalition of the champions themselves. The partisans of each being thus suddenly left in the lurch, and mutually heated with disgust at the measure, felt no other relief than uniting in a common execration against both. A higher stimulus or resentment being thus excited than what the contest on prerogatives occasioned, the nation quitted all former objects of rights and wrongs, and sought only that of gratification. The indignation at the Coalition so effectually superseded the indignation against the Court as to extinguish it; and without any change of principles on the part of the Court, the same people who had reprobated its despotism united with it to revenge themselves on the Coalition Parliament. The case was not, which they liked best, but which they hated most; and the least hated passed for love. The dissolution of the Coalition Parliament, as it afforded the means of gratifying the resentment of the Nation, could not fail to be popular; and from hence arose the popularity of the Court.

Transitions of this kind exhibit a Nation under the government of temper, instead of a fixed and steady principle; and having once committed itself, however rashly, it feels itself urged along to justify by continuance its first proceeding. Measures which at other times it would censure it now approves, and acts persuasion upon itself to suffocate its judgment.

On the return of a new Parliament, the new Minister, Mr. Pitt, found himself in a secure majority; and the Nation gave him credit, not out of regard to himself, but because it had resolved to do it out of resentment to another. He introduced himself to public notice by a proposed Reform of Parliament, which in its operation would have amounted to a public justification of corruption. The Nation was to be at the expence of buying up the rotten boroughs, whereas it ought to punish the persons who deal in the traffic.

Passing over the two bubbles of the Dutch business and the million a-year to sink the national debt, the matter which most presents itself, is the affair of the Regency. Never, in the course of my observation, was delusion more successfully acted, nor a nation more completely deceived. But, to make this appear, it will be necessary to go over the circumstances.

Mr. Fox had stated in the House of Commons, that the Prince of Wales, as heir in succession, had a right in himself to assume the Government. This was opposed by Mr. Pitt; and, so far as the opposition was confined to the doctrine, it was just. But the principles which Mr. Pitt maintained on the contrary side were as bad, or worse in their extent, than those of Mr. Fox; because they went to establish an aristocracy over the nation, and over the small representation it has in the House of Commons.

Whether the English form of Government be good or bad, is not in this case the question; but, taking it as it stands, without regard to its merits or demerits, Mr. Pitt was farther from the point than Mr. Fox.

It is supposed to consist of three parts:—while therefore the Nation is disposed to continue this form, the parts have a *national standing*, independent of each other, and are not the creatures of each other. Had Mr. Fox passed through Parliament, and said that the person alluded to claimed on the ground of the Nation, Mr. Pitt must then have contended what he called the right of the Parliament against the right of the Nation.

By the appearance which the contest made, Mr. Fox took the hereditary ground, and Mr. Pitt the Parliamentary ground; but the fact is, they both took hereditary ground, and Mr. Pitt took the worst of the two.

What is called the Parliament is made up of two Houses, one of which is more hereditary, and more beyond the controul of the Nation than what the Crown (as it is called) is supposed to be. It is an hereditary aristocracy, assuming and asserting indefeasible, irrevocable, rights and authority, wholly independent of the Nation. Where, then, was the merited popularity of exalting this hereditary power over another hereditary power less independent of the Nation than what itself assumed to be, and of absorbing the rights of the Nation into a House over which it has neither election nor controul?

The general impulse of the Nation was right; but it acted without reflection. It approved the opposition made to the right set up by Mr. Fox, without perceiving that Mr. Pitt was supporting another indefeasible right more remote from the Nation, in opposition to it.

With respect to the House of Commons, it is elected but by a small part of the Nation; but were the election as universal as taxation, which it ought to be, it would still be only the organ of the Nation, and cannot possess inherent rights.—When the National Assembly of France resolves a matter, the resolve is made in right of the Nation; but Mr. Pitt, on all national questions, so far as they refer to the House of Commons, absorbs the rights of the Nation into the organ, and makes the organ into a Nation, and the Nation itself into a cypher.

In a few words, the question on the Regency was a question of a million a-year, which is appropriated to the executive department: and Mr. Pitt could not possess himself of any management of this sum, without setting up the supremacy of Parliament; and when this was accomplished, it was indifferent who should be Regent, as he must be Regent at his own cost. Among the curiosities which this contentious debate afforded, was that of making the Great Seal into a King, the affixing of which to an act was to be royal authority. If, therefore, Royal Authority is a Great Seal, it consequently is in itself nothing; and a good Constitution would be of infinitely more value to the Nation than what the three Nominal Powers, as they now stand, are worth.

The continual use of the word *Constitution* in the English Parliament shews there is none; and that the whole is merely a form of government without a Constitution, and constituting itself with what powers it pleases. If there were a Constitution, it certainly could be referred to; and the debate on any constitutional point would terminate by producing the Constitution. One member says this is Constitution, and another says that is Constitution—To-day it is one thing; and to-morrow something else—while the maintaining of the debate proves there is none. Constitution is now the cant word of Parliament, tuning itself to the ear of the Nation. Formerly it was the *universal supremacy of Parliament—the omnipotence of Parliament:* But since the progress of Liberty in France, those phrases have a despotic harshness in their note; and the English Parliament have catched the fashion from the National Assembly, but without the substance, of speaking of *Constitution*.

As the present generation of the people in England did not make the Government, they are not accountable for any of its defects; but, that sooner or later, it must come into their hands to undergo a constitutional reformation, is as certain as that the same thing has happened in France. If France, with a revenue of nearly twenty-four millions sterling, with an extent of rich and fertile country above four times larger than England, with a population of twenty-four millions of inhabitants to support taxation, with upwards of ninety millions sterling of gold and silver circulating in the nation, and with a debt less than the present debt of England—still found it necessary, from whatever cause, to come to a settlement of its affairs, it solves the problem of funding for both countries.

It is out of the question to say how long what is called the

English constitution has lasted, and to argue from thence how long it is to last; the question is, how long can the funding system last? It is a thing but of modern invention, and has not yet continued beyond the life of a man; yet in that short space it has so far accumulated, that, together with the current expenses, it requires an amount of taxes at least equal to the whole landed rental of the nation in acres to defray the annual expenditure. That a government could not have always gone on by the same system which has been followed for the last seventy years, must be evident to every man; and for the same reason it cannot always go on.

The funding system is not money; neither is it, properly speaking, credit. It, in effect, creates upon paper the sum which it appears to borrow, and lays on a tax to keep the imaginary capital alive by the payment of interest and sends the annuity to market, to be sold for paper already in circulation. If any credit is given, it is to the disposition of the people to pay the tax, and not to the government, which lays it on. When this disposition expires, what is supposed to be the credit of Government expires with it. The instance of France under the former Government shews that it is impossible to compel the payment of taxes by force, when a whole nation is determined to take its stand upon that ground.

Mr. Burke, in his review of the finances of France, states the quantity of gold and silver in France, at about eighty-eight millions sterling. In doing this, he has, I presume, divided by the difference of exchange, instead of the standard of twenty-four livres to a pound sterling; for M. Neckar's statement, from which Mr. Burke's is taken, is *two thousand two hundred millions of livres*, which is upwards of ninety-one millions and a half sterling.

M. Neckar in France, and Mr. George Chalmers at the Office of Trade and Plantation in England, of which Lord Hawkesbury is president, published nearly about the same time (1786) an account of the quantity of money in each nation, from the returns of the Mint of each Nation. Mr. Chalmers, from the returns of the English Mint at the Tower of London, states the quantity of money in England, including Scotland and Ireland, to be twenty millions sterling.*

---

*See "Estimate of the Comparative Strength of Great Britain," by G. Chalmers [Author's note].

M. Neckar* says that the amount of money in France, recoined from the old coin which was called in, was two thousand five hundred millions of livres (upwards of one hundred and four millions sterling); and, after deducting for waste, and what may be in the West Indies and other possible circumstances, states the circulation quantity at home to be ninety-one millions and a half sterling; but, taking it as Mr. Burke has put it, it is sixty-eight millions more than the national quantity in England.

That the quantity of money in France cannot be under this sum, may at once be seen from the state of the French Revenue, without referring to the records of the French Mint for proofs. The revenue of France, prior to the Revolution, was nearly twenty-four millions sterling; and as paper had then no existence in France the whole revenue was collected upon gold and silver; and it would have been impossible to have collected such a quantity of revenue upon a less national quantity than M. Neckar has stated. Before the establishment of paper in England, the revenue was about a fourth part of the national amount of gold and silver, as may be known by referring to the revenue prior to King William, and the quantity of money stated to be in the nation at that time, which was nearly as much as it is now.

It can be of no real service to a nation, to impose upon itself, or to permit itself to be imposed upon; but the prejudices of some, and the imposition of others, have always represented France as a nation possessing but little money—whereas the quantity is not only more than four times what the quantity is in England, but is considerably greater on a proportion of numbers. To account for this deficiency on the part of England, some reference should be had to the English system of funding. It operates to multiply paper, and to substitute it in the room of money, in various shapes; and the more paper is multiplied, the more opportunities are offered to export the specie; and it admits of a possibility (by extending it to small notes) of increasing paper till there is no money left.

I know this is not a pleasant subject to English readers; but the

*See "Administration of the Finances of France," vol. iii., by M. Neckar [Author's note].

matters I am going to mention, are so important in themselves, as to require the attention of men interested in money transactions of a public nature. There is a circumstance stated by M. Neckar, in his treatise on the administration of the finances, which has never been attended to in England, but which forms the only basis whereon to estimate the quantity of money (gold and silver) which ought to be in every nation in Europe, to preserve a relative proportion with other nations.

Lisbon and Cadiz are the two ports into which (money) gold and silver from South America are imported, and which afterwards divide and spread themselves over Europe by means of commerce, and increase the quantity of money in all parts of Europe. If, therefore, the amount of the annual importation into Europe can be known, and the relative proportion of the foreign commerce of the several nations by which it can be distributed can be ascertained, they give a rule sufficiently true, to ascertain the quantity of money which ought to be found in any nation, at any given time.

M. Neckar shews from the registers of Lisbon and Cadiz, that the importation of gold and silver into Europe, is five millions sterling annually. He has not taken it on a single year, but on an average of fifteen succeeding years, from 1763 to 1777, both inclusive; in which time, the amount was one thousand eight hundred million livres, which is seventy-five millions sterling.*

From the commencement of the Hanover succession in 1714 to the time Mr. Chalmers published, is seventy-two years; and the quantity imported into Europe, in that time, would be three hundred and sixty millions sterling.

If the foreign commerce of Great Britain be stated at a sixth part of what the whole foreign commerce of Europe amounts to (which is probably an inferior estimation to what the gentlemen at the Exchange would allow) the proportion which Britain should draw by commerce of this sum, to keep herself on a proportion with the rest of Europe, would be also a sixth part which is sixty millions sterling; and if the same allowance for waste and accident be made for England which M. Neckar makes for France, the quantity remaining after these deductions would be fifty-two millions; and this sum ought to

---

* "Administration of the Finances of France," vol. iii [Author's note].

have been in the nation (at the time Mr. Chalmers published), in addition to the sum which was in the nation at the commencement of the Hanover succession, and to have made in the whole at least sixty-six millions sterling; instead of which there were but twenty millions, which is forty-six millions below its proportionate quantity.

As the quantity of gold and silver imported into Lisbon and Cadiz is more exactly ascertained than that of any commodity imported into England, and as the quantity of money coined at the Tower of London is still more positively known, the leading facts do not admit of controversy. Either, therefore, the commerce of England is unproductive of profit, or the gold and silver which it brings in leak continually away by unseen means at the average rate of about three-quarters of a million a year, which, in the course of seventy-two years, accounts for the deficiency; and its absence is supplied by paper.*

---

*Whether the English commerce does not bring in money, or whether the government sends it out after it is brought in, is a matter which the parties concerned can best explain; but that the deficiency exists, is not in the power of either to disprove. While Dr. Price, Mr. Eden, (now Auckland,) Mr. Chalmers, and others, were debating whether the quantity of money in England was greater or less than at the Revolution, the circumstance was not adverted to, that since the Revolution, there cannot have been less than four hundred millions sterling imported into Europe; and therefore the quantity in England ought at least to have been four times greater than it was at the Revolution, to be on a proportion with Europe. What England is now doing by paper, is what she would have been able to do by solid money, if gold and silver had come into the nation in the proportion it ought, or had not been sent out; and she is endeavoring to restore by paper, the balance she has lost by money. It is certain, that the gold and silver which arrive annually in the register-ships to Spain and Portugal, do not remain in those countries. Taking the value half in gold and half in silver, it is about four hundred tons annually; and from the number of ships and galloons employed in the trade of bringing those metals from South-America to Portugal and Spain, the quantity sufficiently proves itself, without referring to the registers.

In the situation England now is, it is impossible she can increase in money. High taxes not only lessen the property of the individuals, but they lessen also the money capital of the nation, by inducing smuggling, which can only be carried on by gold and silver. By the politics which the British Government have carried on with the Inland Powers of Germany and the Continent, it has made an enemy of all the Maritime Powers, and is therefore obliged to keep up a large navy; but though the navy is built in England, the naval stores must be purchased from abroad, and that from countries where the greatest part must be paid for in gold and silver. Some fallacious rumours have been set afloat in England to induce a belief in money, and, among

The Revolution of France is attended with many novel circumstances, not only in the political sphere, but in the circle of money transactions. Among others, it shows that a government may be in a state of insolvency and a nation rich. So far as the fact is confined to the late Government of France, it was insolvent; because the nation would no longer support its extravagance, and therefore it could no longer support itself—but with respect to the nation all the means existed. A government may be said to be insolvent every time it applies to the nation to discharge its arrears. The insolvency of the late Government of France and the present of England differed in no other respect than as the dispositions of the people differ. The people of France refused their aid to the old Government; and the people of England submit to taxation without inquiry. What is called the Crown in England has been insolvent several times; the last of which, publicly known, was in May, 1777, when it applied to the nation to discharge upwards of £600,000 private debts, which otherwise it could not pay.

It was the error of Mr. Pitt, Mr. Burke, and all those who were unacquainted with the affairs of France to confound the French nation with the French Government. The French nation, in effect, endeavoured to render the late Government insolvent for the purpose of taking government into its own hands: and it reserved its means for the support of the new Government. In a country of such vast extent and population as France the natural means cannot be wanting, and the political means appear the instant the nation is disposed

---

others, that of the French refugees bringing great quantities. The idea is ridiculous. The general part of the money in France is silver; and it would take upwards of twenty of the largest broad wheel wagons, with ten horses each, to remove one million sterling of silver. Is it then to be supposed, that a few people fleeing on horseback or in post-chaises, in a secret manner, and having the French Custom-House to pass, and the sea to cross, could bring even a sufficiency for their own expences?

When millions of money are spoken of, it should be recollected, that such sums can only accumulate in a country by slow degrees, and a long procession of time. The most frugal system that England could now adopt, would not recover in a century the balance she has lost in money since the commencement of the Hanover succession. She is seventy millions behind France, and she must be in some considerable proportion behind every country in Europe, because the returns of the English mint do not shew an increase of money, while the registers of Lisbon and Cadiz shew an European increase of between three and four hundred millions sterling [Author's note].

to permit them. When Mr. Burke, in a speech last winter in the British Parliament, "cast his eyes over the map of Europe, and saw a chasm that once was France," he talked like a dreamer of dreams. The same natural France existed as before, and all the natural means existed with it. The only chasm was that the extinction of despotism had left, and which was to be filled up with the Constitution more formidable in resources than the power which had expired.

Although the French Nation rendered the late Government insolvent, it did not permit the insolvency to act towards the creditors; and the creditors, considering the Nation as the real pay-master, and the Government only as the agent, rested themselves on the nation, in preference to the Government. This appears greatly to disturb Mr. Burke, as the precedent is fatal to the policy by which governments have supposed themselves secure. They have contracted debts, with a view of attaching what is called the monied interest of a Nation to their support; but the example in France shews that the permanent security of the creditor is in the Nation, and not in the Government; and that in all possible revolutions that may happen in Governments, the means are always with the Nation, and the Nation always in existence. Mr. Burke argues that the creditors ought to have abided the fate of the Government which they trusted; but the National Assembly considered them as the creditors of the Nation, and not of the Government—of the master, and not of the steward.

Notwithstanding the late government could not discharge the current expenses, the present government has paid off a great part of the capital. This has been accomplished by two means; the one by lessening the expenses of government, and the other by the sale of the monastic and ecclesiastical landed estates. The devotees and penitent debauchees, extortioners and misers of former days, to ensure themselves a better world than that they were about to leave, had bequeathed immense property in trust to the priesthood for *pious uses;* and the priesthood kept it for themselves. The National Assembly has ordered it to be sold for the good of the whole nation, and the priesthood to be decently provided for.

In consequence of the revolution, the annual interest of the debt of France will be reduced at least six millions sterling, by paying off upwards of one hundred millions of the capital; which, with lessening the former expenses of government at least three millions, will place France in a situation worthy the imitation of Europe.

Upon a whole review of the subject, how vast is the contrast! While Mr. Burke has been talking of a general bankruptcy in France, the National Assembly has been paying off the capital of its debt; and while taxes have increased near a million a year in England, they have lowered several millions a year in France. Not a word has either Mr. Burke or Mr. Pitt said about the French affairs, or the state of the French finances, in the present Session of Parliament. The subject begins to be too well understood, and imposition serves no longer.

There is a general enigma running through the whole of Mr. Burke's book. He writes in a rage against the National Assembly; but what is he enraged about? If his assertions were as true as they are groundless, and that France by her Revolution, had annihilated her power, and become what he calls a *chasm*, it might excite the grief of a Frenchman (considering himself as a national man), and provoke his rage against the National Assembly; but why should it excite the rage of Mr. Burke? Alas! it is not the nation of France that Mr. Burke means, but the Court; and every Court in Europe, dreading the same fate, is in mourning. He writes neither in the character of a Frenchman nor an Englishman, but in the fawning character of that creature known in all countries, and a friend to none— a courtier. Whether it be the Court of Versailles, or the Court of St. James, or Carlton-House, or the Court in expectation, signifies not; for the caterpillar principle of all Courts and Courtiers are alike. They form a common policy throughout Europe, detached and separate from the interest of Nations: and while they appear to quarrel, they agree to plunder. Nothing can be more terrible to a Court or Courtier than the Revolution of France. That which is a blessing to Nations is bitterness to them: and as their existence depends on the duplicity of a country, they tremble at the approach of principles, and dread the precedent that threatens their overthrow.

CONCLUSION.

REASON AND IGNORANCE, the opposites of each other, influence the great bulk of mankind. If either of these can be rendered sufficiently extensive in a country, the machinery of Government goes easily on. Reason obeys itself; and Ignorance submits to whatever is dictated to it.

The two modes of the Government which prevail in the world, are, *first*, Government by election and representation: *Secondly*, Government by hereditary succession. The former is generally known by the name of republic; the latter by that of monarchy and aristocracy.

Those two distinct and opposite forms, erect themselves on the two distinct and opposite bases of Reason and Ignorance.—As the exercise of Government requires talents and abilities, and as talents and abilities cannot have hereditary descent, it is evident that hereditary succession requires a belief from man to which his reason cannot subscribe, and which can only be established upon his ignorance; and the more ignorant any country is, the better it is fitted for this species of Government.

On the contrary, Government, in a well-constituted republic, requires no belief from man beyond what his reason can give. He sees the *rationale* of the whole system, its origin and its operation; and as it is best supported when best understood, the human faculties act with boldness, and acquire, under this form of government, a gigantic manliness.

As, therefore, each of those forms acts on a different base, the one moving freely by the aid of reason, the other by ignorance; we have next to consider, what it is that gives motion to that species of Government which is called mixed Government, or, as it is sometimes ludicrously stiled, a Government of *this, that* and *t'other*.

The moving power in this species of Government, is of necessity, Corruption. However imperfect election and representation may be in mixed Governments, they still give exercise to a greater portion of reason than is convenient to the hereditary Part; and therefore it becomes necessary to buy the reason up. A mixed Government is an imperfect everything, cementing and soldering the discordant parts together by corruption, to act as a whole. Mr. Burke appears highly disgusted that France, since she had resolved on a revolution, did not adopt what he calls "*A British Constitution*"; and the regretful manner in which he expresses himself on this occasion implies a suspicion that the British Constitution needed something to keep its defects in countenance.

In mixed Governments there is no responsibility: the parts cover each other till responsibility is lost; and the corruption which moves the machine, contrives at the same time its own escape. When it is laid down as a maxim, that *a King can do no wrong*, it places him in a state of similar security with that of ideots and persons insane, and responsibility is out of the question with respect to himself. It then descends upon the Minister, who shelters himself under a majority in Parliament, which, by places, pensions, and corruption, he can always command; and that majority justifies itself by the same authority with which it protects the Minister. In this rotatory motion, responsibility is thrown off from the parts, and from the whole.

When there is a Part in a Government which can do no wrong, it implies that it does nothing; and is only the machine of another power, by whose advice and direction it acts. What is supposed to be the King in the mixed Governments, is the Cabinet; and as the Cabinet is always a part of the Parliament, and the members justifying in one character what they advise and act in another, a mixed Government becomes a continual enigma; entailing upon a country by the quantity of corruption necessary to solder the parts, the expence of supporting all the forms of government at once, and finally resolving itself into a Government by Committee; in which the advisers, the actors, the approvers, the justifiers, the persons responsible, and the persons not responsible, are the same persons.

By this pantomimical contrivance, and change of scene and character, the parts help each other out in matters which neither of them singly would assume to act. When money is to be obtained, the mass of variety apparently dissolves, and a profusion of parliamentary praises passes between the parts. Each admires with astonishment, the wisdom, the liberality, the disinterestedness of the other: and all of them breathe a pitying sigh at the burthens of the Nation.

But in a well-constituted republic, nothing of this soldering, praising, and pitying, can take place; the representation being equal throughout the country, and compleat in itself, however it may be arranged into legislative and executive, they have all one and the same natural source. The parts are not foreigners to each other, like democracy, aristocracy, and monarchy. As there are no discordant distinctions, there is nothing to corrupt by compromise, nor confound by contrivance. Public measures appeal of themselves to the understanding of the Nation, and, resting on their own merits, disown any flattering applications to vanity. The continual whine of lamenting the burden of taxes, however successfully it may be practised in mixed Governments, is inconsistent with the sense and spirit of a republic. If taxes are necessary, they are of course advantageous; but if they require an apology, the apology itself implies an impeachment. Why, then, is man thus imposed upon, or why does he impose upon himself?

When men are spoken of as kings and subjects, or when Government is mentioned under the distinct and combined heads of monarchy, aristocracy, and democracy, what is it that *reasoning* man is to understand by the terms? If there really existed in the world two or more distinct and separate *elements* of human power, we should then see the several origins to which those terms would descriptively apply; but as there is but one species of man, there can be but one element of human power; and that element is man himself. Monarchy, aristocracy, and democracy, are but creatures of imagination; and a thousand such may be contrived as well as three.

* * * *

From the Revolutions of America and France, and the symptoms that have appeared in other countries, it is evident that the opinion of the world is changing with respect to systems of Government, and that revolutions are not within the compass of political calculations. The progress of time and circumstances, which men assign to the accomplishment of great changes, is too mechanical to measure the force of the mind, and the rapidity of reflection, by which revolutions are generated: All the old governments have received a shock from those that already appear, and which were once more improbable, and are a greater subject of wonder, than a general revolution in Europe would be now.

When we survey the wretched condition of man, under the monarchical and hereditary systems of Government, dragged from his home by one power, or driven by another, and impoverished by taxes more than by enemies, it becomes evident that those systems are bad, and that a general revolution in the principle and construction of Governments is necessary.

What is government more than the management of the affairs of a Nation? It is not, and from its nature cannot be, the property of any particular man or family, but of the whole community, at whose expence it is supported; and though by force and contrivance it has been usurped into an inheritance, the usurpation cannot alter the right of things. Sovereignty, as a matter of right, appertains to the Nation only, and not to any individual; and a Nation has at all times an inherent indefeasible right to abolish any form of Government it finds inconvenient, and to establish such as accords with its interest, disposition and happiness. The romantic and barbarous distinction of men into Kings and subjects, though it may suit the condition of courtiers, cannot that of citizens; and is exploded by the principle upon which Governments are now founded. Every citizen is a member of the Sovereignty, and, as such, can acknowledge no personal subjection; and his obedience can be only to the laws.

When men think of what Government is, they must necessarily suppose it to possess a knowledge of all the objects and matters upon which its authority is to be exercised. In this view of Government, the republican system, as established by America and France, operates to embrace the whole of a Nation; and the knowledge necessary to the interest of all the parts, is to be found in the center, which the parts by representation form: But the old Governments are on a construction that excludes knowledge as well as happiness; Government by Monks, who knew nothing of the world beyond the walls of a Convent, is as consistent as government by Kings.

What were formerly called Revolutions, were little more than a change of persons, or an alteration of local circumstances. They rose and fell like things of course, and had nothing in their existence or their fate that could influence beyond the spot that produced them. But what we now see in the world, from the Revolutions of America and France, are a renovation of the natural order of things, a system of principles as universal as truth and the existence of man, and combining moral with political happiness and national prosperity.

"I. *Men are born, and always continue, free and equal in respect of their rights. Civil distinctions, therefore, can be founded only on public utility.*

"II. *The end of all political associations is the preservation of the natural and imprescriptible rights of man; and these rights are liberty, property, security, and resistance of oppression.*

"III. *The nation is essentially the source of all sovereignty; nor can any* INDIVIDUAL, *or* ANY BODY OF MEN, *be entitled to any authority which is not expressly derived from it.*"

In these principles, there is nothing to throw a Nation into confusion by inflaming ambition. They are calculated to call forth wisdom and abilities, and to exercise them for the public good, and not for the emolument or aggrandisement of particular descriptions of men or families. Monarchical sovereignty, the enemy of mankind, and the source of misery, is abolished; and the sovereignty itself is restored to its natural and original place, the Nation. Were this the case throughout Europe, the cause of wars would be taken away.

It is attributed to Henry the Fourth of France, a man of enlarged and benevolent heart, that he proposed, about the year 1610, a plan for abolishing war in Europe. The plan consisted in constituting an European Congress, or as the French authors stile it, a Pacific Republic; by appointing delegates from the several Nations who were to act as a Court of arbitration in any disputes that might arise between nation and nation.

Had such a plan been adopted at the time it was proposed, the taxes of England and France, as two of the parties, would have been at least ten millions sterling annually to each Nation less than they were at the commencement of the French Revolution.

To conceive a cause why such a plan has not been adopted (and that instead of a Congress for the purpose of *preventing* war, it has been called only to *terminate* a war, after a fruitless expence of several years) it will be necessary to consider the interest of Governments as a distinct interest to that of Nations.

Whatever is the cause of taxes to a Nation, becomes also the means of revenue to Government. Every war terminates with an addition of taxes, and consequently with an addition of revenue; and in any event of war, in the manner they are now commenced and concluded, the power and interest of Governments are increased. War, therefore, from its productiveness, as it easily furnishes the pretence of necessity for taxes and appointments to places and offices, becomes a principal part of the system of old Governments; and to establish any mode to abolish war, however advantageous it might be to Nations, would be to take from such Government the most lucrative of its branches. The frivolous matters upon which war is made, shew the disposition and avidity of Governments to uphold the system of war, and betray the motives upon which they act.

Why are not Republics plunged into war, but because the nature of their Government does not admit of an interest distinct from that of the Nation? Even Holland, though an ill-constructed Republic, and with a commerce extending over the world, existed nearly a century without war: and the instant the form of Government was changed in France, the republican principles of peace and domestic prosperity and œconomy arose with the new Government; and the same consequences would follow the cause in other Nations.

As war is the system of Government on the old construction, the animosity which Nations reciprocally entertain, is nothing more than what the policy of their Governments excites to keep up the spirit of the system. Each Government accuses the other of perfidy, intrigue, and ambition, as a means of heating the imagination of their respective Nations, and incensing them to hostilities. Man is not the enemy of man, but through the medium of a false system of Government. Instead, therefore, of exclaiming against the ambition of Kings, the exclamation should be directed against the principle of such Governments; and instead of seeking to reform the individual, the wisdom of a Nation should apply itself to reform the system.

Whether the forms and maxims of Governments which are still in practice, were adapted to the condition of the world at the period they were established, is not in this case the question. The older they are, the less correspondence can they have with the present state of things. Time, and change of circumstances and opinions, have the same progressive effect in rendering modes of Government obsolete as they have upon customs and manners.—Agriculture, commerce, manufactures, and the tranquil arts, by which the prosperity of Nations is best promoted, require a different system of Government, and a different species of knowledge to direct its operations, than what might have been required in the former condition of the world.

As it is not difficult to perceive, from the enlightened state of mankind, that hereditary Governments are verging to their decline, and that Revolutions on the broad basis of national sovereignty and Government by representation, are making their way in Europe, it would be an act of wisdom to anticipate their approach, and produce Revolutions by reason and accommodation, rather than commit them to the issue of convulsions.

From what we now see, nothing of reform in the political world ought to be held improbable. It is an age of Revolutions, in which everything may be looked for. The intrigue of Courts, by which the system of war is kept up, may provoke a confederation of Nations to abolish it: and an European Congress to patronise the progress of free Government, and promote the civilisation of Nations with each other, is an event nearer in probability, than once were the revolutions and alliance of France and America.

RIGHTS OF MAN

[Part the Second]

COMBINING
PRINCIPLE AND PRACTICE.

BY

THOMAS PAINE

FRENCH TRANSLATOR'S PREFACE.

(1792.)

THE WORK OF WHICH we offer a translation to the public has created the greatest sensation in England. Paine, that man of freedom, who seems born to preach "Common Sense" to the whole world with the same success as in America, explains in it to the people of England the theory of the practice of the Rights of Man.

Owing to the prejudices that still govern *that nation*, the author has been obliged to condescend to answer Mr. Burke. He has done so more especially in an extended preface which is nothing but a piece of very tedious controversy, in which he shows himself very sensitive to criticisms that do not really affect him. To translate it seemed an insult to the *free French people*, and similar reasons have led the editors to suppress also a dedicatory epistle addressed by Paine to Lafayette.

The French can no longer endure dedicatory epistles. A man should write privately to those he esteems: when he publishes a book his thoughts should be offered to the public alone. Paine, that uncorrupted friend of freedom, believed too in the sincerity of Lafayette. So easy is it to deceive men of single-minded purpose! Bred at a distance from courts, that austere American does not seem any more on his guard against the artful ways and speech of courtiers than some Frenchmen who resemble him.

To M. De La Fayette.

AFTER AN ACQUAINTANCE OF nearly fifteen years in difficult situations in America, and various consultations in Europe, I feel a pleasure in presenting to you this small treatise, in gratitude for your services to my beloved America, and as a testimony of my esteem for the virtues, public and private, which I know you too possess.

The only point upon which I could ever discover that we differed was not as to principles of government, but as to time. For my own part I think it equally as injurious to good principles to permit them to linger, as to push them on too fast. That which you suppose accomplishable in fourteen or fifteen years, I may believe practicable in a much shorter period. Mankind, as it appears to me, are always ripe enough to understand their true interest, provided it be presented clearly to their understanding, and that in a manner not to create suspicion by anything like self-design, nor offend by assuming too much. Where we would wish to reform we must not reproach.

When the American revolution was established I felt a disposition to sit serenely down and enjoy the calm. It did not appear to me that any object could afterwards arise great enough to make me quit tranquility and feel as I had felt before. But when principle, and not place, is the energetic cause of action, a man, I find, is everywhere the same.

I am now once more in the public world; and as I have not a right to contemplate on so many years of remaining life as you have, I have resolved to labour as fast as I can; and as I am anxious for your aid and your company, I wish you to hasten your principles and overtake me.

If you make a campaign the ensuing spring, which it is most probable there will be no occasion for, I will come and join you. Should the campaign commence, I hope it will terminate in the extinction of German despotism, and in establishing the freedom of all Germany. When France shall be surrounded with revolutions she will be in peace and safety, and her taxes, as well as those of Germany, will consequently become less.

>   Your sincere,
>   Affectionate Friend,
>
>   THOMAS PAINE.

LONDON, FEB. 9, 1792.

PREFACE.

WHEN I BEGAN THE chapter entitled the *"Conclusion"* in the former part of the RIGHTS OF MAN, published last year, it was my intention to have extended it to a greater length; but in casting the whole matter in my mind, which I wish to add, I found that it must either make the work too bulky, or contract my plan too much. I therefore brought it to a close as soon as the subject would admit, and reserved what I had further to say to another opportunity.

Several other reasons contributed to produce this determination. I wished to know the manner in which a work, written in a style of thinking and expression different to what had been customary in England, would be received before I proceeded farther. A great field was opening to the view of mankind by means of the French Revolution. Mr. Burke's outrageous opposition thereto brought the controversy into England. He attacked principles which he knew (from information) I would contest with him, because they are principles I believe to be good, and which I have contributed to establish, and conceive myself bound to defend. Had he not urged the controversy, I had most probably been a silent man.

Another reason for deferring the remainder of the work was, that Mr. Burke promised in his first publication to renew the subject at another opportunity, and to make a comparison of what he called the English and French Constitutions. I therefore held myself in reserve for him. He has published two works since, without doing this: which he certainly would not have omitted, had the comparison been in his favour.

In his last work, his *"Appeal from the New to the Old Whigs,"* he has quoted about ten pages from the RIGHTS OF MAN, and having given himself the trouble of doing this, says he "shall not attempt in the smallest degree to refute them," meaning the principles therein contained. I am enough acquainted with Mr. Burke to know that he would if he could. But instead of contesting them, he immediately after consoles himself with saying that "he has done his part."—He has not done his part. He has not performed his promise of a comparison of constitutions. He started the controversy, he gave the challenge, and has fled from it; and he is now a *case in point* with his own opinion that *"the age of chivalry is gone!"*

The title, as well as the substance of his last work, his *"Appeal,"* is his condemnation. Principles must stand on their own merits, and if they are good they certainly will. To put them under the shelter of other men's authority, as Mr. Burke has done, serves to bring them into suspicion. Mr. Burke is not very fond of dividing his honours, but in this case he is artfully dividing the disgrace.

But who are those to whom Mr. Burke has made his appeal? A set of childish thinkers, and half-way politicians born in the last century, men who went no farther with any principle than as it suited their purposes as a party; the nation was always left out of the question; and this has been the character of every party from that day to this. The nation sees nothing of such works, or such politics, worthy its attention. A little matter will move a party, but it must be something great that moves a nation.

Though I see nothing in Mr. Burke's "Appeal" worth taking much notice of, there is, however, one expression upon which I shall offer a few remarks. After quoting largely from the RIGHTS OF MAN, and declining to contest the principles contained in that work, he says: "This will most probably be done (*if such writings shall be thought to deserve any other refutation than that of criminal justice*) by others, who may think with Mr. Burke and with the same zeal."

In the first place, it has not yet been done by anybody. Not less, I believe than eight or ten pamphlets intended as answers to the former part of the RIGHTS OF MAN have been published by different persons, and not one of them to my knowledge, has extended to a second edition, nor are even the titles of them so much as generally remembered. As I am averse to unnecessary multiplying publications, I have answered none of them. And as I believe that a man may write himself out of reputation when nobody else can do it, I am careful to avoid that rock.

But as I would decline unnecessary publications on the one hand, so would I avoid everything that might appear like sullen pride on the other. If Mr. Burke, or any person on his side the question, will produce an answer to the RIGHTS OF MAN that shall extend to a half, or even to a fourth part of the number of copies to which the RIGHTS OF MAN extended, I will reply to his work. But until this be done, I shall so far take the sense of the public for my guide (and the world knows I am not a flatterer) that what they do not think worth while to read, is not worth mine to answer. I suppose the number of copies to which the first part of the RIGHTS OF MAN extended, taking England, Scotland, and Ireland, is not less than between forty and fifty thousand.

I now come to remark on the remaining part of the quotation I have made from Mr. Burke.

"If," says he, "such writing shall be thought to deserve any other refutation than that of *criminal* justice."

Pardoning the pun, it must be *criminal* justice indeed that should condemn a work as a substitute for not being able to refute it. The greatest condemnation that could be passed upon it would be a refutation. But in proceeding by the method Mr. Burke alludes to, the condemnation would, in the final event, pass upon the criminality of the process and not upon the work, and in this case, I had rather be the author, than be either the judge or the jury that should condemn it.

But to come at once to the point. I have differed from some professional gentlemen on the subject of prosecutions, and I since find they are falling into my opinion, which I will here state as fully, but as concisely as I can.

I will first put a case with respect to any law, and then compare it with a government, or with what in England is, or has been, called a constitution.

It would be an act of despotism, or what in England is called arbitrary power, to make a law to prohibit investigating the principles, good or bad, on which such a law, or any other is founded.

If a law be bad it is one thing to oppose the practice of it, but it is quite a different thing to expose its errors, to reason on its defects, and to shew cause why it should be repealed, or why another ought to be substituted in its place. I have always held it an opinion (making it also my practice) that it is better to obey a bad law, making use at the same time of every argument to shew its errors and procure its repeal, than forcibly to violate it; because the precedent of breaking a bad law might weaken the force, and lead to a discretionary violation, of those which are good.

The case is the same with respect to principles and forms of government, or to what are called constitutions and the parts of which they are composed.

It is for the good of nations and not for the emolument or aggrandisement of particular individuals, that government ought to be established, and that mankind are at the expence of supporting it. The defects of every government and constitution, both as to principle and form, must, on a parity of reasoning, be as open to discussion as the defects of a law, and it is a duty which every man owes to society to point them out. When those defects, and the means of remedying them, are generally seen by a nation, that nation will reform its government or its constitution in the one case, as the government repealed or reformed the law in the other. The operation of government is restricted to the making and the administering of laws; but it is to a nation that the right of forming or reforming, generating or regenerating constitutions and governments belong; and consequently those subjects, as subjects of investigation, are always before a country *as a matter of right*, and cannot, without invading the general rights of that country, be made subjects for prosecution. On this ground I will meet Mr. Burke whenever he please. It is better that the whole argument should come out than to seek to stifle it. It was himself that opened the controversy, and he ought not to desert it.

I do not believe that monarchy and aristocracy will continue seven years longer in any of the enlightened countries in Europe. If better reasons can be shewn for them than against them, they will stand; if the contrary, they will not. Mankind are not now to be told they shall not think, or they shall not read; and publications that go no farther than to investigate principles of government, to invite men to reason and to reflect, and to shew the errors and excellences of different systems, have a right to appear. If they do not excite attention, they are not worth the trouble of a prosecution; and if they do, the prosecution will amount to nothing, since it cannot amount to a prohibition of reading. This would be a sentence on the public, instead of the author, and would also be the most effectual mode of making or hastening revolutions.

On all cases that apply universally to a nation, with respect to systems of government, a jury of *twelve* men is not competent to decide. Where there are no witnesses to be examined, no facts to be proved, and where the whole matter is before the whole public, and the merits or demerits of it resting on their opinion; and where there is nothing to be known in a court, but what every body knows out of it, every twelve men is equally as good a jury as the other, and would most probably reverse each other's verdict; or, from the variety of their opinions, not be able to form one. It is one case, whether a nation approve a work, or a plan; but it is quite another case, whether it will commit to any such jury the power of determining whether that nation have a right to, or shall reform its government or not. I mention those cases that Mr. Burke may see I have not written on Government without reflecting on what is Law, as well as on what are Rights.—The only effectual jury in such cases would be, a convention of the whole nation fairly elected; for in all such cases the whole nation is the vicinage. If Mr. Burke will propose such a jury, I will wave all privileges of being the citizen of another country, and, defending its principles, abide the issue, provided he will do the same; for my opinion is, that his work and his principles would be condemned instead of mine.

As to the prejudices which men have from education and habit, in favour of any particular form or system of government, those prejudices have yet to stand the test of reason and reflection. In fact, such prejudices are nothing. No man is prejudiced in favour of a thing, knowing it to be wrong. He is attached to it on the belief of its being right; and when he sees it is not so, the prejudice will be gone. We have but a defective idea of what prejudice is. It *might be said*, that until men think for themselves the whole is prejudice, and *not opinion;* for that only is opinion which is the result of reason and reflection. I offer this remark, that Mr. Burke may not confide too much in what have been the customary prejudices of the country.

I do not believe that the people of England have ever been fairly and candidly dealt by. They have been imposed upon by parties, and by men assuming the character of leaders. It is time that the nation should rise above those trifles. It is time to dismiss that inattention which has so long been the encouraging cause of stretching taxation to excess. It is time to dismiss all those songs and toasts which are calculated to enslave, and operate to suffocate reflection. On all such subjects men have but to think, and they will neither act wrong nor be misled. To say that any people are not fit for freedom, is to make poverty their choice, and to say they had rather be loaded with taxes than not. If such a case could be proved, it would equally prove, that those who govern are not fit to govern them, for they are a part of the same national mass.

But admitting governments to be changed all over Europe; it certainly may be done without convulsion or revenge. It is not worth making changes or revolutions, unless it be for some great national benefit: and when this shall appear to a nation, the danger will be, as in America and France, to those who oppose; and with this reflection I close my Preface.

Thomas Paine.

London, Feb. 9, 1792.

RIGHTS OF MAN.

Introduction.

WHAT ARCHIMEDES* SAID OF the mechanical powers, may be applied to Reason and Liberty. *"Had we,"* said he, *"a place to stand upon, we might raise the world."*

The revolution of America presented in politics what was only theory in mechanics. So deeply rooted were all the governments of the old world, and so effectually had the tyranny and the antiquity of habit established itself over the mind, that no beginning could be made in Asia, Africa, or Europe, to reform the political condition of man. Freedom had been hunted round the globe; reason was considered as rebellion; and the slavery of fear had made men afraid to think.

But such is the irresistible nature of truth, that all it asks,—and all it wants,—is the liberty of appearing. The sun needs no inscription to distinguish him from darkness; and no sooner did the American governments display themselves to the world, than despotism felt a shock and man began to contemplate redress.

The independence of America, considered merely as a separation from England, would have been a matter but of little importance, had it not been accompanied by a revolution in the principles and practice of governments. She made a stand, not for herself only, but for the world, and looked beyond the advantages herself could receive. Even the Hessian,† though hired to fight against her, may live to bless his defeat; and England, condemning the viciousness of its government, rejoice in its miscarriage.

---

*Ancient Greek mathematician, physicist, and inventor (c.287–212 B.C.).
†German mercenary hired by the British to serve with their forces during the American Revolution.

As America was the only spot in the political world where the principle of universal reformation could begin, so also was it the best in the natural world. An assemblage of circumstances conspired, not only to give birth, but to add gigantic maturity to its principles. The scene which that country presents to the eye of a spectator, has something in it which generates and encourages great ideas. Nature appears to him in magnitude. The mighty objects he beholds, act upon his mind by enlarging it, and he partakes of the greatness he contemplates.—Its first settlers were emigrants from different European nations, and of diversified professions of religion, retiring from the governmental persecutions of the old world, and meeting in the new, not as enemies, but as brothers. The wants which necessarily accompany the cultivation of a wilderness produced among them a state of society, which countries long harassed by the quarrels and intrigues of governments, had neglected to cherish. In such a situation man becomes what he ought. He sees his species, not with the inhuman idea of a natural enemy, but as kindred; and the example shews to the artificial world, that man must go back to Nature for information.

From the rapid progress which America makes in every species of improvement, it is rational to conclude that, if the governments of Asia, Africa, and Europe had begun on a principle similar to that of America, or had not been very early corrupted therefrom, those countries must by this time have been in a far superior condition to what they are. Age after age has passed away, for no other purpose than to behold their wretchedness. Could we suppose a spectator who knew nothing of the world, and who was put into it merely to make his observations, he would take a great part of the old world to be new, just struggling with the difficulties and hardships of an infant settlement. He could not suppose that the hordes of miserable poor with which old countries abound could be any other than those who had not yet had time to provide for themselves. Little would he think they were the consequence of what in such countries they call government.

If, from the more wretched parts of the old world, we look at those which are in an advanced stage of improvement we still find the greedy hand of government thrusting itself into every corner and crevice of industry, and grasping the spoil of the multitude. Invention is continually exercised to furnish new pretences for revenue and taxation. It watches prosperity as its prey, and permits none to escape without a tribute.

As revolutions have begun, (and as the probability is always greater against a thing beginning, than of proceeding after it has begun) it is natural to expect that other revolutions will follow. The amazing and still increasing expences with which old governments are conducted, the numerous wars they engage in or provoke, the embarrassments they throw in the way of universal civilization and commerce, and the oppression and usurpation acted at home, have wearied out the patience, and exhausted the property of the world. In such a situation, and with such examples already existing, revolutions are to be looked for. They are become subjects of universal conversation, and may be considered as the *Order of the day*.

If systems of government can be introduced less expensive and more productive of general happiness than those which have existed, all attempts to oppose their progress will in the end be fruitless. Reason, like time, will make its own way, and prejudice will fall in a combat with interest. If universal peace, civilisation, and commerce are ever to be the happy lot of man, it cannot be accomplished but by a revolution in the system of governments. All the monarchical governments are military. War is their trade, plunder and revenue their objects. While such governments continue, peace has not the absolute security of a day. What is the history of all monarchical governments but a disgustful picture of human wretchedness, and the accidental respite of a few years' repose? Wearied with war, and tired with human butchery, they sat down to rest, and called it peace. This certainly is not the condition that heaven intended for man; and if *this be monarchy*, well might monarchy be reckoned among the sins of the Jews.

The revolutions which formerly took place in the world had nothing in them that interested the bulk of mankind. They extended only to a change of persons and measures, but not of principles, and rose or fell among the common transactions of the moment. What we now behold may not improperly be called a "*counter revolution*." Conquest and tyranny, at some earlier period, dispossessed man of his rights, and he is now recovering them. And as the tide of all human affairs has its ebb and flow in directions contrary to each other, so also is it in this. Government founded on a *moral theory, on a system of universal peace, on the indefeasible hereditary Rights of Man*, is now revolving from west to east by a stronger impulse than the government of the sword revolved from east to west. It interests not particular individuals, but nations in its progress, and promises a new era to the human race.

The danger to which the success of revolutions is most exposed is that of attempting them before the principles on which they proceed, and the advantages to result from them, are sufficiently seen and understood. Almost everything appertaining to the circumstances of a nation, has been absorbed and confounded under the general and mysterious word *government*. Though it avoids taking to its account the errors it commits, and the mischiefs it occasions, it fails not to arrogate to itself whatever has the appearance of prosperity. It robs industry of its honours, by pedanticly making itself the cause of its effects; and purloins from the general character of man, the merits that appertain to him as a social being.

It may therefore be of use in this day of revolutions to discriminate between those things which are the effect of government, and those which are not. This will best be done by taking a review of society and civilisation, and the consequences resulting therefrom, as things distinct from what are called governments. By beginning with this investigation, we shall be able to assign effects to their proper causes and analize the mass of common errors.

CHAPTER I.

Of Society and Civilisation.

GREAT PART OF THAT order which reigns among mankind is not the effect of government. It has its origin in the principles of society and the natural constitution of man. It existed prior to government, and would exist if the formality of government was abolished. The mutual dependence and reciprocal interest which man has upon man, and all the parts of civilised community upon each other, create that great chain of connection which holds it together. The landholder, the farmer, the manufacturer, the merchant, the tradesman, and every occupation, prospers by the aid which each receives from the other, and from the whole. Common interest regulates their concerns, and forms their law; and the laws which common usage ordains, have a greater influence than the laws of government. In fine society performs for itself almost everything which is ascribed to government.

To understand the nature and quantity of government proper for man, it is necessary to attend to his character. As Nature created him for social life, she fitted him for the station she intended. In all cases she made his natural wants greater than his individual powers. No one man is capable, without the aid of society, of supplying his own wants; and those wants, acting upon every individual, impel the whole of them into society, as naturally as gravitation acts to a centre.

But she has gone further. She has not only forced man into society by a diversity of wants which the reciprocal aid of each other can supply, but she has implanted in him a system of social affections, which, though not necessary to his existence, are essential to his happiness. There is no period in life when this love for society ceases to act. It begins and ends with our being.

If we examine with attention into the composition and constitution of man, the diversity of his wants, and the diversity of talents in different men for reciprocally accommodating the wants of each other, his propensity to society, and consequently to preserve the advantages resulting from it, we shall easily discover, that a great part of what is called government is mere imposition.

Government is no farther necessary than to supply the few cases to which society and civilisation are not conveniently competent; and instances are not wanting to show, that everything which government can usefully add thereto, has been performed by the common consent of society, without government.

For upwards of two years from the commencement of the American War, and to a longer period in several of the American States, there were no established forms of government. The old governments had been abolished, and the country was too much occupied in defence to employ its attention in establishing new governments; yet during this interval order and harmony were preserved as inviolate as in any country in Europe. There is a natural aptness in man, and more so in society, because it embraces a greater variety of abilities and resource, to accommodate itself to whatever situation it is in. The instant formal government is abolished, society begins to act: a general association takes place, and common interest produces common security.

So far is it from being true, as has been pretended, that the abolition of any formal government is the dissolution of society, that it acts by a contrary impulse, and brings the latter the closer together. All that part of its organisation which it had committed to its government, devolves again upon itself, and acts through its medium. When men, as well from natural instinct as from reciprocal benefits, have habituated themselves to social and civilised life, there is always enough of its principles in practice to carry them through any changes they may find necessary or convenient to make in their government. In short, man is so naturally a creature of society that it is almost impossible to put him out of it.

Formal government makes but a small part of civilised life; and when even the best that human wisdom can devise is established, it is a thing more in name and idea than in fact. It is to the great and fundamental principles of society and civilisation—to the common usage universally consented to, and mutually and reciprocally maintained—to the unceasing circulation of interest, which, passing through its million channels, invigorates the whole mass of civilised man—it is to these things, infinitely more than to anything which even the best instituted government can perform, that the safety and prosperity of the individual and of the whole depends.

The more perfect civilisation is, the less occasion has it for government, because the more does it regulate its own affairs, and govern itself; but so contrary is the practice of old governments to the reason of the case, that the expences of them increase in the proportion they ought to diminish. It is but few general laws that civilised life requires, and those of such common usefulness, that whether they are enforced by the forms of government or not, the effect will be nearly the same. If we consider what the principles are that first condense men into society, and what are the motives that regulate their mutual intercourse afterwards, we shall find, by the time we arrive at what is called government, that nearly the whole of the business is performed by the natural operation of the parts upon each other.

Man, with respect to all those matters, is more a creature of consistency than he is aware, or than governments would wish him to believe. All the great laws of society are laws of nature. Those of trade and commerce, whether with respect to the intercourse of individuals or of nations, are laws of mutual and reciprocal interest. They are followed and obeyed, because it is the interest of the parties so to do, and not on account of any formal laws their governments may impose or interpose.

But how often is the natural propensity to society disturbed or destroyed by the operations of government! When the latter, instead of being ingrafted on the principles of the former, assumes to exist for itself, and acts by partialities of favour and oppression, it becomes the cause of the mischiefs it ought to prevent.

If we look back to the riots and tumults which at various times have happened in England, we shall find that they did not proceed from the want of a government, but that government was itself the generating cause; instead of consolidating society it divided it; it deprived it of its natural cohesion, and engendered discontents and disorders which otherwise would not have existed. In those associations which men promiscuously form for the purpose of trade, or of any concern in which government is totally out of the question, and in which they act merely on the principles of society, we see how naturally the various parties unite; and this shews, by comparison, that governments, so far from being always the cause or means of order, are often the destruction of it. The riots of 1780 had no other source than the remains of those prejudices which the government itself had encouraged. But with respect to England there are also other causes.

Excess and inequality of taxation, however disguised in the means, never fail to appear in their effects. As a great mass of the community are thrown thereby into poverty and discontent, they are constantly on the brink of commotion; and deprived, as they unfortunately are, of the means of information, are easily heated to outrage. Whatever the apparent cause of any riots may be, the real one is always want of happiness. It shews that something is wrong in the system of government that injures the felicity by which society is to be preserved.

But as a fact is superior to reasoning, the instance of America presents itself to confirm these observations. If there is a country in the world where concord, according to common calculation, would be least expected, it is America. Made up as it is of people from different nations,* accustomed to different forms and habits of government, speaking different languages, and more different in their modes of worship, it would appear that the union of such a people was impracticable; but by the simple operation of constructing government on the principles of society and the rights of man, every difficulty retires, and all the parts are brought into cordial unison. There the poor are not oppressed, the rich are not privileged. In-

---

*That part of America which is generally called New-England, including New-Hampshire, Massachusetts, Rhode-Island, and Connecticut, is peopled chiefly by English descendants. In the state of New-York about half are Dutch, the rest English, Scotch, and Irish. In New-Jersey. a mixture of English and Dutch, with some Scotch and Irish. In Pennsylvania about one third are English, another Germans, and the remainder Scotch and Irish, with some Swedes. The States to the southward have a greater proportion of English than the middle States, but in all of them there is a mixture; and besides those enumerated, there are a considerable number of French, and some few of all the European nations, lying on the coast. The most numerous religious denomination are the Presbyterians; but no one sect is established above another, and all men are equally citizens [Author's note].

dustry is not mortified by the splendid extravagance of a court riot-ing at its expence. Their taxes are few, because their government is just: and as there is nothing to render them wretched, there is noth-ing to engender riots and tumults.

A metaphysical man, like Mr. Burke, would have tortured his in-vention to discover how such a people could be governed. He would have supposed that some must be managed by fraud, others by force, and all by some contrivance; that genius must be hired to impose upon ignorance, and shew and parade to fascinate the vulgar. Lost in the abundance of his researches, he would have resolved and re-resolved, and finally overlooked the plain and easy road that lay di-rectly before him.

One of the great advantages of the American Revolution has been, that it led to a discovery of the principles, and laid open the imposition, of governments. All the revolutions till then had been worked within the atmosphere of a court, and never on the grand floor of a nation. The parties were always of the class of courtiers; and whatever was their rage for reformation, they carefully pre-served the fraud of the profession.

In all cases they took care to represent government as a thing made up of mysteries, which only themselves understood; and they hid from the understanding of the nation the only thing that was beneficial to know, namely, *That government is nothing more than a national association acting on the principles of society.*

Having thus endeavored to show that the social and civilised state of man is capable of performing within itself almost everything nec-essary to its protection and government, it will be proper, on the other hand, to take a review of the present old governments, and examine whether their principles and practice are correspondent thereto.

CHAPTER II.

Of the Origin of the Present Old Governments.

IT IS IMPOSSIBLE THAT such governments as have hitherto ex-isted in the world, could have commenced by any other means than a total violation of every principle sacred and moral. The obscurity in which the origin of all the present old governments is buried, implies the iniquity and disgrace with which they began. The origin of the present government of America and France will ever be remembered, because it is honourable to record it; but with respect to the rest, even Flattery has consigned them to the tomb of time, without an inscription.

It could have been no difficult thing in the early and solitary ages of the world, while the chief employment of men was that of attending flocks and herds, for a banditti of ruffians to overrun a country, and lay it under contributions. Their power being thus established, the chief of the band contrived to lose the name of Robber in that of Monarch; and hence the origin of Monarchy and Kings.

The origin of the Government of England, so far as relates to what is called its line of monarchy, being one of the latest, is perhaps the best recorded. The hatred which the Norman invasion* and tyranny begat, must have been deeply rooted in the nation, to have outlived the contrivance to obliterate it. Though not a courtier will talk of the curfeubell,† not a village in England has forgotten it.

Those bands of robbers having parcelled out the world, and divided it into dominions, began, as is naturally the case, to quarrel with each other. What at first was obtained by violence was considered by others as lawful to be taken, and a second plunderer succeeded the first. They alternately invaded the dominions which each had assigned to himself, and the brutality with which they treated each other explains the original character of monarchy. It was ruffian torturing ruffian. The conqueror considered the conquered, not as his prisoner, but his property. He led him in triumph rattling in chains, and doomed him, at pleasure, to slavery or death. As time obliterated the history of their beginning, their successors assumed new appearances, to cut off the entail of their disgrace, but their

---

*In 1066 William I of Normandy, known as William the Conqueror (1027?–1087), invaded England and became its king.
†Reputedly introduced in England by William of Normandy as a means of political repression.

principles and objects remained the same. What at first was plunder, assumed the softer name of revenue; and the power originally usurped, they affected to inherit.

From such beginning of governments, what could be expected but a continued system of war and extortion? It has established itself into a trade. The vice is not peculiar to one more than to another, but is the common principle of all. There does not exist within such governments sufficient stamina whereon to engraft reformation; and the shortest and most effectual remedy is to begin anew on the ground of the nation.

What scenes of horror, what perfection of iniquity, present themselves in contemplating the character and reviewing the history of such governments! If we would delineate human nature with a baseness of heart and hypocrisy of countenance that reflexion would shudder at and humanity disown, it is kings, courts and cabinets that must sit for the portrait. Man, naturally as he is, with all his faults about him, is not up to the character.

Can we possibly suppose that if governments had originated in a right principle, and had not an interest in pursuing a wrong one, the world could have been in the wretched and quarrelsome condition we have seen it? What inducement has the farmer, while following the plough, to lay aside his peaceful pursuit, and go to war with the farmer of another country? or what inducement has the manufacturer? What is dominion to them, or to any class of men in a nation? Does it add an acre to any man's estate, or raise its value? Are not conquest and defeat each of the same price, and taxes the never-failing consequence?—Though this reasoning may be good to a nation, it is not so to a government. War is the Pharo-table* of governments, and nations the dupes of the game.

If there is anything to wonder at in this miserable scene of governments more than might be expected, it is the progress which the peaceful arts of agriculture, manufacture and commerce have made beneath such a long accumulating load of discouragement and oppression. It serves to shew that instinct in animals does not act with

---

*Place to play faro, a gambling card game.

stronger impulse than the principles of society and civilisation operate in man. Under all discouragements, he pursues his object, and
yields to nothing but impossibilities.

CHAPTER III.

Of the Old and New Systems of Government.

NOTHING CAN APPEAR MORE contradictory than the principles
on which the old governments began, and the condition to which
society, civilisation and commerce are capable of carrying mankind.
Government, on the old system, is an assumption of power, for the
aggrandisement of itself; on the new, a delegation of power for the
common benefit of society. The former supports itself by keeping
up a system of war; the latter promotes a system of peace, as the true
means of enriching a nation. The one encourages national prejudices; the other promotes universal society, as the means of universal commerce. The one measures its prosperity, by the quantity of
revenue it extorts; the other proves its excellence, by the small quantity of taxes it requires.

Mr. Burke has talked of old and new whigs. If he can amuse himself with childish names and distinctions, I shall not interrupt his
pleasure. It is not to him, but to the Abbé Sieyès,* that I address this
chapter. I am already engaged to the latter gentleman to discuss the
subject of monarchical government; and as it naturally occurs in
comparing the old and new systems, I make this the opportunity of
presenting to him my observations. I shall occasionally take Mr.
Burke in my way.

Though it might be proved that the system of government now
called the NEW, is the most ancient in principle of all that have existed, being founded on the original, inherent Rights of Man: yet, as
tyranny and the sword have suspended the exercise of those rights

---

*Emmanuel Joseph Sieyès (1748–1836), French Revolutionary leader and radical
pamphleteer.

for many centuries past, it serves better the purpose of distinction to call it the *new*, than to claim the right of calling it the old.

The first general distinction between those two systems, is, that the one now called the old is *hereditary*, either in whole or in part; and the new is entirely *representative*. It rejects all hereditary government:

First, As being an imposition on mankind.

Secondly, As inadequate to the purposes for which government is necessary.

With respect to the first of these heads—It cannot be proved by what right hereditary government could begin; neither does there exist within the compass of mortal power a right to establish it. Man has no authority over posterity in matters of personal right; and, therefore, no man, or body of men, had, or can have, a right to set up hereditary government. Were even ourselves to come again into existence, instead of being succeeded by posterity, we have not now the right of taking from ourselves the rights which would then be ours. On what ground, then, do we pretend to take them from others?

All hereditary government is in its nature tyranny. An heritable crown, or an heritable throne, or by what other fanciful name such things may be called, have no other significant explanation than that mankind are heritable property. To inherit a government, is to inherit the people, as if they were flocks and herds.

With respect to the second head, that of being inadequate to the purposes for which government is necessary, we have only to consider what government essentially is, and compare it with the circumstances to which hereditary succession is subject.

Government ought to be a thing always in full maturity. It ought to be so constructed as to be superior to all the accidents to which individual man is subject; and, therefore, hereditary succession, by being *subject to them all*, is the most irregular and imperfect of all the systems of government.

We have heard the *Rights of Man* called a *levelling* system; but the only system to which the word *levelling* is truly applicable, is the hereditary monarchical system. It is a system of *mental levelling*. It indiscriminately admits every species of character to the same authority. Vice and virtue, ignorance and wisdom, in short, every quality, good or bad, is put on the same level. Kings succeed each other, not as rationals, but as animals. It signifies not what their mental or moral characters are. Can we then be surprised at the abject state of the human mind in monarchical countries, when the government itself is formed on such an abject levelling system?—It has no fixed character. To-day it is one thing; to-morrow it is something else. It changes with the temper of every succeeding individual, and is subject to all the varieties of each. It is government through the medium of passions and accidents. It appears under all the various characters of childhood, decrepitude, dotage, a thing at nurse, in leading-strings, or in crutches. It reverses the wholesome order of nature. It occasionally puts children over men, and the conceits of non-age over wisdom and experience. In short, we cannot conceive a more ridiculous figure of government, than hereditary succession, in all its cases, presents.

Could it be made a decree in nature, or an edict registered in heaven, and man could know it, that virtue and wisdom should invariably appertain to hereditary succession, the objection to it would be removed; but when we see that nature acts as if she disowned and sported with the hereditary system; that the mental character of successors, in all countries, is below the average of human understanding; that one is a tyrant, another an idiot, a third insane, and some all three together, it is impossible to attach confidence to it, when reason in man has power to act.

It is not to the Abbé Sieyès that I need apply this reasoning; he has already saved me that trouble by giving his own opinion upon the case. "If it be asked," says he, "what is my opinion with respect to hereditary right, I answer without hesitation, That in good theory, an hereditary transmission of any power of office, can never accord with the laws of a true representation. Hereditaryship is, in this sense, as much an attaint upon principle, as an outrage upon society. But let us," continues he, "refer to the history of all elective monarchies and principalities: is there one in which the elective mode is not worse than the hereditary succession?"

As to debating on which is the worst of the two, it is admitting both to be bad; and herein we are agreed. The preference which the Abbé has given, is a condemnation of the thing that he prefers. Such a mode of reasoning on such a subject is inadmissible, because it finally amounts to an accusation upon Providence, as if she had left to man no other choice with respect to government than between two evils, the best of which he admits to be "*an attaint upon principle, and an outrage upon society.*"

Passing over, for the present, all the evils and mischiefs which monarchy has occasioned in the world, nothing can more effectually prove its uselessness in a state of *civil government*, than making it hereditary. Would we make any office hereditary that required wisdom and abilities to fill it? And where wisdom and abilities are not necessary, such an office, whatever it may be, is superfluous or insignificant.

Hereditary succession is a burlesque upon monarchy. It puts it in the most ridiculous light, by presenting it as an office which any child or ideot may fill. It requires some talents to be a common mechanic; but to be a king requires only the animal figure of man—a sort of breathing automaton. This sort of superstition may last a few years more, but it cannot long resist the awakened reason and interest of man.

As to Mr. Burke, he is a stickler for monarchy, not altogether as a pensioner, if he is one, which I believe, but as a political man. He has taken up a contemptible opinion of mankind, who, in their turn, are taking up the same of him. He considers them as a herd of beings that must be governed by fraud, effigy, and show; and an idol would be as good a figure of monarchy with him, as a man. I will, however, do him the justice to say that, with respect to America, he has been very complimentary. He always contended, at least in my hearing, that the people of America were more enlightened than those of England, or of any country in Europe; and that therefore the imposition of shew was not necessary in their governments.

Though the comparison between hereditary and elective monarchy, which the Abbé has made, is unnecessary to the case, because the representative system rejects both: yet, were I to make the comparison, I should decide contrary to what he has done.

The civil wars which have originated from contested hereditary claims, are more numerous, and have been more dreadful, and of longer continuance, than those which have been occasioned by election. All the civil wars in France arose from the hereditary system; they were either produced by hereditary claims, or by the imperfection of the hereditary form, which admits of regencies or monarchy at nurse. With respect to England, its history is full of the same misfortunes. The contests for succession between the houses of York and Lancaster, lasted a whole century; and others of a similar nature, have renewed themselves since that period. Those of 1715 and 1745,* were of the same kind. The succession war for the crown of Spain,† embroiled almost half Europe. The disturbances of Holland are generated from the hereditaryship of the Stadtholder. A government calling itself free, with an hereditary office, is like a thorn in the flesh, that produces a fermentation which endeavours to discharge it.

But I might go further, and place also foreign wars, of whatever kind, to the same cause. It is by adding the evil of hereditary succession to that of monarchy, that a permanent family interest is created, whose constant objects are dominion and revenue. Poland, though an elective monarchy, has had fewer wars than those which are hereditary; and it is the only government that has made a voluntary essay, though but a small one, to reform the condition of the country.

Having thus glanced at a few of the defects of the old, or hereditary systems of government, let us compare it with the new, or representative system.

The representative system takes society and civilisation for its basis; nature, reason, and experience, for its guide.

Experience, in all ages, and in all countries, has demonstrated that it is impossible to controul Nature in her distribution of mental powers. She gives them as she pleases. Whatever is the rule by which she, apparently to us, scatters them among mankind, that rule remains a secret to man. It would be as ridiculous to attempt to fix the hereditaryship of human beauty, as of wisdom. Whatever wisdom constituently is, it is like a seedless plant; it may be reared when it appears, but it cannot be voluntarily produced. There is always a sufficiency somewhere in the general mass of society for all purposes; but with respect to the parts of society, it is continually

---

*Two rebellions attempting to restore the exiled Stuart line to the English throne.
†When Charles II of Spain (1665–1700) died childless, Europe became embroiled in the War of the Spanish Succession (1701–1714) to determine whether the throne should go to France or Austria.

changing its place. It rises in one to-day, in another to-morrow, and has most probably visited in rotation every family of the earth, and again withdrawn.

As this is in the order of nature, the order of government must necessarily follow it, or government will, as we see it does, degenerate into ignorance. The hereditary system, therefore, is as repugnant to human wisdom as to human rights; and is as absurd as it is unjust.

As the republic of letters brings forward the best literary productions, by giving to genius a fair and universal chance; so the representative system of government is calculated to produce the wisest laws, by collecting wisdom from where it can be found. I smile to myself when I contemplate the ridiculous insignificance into which literature and all the sciences would sink, were they made hereditary; and I carry the same idea into governments. An hereditary governor is as inconsistent as an hereditary author. I know not whether Homer or Euclid* had sons; but I will venture an opinion that if they had, and had left their works unfinished, those sons could not have completed them.

Do we need a stronger evidence of the absurdity of hereditary government than is seen in the descendants of those men, in any line of life, who once were famous? Is there scarcely an instance in which there is not a total reverse of the character? It appears as if the tide of mental faculties flowed as far as it could in certain channels, and then forsook its course, and arose in others. How irrational then is the hereditary system, which establishes channels of power, in company with which wisdom refuses to flow! By continuing this absurdity, man is perpetually in contradiction with himself; he accepts, for a king, or a chief magistrate, or a legislator, a person whom he would not elect for a constable.

It appears to general observation, that revolutions create genius and talents; but those events do no more than bring them forward. There is existing in man, a mass of sense lying in a dormant state, and which, unless something excites it to action, will descend with

---

*Two renowned ancient Greeks: Homer (approx. ninth century B.C.) was an epic poet to whom the *Iliad* and the *Odyssey* are attributed; Euclid (flourished c.300 B.C.) was a geometrician.

him, in that condition, to the grave. As it is to the advantage of society that the whole of its faculties should be employed, the construction of government ought to be such as to bring forward, by a quiet and regular operation, all that extent of capacity which never fails to appear in revolutions.

This cannot take place in the insipid state of hereditary government, not only because it prevents, but because it operates to benumb. When the mind of a nation is bowed down by any political superstition in its government, such as hereditary succession is, it loses a considerable portion of its powers on all other subjects and objects. Hereditary succession requires the same obedience to ignorance, as to wisdom; and when once the mind can bring itself to pay this indiscriminate reverence, it descends below the stature of mental manhood. It is fit to be great only in little things. It acts a treachery upon itself, and suffocates the sensations that urge the detection.

Though the ancient governments present to us a miserable picture of the condition of man, there is one which above all others exempts itself from the general description. I mean the democracy of the Athenians.* We see more to admire, and less to condemn, in that great, extraordinary people, than in anything which history affords.

Mr. Burke is so little acquainted with constituent principles of government, that he confounds democracy and representation together. Representation was a thing unknown in the ancient democracies. In those the mass of the people met and enacted laws (grammatically speaking) in the first person. Simple democracy was no other than the common hail of the ancients. It signifies the *form*, as well as the public principle of the government. As those democracies increased in population, and the territory extended, the simple democratical form became unwieldy and impracticable; and as the system of representation was not known, the consequence was, they either degenerated convulsively into monarchies, or became absorbed into such as then existed. Had the system of representation been then understood, as it now is, there is no reason to believe that those forms of government, now called monarchical or aristocrati-

---

*Athens was a city-state in ancient Greece.

cal, would ever have taken place. It was the want of some method to consolidate the parts of society, after it became too populous, and too extensive for the simple democratical form, and also the lax and solitary condition of shepherds and herdsmen in other parts of the world, that afforded opportunities to those unnatural modes of government to begin.

As it is necessary to clear away the rubbish of errors, into which the subject of government has been thrown, I will proceed to remark on some others.

It has always been the political craft of courtiers and court-governments, to abuse something which they called republicanism; but what republicanism was, or is, they never attempt to explain. Let us examine a little into this case.

The only forms of government are, the democratical, the aristocratical, the monarchical, and what is now called the representative.

What is called a *republic* is not any *particular form* of government. It is wholly characteristical of the purport, matter or object for which government ought to be instituted, and on which it is to be employed, RES-PUBLICA, the public affairs, or the public good; or, literally translated, the *public thing*. It is a word of a good original, referring to what ought to be the character and business of government; and in this sense it is naturally opposed to the word *monarchy*, which has a base original signification. It means arbitrary power in an individual person; in the exercise of which, *himself*, and not the *res-publica*, is the object.

Every government that does not act on the principle of a *Republic*, or in other words, that does not make the *res-republica* its whole and sole object, is not a good government. Republican government is no other than government established and conducted for the interest of the public, as well individually as collectively. It is not necessarily connected with any particular form, but it most naturally associates with the representative form, as being best calculated to secure the end for which a nation is at the expense of supporting it.

Various forms of government have affected to style themselves a republic. Poland calls itself a republic, which is an hereditary aristocracy, with what is called an elective monarchy. Holland calls itself a republic, which is chiefly aristocratical, with an hereditary stadtholdership. But the government of America, which is wholly on the system of representation, is the only real Republic, in character and in practice, that now exists. Its government has no other object than the public business of the nation, and therefore it is properly a republic; and the Americans have taken care that THIS, and no other, shall always be the object of their government, by their rejecting everything hereditary, and establishing governments on the system of representation only. Those who have said that a republic is not a *form* of government calculated for countries of great extent, mistook, in the first place, the *business* of a government, for a *form* of government; for the *res-republica* equally appertains to every extent of territory and population. And, in the second place, if they meant anything with respect to *form*, it was the simple democratical form, such as was the mode of government in the ancient democracies, in which there was no representation. The case, therefore, is not, that a republic cannot be extensive, but that it cannot be extensive on the simple democratical form; and the question naturally presents itself, *What is the best form of government for conducting the* RES-PUBLICA, *or the* PUBLIC BUSINESS *of a nation, after it becomes too extensive and populous for the simple democratical form?* It cannot be monarchy, because monarchy is subject to an objection of the same amount to which the simple democratical form was subject.

It is possible that an individual may lay down a system of principles, on which government shall be constitutionally established to any extent of territory. This is no more than an operation of the mind, acting by its own powers. But the practice upon those principles, as applying to the various and numerous circumstances of a nation, its agriculture, manufacture, trade, commerce, etc., etc., requires a knowledge of a different kind, and which can be had only from the various parts of society. It is an assemblage of practical knowledge, which no individual can possess; and therefore the monarchical form is as much limited, in useful practice, from the incompetency of knowledge, as was the democratical form, from the multiplicity of population. The one degenerates, by extension, into confusion; the other, into ignorance and incapacity, of which all the great monarchies are an evidence. The monarchical form, therefore, could not be a substitute for the democratical, because it has equal inconveniences.

Much less could it when made hereditary. This is the most effec-

tual of all forms to preclude knowledge. Neither could the high democratical mind have voluntarily yielded itself to be governed by
children and ideots, and all the motley insignificance of character,
which attends such a mere animal system, the disgrace and the reproach of reason and of man.

As to the aristocratical form, it has the same vices and defects
with the monarchical, except that the chance of abilities is better
from the proportion of numbers, but there is still no security for the
right use and application of them.*

Referring them to the original simple democracy, it affords the
true data from which government on a large scale can begin. It is
incapable of extension, not from its principle, but from the inconvenience of its form; and monarchy and aristocracy, from their incapacity. Retaining, then, democracy as the ground, and rejecting the
corrupt systems of monarchy and aristocracy, the representative system naturally presents itself; remedying at once the defects of the
simple democracy as to form, and the incapacity of the other two
with respect to knowledge.

Simple democracy was society governing itself without the aid of
secondary means. By ingrafting representation upon democracy, we
arrive at a system of government capable of embracing and confed-
erating all the various interests and every extent of territory and
population; and that also with advantages as much superior to
hereditary government, as the republic of letters is to hereditary literature.

It is on this system that the American government is founded. It
is representation ingrafted upon democracy. It has fixed the form by
a scale parallel in all cases to the extent of the principle. What
Athens was in miniature America will be in magnitude. The one
was the wonder of the ancient world; the other is becoming the admiration of the present. It is the easiest of all the forms of government to be understood and the most eligible in practice; and
excludes at once the ignorance and insecurity of the hereditary
mode, and the inconvenience of the simple democracy.

It is impossible to conceive a system of government capable of

---

*For a character of aristocracy, the reader is referred to *Rights of Man*, Part I. [Au-
thor's note].

acting over such an extent of territory, and such a circle of interests, as is immediately produced by the operation of representation. France, great and populous as it is, is but a spot in the capaciousness of the system. It is preferable to simple democracy even in small territories. Athens, by representation, would have outrivalled her own democracy.

That which is called government, or rather that which we ought to conceive government to be, is no more than some common center in which all the parts of society unite. This cannot be accomplished by any method so conducive to the various interests of the community, as by the representative system. It concentrates the knowledge necessary to the interest of the parts, and of the whole. It places government in a state of constant maturity. It is, as has already been observed, never young, never old. It is subject neither to nonage, nor dotage. It is never in the cradle, nor on crutches. It admits not of a separation between knowledge and power, and is superior, as government always ought to be, to all the accidents of individual man, and is therefore superior to what is called monarchy.

A nation is not a body, the figure of which is to be represented by the human body; but is like a body contained within a circle, having a common center, in which every radius meets; and that center is formed by representation. To connect representation with what is called monarchy, is eccentric government. Representation is of itself the delegated monarchy of a nation, and cannot debase itself by dividing it with another.

Mr. Burke has two or three times, in his parliamentary speeches, and in his publications, made use of a jingle of words that convey no ideas. Speaking of government, he says, "It is better to have monarchy for its basis, and republicanism for its corrective, than republicanism for its basis, and monarchy for its corrective."—If he means that it is better to correct folly with wisdom, than wisdom with folly, I will no otherwise contend with him, than that it would be much better to reject the folly entirely.

But what is this thing which Mr. Burke calls monarchy? Will he explain it? All men can understand what representation is; and that it must necessarily include a variety of knowledge and talents. But what security is there for the same qualities on the part of monarchy? or, when the monarchy is a child, where then is the wisdom?

What does it know about government? Who then is the monarch, or where is the monarchy? If it is to be performed by regency, it proves to be a farce. A regency is a mock species of republic, and the whole of monarchy deserves no better description. It is a thing as various as imagination can paint. It has none of the stable character that government ought to possess. Every succession is a revolution, and every regency a counter-revolution. The whole of it is a scene of perpetual court cabal and intrigue, of which Mr. Burke is himself an instance. To render monarchy consistent with government, the next in succession should not be born a child, but a man at once, and that man a Solomon. It is ridiculous that nations are to wait and government be interrupted till boys grow to be men.

Whether I have too little sense to see, or too much to be imposed upon; whether I have too much or too little pride, or of anything else, I leave out of the question; but certain it is, that what is called monarchy, always appears to me a silly, contemptible thing. I compare it to something kept behind a curtain, about which there is a great deal of bustle and fuss, and a wonderful air of seeming solemnity; but when, by any accident, the curtain happens to be open— and the company see what it is, they burst into laughter.

In the representative system of government, nothing of this can happen. Like the nation itself, it possesses a perpetual stamina, as well of body as of mind, and presents itself on the open theatre of the world in a fair and manly manner. Whatever are its excellences or defects, they are visible to all. It exists not by fraud and mystery; it deals not in cant and sophistry; but inspires a language that, passing from heart to heart, is felt and understood.

We must shut our eyes against reason, we must basely degrade our understanding, not to see the folly of what is called monarchy. Nature is orderly in all her works; but this is a mode of government that counteracts nature. It turns the progress of the human faculties upside down. It subjects age to be governed by children, and wisdom by folly.

On the contrary, the representative system is always parallel with the order and immutable laws of nature, and meets the reason of man in every part. For example:

In the American Federal Government, more power is delegated to the President of the United States than to any other individual member of Congress. He cannot, therefore, be elected to this office under the age of thirty-five years. By this time the judgment of man becomes more matured, and he has lived long enough to be acquainted with men and things, and the country with him.—But on the monarchial plan (exclusive of the numerous chances there are against every man born into the world, of drawing a prize in the lottery of human faculties), the next in succession, whatever he may be, is put at the head of a nation, and of a government, at the age of eighteen years. Does this appear like an action of wisdom? Is it consistent with the proper dignity and the manly character of a nation? Where is the propriety of calling such a lad the father of the people?—In all other cases, a person is a minor until the age of twenty-one years. Before this period, he is not trusted with the management of an acre of land, or with the heritable property of a flock of sheep, or an herd of swine; but, wonderful to tell! he may, at the age of eighteen years, be trusted with a nation.

That monarchy is all a bubble, a mere court artifice to procure money, is evident (at least to me,) in every character in which it can be viewed. It would be impossible, on the rational system of representative government, to make out a bill of expences to such an enormous amount as this deception admits. Government is not of itself a very chargeable institution. The whole expence of the federal government of America, founded, as I have already said, on the system of representation, and extending over a country nearly ten times as large as England, is but six hundred thousand dollars, or one hundred and thirty-five thousand pounds sterling.

I presume, that no man in his sober senses, will compare the character of any of the kings of Europe with that of General Washington. Yet, in France, and also in England, the expence of the civil list only, for the support of one man, is eight times greater than the whole expence of the federal government in America. To assign a reason for this, appears almost impossible. The generality of people in America, especially the poor, are more able to pay taxes, than the generality of people either in France or England.

But the case is, that the representative system diffuses such a body of knowledge throughout a nation, on the subject of government, as to explode ignorance and preclude imposition. The craft of courts cannot be acted on that ground. There is no place for mystery; nowhere for it to begin. Those who are not in the representation, know as much of the nature of business as those who are. An affectation of mysterious importance would there be scouted. Nations can have no secrets; and the secrets of courts, like those of individuals, are always their defects.

In the representative system, the reason for everything must publicly appear. Every man is a proprietor in government, and considers it a necessary part of his business to understand. It concerns his interest, because it affects his property. He examines the cost, and compares it with the advantages; and above all, he does not adopt the slavish custom of following what in other governments are called LEADERS.

It can only be by blinding the understanding of man, and making him believe that government is some wonderful mysterious thing, that excessive revenues are obtained. Monarchy is well calculated to ensure this end. It is the popery of government; a thing kept up to amuse the ignorant, and quiet them into taxes.

The government of a free country, properly speaking, is not in the persons, but in the laws. The enacting of those requires no great expence; and when they are administered, the whole of civil government is performed—the rest is all court contrivance.

CHAPTER IV.

Of Constitutions.

THAT MEN MEAN DISTINCT and separate things when they speak of constitutions and of governments, is evident; or why are those terms distinctly and separately used? A constitution is not the act of a government, but of a people constituting a government; and government without a constitution, is power without a right.

All power exercised over a nation, must have some beginning. It must either be delegated or assumed. There are no other sources. All delegated power is trust, and all assumed power is usurpation. Time does not alter the nature and quality of either.

In viewing this subject, the case and circumstances of America present themselves as in the beginning of a world; and our enquiry into the origin of government is shortened, by referring to the facts that have arisen in our own day. We have no occasion to roam for information into the obscure field of antiquity, nor hazard ourselves upon conjecture. We are brought at once to the point of seeing government begin, as if we had lived in the beginning of time. The real volume, not of history, but of facts, is directly before us, unmutilated by contrivance, or the errors of tradition.

I will here concisely state the commencement of the American constitutions; by which the difference between constitutions and governments will sufficiently appear.

It may not appear improper to remind the reader that the United States of America consist of thirteen separate states, each of which established a government for itself, after the declaration of independence, done the 4th of July, 1776. Each state acted independently of the rest, in forming its governments; but the same general principle pervades the whole. When the several state governments were formed, they proceeded to form the federal government, that acts over the whole in all matters which concern the interest of the whole, or which relate to the intercourse of the several states with each other, or with foreign nations. I will begin with giving an instance from one of the state governments (that of Pennsylvania) and then proceed to the federal government.

The State of Pennsylvania, though nearly of the same extent of territory as England, was then divided into only twelve counties. Each of those counties had elected a committee at the commencement of the dispute with the English government; and as the city of Philadelphia, which also had its committee, was the most central for intelligence, it became the center of communication to the several county committees. When it became necessary to proceed to the formation of a government, the committee of Philadelphia proposed a conference of all the committees, to be held in that city, and which met the latter end of July, 1776.

Though these committees had been duly elected by the people, they were not elected expressly for the purpose, nor invested with the authority of forming a constitution; and as they could not, consistently with the American idea of rights, assume such a power, they could only confer upon the matter, and put it into a train of operation. The conferees, therefore, did no more than state the case, and recommend to the several counties to elect six representatives for each county, to meet in convention at Philadelphia, with powers to form a constitution, and propose it for public consideration.

This convention, of which Benjamin Franklin was president, having met and deliberated, and agreed upon a constitution, they next ordered it to be published, not as a thing established, but for the consideration of the whole people, their approbation or rejection, and then adjourned to a stated time. When the time of adjournment was expired, the convention re-assembled; and as the general opinion of the people in approbation of it was then known, the constitution was signed, sealed, and proclaimed on the *authority of the people* and the original instrument deposited as a public record. The convention then appointed a day for the general election of the representatives who were to compose the government, and the time it should commence; and having done this they dissolved, and returned to their several homes and occupations.

In this constitution were laid down, first, a declaration of rights; then followed the form which the government should have, and the powers it should possess—the authority of the courts of judicature, and of juries—the manner in which elections should be conducted, and the proportion of representatives to the number of electors—the time which each succeeding assembly should continue, which was one year—the mode of levying, and of accounting for the expenditure, of public money—of appointing public officers, etc., etc., etc.

No article of this constitution could be altered or infringed at the discretion of the government that was to ensue. It was to that government a law. But as it would have been unwise to preclude the benefit of experience, and in order also to prevent the accumulation of errors, if any should be found, and to preserve an unison of government with the circumstances of the State at all times, the constitution provided, that, at the expiration of every seven years, a convention should be elected, for the express purpose of revising the constitution, and making alterations, additions, or abolitions therein, if any such should be found necessary.

Here we see a regular process—a government issuing out of a constitution, formed by the people in their original character; and that constitution serving, not only as an authority, but as an law of controul to the government. It was the political bible of the state.

Scarcely a family was without it. Every member of the government had a copy; and nothing was more common, when any debate arose on the principle of a bill, or on the extent of any species of authority, than for the members to take the printed constitution out of their pocket, and read the chapter with which such matter in debate was connected.

Having thus given an instance from one of the states, I will shew the proceedings by which the federal constitution of the United States arose and was formed.

Congress, at its two first meetings, in September 1774, and May 1775, was nothing more than a deputation from the legislatures of the several provinces, afterwards states; and had no other authority than what arose from common consent, and the necessity of its acting as a public body. In everything which related to the internal affairs of America, congress went no further than to issue recommendations to the several provincial assemblies, who at discretion adopted them or not. Nothing on the part of congress was compulsive; yet, in this situation, it was more faithfully and affectionately obeyed than was any government in Europe. This instance, like that of the national assembly in France, sufficiently shows, that the strength of government does not consist in any thing WITHIN itself, but in the attachment of a nation, and the interest which a people feel in supporting it. When this is lost, government is but a child in power; and though, like the old government in France, it may harrass individuals for a while, it but facilitates its own fall.

After the declaration of independence, it became consistent with the principle on which representative government is founded, that the authority of congress should be defined and established. Whether that authority should be more or less than congress then discretionarily exercised was not the question. It was merely the rectitude of the measure.

For this purpose, the act, called the act of confederation, (which was a sort of imperfect federal constitution), was proposed, and, after long deliberation, was concluded in the year 1781. It was not the act of congress, because it is repugnant to the principles of representative government that a body should give power to itself. Congress first informed the several states, of the powers which it conceived were necessary to be invested in the union, to enable it to perform the duties and services required from it; and the states severally agreed with each other, and concentrated in congress those powers.

It may not be improper to observe, that in both those instances, (the one of Pennsylvania, and the other of the United States), there is no such thing as the idea of a compact between the people on one side, and the government on the other. The compact was that of the people with each other, to produce and constitute a government. To suppose that any government can be a party in a compact with the whole people, is to suppose it to have existence before it can have a right to exist. The only instance in which a compact can take place between the people and those who exercise the government, is, that the people shall pay them, while they chuse to employ them.

Government is not a trade which any man, or any body of men, has a right to set up and exercise for his own emolument, but is altogether a trust, in right of those by whom that trust is delegated, and by whom it is always resumeable. It has of itself no rights; they are altogether duties.

Having thus given two instances of the original formation of a constitution, I will shew the manner in which both have been changed since their first establishment.

The powers vested in the governments of the several states, by the state constitutions, were found, upon experience, to be too great; and those vested in the federal government, by the act of confederation, too little. The defect was not in the principle, but in the distribution of power.

Numerous publications, in pamphlets and in the newspapers, appeared, on the propriety and necessity of new modelling the federal government. After some time of public discussion, carried on through the channel of the press, and in conversations, the state of Virginia, experiencing some inconvenience with respect to commerce, proposed holding a continental conference; in consequence of which, a deputation from five or six state assemblies met at Annapolis, in Maryland, in 1786. This meeting, not conceiving itself sufficiently authorised to go into the business of a reform, did no more than state their general opinions of the propriety of the measure, and recommend that a convention of all the states should be held the year following.

The convention met at Philadelphia in May, 1787, of which General Washington was elected president. He was not at that time connected with any of the state governments, or with congress. He delivered up his commission when the war ended, and since then had lived a private citizen.

The Convention went deeply into all the subjects; and having, after a variety of debate and investigation, agreed among themselves upon the several parts of a federal constitution, the next question was, the manner of giving it authority and practice.

For this purpose they did not, like a cabal of courtiers, send for a Dutch Stadtholder, or a German Elector;* but they referred the whole matter to the sense and interest of the country.

They first directed that the proposed constitution should be published. Secondly, that each state should elect a convention, expressly for the purpose of taking it into consideration, and of ratifying or rejecting it; and that as soon as the approbation and ratification of any nine states should be given, that those states shall proceed to the election of their proportion of members to the new federal government; and that the operation of it should then begin, and the former federal government cease.

The several States proceeded accordingly to elect their conventions. Some of those conventions ratified the constitution by very large majorities, and two or three unanimously. In others there were much debate and division of opinion. In the Massachussetts convention, which met at Boston, the majority was not above nineteen or twenty, in about three hundred members; but such is the nature of representative government, that it quietly decides all matters by majority. After the debate in the Massachussetts convention was closed, and the vote taken, the objecting members rose and declared, *"That though they had argued and voted against it, because certain parts appeared to them in a different light to what they appeared to other members; yet, as the vote had decided in favour of the constitution as proposed, they should give it the same practical support as if they had voted for it."*

As soon as nine states had concurred (and the rest followed in the

*Chief magistrate of the Dutch republic, and a German prince entitled to elect the Holy Roman Emperor.

order their conventions were elected), the old fabric of the federal government was taken down, and the new one erected, of which General Washington is president.—In this place I cannot help remarking, that the character and services of this gentleman are sufficient to put all those men called kings to shame. While they are receiving from the sweat and labours of mankind, a prodigality of pay, to which neither their abilities nor their services can entitle them, he is rendering every service in his power, and refusing every pecuniary reward. He accepted no pay as commander-in-chief; he accepts none as president of the United States.

After the new federal constitution was established, the state of Pennsylvania, conceiving that some parts of its own constitution required to be altered, elected a convention for that purpose. The proposed alterations were published, and the people concurring therein, they were established.

In forming those constitutions, or in altering them, little or no inconvenience took place. The ordinary course of things was not interrupted, and the advantages have been much. It is always the interest of a far greater number of people in a nation to have things right, than to let them remain wrong; and when public matters are open to debate, and the public judgment free, it will not decide wrong, unless it decides too hastily.

In the two instances of changing the constitutions, the governments then in being were not actors either way. Government has no right to make itself a party in any debate respecting the principles or modes of forming, or of changing, constitutions. It is not for the benefit of those who exercise the powers of government that constitutions, and the governments issuing from them, are established. In all those matters the right of judging and acting are in those who pay, and not in those who receive.

A constitution is the property of a nation, and not of those who exercise the government. All the constitutions of America are declared to be established on the authority of the people. In France, the word nation is used instead of the people; but in both cases, a constitution is a thing antecedent to the government, and always distinct therefrom.

In England it is not difficult to perceive that everything has a constitution, except the nation. Every society and association that is established, first agreed upon a number of original articles, digested into form, which are its constitution. It then appointed its officers, whose powers and authorities are described in that constitution, and the government of that society then commenced. Those officers, by whatever name they are called, have no authority to add to, alter, or abridge the original articles. It is only to the constituting power that this right belongs.

From the want of understanding the difference between a constitution and a government, Dr. Johnson,* and all writers of his description, have always bewildered themselves. They could not but perceive, that there must necessarily be a *controuling* power existing somewhere, and they placed this power in the discretion of the persons exercising the government, instead of placing it in a constitution formed by the nation. When it is in a constitution, it has the nation for its support, and the natural and the political controuling powers are together. The laws which are enacted by governments, controul men only as individuals, but the nation, through its constitution, controuls the whole government, and has a natural ability to do so. The final controuling power, therefore, and the original constituting power, are one and the same power.

Dr. Johnson could not have advanced such a position in any country where there was a constitution; and he is himself an evidence that no such thing as a constitution exists in England. But it may be put as a question, not improper to be investigated, that if a constitution does not exist, how came the idea of its existence so generally established?

In order to decide this question, it is necessary to consider a constitution in both its cases:—First, as creating a government and giving it powers. Secondly, as regulating and restraining the powers so given.

If we begin with William of Normandy, we find that the government of England was originally a tyranny, founded on an invasion and conquest of the country. This being admitted, it will then appear, that the exertion of the nation, at different periods, to abate that tyranny, and render it less intolerable, has been credited for a constitution.

---

*Samuel Johnson (1709–1784), English lexicographer, poet, and essayist.

Magna Charta,* as it was called (it is now like an almanack of the same date), was no more than compelling the government to renounce a part of its assumptions. It did not create and give powers to government in a manner a constitution does; but was, as far as it went, of the nature of a re-conquest, and not a constitution; for could the nation have totally expelled the usurpation, as France has done its despotism, it would then have had a constitution to form.

The history of the Edwards and the Henries, and up to the commencement of the Stuarts,† exhibits as many instances of tyranny as could be acted within the limits to which the nation had restricted it. The Stuarts endeavoured to pass those limits, and their fate is well known.‡ In all those instances we see nothing of a constitution, but only of restrictions on assumed power.

After this, another William, descended from the same stock, and claiming from the same origin, gained possession; and of the two evils, *James* and *William*,§ the nation preferred what it thought the least; since, from circumstances, it must take one. The act, called the Bill of Rights, comes here into view. What is it, but a bargain, which the parts of the government made with each other to divide powers, profits, and privileges? You shall have so much, and I will have the rest; and with respect to the nation, it said, for *your share*, YOU *shall have the right of petitioning*. This being the case, the bill of rights is more properly a bill of wrongs, and of insult. As to what is called the convention parliament, it was a thing that made itself, and then made the authority by which it acted. A few persons got together, and called themselves by that name. Several of them had never been elected, and none of them for the purpose.

From the time of William a species of government arose, issuing out of this coalition bill of rights; and more so, since the corruption in-

---

*The "Great Charter" (1215) the English barons forced King John to sign, limiting royal power by law.

†Paine refers to the kings from the houses of Plantagenet, Lancaster, York, Tudor, and Stuart who ruled after the Magna Charta was signed.

‡Charles I was beheaded in 1649 during the Puritan Revolution; James II was deposed in 1688.

§England deposed James II in favor of his nephew and son-in-law William of Orange.

troduced at the Hanover succession by the agency of Walpole;* that can be described by no other name than a despotic legislation. Though the parts may embarrass each other, the whole has no bounds; and the only right it acknowledges out of itself, is the right of petitioning. Where then is the constitution either that gives or restrains power?

It is not because a part of the government is elective, that makes it less a despotism, if the persons so elected possess afterwards, as a parliament, unlimited powers. Election, in this case, becomes separated from representation, and the candidates are candidates for despotism.

I cannot believe that any nation, reasoning on its own rights, would have thought of calling these things *a constitution*, if the cry of constitution had not been set up by the government. It has got into circulation like the words *bore* and *quoz* [*quiz*], by being chalked up in the speeches of parliament, as those words were on window shutters and doorposts; but whatever the constitution may be in other respects, it has undoubtedly been *the most productive machine of taxation that was ever invented.* The taxes in France, under the new constitution, are not quite thirteen shillings per head,† and the taxes in England, under what is called its present constitution, are forty-eight shillings and sixpence per head—men, women, and children—amounting to nearly seventeen millions sterling, besides the expence of collecting, which is upwards of a million more.

In a country like England, where the whole of the civil Government is executed by the people of every town and county, by means of parish officers, magistrates, quarterly sessions, juries, and assize; without any trouble to what is called the government or any other expence to the revenue than the salary of the judges, it is astonishing how such a mass of taxes can be employed. Not even the inter-

---

*Sir Robert Walpole (1676–1745), regarded as England's first prime minister; he was very powerful during the reigns of George I and II.

†The whole amount of the assessed taxes of France, for the present year, is three hundred millions of francs, which is twelve millions and a half sterling; and the incidental taxes are estimated at three millions, making in the whole fifteen millions and a half; which among twenty-four millions of people, is not quite thirteen shillings per head. France has lessened her taxes since the revolution, nearly nine millions sterling annually. Before the revolution, the city of Paris paid a duty of upwards of thirty per cent. on all articles brought into the city. This tax was collected at the city gates. It was taken off on the first of last May, and the gates taken down [Author's note].

nal defence of the country is paid out of the revenue. On all occasions, whether real or contrived, recourse is continually had to new loans and new taxes. No wonder, then, that a machine of government so advantageous to the advocates of a court, should be so triumphantly extolled! No wonder, that St. James's or St. Stephen's should echo with the continual cry of constitution; no wonder, that the French revolution should be reprobated, and the *res-publica* treated with reproach! The *red book* of England, like the red book of France, will explain the reason.*

I will now, by way of relaxation, turn a thought or two to Mr. Burke. I ask his pardon for neglecting him so long.

"America," says he (in his speech on the Canada Constitution bill), "never dreamed of such absurd doctrine as the *Rights of Man.*"

Mr. Burke is such a bold presumer, and advances his assertions and his premises with such a deficiency of judgment, that, without troubling ourselves about principles of philosophy or politics, the mere logical conclusions they produce, are ridiculous. For instance,

If governments, as Mr. Burke asserts, are not founded on the Rights of MAN, and are founded on *any rights* at all, they consequently must be founded on the right of *something* that is *not man*. What then is that something?

Generally speaking, we know of no other creatures that inhabit the earth than man and beast; and in all cases, where only two things offer themselves, and one must be admitted, a negation proved on any one, amounts to an affirmative on the other; and therefore, Mr. Burke, by proving against the Rights of *Man*, proves in behalf of the *beast;* and consequently, proves that government is a beast; and as difficult things sometimes explain each other, we now see the origin of keeping wild beasts in the Tower; for they certainly can be of no other use than to shew the origin of the government. They are in the place of a constitution. O John Bull,[†] what honours thou hast lost by not being a wild beast. Thou mightest, on Mr. Burke's system, have been in the Tower for life.

---

*What was called the *livre rouge*, or the red book, in France, was not exactly similar to the court calender in England; but it sufficiently showed how a great part of the taxes was lavished [Author's note].

[†]Personification of England, as a bullheaded but kind farmer.

If Mr. Burke's arguments have not weight enough to keep one serious, the fault is less mine than his; and as I am willing to make an apology to the reader for the liberty I have taken, I hope Mr. Burke will also make his for giving the cause.

Having thus paid Mr. Burke the compliment of remembering him, I return to the subject.

From the want of a constitution in England to restrain and regulate the wild impulse of power, many of the laws are irrational and tyrannical, and the administration of them vague and problematical.

The attention of the government of England (for I rather chuse to call it by this name than the English government) appears, since its political connection with Germany, to have been so completely engrossed and absorbed by foreign affairs, and the means of raising taxes, that it seems to exit for no other purposes. Domestic concerns are neglected; and with respect to regular law, there is scarcely such a thing.

Almost every case must now be determined by some precedent, be that precedent good or bad, or whether it properly applies or not; and the practice is become so general as to suggest a suspicion, that it proceeds from a deeper policy than at first sight appears.

Since the revolution of America, and more so since that of France, this preaching up the doctrines of precedents, drawn from times and circumstances antecedent to those events, has been the studied practice of the English government. The generality of those precedents are founded on principles and opinions, the reverse of what they ought; and the greater distance of time they are drawn from, the more they are to be suspected. But by associating those precedents with a superstitious reverence for ancient things, as monks shew relics and call them holy, the generality of mankind are deceived into the design. Governments now act as if they were afraid to awaken a single reflection in man. They are softly leading him to the sepulchre of precedents, to deaden his faculties and call attention from the scene of revolutions. They feel that he is arriving at knowledge faster than they wish, and their policy of precedents is the barometer of their fears. This political popery, like the ecclesiastical popery of old, has had its day, and is hastening to its exit. The ragged relic and the antiquated precedent, the monk and the monarch, will moulder together.

Government by precedent, without any regard to the principle of the precedent, is one of the vilest systems that can be set up. In numerous instances, the precedent ought to operate as a warning, and not as an example, and requires to be shunned instead of imitated; but instead of this, precedents are taken in the lump, and put at once for constitution and for law.

Either the doctrine of precedents is policy to keep a man in a state of ignorance, or it is a practical confession that wisdom degenerates in governments as governments increase in age, and can only hobble along by the stilts and crutches of precedents. How is it that the same persons who would proudly be thought wiser than their predecessors, appear at the same time only as the ghosts of departed wisdom? How strangely is antiquity treated! To some purposes it is spoken of as the times of darkness and ignorance, and to answer others, it is put for the light of the world.

If the doctrine of precedents is to be followed, the expences of government need not continue the same. Why pay men extravagantly, who have but little to do? If everything that can happen is already in precedent, legislation is at an end, and precedent, like a dictionary, determines every case. Either, therefore, government has arrived at its dotage, and requires to be renovated, or all the occasions for exercising its wisdom have occurred.

We now see all over Europe, and particularly in England, the curious phenomenon of a nation looking one way, and the government the other—the one forward and the other backward. If governments are to go on by precedent, while nations go on by improvement, they must at last come to a final separation; and the sooner, and the more civilly they determine this point, the better.*

---

*In England the improvements in agriculture, useful arts, manufactures, and commerce, have been made in opposition to the genius of its government, which is that of following precedents. It is from the enterprise and industry of the individuals, and their numerous associations, in which, tritely speaking, government is neither pillow nor bolster, that these improvements have proceeded. No man thought about government, or who was *in*, or who was *out*, when he was planning or executing those things; and all he had to hope, with respect to government, was, *that it would let him alone.* Three or four very silly ministerial newspapers are continually offending against the spirit of national improvement, by ascribing it to a minister. They may with as much truth ascribe this book to a minister [Author's note].

Having thus spoken of constitutions generally, as things distinct from actual governments, let us proceed to consider the parts of which a constitution is composed.

Opinions differ more on this subject than with respect to the whole. That a nation ought to have a constitution, as a rule for the conduct of its government, is a simple question in which all men, not directly courtiers, will agree. It is only on the component parts that questions and opinions multiply.

But this difficulty, like every other, will diminish when put into a train of being rightly understood.

The first thing is, that a nation has a right to establish a constitution.

Whether it exercises this right in the most judicious manner at first is quite another case. It exercises it agreeably to the judgment it possesses; and by continuing to do so, all errors will at last be exploded.

When this right is established in a nation, there is no fear that it will be employed to its own injury. A nation can have no interest in being wrong.

Though all the constitutions of America are on one general principle, yet no two of them are exactly alike in their component parts, or in the distribution of the powers which they give to the actual governments. Some are more, and others less complex.

In forming a constitution, it is first necessary to consider what are the ends for which government is necessary? Secondly, what are the best means, and the least expensive, for accomplishing those ends?

Government is nothing more than a national association; and the object of this association is the good of all, as well individually as collectively. Every man wishes to pursue his occupation, and to enjoy the fruits of his labours and the produce of his property in peace and safety, and with the least possible expence. When these things are accomplished, all the objects for which government ought to be established are answered.

It has been customary to consider government under three distinct general heads. The legislative, the executive, and the judicial.

But if we permit our judgment to act unincumbered by the habit of multiplied terms, we can perceive no more than two divisions of power, of which civil government is composed, namely, that of legislating or enacting laws, and that of executing or administering them. Everything, therefore, appertaining to civil government, classes itself under one or other of these two divisions.

So far as regards the execution of the laws, that which is called the judicial power, is strictly and properly the executive power of every country. It is that power to which every individual has appeal, and which causes the laws to be executed; neither have we any other clear idea with respect to the official execution of the laws. In England, and also in America and France, this power begins with the magistrate, and proceeds up through all the courts of judicature.

I leave to courtiers to explain what is meant by calling monarchy the executive power. It is merely a name in which acts of government are done; and any other, or none at all, would answer the same purpose. Laws have neither more nor less authority on this account. It must be from the justness of their principles, and the interest which a nation feels therein, that they derive support; if they require any other than this, it is a sign that something in the system of government is imperfect. Laws difficult to be executed cannot be generally good.

With respect to the organization of the *legislative power*, different modes have been adopted in different countries. In America it is generally composed of two houses. In France it consists but of one, but in both countries, it is wholly by representation.

The case is, that mankind (from the long tyranny of assumed power) have had so few opportunities of making the necessary trials on modes and principles of government, in order to discover the best, *that government is but now beginning to be known*, and experience is yet wanting to determine many particulars.

The objections against two houses are, first, that there is an inconsistency in any part of a whole legislature, coming to a final determination by vote on any matter, whilst *that matter*, with respect to *that whole*, is yet only in a train of deliberation, and consequently open to new illustrations.

Secondly, That by taking the vote on each, as a separate body, it always admits of the possibility, and is often the case in practice, that the minority governs the majority, and that, in some instances, to a degree of great inconsistency.

Thirdly, That two houses arbitrarily checking or controuling each other is inconsistent; because it cannot be proved on the principles of just representation, that either should be wiser or better than the other. They may check in the wrong as well as in the right—and therefore to give the power where we cannot give the wisdom to use it, nor be assured of its being rightly used, renders the hazard at least equal to the precaution.*

The objection against a single house is, that it is always in a condition of committing itself too soon.—But it should at the same time be remembered, that when there is a constitution which defines the power, and establishes the principles within which a legislature shall act, there is already a more effectual check provided, and more powerfully operating, than any other check can be. For example,

Were a Bill to be brought into any of the American legislatures similar to that which was passed into an act by the English parliament, at the commencement of George the First, to extend the du-

---

*With respect to the two houses, of which the English parliament is composed, they appear to be effectually influenced into one, and, as a legislature, to have no temper of its own. The minister, whoever he at any time may be, touches it as with an opium wand, and it sleeps obedience.

But if we look at the distinct abilities of the two houses, the difference will appear so great, as to show the inconsistency of placing power where there can be no certainty of the judgment to use it. Wretched as the state of representation is in England, it is manhood compared with what is called the house of Lords; and so little is this nick-named house regarded, that the people scarcely inquire at any time what it is doing. It appears also to be most under influence, and the furthest removed from the general interest of the nation. In the debate on engaging in the Russian and Turkish war, the majority in the house of peers in favor of it was upwards of ninety, when in the other house; which was more than double its numbers, the majority was sixty-three.

The proceedings on Mr. Fox's bill, respecting the rights of juries, merits also to be noticed. The persons called the peers were not the objects of that bill. They are already in possession of more privileges than that bill gave to others. They are their own jury, and if any one of that house were prosecuted for a libel, he would not suffer, even upon conviction, for the first offence. Such inequality in laws ought not to exist in any country. The French constitution says, that *the law is the same to every individual, whether to protect or to punish. All are equal in its sight* [Author's note].

ration of the assemblies to a longer period than they now sit, the check is in the constitution, which in effect says, Thus far shalt thou go and no further.

But in order to remove the objection against a single house, (that of acting with too quick an impulse,) and at the same time to avoid the inconsistencies, in some cases absurdities, arising from two houses, the following method has been proposed as an improvement upon both.

First, To have but one representation.

Secondly, To divide that representation, by lot, into two or three parts.

Thirdly, That every proposed bill, shall be first debated in those parts by succession, that they may become the hearers of each other, but without taking any vote. After which the whole representation to assemble for a general debate and determination by vote.

To this proposed improvement has been added another, for the purpose of keeping the representation in the state of constant renovation; which is, that one-third of the representation of each county, shall go out at the expiration of one year, and the number be replaced by new elections. Another third at the expiration of the second year replaced in like manner, and every third year to be a general election.*

But in whatever manner the separate parts of a constitution may be arranged, there is *one* general principle that distinguishes freedom from slavery, which is, that all *hereditary government over a people is to them a species of slavery, and representative government is freedom.*

Considering government in the only light in which it should be considered, that of a NATIONAL ASSOCIATION, it ought to be so constructed as not to be disordered by any accident happening among the parts; and, therefore, no extraordinary power, capable of producing such an effect, should be lodged in the hands of any

---

*As to the state of representation in England, it is too absurd to be reasoned upon. Almost all the represented parts are decreasing in population, and the unrepresented parts are increasing. A general convention of the nation is necessary to take the whole form of government into consideration [Author's note].

individual. The death, sickness, absence or defection, of any one individual in a government, ought to be a matter of no more consequence, with respect to the nation, than if the same circumstance had taken place in a member of the English Parliament, or the French National Assembly.

Scarcely anything presents a more degrading character of national greatness, than its being thrown into confusion, by anything happening to or acted by any individual; and the ridiculousness of the scene is often increased by the natural insignificance of the person by whom it is occasioned. Were a government so constructed, that it could not go on unless a goose or a gander were present in the senate, the difficulties would be just as great and as real, on the flight or sickness of the goose, or the gander, as if it were called a King. We laugh at individuals for the silly difficulties they make to themselves, without perceiving that the greatest of all ridiculous things are acted in governments.*

All the constitutions of America are on a plan that excludes the childish embarrassments which occur in monarchical countries. No suspension of government can there take place for a moment, from any circumstances whatever. The system of representation provides for everything, and is the only system in which nations and governments can always appear in their proper character.

As extraordinary power ought not to be lodged in the hands of any individual, so ought there to be no appropriations of public money to any person, beyond what his services in a state may be

---

*It is related that in the canton of Berne, in Switzerland, it has been customary, from time immemorial, to keep a bear at the public expense, and the people had been taught to believe, that if they had not a bear they should all be undone. It happened some years ago that the bear, then in being, was taken sick, and died too suddenly to have his place immediately supplied with another. During this interregnum the people discovered that the corn grew, and the vintage flourished, and the sun and moon continued to rise and set, and everything went on the same as before, and taking courage from these circumstances, they resolved not to keep any more bears; for, said they, "a bear is a very voracious expensive animal, and we were obliged to pull out his claws, lest he should hurt the citizens." The story of the bear of Berne was related in some of the French newspapers, at the time of the flight of Louis XVI., and the application of it to monarchy could not be mistaken in France; but it seems that the aristocracy of Berne applied it to themselves, and have since prohibited the reading of French newspapers [Author's note].

worth. It signifies not whether a man be called a president, a king, an emperor, a senator, or by any other name which propriety or folly may devise or arrogance assume; it is only a certain service he can perform in the state; and the service of any such individual in the routine of office, whether such office be called monarchical, presidential, senatorial, or by any other name or title, can never exceed the value of ten thousand pounds a year. All the great services that are done in the world are performed by volunteer characters, who accept nothing for them; but the routine of office is always regulated to such a general standard of abilities as to be within the compass of numbers in every country to perform, and therefore cannot merit very extraordinary recompense. *Government*, says Swift,* *is a plain thing, and fitted to the capacity of many heads.*

It is inhuman to talk of a million sterling a year, paid out of the public taxes of any country, for the support of any individual, whilst thousands who are forced to contribute thereto, are pining with want, and struggling with misery. Government does not consist in a contrast between prisons and palaces, between poverty and pomp; it is not instituted to rob the needy of his mite, and increase the wretchedness of the wretched.—But on this part of the subject I shall speak hereafter, and confine myself at present to political observations.

When extraordinary power and extraordinary pay are allotted to any individual in a government, he becomes the center, round which every kind of corruption generates and forms. Give to any man a million a-year, and add thereto the power of creating and disposing of places, at the expence of a country, and the liberties of that country are no longer secure. What is called the splendor of a throne is no other than the corruption of the state. It is made up of a band of parasites, living in luxurious indolence, out of the public taxes.

When once such a vicious system is established it becomes the guard and protection of all inferior abuses. The man who is in the receipt of a million a year is the last person to promote a spirit of re-

---

*Jonathan Swift (1667–1745), English satirist and political writer.

form, lest, in the event, it should reach to himself. It is always his interest to defend inferior abuses, as so many outworks to protect the citadel; and on this species of political fortification, all the parts have such a common dependence that it is never to be expected they will attack each other.*

Monarchy would not have continued so many ages in the world, had it not been for the abuses it protects. It is the master-fraud, which shelters all others. By admitting a participation of the spoil, it makes itself friends; and when it ceases to do this it will cease to be the idol of courtiers.

As the principle on which constitutions are now formed rejects all hereditary pretensions to government, it also rejects all that catalogue of assumptions known by the name of prerogatives.

If there is any government where prerogatives might with apparent safety be entrusted to any individual, it is in the federal government of America. The president of the United States of America is elected only for four years. He is not only responsible in the general sense of the word, but a particular mode is laid down in the constitution for trying him. He cannot be elected under thirty-five years of age; and he must be a native of the country.

---

*It is scarcely possible to touch on any subject, that will not suggest an allusion to some corruption in governments. The simile of "*fortifications*," unfortunately involves with it a circumstance, which is directly in point with the matter above alluded to.

Among the numerous instances of abuse which have been acted or protected by governments, ancient or modern, there is not a greater than that of quartering a man and his heirs upon the public, to be maintained at his expence.

Humanity dictates a provision for the poor; but by what right, moral or political, does any government assume to say, that the person called the Duke of Richmond, shall be maintained by the public? Yet, if common report is true, not a beggar in London can purchase his wretched pittance of coal, without paying towards the civil list of the Duke of Richmond. Were the whole produce of this imposition but a shilling a year, the iniquitous principle would be still the same; but when it amounts, as it is said to do, to no less than twenty thousand pounds per annum, the enormity is too serious to be permitted to remain. This is one of the effects of monarchy and aristocracy.

In stating this case I am led by no personal dislike. Though I think it mean in any man to live upon the public, the vice originates in the government; and so general is it become, that whether the parties are in the ministry or in the opposition, it makes no difference: they are sure of the guarantee of each other [Author's note].

In a comparison of these cases with the Government of England, the difference when applied to the latter amounts to an absurdity. In England the person who exercises prerogative is often a foreigner; always half a foreigner, and always married to a foreigner. He is never in full natural or political connexion with the country, is not responsible for anything, and becomes of age at eighteen years; yet such a person is permitted to form foreign alliances, without even the knowledge of the nation, and to make war and peace without its consent.

But this is not all. Though such a person cannot dispose of the government in the manner of a testator, he dictates the marriage connexions, which, in effect, accomplish a great part of the same end. He cannot directly bequeath half the government to Prussia, but he can form a marriage partnership that will produce almost the same thing. Under such circumstances, it is happy for England that she is not situated on the Continent, or she might, like Holland, fall under the dictatorship of Prussia. Holland, by marriage, is as effectually governed by Prussia, as if the old tyranny of bequeathing the government had been the means.

The presidency in America (or, as it is sometimes called, the executive) is the only office from which a foreigner is excluded, and in England it is the only one to which he is admitted. A foreigner cannot be a member of Parliament, but he may be what is called a king. If there is any reason for excluding foreigners, it ought to be from those offices where mischief can most be acted, arid where, by uniting every bias of interest and attachment, the trust is best secured. But as nations proceed in the great business of forming constitutions, they will examine with more precision into the nature and business of that department which is called the executive. What the legislative and judicial departments are every one can see; but with respect to what, in Europe, is called the executive, as distinct from those two, it is either a political superfluity or a chaos of unknown things.

Some kind of official department, to which reports shall be made from the different parts of a nation, or from abroad, to be laid before the national representatives, is all that is necessary; but there is no consistency in calling this the executive; neither can it be considered in any other light than as inferior to the legislative. The sovereign authority in any country is the power of making laws, and everything else is an official department.

Next to the arrangement of the principles and the organization of the several parts of a constitution, is the provision to be made for the support of the persons to whom the nation shall confide the administration of the constitutional powers.

A nation can have no right to the time and services of any person at his own expence, whom it may choose to employ or intrust in any department whatever; neither can any reason be given for making provision for the support of any one part of a government and not for the other.

But admitting that the honour of being entrusted with any part of a government is to be considered a sufficient reward, it ought to be so to every person alike. If the members of the legislature of any country are to serve at their own expence that which is called the executive, whether monarchical or by any other name, ought to serve in like manner. It is inconsistent to pay the one, and accept the service of the other gratis.

In America, every department in the government is decently provided for; but no one is extravagantly paid. Every member of Congress, and of the Assemblies, is allowed a sufficiency for his expences. Whereas in England, a most prodigal provision is made for the support of one part of the Government, and none for the other, the consequence of which is that the one is furnished with the means of corruption and the other is put into the condition of being corrupted. Less than a fourth part of such expence, applied as it is in America, would remedy a great part of the corruption.

Another reform in the American constitution is the exploding all oaths of personality. The oath of allegiance in America is to the nation only. The putting any individual as a figure for a nation is improper. The happiness of a nation is the superior object, and therefore the intention of an oath of allegiance ought not to be obscured by being figuratively taken, to, or in the name of, any person. The oath, called the civic oath, in France, viz., *"the nation, the law, and the king,"* is improper. If taken at all, it ought to be as in America, to the nation only. The law may or may not be good; but, in this place, it can have no other meaning, than as being conducive to the happiness of a nation, and therefore is included in it. The remainder of the oath is improper, on the ground, that all personal oaths ought to be abolished. They are the remains of tyranny on one part and slavery on the other; and the name of the CREATOR ought not to be introduced to witness the degradation of his creation; or if taken, as is already mentioned, as figurative of the nation, it is in this place redundant. But whatever apology may be made for oaths at the first establishment of a government, they ought not to be permitted afterwards. If a government requires the support of oaths, it is a sign that it is not worth supporting, and ought not to be supported. Make government what it ought to be, and it will support itself.

To conclude this part of the subject:—One of the greatest improvements that have been made for the perpetual security and progress of constitutional liberty, is the provision which the new constitutions make for occasionally revising, altering, and amending them.

The principle upon which Mr. Burke formed his political creed, that of "*binding and controuling posterity to the end of time*, and of *renouncing and abdicating the rights of all posterity, for ever*," is now become too detestable to be made a subject of debate; and therefore, I pass it over with no other notice than exposing it.

Government is but now beginning to be known. Hitherto it has been the mere exercise of power, which forbad all effectual enquiry into rights, and grounded itself wholly on possession. While the enemy of liberty was its judge, the progress of its principles must have been small indeed.

The constitutions of America, and also that of France, have either affixed a period for their revision, or laid down the mode by which improvement shall be made. It is perhaps impossible to establish anything that combines principles with opinions and practice, which the progress of circumstances, through a length of years, will not in some measure derange, or render inconsistent; and, therefore, to prevent inconveniencies accumulating, till they discourage reformations or provoke revolutions, it is best to provide the means of regulating them as they occur. The Rights of Man are the rights of all generations of men, and cannot be monopolised by any. That which is worth following, will be followed for the sake of its worth, and it is in this that its security lies, and not in any conditions with which it may be encumbered. When a man leaves property to his heirs, he does not connect it with an obligation that they shall accept it. Why, then, should we do otherwise with respect to constitutions? The best constitution that could now be devised, consistent with the condition of the present moment, may be far short of that excellence which a few years may afford. There is a morning of reason rising upon man on the subject of government, that has not appeared before. As the barbarism of the present old governments expires, the moral conditions of nations with respect to each other will be changed. Man will not be brought up with the savage idea of considering his species as his enemy, because the accident of birth gave the individuals existence in countries distinguished by different names; and as constitutions have always some relation to external as well as to domestic circumstances, the means of benefitting by every change, foreign or domestic, should be a part of every constitution. We already see an alteration in the national disposition of England and France towards each other, which, when we look back to only a few years, is itself a Revolution. Who could have foreseen, or who could have believed, that a French National Assembly would ever have been a popular toast in England, or that a friendly alliance of the two nations should become the wish of either? It shews, that man, were he not corrupted by governments, is naturally the friend of man, and that human nature is not of itself vicious. That spirit of jealousy and ferocity, which the governments of the two countries inspired, and which they rendered subservient to the purpose of taxation, is now yielding to the dictates of reason, interest, and humanity. The trade of courts is beginning to be understood, and the affectation of mystery, with all the artificial sorcery by which they imposed upon mankind, is on the decline. It has received its death-wound; and though it may linger, it will expire. Government ought to be as much open to improvement as anything which appertains to man, instead of which it has been monopolised from age to age, by the most ignorant and vicious of the human race. Need we any other proof of their wretched management, than the excess of debts and taxes with which every nation groans, and the quarrels into which they have precipitated the world? Just emerging from such a barbarous condition, it is too soon to determine to what extent of improvement government may yet be carried. For what we can foresee, all Europe may form but one great Republic, and man be free of the whole.

CHAPTER V.

Ways and Means of Improving the Condition of Europe,
Interspersed with Miscellaneous Observations.

IN CONTEMPLATING A SUBJECT that embraces with equatorial magnitude the whole region of humanity it is impossible to confine the pursuit in one single direction. It takes ground on every character and condition that appertains to man, and blends the individual, the nation, and the world. From a small spark, kindled in America, a flame has arisen not to be extinguished. Without consuming, like the *Ultima Ratio Regum,** it winds its progress from nation to nation, and conquers by a silent operation. Man finds himself changed, he scarcely perceives how. He acquires a knowledge of his rights by attending justly to his interest, and discovers in the event that the strength and powers of despotism consist wholly in the fear of resisting it, and that, in order *"to be free, it is sufficient that he wills it."*

Having in all the preceding parts of this work endeavoured to establish a system of principles as a basis on which governments ought to be erected, I shall proceed in this, to the ways and means of rendering them into practice. But in order to introduce this part of the subject with more propriety, and stronger effect, some preliminary observations, deducible from, or connected with, those principles, are necessary.

Whatever the form or constitution of government may be, it ought to have no other object than the *general* happiness. When, in-

---

*"The final argument of kings"; a resort to force; motto engraved on Louis XIV's cannon.

stead of this, it operates to create and encrease wretchedness in any of the parts of society, it is on a wrong system, and reformation is necessity. Customary language has classed the condition of man under the two descriptions of civilised and uncivilised life. To the one it has ascribed felicity and affluence; to the other hardship and want. But, however our imagination may be impressed by painting and comparison, it is nevertheless true, that a great portion of mankind, in what are called civilised countries, are in a state of poverty and wretchedness, far below the condition of an Indian. I speak not of one country, but of all. It is so in England, it is so all over Europe. Let us enquire into the cause.

It lies not in any natural defect in the principles of civilisation, but in preventing those principles having a universal operation; the consequence of which is, a perpetual system of war and expence, that drains the country, and defeats the general felicity of which civilisation is capable. All the European governments (France now excepted) are constructed not on the principle of universal civilisation, but on the reverse of it. So far as those governments relate to each other, they are in the same condition as we conceive of savage uncivilised life; they put themselves beyond the law as well of GOD as of man, and are, with respect to principle and reciprocal conduct, like so many individuals in a state of nature. The inhabitants of every country, under the civilisation of laws, easily civilise together, but governments being yet in an uncivilised state, and almost continually at war, they pervert the abundance which civilised life produces to carry on the uncivilised part to a greater extent. By thus engrafting the barbarism of government upon the internal civilisation of a country, it draws from the latter, and more especially from the poor, a great portion of those earnings, which should be applied to their own subsistence and comfort. Apart from all reflections of morality and philosophy, it is a melancholy fact that more than one-fourth of the labour of mankind is annually consumed by this barbarous system. What has served to continue this evil, is the pecuniary advantage which all the governments of Europe have found in keeping up this state of uncivilisation. It affords to them pretences for power, and revenue, for which there would be neither occasion nor apology, if the circle of civilisation were rendered complete. Civil government alone, or the government of laws, is not productive of pretences for many taxes; it operates at home, directly under the eye of the country, and precludes the possibility of much imposition. But when the scene is laid in the uncivilised contention of governments, the field of pretences is enlarged, and the country, being no longer a judge, is open to every imposition, which governments please to act. Not a thirtieth, scarcely a fortieth, part of the taxes which are raised in England are either occasioned by, or applied to, the purpose of civil government. It is not difficult to see, that the whole which the actual government does in this respect, is to enact laws, and that the country administers and executes them, at its own expence, by means of magistrates, juries, sessions, and assize, over and above the taxes which it pays. In this view of the case, we have two distinct characters of government; the one the civil government, or the government of laws, which operates at home, the other the court or cabinet government, which operates abroad, on the rude plan of uncivilised life; the one attended with little charge, the other with boundless extravagance; and so distinct are the two, that if the latter were to sink, as it were, by a sudden opening of the earth, and totally disappear, the former would not be deranged. It would still proceed, because it is the common interest of the nation that it should, and all the means are in practice. Revolutions, then, have for their object a change in the moral condition of governments, and with this change the burthen of public taxes will lessen, and civilisation will be left to the enjoyment of that abundance, of which it is now deprived. In contemplating the whole of this subject, I extend my views into the department of commerce. In all my publications, where the matter would admit, I have been an advocate for commerce, because I am a friend to its effects. It is a pacific system, operating to cordialise mankind, by rendering nations, as well as individuals, useful to each other. As to the mere theoretical reformation, I have never preached it up. The most effectual process is that of improving the condition of man by means of his interest; and it is on this ground that I take my stand. If commerce were permitted to act to the universal extent it is capable, it would extirpate the system of war, and produce a revolution in the uncivilised state of governments. The invention of commerce has arisen since those governments began, and is the greatest approach towards universal civilisation that has yet been made by any means not immediately flowing from moral principles. Whatever has a tendency to promote the civil intercourse of nations by an exchange of benefits, is a subject as worthy of philosophy as of politics. Commerce is no other than the traffic of two individuals, multiplied on a scale of numbers; and by the same rule that nature intended for the intercourse of two, she intended that of all. For this purpose she has distributed the materials of manufactures and commerce, in various and distant parts of a nation and of the world; and as they cannot be procured by war so cheaply or so commodiously as by commerce, she has rendered the latter the means of extirpating the former. As the two are nearly the opposite of each other, consequently, the uncivilised state of the European governments is injurious to commerce. Every kind of destruction or embarrassment serves to lessen the quantity, and it matters but little in what part of the commercial world the reduction begins. Like blood, it cannot be taken from any of the parts, without being taken from the whole mass in circulation, and all partake of the loss. When the ability in any nation to buy is destroyed, it equally involves the seller. Could the government of England destroy the commerce of all other nations, she would most effectually ruin her own. It is possible that a nation may be the carrier for the world, but she cannot be the merchant. She cannot be the seller and buyer of her own merchandise. The ability to buy must reside out of herself; and, therefore, the prosperity of any commercial nation is regulated by the prosperity of the rest. If they are poor she cannot be rich, and her condition, be what it may, is an index of the height of the commercial tide in other nations. That the principles of commerce, and its universal operation may be understood, without understanding the practice, is a position that reason will not deny; and it is on this ground only that I argue the subject. It is one thing in the counting-house, in the world it is another. With respect to its operation it must necessarily be contemplated as a reciprocal thing; that only one-half its powers resides within the nation, and that the whole is as effectually destroyed by the destroying the half that resides without, as if the destruction had been committed on that which is within; for neither can act without the other. When in the last, as well as in former wars, the commerce of England sunk, it was because the quantity was lessened everywhere; and it now rises, because commerce is in a rising state in every nation. If England, at this day, imports and exports more than at any former period, the nations with which she trades must necessarily do the same; her imports are their exports, and *vice versa*. There can be no such thing as a nation flourishing alone in commerce: she can only participate; and the destruction of it in any part must necessarily affect all. When, therefore, governments are at war, the attack is made upon a common stock of commerce, and the consequence is the same as if each had attacked his own. The present increase of commerce is not to be attributed to ministers, or to any political contrivances, but to its own natural operation in consequence of peace. The regular markets had been destroyed, the channels of trade broken up, the high road of the seas infested with robbers of every nation, and the attention of the world called to other objects. Those interruptions have ceased, and peace has restored the deranged condition of things to their proper order.* It is worth remarking that every nation reckons the balance of trade in its own favour; and therefore something must be irregular in the common ideas upon this subject. The fact, however, is true, according to what is called a balance; and it is from this cause that commerce is universally supported. . . .

Cases are continually occurring in a metropolis, different from those which occur in the country, and for which a different, or rather an additional, mode of relief is necessary. In the country, even in large towns, people have a knowledge of each other, and distress never rises to that extreme height it sometimes does in a metropo-

---

*In America the increase of commerce is greater in proportion than in England. It is, at this time, at least one half more than at any period prior to the revolution. The greatest number of vessels cleared out of the port of Philadelphia, before the commencement of the war, was between eight and nine hundred. In the year 1788, the number was upwards of twelve hundred. As the State of Pennsylvania is estimated at an eighth part of the United States in population, the whole number of vessels must now be nearly ten thousand [Author's note].

lis. There is no such thing in the country as persons, in the literal sense of the word, starved to death, or dying with cold from the want of a lodging. Yet such cases, and others equally as miserable, happen in London.

Many a youth comes up to London full of expectations, and with little or no money, and unless he get immediate employment he is already half undone; and boys bred up in London without any means of a livelihood, and as it often happens of dissolute parents, are in a still worse condition; and servants long out of place are not much better off. In short, a world of little cases is continually arising, which busy or affluent life knows not of, to open the first door to distress. Hunger is not among the postponable wants, and a day, even a few hours, in such a condition is often the crisis of a life of ruin.

These circumstances which are the general cause of the little thefts and pilferings that lead to greater, may be prevented. There yet remain twenty thousand pounds out of the four millions of surplus taxes, which with another fund hereafter to be mentioned, amounting to about twenty thousand pounds more, cannot be better applied than to this purpose. The plan will then be:

First,—To erect two or more buildings, or take some already erected, capable of containing at least six thousand persons, and to have in each of these places as many kinds of employment as can be contrived, so that every person who shall come may find something which he or she can do.

Secondly,—To receive all who shall come, without enquiring who or what they are. The only condition to be, that for so much, or so many hours' work, each person shall receive so many meals of wholesome food, and a warm lodging, at least as good as a barrack. That a certain portion of what each person's work shall be worth shall be reserved, and given to him or her, on their going away; and that each person shall stay as long or as short a time, or come as often as he chuse, on these conditions.

If each person staid three months, it would assist by rotation twenty-four thousand persons annually, though the real number, at all times, would be but six thousand. By establishing an asylum of this kind, such persons to whom temporary distresses occur, would have an opportunity to recruit themselves, and be enabled to look out for better employment.

Allowing that their labor paid but one half the expence of supporting them, after reserving a portion of their earnings for themselves, the sum of forty thousand pounds additional would defray all other charges for even a greater number than six thousand.

The fund very properly convertible to this purpose, in addition to the twenty thousand pounds, remaining of the former fund, will be the produce of the tax upon coals, so iniquitously and wantonly applied to the support of the Duke of Richmond. It is horrid that any man, more especially at the price coals now are, should live on the distresses of a community; and any government permitting such an abuse, to be dismissed. This fund is said to be about twenty thousand pounds *per annum*.

I shall now conclude this plan with enumerating the several particulars, and then proceed to other matters.

The enumeration is as follows:—

First—Abolition of two millions poor-rates.

Secondly—Provision for two hundred and fifty thousand poor families.

Thirdly—Education for one million and thirty thousand children.

Fourthly—Comfortable provision for one hundred and forty thousand aged persons.

Fifthly—Donation of twenty shillings each for fifty thousand births.

Sixthly—Donation of twenty shillings each for twenty thousand marriages.

Seventhly—Allowance of twenty thousand pounds for the funeral expences of persons travelling for work, and dying at a distance from their friends.

Eighthly—Employment, at all times, for the casual poor in the cities of London and Westminster.

By the operation of this plan, the poor laws, those instruments of civil torture, will be superseded, and the wasteful expence of litigation prevented. The hearts of the humane will not be shocked by ragged and hungry children, and persons of seventy and eighty years of age, begging for bread. The dying poor will not be dragged from place to place to breathe their last, as a reprisal of parish upon parish. Widows will have a maintenance for their children, and not be carted away, on the death of their husbands, like culprits and criminals; and children will no longer be considered as encreasing the distresses of their parents. The haunts of the wretched will be known, because it will be to their advantage; and the number of petty crimes, the offspring of distress and poverty, will be lessened. The poor, as well as the rich, will then be interested in the support of government, and the cause and apprehension of riots and tumults will cease.—Ye who sit in ease, and solace yourselves in plenty, and such there are in Turkey and Russia, as well as in England, and who say to yourselves, "Are we not well off?" have ye thought of these things? When ye do, ye will cease to speak and feel for yourselves alone.

The plan is easy in practice. It does not embarrass trade by a sudden interruption in the order of taxes, but effects the relief by changing the application of them; and the money necessary for the purpose can be drawn from the excise collections, which are made eight times a year in every market town in England.

Having now arranged and concluded this subject, I proceed to the next.

Taking the present current expences at seven millions and an half, which is the least amount they are now at, there will remain (after the sum of one million and an half be taken for the new current expenses and four millions for the before-mentioned service) the sum of two millions; part of which to be applied as follows:

Though fleets and armies, by an alliance with France, will, in a great measure, become useless, yet the persons who have devoted themselves to those services, and have thereby unfitted themselves for other lines of life, are not to be sufferers by the means that make others happy. They are a different description of men from those who form or hang about a court.

A part of the army will remain, at least for some years, and also of the navy, for which a provision is already made in the former part of this plan of one million, which is almost half a million more than the peace establishment of the army and navy in the prodigal times of Charles the Second.

Suppose, then, fifteen thousand soldiers to be disbanded, and that an allowance be made to each of three shillings a week during life, clear of all deductions, to be paid in the same manner as the Chelsea College pensioners* are paid, and for them to return to their trades and their friends; and also that an addition of fifteen thousand sixpences per week be made to the pay of the soldiers who shall remain; the annual expences will be, to the pay of—

Fifteen thousand disbanded soldiers at 3s. per week £117,000
Additional pay to the remaining soldiers 19,000
Suppose that the pay to the officers of the disbanded corps
    be the same amount as to the men 117,000
To prevent bulky estimations, admit the same sum to the
    disbanded navy as to the army, and the same increase
    of pay 253,500
               Total £507,000

Every year some part of this sum of half a million (I omit the odd seven thousand pounds for the purpose of keeping the account unembarrassed) will fall in, and the whole of it in time, as it is on the ground of life annuities, except the encreased pay of twenty-nine thousand pounds. As it falls in, part of the taxes may be taken off; and as, for instance, when thirty thousand pounds fall in, the duty on hops may be wholly taken off; and as other parts fall in, the duties on candles and soap may be lessened, till at last they will totally cease. There now remains at least one million and a half of surplus taxes.

The tax on houses and windows is one of those direct taxes, which, like the poor rates, is not confounded with trade; and, when taken off, the relief will be instantly felt. This tax falls heavy on the middle class of people. The amount of this tax, by the returns of 1788, was: by the act of 1766, £385,459 11 7; by the act of 1779, £130,739 14 5½; total, £516,199 6 0½.

If this tax be struck off, there will then remain about one million of surplus taxes; and as it is always proper to keep a sum in reserve, for incidental matters, it may be best not to extend reductions fur-

---

*Army pensioners in the Royal Hospital, London.

ther in the first instance, but to consider what may be accomplished by other modes of reform.

Among the taxes most heavily felt is the commutation-tax. I shall therefore offer a plan for its abolition, by substituting another in its place, which will effect three objects at once: 1, that of removing the burthen to where it can best be borne; 2, restoring justice among families by a distribution of property; 3, extirpating the overgrown influence arising from the unnatural law of primogeniture, which is one of the principal sources of corruption at elections. The amount of commutation-tax by the returns of 1788, was £771,657.

When taxes are proposed, the country is amused by the plausible language of taxing luxuries. One thing is called a luxury at one time, and something else at another; but the real luxury does not consist in the article, but in the means of procuring it, and this is always kept out of sight.

I know not why any plant or herb of the field should be a greater luxury in one country than another; but an overgrown estate in either is a luxury at all times, and, as such, is the proper object of taxation. It is, therefore, right to take those kind tax-making gentlemen up on their own word, and argue on the principle themselves have laid down, that of *taxing luxuries*. If they or their champion, Mr. Burke, who, I fear, is growing out of date, like the man in armor; can prove that an estate of twenty, thirty, or forty thousand pounds a year is not a luxury, I will give up the argument.

Admitting that any annual sum, say, for instance, one thousand pounds, is necessary or sufficient for the support of a family, consequently the second thousand is of the nature of a luxury, the third still more so, and by proceeding on, we shall at last arrive at a sum that may not improperly be called a prohibitable luxury. It would be impolitic to set bounds to property acquired by industry, and therefore it is right to place the prohibition beyond the probable acquisition to which industry can extend; but there ought to be a limit to property or the accumulation of it by bequest. It should pass in some other line. The richest in every nation have poor relations, and those often very near in consanguinity.

The following table of progressive taxation is constructed on the above principles, and as a substitute for the commutation tax. It will reach the point of prohibition by a regular operation, and thereby supercede the aristocratical law of primogeniture.

TABLE I.

A tax on all estates of the clear yearly value of £50, after deducting the land tax, and up

		per s. d. pound				per s. d. pound
To £500	..	o 3 "	On the twelfth thousand.		9 0	"
From £500 to £1,000....		o 6 "	On the thirteenth	"	10 0	"
On the second thousand.		o 9 "	On the fourteenth	"	11 0	"
On the third	"	1 0 "	On the fifteenth	"	12 0	"
On the fourth	"	1 6 "	On the sixteenth	"	13 0	"
On the fifth	"	2 0 "	On the seventeenth	"	14 0	"
On the sixth	"	3 0 "	On the eighteenth	"	15 0	"
On the seventh	"	4 0 "	On the nineteenth	"	16 0	"
On the eighth	"	5 0 "	On the twentieth	"	17 0	"
On the ninth	"	6 0 "	On the twenty-first	"	18 0	"
On the tenth	"	7 0 "	On the twenty-second	"	19 0	"
On the eleventh	"	8 0 "	On the twenty-third	"	20 0	"

The foregoing table shows the progression per pound on every progressive thousand. The following table shows the amount of the tax on every thousand separately, and in the last column the total amount of all the separate sums collected.

TABLE II.

An estate of

£50 *per annum*, at 3d., pays,	£0	12	6	£300 *per annum*, at 3d., pays,	£3	15	0
100 " " "	1	5	0	400 " " "	5	0	0
200 " " "	2	10	0	500 " " "	7	5	0

After £500, the tax of 6d. per pound takes place on the second £500; consequently an estate of £1,000 *per annum* pays £21, 15s, and so on.

For the

	£	s.	d.	£	s.	£	s.
1st £500 at	0	3—		7	5	} 21 15	
2nd "	0	6—		14	10		
2nd 1000 at	0	9—		37	11	59	5
3rd "	1	0—		50	0	109	5
4th "	1	6—		75	0	184	5
5th "	2	0—	100	0		284	5
6th "	3	0—	150	0		434	5
7th "	4	0—	200	0		634	5
8th "	5	0—	250	0		880	5
9th "	6	0—	300	0		1100	5
10th "	7	0—	350	0		1530	5
11th "	8	0—	400	0		1930	5

	£	s.	d.	£	s.	£	s.
12th 1000 at	9	0—		450	0	2380	5
13th "	10	0—		500	0	2880	5
14th "	11	0—		550	0	3430	5
15th "	12	0—		600	0	4030	5
16th "	13	0—		650	0	4680	5
17th "	14	0—		700	0	5380	5
18th "	15	0—		750	0	6130	5
19th "	16	0—		800	0	6930	5
20th "	17	0—		850	0	7780	5
21st "	18	0—		900	0	8680	5
22nd "	19	0—		950	0	9630	5
23rd "	20	0—	1000	0		10630	5

At the twenty-third thousand the tax becomes 20s. in the pound, and consequently every thousand beyond that sum can produce no profit but by dividing the estate. Yet formidable as this tax appears, it will not, I believe, produce so much as the commutation tax; should it produce more, it ought to be lowered to that amount upon estates under two or three thousand a year.

On small and middling estates it is lighter (as it is intended to be) than the commutation tax. It is not till after seven or eight thousand a-year, that it begins to be heavy. The object is not so much the produce of the tax as the justice of the measure. The aristocracy has screened itself too much, and this serves to restore a part of the lost equilibrium.

As an instance of its screening itself, it is only necessary to look back to the first establishment of the excise laws, at what is called the Restoration, or the coming of Charles the Second.* The aristocratical interest then in power, commuted the feudal services itself was under, by laying a tax on beer brewed for sale; that is, they compounded with Charles for an exemption from those services for themselves and their heirs, by a tax to be paid by other people. The aristocracy do not purchase beer brewed for sale, but

---

*Restoration of the English monarchy in 1660, on the accession of Charles II (1630–1685).

brew their own beer free of the duty, and if any commutation at that time were necessary, it ought to have been at the expence of those for whom the exemptions from those services were intended*; instead of which, it was thrown on an entirely different class of men.

But the chief object of this progressive tax (besides the justice of rendering taxes more equal than they are) is, as already stated, to extirpate the overgrown influence arising from the unnatural law of primogeniture, and which is one of the principal sources of corruption at elections.

It would be attended with no good consequences to enquire how such vast estates as thirty, forty, or fifty thousand a-year could commence, and that at a time when commerce and manufactures were not in a state to admit of such acquisitions. Let it be sufficient to remedy the evil by putting them in a condition of descending again to the community by the quiet means of apportioning them among all the heirs and heiresses of those families. This will be the more necessary, because hitherto the aristocracy have quartered their younger children and connexions upon the public in useless posts, places and offices, which when abolished will leave them destitute, unless the law of primogeniture be also abolished or superceded.

A progressive tax will, in a great measure, effect this object, and that as a matter of interest to the parties most immediately concerned, as will be seen by the following table; which shews the nett produce upon every estate, after subtracting the tax. By this it will appear, that after an estate exceeds thirteen or fourteen thousand a-year, the remainder produces but little profit to the holder, and consequently, will pass either to the younger children, or to other kindred.

---

*The tax on beer brewed for sale, from which the aristocracy are exempt, is almost one million more than the present commutation tax, being by the returns of 1788, 1,666,152*l.*—and, consequently, they ought to take on themselves the amount of the commutation tax, as they are already exempted from one which is almost a million greater [Author's note].

TABLE III.

Shewing the nett produce of every estate from one thousand to
twenty-three thousand pounds a year.

No. of thousands per ann.	Total tax subtracted.	Nett produce.
1000*l.*	21*l.*	979*l.*
2000	59	1941
3000	109	2891
4000	184	3861
5000	284	4716
6000	434	5566
7000	634	6366
8000	880	7120
9000	1100	7820
10,000	1530	8470
11,000	1930	9070
12,000	2380	9620
13,000	2880	10,120
14,000	3430	10,570
15,000	4030	10,970
16,000	4680	11,320
17,000	5380	11,620
18,000	6130	11,870
19,000	6930	12,170
20,000	7780	12,220
21,000	8680	12,320
22,000	9630	12,370
23,000	10,630	12,370

N. B. The odd shillings are dropped in this table.

According to this table, an estate cannot produce more than
12,370*l.* clear of the land tax and the progressive tax, and therefore
the dividing such estates will follow as a matter of family interest.
An estate of 23,000*l.* a year, divided into five estates of four thousand each and one of three, will be charged only 1129*l.* which is but
five *per cent.*, but if held by one possessor, will be charged 10,630*l.*

Although an enquiry into the origin of those estates be unnecessary, the continuation of them in their present state is another subject. It is a matter of national concern. As hereditary estates, the law

has created the evil, and it ought also to provide the remedy. Primogeniture ought to be abolished, not only because it is unnatural and unjust, but because the country suffers by its operation. By cutting off (as before observed) the younger children from their proper portion of inheritance, the public is loaded with the expence of maintaining them; and the freedom of elections violated by the overbearing influence which this unjust monopoly of family property produces. Nor is this all. It occasions a waste of national property. A considerable part of the land of the country is rendered unproductive, by the great extent of parks and chases which this law serves to keep up, and this at a time when the annual production of grain is not equal to the national consumption.*—In short, the evils of the aristocratical system are so great and numerous, so inconsistent with every thing that is just, wise, natural, and beneficent, that when they are considered, there ought not to be a doubt that many, who are now classed under that description, will wish to see such a system abolished.

What pleasure can they derive from contemplating the exposed condition, and almost certain beggary of their younger offspring? Every aristocratical family has an appendage of family beggars hanging round it, which in a few ages, or a few generations, are shook off, and console themselves with telling their tale in almshouses, workhouses, and prisons. This is the natural consequence of aristocracy. The peer and the beggar are often of the same family. One extreme produces the other: to make one rich many must be made poor: neither can the system be supported by other means.

There are two classes of people to whom the laws of England are particularly hostile, and those the most helpless; younger children, and the poor. Of the former I have just spoken; of the latter I shall mention one instance out of the many that might be produced, and with which I shall close this subject.

Several laws are in existence for regulating and limiting workmen's wages. Why not leave them as free to make their own bargains, as the law-makers are to let their farms and houses? Personal

---

*See the Reports on the Corn Trade [Author's note].

labour is all the property they have. Why is that little, and the little freedom they enjoy, to be infringed? But the injustice will appear stronger, if we consider the operation and effect of such laws. When wages are fixed by what is called a law, the legal wages remain stationary, while every thing else is in progression; and as those who make that law, still continue to lay on new taxes by other laws, they encrease the expence of living by one law, and take away the means by another.

But if these gentlemen law-makers and tax-makers thought it right to limit the poor pittance which personal labour can produce, and on which a whole family is to be supported, they certainly must feel themselves happily indulged in a limitation on their own part, of not less than twelve thousand a-year, and that of property they never acquired, (nor probably any of their ancestors) and of which they have made so ill a use.

Having now finished this subject, I shall bring the several particulars into one view, and then proceed to other matters.

The first eight articles are brought forward from p. 237:

1. Abolition of two millions poor-rates.

2. Provision for two hundred and fifty-two thousand poor families, at the rate of four pounds per head for each child under fourteen years of age; which, with the addition of two hundred and fifty thousand pounds, provides also education for one million and thirty thousand children.

3. Annuity of six pounds (per annum) each for all poor persons, decayed tradesmen, and others (supposed seventy thousand) of the age of fifty years, and until sixty.

4. Annuity of ten pounds each for life for all poor persons, decayed tradesmen, and others (supposed seventy thousand) of the age of sixty years.

5. Donation of twenty shillings each for fifty thousand births.

6. Donation of twenty shillings each for twenty thousand marriages.

7. Allowance of twenty thousand pounds for the funeral expenses of persons travelling for work, and dying at a distance from their friends.

8. Employment at all times for the casual poor in the cities of London and Westminster.

Second enumeration:

9. Abolition of the tax on houses and windows.

10. Allowance of three shillings per week for life to fifteen thousand disbanded soldiers, and a proportionate allowance to the officers of the disbanded corps.

11. Encrease of pay to the remaining soldiers of 19,500*l.* annually.

12. The same allowance to the disbanded navy, and the same encrease of pay, as to the army.

13. Abolition of the commutation tax.

14. Plan of a progressive tax, operating to extirpate the unjust and unnatural law of primogeniture, and the vicious influence of the aristocratical system*

There yet remains, as already stated, one million of surplus taxes. Some part of this will be required for circumstances that do not immediately present themselves, and such part as shall not be wanted, will admit of a further reduction of taxes equal to that amount.

Among the claims that justice requires to be made, the condition of the inferior revenue-officers will merit attention. It is a reproach to any government to waste such an immensity of revenue in

---

*When inquiries are made into the condition of the poor, various degrees of distress will most probably be found, to render a different arrangement preferable to that which is already proposed. Widows with families will be in greater want than where there are husbands living. There is also a difference in the expence of living in different counties: and more so in fuel.

Suppose then fifty thousand extraordinary cases, at the rate of ten pounds per family per ann	500,000*l.*
100,000 families, at 8*l.* per family per ann	800,000
100,000 families, at 7*l.* per ” ”	700,000
104,000 families, at 5*l.* per ” ”	520,000
And instead of ten shillings per head for the education of other children, to allow fifty shillings per family for that purpose to fifty thousand families	250,000
	2,770,000
140,000 aged persons as before,	1,120,000
	3,890,000*l.*

This arrangement amounts to the same sum as stated in p. 489, including the 250,000*l.* for education; but it provides (including the aged people) for four hundred and four thousand families, which is almost one third of all the families in England [Author's note].

sinecures and nominal and unnecessary places and officers, and not allow even a decent livelihood to those on whom the labour falls. The salary of the inferior officers of the revenue has stood at the petty pittance of less than fifty pounds a year for upwards of one hundred years. It ought to be seventy. About one hundred and twenty thousand pounds applied to this purpose, will put all those salaries in a decent condition.

This was proposed to be done almost twenty years ago, but the treasury-board then in being, startled at it, as it might lead to similar expectations from the army and navy; and the event was, that the King, or somebody for him, applied to parliament to have his own salary raised an hundred thousand pounds a year, which being done, every thing else was laid aside. . . .

Never did so great an opportunity offer itself to England, and to all Europe, as is produced by the two Revolutions of America and France. By the former, freedom has a national champion in the western world; and by the latter, in Europe. When another nation shall join France, despotism and bad government will scarcely dare to appear. To use a trite expression, the iron is becoming hot all over Europe. The insulted German and the enslaved Spaniard, the Russ and the Pole, are beginning to think. The present age will hereafter merit to be called the Age of reason, and the present generation will appear to the future as the Adam of a new world.

When all the governments of Europe shall be established on the representative system, nations will become acquainted, and the animosities and prejudices fomented by the intrigue and artifice of courts, will cease. The oppressed soldier will become a freeman; and the tortured sailor, no longer dragged through the streets like a felon, will pursue his mercantile voyage in safety. It would be better that nations should continue the pay of their soldiers during their lives, and give them their discharge and restore them to freedom and their friends, and cease recruiting, than retain such multitudes at the same expence, in a condition useless to society and to themselves. As soldiers have hitherto been treated in most countries, they might be said to be without a friend. Shunned by the citizen on an apprehension of their being enemies to liberty, and too often insulted by those who commanded them, their condition was a double oppression. But where genuine principles of liberty pervade a people, every thing is restored to order; and the soldier civilly treated, returns the civility.

In contemplating revolutions, it is easy to perceive that they may arise from two distinct causes; the one, to avoid or get rid of some great calamity; the other, to obtain some great and positive good; and the two may be distinguished by the names of active and passive revolutions. In those which proceed from the former cause, the temper becomes incensed and sowered; and the redress, obtained by danger, is too often sullied by revenge. But in those which proceed from the latter, the heart, rather animated than agitated, enters serenely upon the subject. Reason and discussion, persuasion and conviction, become the weapons in the contest, and it is only when those are attempted to be suppressed that recourse is had to violence. When men unite in agreeing that a *thing is good*, could it be obtained, such for instance as relief from a burden of taxes and the extinction of corruption, the object is more than half accomplished. What they approve as the end, they will promote in the means.

Will any man say, in the present excess of taxation, falling so heavily on the poor, that a remission of five pounds annually of taxes to one hundred and four thousand poor families is not a *good thing*? Will he say, that a remission of seven pounds annually to one hundred thousand other poor families—of eight pounds annually to another hundred thousand poor families, and of ten pounds annually to fifty thousand poor and widowed families, are not *good things*? And, to proceed a step further in this climax, will he say, that to provide against the misfortunes to which all human life is subject, by securing six pounds annually for all poor, distressed, and reduced persons of the age of fifty and until sixty, and of ten pounds annually after sixty, is not a *good thing*?

Will he say, that an abolition of two millions of poor-rates to the house-keepers, and of the whole of the house and window-light tax and of the commutation tax is not a *good thing*? Or will he say, that to abolish corruption is a *bad thing*?

If, therefore, the good to be obtained be worthy of a passive, rational, and costless revolution, it would be bad policy to prefer waiting for a calamity that should force a violent one. I have no idea, considering the reforms which are now passing and spreading throughout Europe, that England will permit herself to be the last;

and where the occasion and the opportunity quietly offer, it is better than to wait for a turbulent necessity. It may be considered as an honour to the animal faculties of man to obtain redress by courage and danger, but it is far greater honour to the rational faculties to accomplish the same object by reason, accommodation, and general consent.*

As reforms, or revolutions, call them which you please, extend themselves among nations, those nations will form connections and conventions, and when a few are thus confederated, the progress will be rapid, till despotism and corrupt government be totally expelled, at least out of two quarters of the world, Europe and America. The Algerine piracy† may then be commanded to cease, for it is only by the malicious policy of old governments, against each other that it exists.

Throughout this work, various and numerous as the subjects are, which I have taken up and investigated, there is only a single paragraph upon religion, *viz.* "*that every religion is good that teaches man to be good.*"

I have carefully avoided to enlarge upon the subject, because I am inclined to believe, that what is called the present ministry, wish to see contentions about religion kept up, to prevent the nation turning its attention to subjects of government. It is, as if they were to say, "*Look that way, or any way, but this.*"

---

*I know it is the opinion of many of the most enlightened characters in France (there always will be those who see further into events than others,) not only among the general mass of citizens, but of many of the principal members of the former National Assembly, that the monarchical plan will not continue many years in that country. They have found out, that as wisdom cannot be made hereditary, power ought not; and that, for a man to merit a million sterling a year from a nation, he ought to have a mind capable of comprehending from an atom to a universe, which, if he had, he would be above receiving the pay. But they wished not to appear to lead the nation faster than its own reason and interest dictated. In all the conversations where I have been present upon this subject, the idea always was, that when such a time, from the general opinion of the nation, shall arrive, that the honourable and liberal method would be, to make a handsome present in fee simple to the person, whoever he may be, that shall then be in the monarchical office, and for him to retire to the enjoyment of private life, possessing his share of general rights and privileges, and to be no more accountable to the public for his time and his conduct than any other citizen [Author's note].

†Plundering like that of the pirates of Algeria.

But as religion is very improperly made a political machine, and the reality of it is thereby destroyed, I will conclude this work with stating in what light religion appears to me.

If we suppose a large family of children, who, on any particular day, or particular circumstance, made it a custom to present to their parents some token of their affection and gratitude, each of them would make a different offering, and most probably in a different manner. Some would pay their congratulations in themes of verse and prose, by some little devices, as their genius dictated, or according to what they thought would please; and, perhaps, the least of all, not able to do any of those things, would ramble into the garden, or the field, and gather what it thought the prettiest flower it could find, though, perhaps, it might be but a simple weed. The parent would be more gratified by such a variety, than if the whole of them had acted on a concerted plan, and each had made exactly the same offering. This would have the cold appearance of contrivance, or the harsh one of controul. But of all unwelcome things, nothing could more afflict the parent than to know, that the whole of them had afterwards gotten together by the ears, boys and girls, fighting, scratching, reviling, and abusing each other about which was the best or the worst present.

Why may we not suppose, that the great Father of all is pleased with variety of devotion; and that the greatest offence we can act, is that by which we seek to torment and render each other miserable? For my own part, I am fully satisfied that what I am now doing, with an endeavour to conciliate mankind, to render their condition happy, to unite nations that have hitherto been enemies, and to extirpate the horrid practice of war, and break the chains of slavery and oppression is acceptable in his sight, and being the best service I can perform, I act it chearfully.

I do not believe that any two men, on what are called doctrinal points, think alike who think at all. It is only those who have not thought that appear to agree. It is in this case as with what is called the British constitution. It has been taken for granted to be good, and encomiums have supplied the place of proof. But when the nation comes to examine into its principles and the abuses it admits, it will be found to have more defects than I have pointed out in this work and the former.

As to what are called national religions, we may, with as much propriety, talk of national Gods. It is either political craft or the remains of the Pagan system, when every nation had its separate and particular deity. Among all the writers of the English church clergy, who have treated on the general subject of religion, the present Bishop of Landaff* has not been excelled, and it is with much pleasure that I take this opportunity of expressing this token of respect.

I have now gone through the whole of the subject, at least, as far as it appears to me at present. It has been my intention for the five years I have been in Europe, to offer an address to the people of England on the subject of government, if the opportunity presented itself before I returned to America. Mr. Burke has thrown it in my way, and I thank him. On a certain occasion, three years ago, I pressed him to propose a national convention, to be fairly elected, for the purpose of taking the state of the nation into consideration; but I found, that however strongly the parliamentary current was then setting against the party he acted with, their policy was to keep every thing within that field of corruption, and trust to accidents. Long experience had shewn that parliaments would follow any change of ministers, and on this they rested their hopes and their expectations.

Formerly, when divisions arose respecting governments, recourse was had to the sword, and a civil war ensued. That savage custom is exploded by the new system, and reference is had to national conventions. Discussion and the general will arbitrates the question, and to this, private opinion yields with a good grace, and order is preserved uninterrupted.

Some gentlemen have affected to call the principles upon which this work and the former part of *Rights of Man* are founded, "a newfangled doctrine." The question is not whether those principles are new or old, but whether they are right or wrong. Suppose the former, I will shew their effect by a figure easily understood.

It is now towards the middle of February. Were I to take a turn into the country, the trees would present a leafless, wintery appearance. As people are apt to pluck twigs as they walk along, I perhaps

---

*Richard Watson (1737–1816), who wrote a famous answer to Paine's *Age of Reason* in 1796.

might do the same, and by chance might observe, that a *single bud* on that twig had begun to swell. I should reason very unnaturally, or rather not reason at all, to suppose this was the *only* bud in England which had this appearance. Instead of deciding thus, I should instantly conclude, that the same appearance was beginning, or about to begin, every where; and though the vegetable sleep will continue longer on some trees and plants than on others, and though some of them may not *blossom* for two or three years, all will be in leaf in the summer, except those which are *rotten*. What pace the political summer may keep with the natural, no human foresight can determine. It is, however, not difficult to perceive that the spring is begun.— Thus wishing, as I sincerely do, freedom and happiness to all nations, I close the SECOND PART.

THE AGE OF REASON

(selections)

Part I
Part II

[1794]

THE AGE OF REASON.
PART I.

CHAPTER I.

The Author's Profession of Faith.

IT HAS BEEN MY intention, for several years past, to publish my thoughts upon religion; I am well aware of the difficulties that attend the subject, and from that consideration, had reserved it to a more advanced period of life. I intended it to be the last offering I should make to my fellow-citizens of all nations, and that at a time when the purity of the motive that induced me to it could not admit of a question, even by those who might disapprove the work.

The circumstance that has now taken place in France, of the total abolition of the whole national order of priesthood, and of everything appertaining to compulsive systems of religion, and compulsive articles of faith, has not only precipitated my intention, but rendered a work of this kind exceedingly necessary, lest, in the general wreck of superstition, of false systems of government, and false theology, we lose sight of morality, of humanity, and of the theology that is true.

As several of my colleagues, and others of my fellow-citizens of France, have given me the example of making their voluntary and individual profession of faith, I also will make mine; and I do this with all that sincerity and frankness with which the mind of man communicates with itself.

I believe in one God, and no more; and I hope for happiness beyond this life.

I believe the equality of man, and I believe that religious duties consist in doing justice, loving mercy, and endeavouring to make our fellow-creatures happy.

But, lest it should be supposed that I believe many other things in addition to these, I shall, in the progress of this work, declare the things I do not believe, and my reasons for not believing them.

I do not believe in the creed professed by the Jewish church, by the Roman church, by the Greek church, by the Turkish church, by the Protestant church, nor by any church that I know of. My own mind is my own church.

All national institutions of churches, whether Jewish, Christian, or Turkish, appear to me no other than human inventions set up to terrify and enslave mankind, and monopolize power and profit.

I do not mean by this declaration to condemn those who believe otherwise; they have the same right to their belief as I have to mine. But it is necessary to the happiness of man, that he be mentally faithful to himself. Infidelity does not consist in believing, or in disbelieving; it consists in professing to believe what he does not believe.

It is impossible to calculate the moral mischief, if I may so express it, that mental lying has produced in society. When a man has so far corrupted and prostituted the chastity of his mind, as to subscribe his professional belief to things he does not believe, he has prepared himself for the commission of every other crime. He takes up the trade of a priest for the sake of gain, and, in order to qualify himself for that trade, he begins with a perjury. Can we conceive anything more destructive to morality than this?

Soon after I had published the pamphlet COMMON SENSE, in America, I saw the exceeding probability that a revolution in the system of government would be followed by a revolution in the system of religion. The adulterous connection of church and state, wherever it had taken place, whether Jewish, Christian, or Turkish, had so effectually prohibited, by pains and penalties, every discussion upon established creeds, and upon first principles of religion, that until the system of government should be changed, those subjects could not be brought fairly and openly before the world; but that whenever this should be done, a revolution in the system of religion would follow. Human inventions and priest-craft would be detected; and man would return to the pure, unmixed, and unadulterated belief of one God, and no more.

CHAPTER II.

Of Missions and Revelations.

EVERY NATIONAL CHURCH OR religion has established itself by pretending some special mission from God, communicated to certain individuals. The Jews have their Moses; the Christians their Jesus Christ, their apostles and saints; and the Turks their Mahomet; as if the way to God was not open to every man alike.

Each of those churches shows certain books, which they call *revelation*, or the Word of God. The Jews say that their Word of God was given by God to Moses face to face; the Christians say, that their Word of God came by divine inspiration; and the Turks say, that their Word of God (the Koran) was brought by an angel from heaven. Each of those churches accuses the other of unbelief; and, for my own part, I disbelieve them all.

As it is necessary to affix right ideas to words, I will, before I proceed further into the subject, offer some observations on the word *revelation*. Revelation when applied to religion, means something communicated *immediately* from God to man.

No one will deny or dispute the power of the Almighty to make such a communication if he pleases. But admitting, for the sake of a case, that something has been revealed to a certain person, and not revealed to any other person, it is revelation to that person only. When he tells it to a second person, a second to a third, a third to a fourth, and so on, it ceases to be a revelation to all those persons. It is revelation to the first person only, and *hearsay* to every other, and, consequently, they are not obliged to believe it.

It is a contradiction in terms and ideas to call anything a revelation that comes to us at second hand, either verbally or in writing. Revelation is necessarily limited to the first communication. After this, it is only an account of something which that person says was a revelation made to him; and though he may find himself obliged to believe it, it cannot be incumbent on me to believe it in the same manner, for it was not a revelation made to *me*, and I have only his word for it that it was made to *him*.

When Moses told the children of Israel that he received the two tables of the commandments from the hand of God, they were not obliged to believe him, because they had no other authority for it than his telling them so; and I have no other authority for it than some historian telling me so, the commandments carrying no internal evidence of divinity with them. They contain some good moral precepts such as any man qualified to be a lawgiver or a legislator could produce himself, without having recourse to supernatural intervention.*

When I am told that the Koran was written in Heaven, and brought to Mahomet by an angel, the account comes to near the same kind of hearsay evidence and second hand authority as the former. I did not see the angel myself, and therefore I have a right not to believe it.

When also I am told that a woman, called the Virgin Mary, said, or gave out, that she was with child without any cohabitation with a man, and that her betrothed husband, Joseph, said that an angel told him so, I have a right to believe them or not: such a circumstance required a much stronger evidence than their bare word for it: but we have not even this; for neither Joseph nor Mary wrote any such matter themselves. It is only reported by others that *they said so*. It is hearsay upon hearsay, and I do not chuse to rest my belief upon such evidence.

It is, however, not difficult to account for the credit that was given to the story of Jesus Christ being the Son of God. He was born when the heathen mythology had still some fashion and repute in the world, and that mythology had prepared the people for the belief of such a story. Almost all the extraordinary men that lived under the heathen mythology were reputed to be the sons of some of their gods. It was not a new thing at that time to believe a man to have been celestially begotten; the intercourse of gods with women was then a

---

*It is, however, necessary to except the declaration which says that God *visits the sins of the fathers upon the children*. This is contrary to every principle of moral justice [Author's note].

matter of familiar opinion. Their Jupiter, according to their accounts, had cohabited with hundreds; the story therefore had nothing in it either new, wonderful, or obscene; it was conformable to the opinions that then prevailed among the people called Gentiles, or mythologists, and it was those people only that believed it. The Jews, who had kept strictly to the belief of one God, and no more, and who had always rejected the heathen mythology, never credited the story.

It is curious to observe how the theory of what is called the Christian Church, sprung out of the tail of the heathen mythology. A direct incorporation took place in the first instance, by making the reputed founder to be celestially begotten. The trinity of gods that then followed was no other than a reduction of the former plurality, which was about twenty or thirty thousand. The statue of Mary succeeded the statue of Diana of Ephesus.* The deification of heroes changed into the canonization of saints. The Mythologists had gods for everything; the Christian Mythologists had saints for everything. The church became as crouded with the one, as the pantheon had been with the other; and Rome was the place of both. The Christian theory is little else than the idolatry of the ancient mythologists, accommodated to the purposes of power and revenue; and it yet remains to reason and philosophy to abolish the amphibious fraud.

CHAPTER III.

Concerning the Character of Jesus Christ, and His History.

NOTHING THAT IS HERE said can apply, even with the most distant disrespect, to the *real* character of Jesus Christ. He was a virtuous and an amiable man. The morality that he preached and practised was of the most benevolent kind; and though similar systems of morality had been preached by Confucius, and by some of the Greek philosophers, many years before, by the Quakers since, and by many good men in all ages, it has not been exceeded by any.

---

*Statue of a multi-breasted virgin goddess adorning a lavish temple in Turkey that subsequently was rededicated to the Virgin Mary.

Jesus Christ wrote no account of himself, of his birth, parentage, or anything else. Not a line of what is called the New Testament is of his writing. The history of him is altogether the work of other people; and as to the account given of his resurrection and ascension, it was the necessary counterpart to the story of his birth. His historians, having brought him into the world in a supernatural manner, were obliged to take him out again in the same manner, or the first part of the story must have fallen to the ground.

The wretched contrivance with which this latter part is told, exceeds everything that went before it. The first part, that of the miraculous conception, was not a thing that admitted of publicity; and therefore the tellers of this part of the story had this advantage, that though they might not be credited, they could not be detected. They could not be expected to prove it, because it was not one of those things that admitted of proof, and it was impossible that the person of whom it was told could prove it himself.

But the resurrection of a dead person from the grave, and his ascension through the air, is a thing very different, as to the evidence it admits of, to the invisible conception of a child in the womb. The resurrection and ascension, supposing them to have taken place, admitted of public and ocular demonstration, like that of the ascension of a balloon, or the sun at noon day, to all Jerusalem at least. A thing which everybody is required to believe, requires that the proof and evidence of it should be equal to all, and universal; and as the public visibility of this last related act was the only evidence that could give sanction to the former part, the whole of it falls to the ground, because that evidence never was given. Instead of this, a small number of persons, not more than eight or nine, are introduced as proxies for the whole world, to say they saw it, and all the rest of the world are called upon to believe it. But it appears that Thomas did not believe the resurrection; and, as they say, would not believe without having ocular and manual demonstration himself. *So neither will I;* and the reason is as good for me, and for every other person, as for Thomas.*

It is in vain to attempt to palliate or disguise this matter. The

---

*One of the twelve apostles; called "Doubting Thomas" because he doubted Jesus' resurrection; see the Bible, John 20:24–29.

story, so far as relates to the supernatural part, has every mark of fraud and imposition stamped upon the face of it. Who were the authors of it is as impossible for us now to know, as it is for us to be assured that the books in which the account is related were written by the persons whose names they bear. The best surviving evidence we now have respecting this affair is the Jews. They are regularly descended from the people who lived in the time this resurrection and ascension is said to have happened, and they say, *it is not true*. It has long appeared to me a strange inconsistency to cite the Jews as a proof of the truth of the story. It is just the same as if a man were to say, I will prove the truth of what I have told you, by producing the people who say it is false.

That such a person as Jesus Christ existed, and that he was crucified, which was the mode of execution at that day, are historical relations strictly within the limits of probability. He preached most excellent morality, and the equality of man; but he preached also against the corruptions and avarice of the Jewish priests, and this brought upon him the hatred and vengeance of the whole order of priesthood. The accusation which those priests brought against him was that of sedition and conspiracy against the Roman government, to which the Jews were then subject and tributary; and it is not improbable that the Roman government might have some secret apprehension of the effects of his doctrine as well as the Jewish priests; neither is it improbable that Jesus Christ had in contemplation the delivery of the Jewish nation from the bondage of the Romans. Between the two, however, this virtuous reformer and revolutionist lost his life.

CHAPTER IV.

Of the Bases of Christianity.

IT IS UPON THIS plain narrative of facts, together with another case I am going to mention, that the Christian mythologists, calling themselves the Christian Church, have erected their fable, which for absurdity and extravagance is not exceeded by anything that is to be found in the mythology of the ancients.

The ancient mythologists tell us that the race of Giants made war against Jupiter, and that one of them threw a hundred rocks against him at one throw; that Jupiter defeated him with thunder, and confined him afterwards under Mount Etna; and that every time the Giant turns himself, Mount Etna belches fire. It is here easy to see that the circumstance of the mountain, that of its being a volcano, suggested the idea of the fable; and that the fable is made to fit and wind itself up with that circumstance.

The Christian mythologists tell that their Satan made war against the Almighty, who defeated him, and confined him afterwards, not under a mountain, but in a pit. It is here easy to see that the first fable suggested the idea of the second; for the fable of Jupiter and the Giants was told many hundred years before that of Satan.

Thus far the ancient and the Christian mythologists differ very little from each other. But the latter have contrived to carry the matter much farther. They have contrived to connect the fabulous part of the story of Jesus Christ with the fable originating from Mount Etna; and, in order to make all the parts of the story tye together, they have taken to their aid the traditions of the Jews; for the Christian mythology is made up partly from the ancient mythology, and partly from the Jewish traditions.

The Christian mythologists, after having confined Satan in a pit, were obliged to let him out again to bring on the sequel of the fable. He is then introduced into the garden of Eden in the shape of a snake, or a serpent, and in that shape he enters into familiar conversation with Eve, who is no ways surprised to hear a snake talk; and the issue of this tête-à-tête is, that he persuades her to eat an apple, and the eating of that apple damns all mankind.

After giving Satan this triumph over the whole creation, one would have supposed that the church mythologists would have been kind enough to send him back again to the pit, or, if they had not done this, that they would have put a mountain upon him, (for they say that their faith can remove a mountain) or have put him under a mountain, as the former mythologists had done, to prevent his getting again among the women, and doing more mischief. But instead of this, they leave him at large, without even obliging him to give his parole. The secret of which is, that they could not do without him; and after being at the trouble of making him, they bribed him to stay. They promised him ALL the Jews, ALL the Turks by anticipation, nine-tenths of the world beside, and Mahomet into the bargain. After this, who can doubt the bountifulness of the Christian Mythology?

Having thus made an insurrection and a battle in heaven, in which none of the combatants could be either killed or wounded—put Satan into the pit—let him out again—given him a triumph over the whole creation—damned all mankind by the eating of an apple, these Christian mythologists bring the two ends of their fable together. They represent this virtuous and amiable man, Jesus Christ, to be at once both God and man, and also the Son of God, celestially begotten, on purpose to be sacrificed, because they say that Eve in her longing had eaten an apple.

CHAPTER V.

Examination in Detail of the Preceding Bases.

PUTTING ASIDE EVERYTHING THAT might excite laughter by its absurdity, or detestation by its prophaness, and confining ourselves merely to an examination of the parts, it is impossible to conceive a story more derogatory to the Almighty, more inconsistent with his wisdom, more contradictory to his power, than this story is.

In order to make for it a foundation to rise upon, the inventors were under the necessity of giving to the being whom they call Satan a power equally as great, if not greater, than they attribute to the Almighty. They have not only given him the power of liberating himself from the pit, after what they call his fall, but they have made that power increase afterwards to infinity. Before this fall they represent him only as an angel of limited existence, as they represent the rest. After his fall, he becomes, by their account, omnipresent. He exists everywhere, and at the same time. He occupies the whole immensity of space.

Not content with this deification of Satan, they represent him as defeating by stratagem, in the shape of an animal of the creation, all the power and wisdom of the Almighty. They represent him as having compelled the Almighty to the *direct necessity* either of surrendering the whole of the creation to the government and sovereignty of this Satan, or of capitulating for its redemption by coming down upon earth, and exhibiting himself upon a cross in the shape of a man.

Had the inventors of this story told it the contrary way, that is, had they represented the Almighty as compelling Satan to exhibit *himself* on a cross in the shape of a snake, as a punishment for his new transgression, the story would have been less absurd, less contradictory. But, instead of this they make the transgressor triumph, and the Almighty fall.

That many good men have believed this strange fable, and lived very good lives under that belief (for credulity is not a crime) is what I have no doubt of. In the first place, they were educated to believe it, and they would have believed anything else in the same manner. There are also many who have been so enthusiastically enraptured by what they conceived to be the infinite love of God to man, in making a sacrifice of himself, that the vehemence of the idea has forbidden and deterred them from examining into the absurdity and profaneness of the story. The more unnatural anything is, the more is it capable of becoming the object of dismal admiration.

CHAPTER VI.

Of the True Theology.

BUT IF OBJECTS FOR gratitude and admiration are our desire, do they not present themselves every hour to our eyes? Do we not see a fair creation prepared to receive us the instant we are born—a world furnished to our hands, that cost us nothing? Is it we that light up the sun; that pour down the rain; and fill the earth with abundance? Whether we sleep or wake, the vast machinery of the universe still goes on. Are these things, and the blessings they indicate in future, nothing to us? Can our gross feelings be excited by no other subjects than tragedy and suicide? Or is the gloomy pride of man become so intolerable, that nothing can flatter it but a sacrifice of the Creator?

I know that this bold investigation will alarm many, but it would be paying too great a compliment to their credulity to forbear it on that account. The times and the subject demand it to be done. The suspicion that the theory of what is called the Christian church is fabulous, is becoming very extensive in all countries; and it will be a consolation to men staggering under that suspicion, and doubting what to believe and what to disbelieve, to see the subject freely investigated. I therefore pass on to an examination of the books called the Old and the New Testament.

CHAPTER VII.

Examination of the Old Testament.

THESE BOOKS, BEGINNING WITH Genesis and ending with Revelations, (which, by the bye, is a book of riddles that requires a revelation to explain it) are, we are told, the word of God. It is, therefore, proper for us to know who told us so, that we may know what credit to give to the report. The answer to this question is, that nobody can tell, except that we tell one another so. The case, however, historically appears to be as follows:

When the church mythologists established their system, they collected all the writings they could find, and managed them as they pleased. It is a matter altogether of uncertainty to us whether such of the writings as now appear under the name of the Old and the New Testament, are in the same state in which those collectors say they found them; or whether they added, altered, abridged, or dressed them up.

Be this as it may, they decided by *vote* which of the books out of the collection they had made, should be the WORD OF GOD, and which should not. They rejected several; they voted others to be doubtful, such as the books called the Apocrypha;* and those books which had a majority of votes, were voted to be the word of God.

---

*Greek for "hidden"; books included in the Greek Septuagint and Latin Vulgate versions of the Bible, but not in many other versions.

Had they voted otherwise, all the people since calling themselves Christians had believed otherwise; for the belief of the one comes from the vote of the other. Who the people were that did all this, we know nothing of. They call themselves by the general name of the Church; and this is all we know of the matter.

As we have no other external evidence or authority for believing these books to be the word of God, than what I have mentioned, which is no evidence or authority at all, I come, in the next place, to examine the internal evidence contained in the books themselves.

In the former part of this essay, I have spoken of revelation. I now proceed further with that subject, for the purpose of applying it to the books in question.

Revelation is a communication of something, which the person, to whom that thing is revealed, did not know before. For if I have done a thing, or seen it done, it needs no revelation to tell me I have done it, or seen it, nor to enable me to tell it, or to write it.

Revelation, therefore, cannot be applied to anything done upon earth of which man is himself the actor or the witness; and consequently all the historical and anecdotal part of the Bible, which is almost the whole of it, is not within the meaning and compass of the word revelation, and, therefore, is not the word of God.

When Samson* ran off with the gate-posts of Gaza, if he ever did so, (and whether he did or not is nothing to us,) or when he visited his Delilah, or caught his foxes, or did anything else, what has revelation to do with these things? If they were facts, he could tell them himself; or his secretary, if he kept one, could write them, if they were worth either telling or writing; and if they were fictions, revelation could not make them true; and whether true or not, we are neither the better nor the wiser for knowing them.—When we contemplate the immensity of that Being, who directs and governs the incomprehensible WHOLE, of which the utmost ken of human sight can discover but a part, we ought to feel shame at calling such paltry stories the word of God.

As to the account of the creation, with which the book of Genesis opens, it has all the appearance of being a tradition which the Is-

---

*Biblical Israelite of great strength whose feats are recorded in the Bible; see Judges 13–16.

raelites had among them before they came into Egypt; and after their departure from that country, they put it at the head of their history, without telling, as it is most probable that they did not know, how they came by it. The manner in which the account opens, shews it to be traditionary. It begins abruptly. It is nobody that speaks. It is nobody that hears. It is addressed to nobody. It has neither first, second, nor third person. It has every criterion of being a tradition. It has no voucher. Moses does not take it upon himself by introducing it with the formality that he uses on other occasions, such as that of saying, "*The Lord spake unto Moses, saying.*"

Why it has been called the Mosaic account of the creation, I am at a loss to conceive. Moses, I believe, was too good a judge of such subjects to put his name to that account. He had been educated among the Egyptians, who were a people as well skilled in science, and particularly in astronomy, as any people of their day; and the silence and caution that Moses observes, in not authenticating the account, is a good negative evidence that he neither told it nor believed it.—The case is, that every nation of people has been world-makers, and the Israelites had as much right to set up the trade of world-making as any of the rest; and as Moses was not an Israelite, he might not chuse to contradict the tradition. The account, however, is harmless; and this is more than can be said for many other parts of the Bible.

Whenever we read the obscene stories, the voluptuous debaucheries, the cruel and torturous executions, the unrelenting vindictiveness, with which more than half the Bible is filled, it would be more consistent that we called it the word of a demon, than the Word of God. It is a history of wickedness, that has served to corrupt and brutalize mankind; and, for my own part, I sincerely detest it, as I detest everything that is cruel.

We scarcely meet with anything, a few phrases excepted, but what deserves either our abhorrence or our contempt, till we come to the miscellaneous parts of the Bible. In the anonymous publications, the Psalms, and the Book of Job, more particularly in the latter, we find a great deal of elevated sentiment reverentially expressed of the power and benignity of the Almighty; but they stand on no higher rank than many other compositions on similar subjects, as well before that time as since.

The Proverbs which are said to be Solomon's,* though most probably a collection, (because they discover a knowledge of life, which his situation excluded him from knowing) are an instructive table of ethics. They are inferior in keenness to the proverbs of the Spaniards, and not more wise and œconomical than those of the American Franklin.†

All the remaining parts of the Bible, generally known by the name of the Prophets, are the works of the Jewish poets and itinerant preachers, who mixed poetry, anecdote, and devotion together— and those works still retain the air and stile of poetry, though in translation.‡

There is not, throughout the whole book called the Bible, any word that describes to us what we call a poet, nor any word that de-

---

*Biblical king of Israel.
†Benjamin Franklin (1706–1790), publisher of *Poor Richard's Almanack* (1732–1757).
‡As there are many readers who do not see that a composition is poetry, unless it be in rhyme, it is for their information that I add this note.

Poetry consists principally in two things—imagery and composition. The composition of poetry differs from that of prose in the manner of mixing long and short syllables together. Take a long syllable out of a line of poetry and put a short one in the room of it, or put a long syllable where a short one should be, and that line will lose its poetical harmony. It will have an effect upon the line like that of misplacing a note in a song.

The imagery in those books called the Prophets appertains altogether to poetry. It is fictitious, and often extravagant, and not admissible in any other kind of writing than poetry.

To shew that these writings are composed in poetical numbers, I will take ten syllables, as they stand in the book, and make a line of the same number of syllables, (heroic measure) that shall rhyme with the last word. It will then be seen that the composition of those books is poetical measure. The instance I shall first produce is from Isaiah:—

> *"Hear, O ye heavens, and give ear, O earth!"*
> 'T is God himself that calls attention forth.

Another instance I shall quote is from the mournful Jeremiah, to which I shall add two other lines, for the purpose of carrying out the figure, and shewing the intention of the poet.

> *"O, that mine head were waters and mine eyes"*
> Were fountains flowing like the liquid skies;
> Then would I give the mighty flood release
> And weep a deluge for the human race [Author's note].

scribes what we call poetry. The case is, that the word *prophet*, to which later times have affixed a new idea, was the Bible word for poet, and the word *prophesying* meant the art of making poetry. It also meant the art of playing poetry to a tune upon any instrument of music.

We read of prophesying with pipes, tabrets, and horns—of prophesying with harps, with psalteries, with cymbals, and with every other instrument of music then in fashion. Were we now to speak of prophesying with a fiddle, or with a pipe and tabor, the expression would have no meaning, or would appear ridiculous, and to some people contemptuous, because we have changed the meaning of the word.

We are told of Saul* being among the prophets, and also that he prophesied; but we are not told what they prophesied, nor what he prophesied. The case is, there was nothing to tell; for these prophets were a company of musicians and poets, and Saul joined in the concert, and this was called prophesying.

The account given of this affair in the book called Samuel, is, that Saul met a company of prophets; a whole company of them! coming down with a psaltery, a tabret, a pipe, and a harp, and that they prophesied, and that he prophesied with them. But it appears afterwards, that Saul prophesied badly, that is, he performed his part badly; for it is said that an "*evil spirit from God*† came upon Saul, and he prophesied."

Now, were there no other passage in the book called the Bible, than this, to demonstrate to us that we have lost the original meaning of the word *prophesy*, and substituted another meaning in its place, this alone would be sufficient; for it is impossible to use and apply the word *prophesy*, in the place it is here used and applied, if we give to it the sense which later times have affixed to it. The manner in which it is here used strips it of all religious meaning, and shews that a man might then be a prophet, or he might *prophesy*, as

---

*Biblical king of Israel.

†As those men who call themselves divines and commentators are very fond of puzzling one another, I leave them to contest the meaning of the first part of the phrase, that of *an evil spirit of God*. I keep to my text. I keep to the meaning of the word prophesy [Author's note].

he may now be a poet or a musician, without any regard to the morality or the immorality of his character. The word was originally a term of science, promiscuously applied to poetry and to music, and not restricted to any subject upon which poetry and music might be exercised.

Deborah and Barak* are called prophets, not because they predicted anything, but because they composed the poem or song that bears their name, in celebration of an act already done. David† is ranked among the prophets, for he was a musician, and was also reputed to be (though perhaps very erroneously) the author of the Psalms. But Abraham, Isaac, and Jacob‡ are not called prophets; it does not appear from any accounts we have, that they could either sing, play music, or make poetry.

We are told of the greater and the lesser prophets. They might as well tell us of the greater and the lesser God; for there cannot be degrees in prophesying consistently with its modern sense. But there are degrees in poetry, and therefore the phrase is reconcilable to the case, when we understand by it the greater and the lesser poets.

It is altogether unnecessary, after this, to offer any observations upon what those men, stiled prophets, have written. The axe goes at once to the root, by shewing that the original meaning of the word has been mistaken, and consequently all the inferences that have been drawn from those books, the devotional respect that has been paid to them, and the laboured commentaries that have been written upon them, under that mistaken meaning, are not worth disputing about.—In many things, however, the writings of the Jewish poets deserve a better fate than that of being bound up, as they now are, with the trash that accompanies them, under the abused name of the Word of God.

If we permit ourselves to conceive right ideas of things, we must necessarily affix the idea, not only of unchangeableness, but of the utter impossibility of any change taking place, by any means or ac-

---

*Deborah was a Hebrew judge; Barak, a warrior, was her most important ally in combating the Canaanites; see the Bible, Judges 4–5.
†Biblical king of Israel, reputed author of the Psalms.
‡Abraham was the first patriarch of the Hebrew people; Isaac was his son and Jacob his grandson.

cident whatever, in that which we would honour with the name of the Word of God; and therefore the Word of God cannot exist in any written or human language.

The continually progressive change to which the meaning of words is subject, the want of an universal language which renders translation necessary, the errors to which translations are again subject, the mistakes of copyists and printers, together with the possibility of wilful alteration, are of themselves evidences that human language, whether in speech or in print, cannot be the vehicle of the Word of God.—The Word of God exists in something else.

Did the book called the Bible excel in purity of ideas and expression all the books now extant in the world, I would not take it for my rule of faith, as being the Word of God; because the possibility would nevertheless exist of my being imposed upon. But when I see throughout the greatest part of this book scarcely anything but a history of the grossest vices, and a collection of the most paltry and contemptible tales, I cannot dishonour my Creator by calling it by his name.

CHAPTER VIII.

Of the New Testament.

THUS MUCH FOR THE Bible; I now go on to the book called the New Testament. The *new* Testament! that is, the *new* Will, as if there could be two wills of the Creator.

Had it been the object or the intention of Jesus Christ to establish a new religion, he would undoubtedly have written the system himself, or *procured it to be written* in his life time. But there is no publication extant authenticated with his name. All the books called the New Testament were written after his death. He was a Jew by birth and by profession; and he was the son of God in like manner that every other person is; for the Creator is the Father of All.

The first four books, called Matthew, Mark, Luke, and John, do not give a history of the life of Jesus Christ, but only detached anecdotes of him. It appears from these books, that the whole time of his being a preacher was not more than eighteen months; and it was only during this short time that those men became acquainted with him. They make mention of him at the age of twelve years, sitting, they say, among the Jewish doctors, asking and answering them questions. As this was several years before their acquaintance with him began, it is most probable they had this anecdote from his parents. From this time there is no account of him for about sixteen years. Where he lived, or how he employed himself during this interval, is not known. Most probably he was working at his father's trade, which was that of a carpenter. It does not appear that he had any school education, and the probability is, that he could not write, for his parents were extremely poor, as appears from their not being able to pay for a bed when he was born.

It is somewhat curious that the three persons whose names are the most universally recorded were of very obscure parentage. Moses was a foundling; Jesus Christ was born in a stable; and Mahomet was a mule driver. The first and the last of these men were founders of different systems of religion; but Jesus Christ founded no new system. He called men to the practice of moral virtues, and the belief of one God. The great trait in his character is philanthropy.

The manner in which he was apprehended shews that he was not much known at that time; and it shews also that the meetings he then held with his followers were in secret; and that he had given over or suspended preaching publicly. Judas* could no otherways betray him than by giving information where he was, and pointing him out to the officers that went to arrest him; and the reason for employing and paying Judas to do this could arise only from the causes already mentioned, that of his not being much known, and living concealed.

The idea of his concealment, not only agrees very ill with his reputed divinity, but associates with it something of pusillanimity; and his being betrayed, or in other words, his being apprehended, on the information of one of his followers, shews that he did not intend to be apprehended, and consequently that he did not intend to be crucified.

The Christian mythologists tell us that Christ died for the sins of the world, and that he came on *purpose to die*. Would it not then

---

*Judas Iscariot, one of the twelve apostles; after betraying Jesus, he hanged himself.

have been the same if he had died of a fever or of the small pox, of old age, or of anything else?

The declaratory sentence which, they say, was passed upon Adam, in case he ate of the apple, was not, that *thou shalt surely be crucified*, but, *thou shalt surely die*. The sentence was death, and not the manner of dying. Crucifixion, therefore, or any other particular manner of dying, made no part of the sentence that Adam was to suffer, and consequently, even upon their own tactic, it could make no part of the sentence that Christ was to suffer in the room of Adam. A fever would have done as well as a cross, if there was any occasion for either.

This sentence of death, which, they tell us, was thus passed upon Adam, must either have meant dying naturally, that is, ceasing to live, or have meant what these mythologists call damnation; and consequently, the act of dying on the part of Jesus Christ, must, according to their system, apply as a prevention to one or other of these two *things* happening to Adam and to us.

That it does not prevent our dying is evident, because we all die; and if their accounts of longevity be true, men die faster since the crucifixion than before: and with respect to the second explanation, (including with it the *natural death* of Jesus Christ as a substitute for the *eternal death or damnation* of all mankind,) it is impertinently representing the Creator as coming off, or revoking the sentence, by a pun or a quibble upon the word *death*. That manufacturer of quibbles, St. Paul,* if he wrote the books that bear his name, has helped this quibble on by making another quibble upon the word *Adam*. He makes there to be two Adams; the one who sins in fact, and suffers by proxy; the other who sins by proxy, and suffers in fact. A religion thus interlarded with quibble, subterfuge, and pun, has a tendency to instruct its professors in the practice of these arts. They acquire the habit without being aware of the cause.

If Jesus Christ was the being which those mythologists tell us he was, and that he came into this world to *suffer*, which is a word they sometimes use instead of *to die*, the only real suffering he could have endured would have been *to live*. His existence here was a state of

---

*Paul (originally Saul) of Tarsus, early Christian leader.

exilement or transportation from heaven, and the way back to his original country was to die.—In fine, everything in this strange system is the reverse of what it pretends to be. It is the reverse of truth, and I become so tired of examining into its inconsistencies and absurdities, that I hasten to the conclusion of it, in order to proceed to something better.

How much, or what parts of the books called the New Testament, were written by the persons whose names they bear, is what we can know nothing of, neither are we certain in what language they were originally written. The matters they now contain may be classed under two heads: anecdote, and epistolary correspondence.

The four books already mentioned, Matthew, Mark, Luke, and John, are altogether anecdotal. They relate events after they had taken place. They tell what Jesus Christ did and said, and what others did and said to him; and in several instances they relate the same event differently. Revelation is necessarily out of the question with respect to those books; not only because of the disagreement of the writers, but because revelation cannot be applied to the relating of facts by the persons who saw them done, nor to the relating or recording of any discourse or conversation by those who heard it. The book called the Acts of the Apostles (an anonymous work) belongs also to the anecdotal part.

All the other parts of the New Testament, except the book of enigmas, called the Revelations, are a collection of letters under the name of epistles; and the forgery of letters has been such a common practice in the world, that the probability is at least equal, whether they are genuine or forged. One thing, however, is much less equivocal, which is, that out of the matters contained in those books, together with the assistance of some old stories, the church has set up a system of religion very contradictory to the character of the person whose name it bears. It has set up a religion of pomp and of revenue in pretended imitation of a person whose life was humility and poverty.

The invention of a purgatory, and of the releasing of souls therefrom, by prayers, bought of the church with money; the selling of pardons, dispensations, and indulgences, are revenue laws, without bearing that name or carrying that appearance. But the case nevertheless is, that those things derive their origin from the proxysm of the crucifixion, and the theory deduced therefrom, which was, that one person could stand in the place of another, and could perform meritorious services for him. The probability, therefore, is, that the whole theory or doctrine of what is called the redemption (which is said to have been accomplished by the act of one person in the room of another) was originally fabricated on purpose to bring forward and build all those secondary and pecuniary redemptions upon; and that the passages in the books upon which the idea of theory of redemption is built, have been manufactured and fabricated for that purpose. Why are we to give this church credit, when she tells us that those books are genuine in every part, any more than we give her credit for everything else she has told us; or for the miracles she says she has performed? That she *could* fabricate writings is certain, because she could write; and the composition of the writings in question, is of that kind that anybody might do it; and that she *did* fabricate them is not more inconsistent with probability, than that she should tell us, as she has done, that she could and did work miracles.

Since, then, no external evidence can, at this long distance of time, be produced to prove whether the church fabricated the doctrine called redemption or not, (for such evidence, whether for or against, would be subject to the same suspicion of being fabricated,) the case can only be referred to the internal evidence which the thing carries of itself; and this affords a very strong presumption of its being a fabrication. For the internal evidence is, that the theory or doctrine of redemption has for its basis an idea of pecuniary justice, and not that of moral justice.

If I owe a person money, and cannot pay him, and he threatens to put me in prison, another person can take the debt upon himself, and pay it for me. But if I have committed a crime, every circumstance of the case is changed. Moral justice cannot take the innocent for the guilty even if the innocent would offer itself. To suppose justice to do this, is to destroy the principle of its existence, which is the thing itself. It is then no longer justice. It is indiscriminate revenge.

This single reflection will shew that the doctrine of redemption is founded on a mere pecuniary idea corresponding to that of a debt which another person might pay; and as this pecuniary idea corresponds again with the system of second redemptions, obtained through the means of money given to the church for pardons, the probability is that the same persons fabricated both the one and the other of those theories; and that, in truth, there is no such thing as redemption; that it is fabulous; and that man stands in the same relative condition with his Maker he ever did stand, since man existed; and that it is his greatest consolation to think so.

Let him believe this, and he will live more consistently and morally, than by any other system. It is by his being taught to contemplate himself as an out-law, as an out-cast, as a beggar, as a mumper, as one thrown as it were on a dunghill, at an immense distance from his Creator, and who must make his approaches by creeping, and cringing to intermediate beings, that he conceives either a contemptuous disregard for everything under the name of religion, or becomes indifferent, or turns what he calls devout. In the latter case, he consumes his life in grief, or the affectation of it. His prayers are reproaches. His humility is ingratitude. He calls himself a worm, and the fertile earth a dunghill; and all the blessings of life by the thankless name of vanities. He despises the choicest gift of God to man, the GIFT OF REASON; and having endeavoured to force upon himself the belief of a system against which reason revolts, he ungratefully calls it *human reason*, as if man could give reason to himself.

Yet, with all this strange appearance of humility, and this contempt for human reason, he ventures into the boldest presumptions. He finds fault with everything. His selfishness is never satisfied; his ingratitude is never at an end. He takes on himself to direct the Almighty what to do, even in the government of the universe. He prays dictatorially. When it is sunshine, he prays for rain, and when it is rain, he prays for sunshine. He follows the same idea in everything that he prays for; for what is the amount of all his prayers, but an attempt to make the Almighty change his mind, and act otherwise than he does? It is as if he were to say—thou knowest not so well as I.

CHAPTER IX.

In What the True Revelation Consists.

BUT SOME PERHAPS WILL say—Are we to have no word of God—no revelation? I answer yes. There is a Word of God; there is a revelation.

THE WORD OF GOD IS THE CREATION WE BEHOLD: And it is in *this word*, which no human invention can counterfeit or alter, that God speaketh universally to man.

Human language is local and changeable, and is therefore incapable of being used as the means of unchangeable and universal information. The idea that God sent Jesus Christ to publish, as they say, the glad tidings to all nations, from one end of the earth unto the other, is consistent only with the ignorance of those who know nothing of the extent of the world, and who believed, as those world-saviours believed, and continued to believe for several centuries, (and that in contradiction to the discoveries of philosophers and the experience of navigators,) that the earth was flat like a trencher; and that a man might walk to the end of it.

But how was Jesus Christ to make anything known to all nations? He could speak but one language, which was Hebrew; and there are in the world several hundred languages. Scarcely any two nations speak the same language, or understand each other; and as to translations, every man who knows anything of languages, knows that it is impossible to translate from one language into another, not only without losing a great part of the original, but frequently of mistaking the sense; and besides all this, the art of printing was wholly unknown at the time Christ lived.

It is always necessary that the means that are to accomplish any end be equal to the accomplishment of that end, or the end cannot be accomplished. It is in this that the difference between finite and infinite power and wisdom discovers itself. Man frequently fails in accomplishing his end, from a natural inability of the power to the purpose; and frequently from the want of wisdom to apply power properly. But it is impossible for infinite power and wisdom to fail as man faileth. The means it useth are always equal to the end: but human language, more especially as there is not an universal language, is incapable of being used as an universal means of unchangeable and uniform information; and therefore it is not the means that God useth in manifesting himself universally to man.

It is only in the CREATION that all our ideas and conceptions of a *word of God* can unite. The Creation speaketh an universal language, independently of human speech or human language, multiplied and various as they be. It is an ever existing original, which every man can read. It cannot be forged; it cannot be counterfeited; it cannot be lost; it cannot be altered; it cannot be suppressed. It does not depend upon the will of man whether it shall be published or not; it publishes itself from one end of the earth to the other. It preaches to all nations and to all worlds; and this *word of God* reveals to man all that is necessary for man to know of God.

Do we want to contemplate his power? We see it in the immensity of the creation. Do we want to contemplate his wisdom? We see it in the unchangeable order by which the incomprehensible Whole is governed. Do we want to contemplate his munificence? We see it in the abundance with which he fills the earth. Do we want to contemplate his mercy? We see it in his not withholding that abundance even from the unthankful. In fine, do we want to know what God is? Search not the book called the scripture, which any human hand might make, but the scripture called the Creation.

CHAPTER X.

Concerning God, and the Lights Cast on His Existence and Attributes by the Bible.

THE ONLY IDEA MAN can affix to the name of God, is that of a *first cause*, the cause of all things. And, incomprehensibly difficult as it is for a man to conceive what a first cause is, he arrives at the belief of it, from the tenfold greater difficulty of disbelieving it. It is difficult beyond description to conceive that space can have no end; but it is more difficult to conceive an end. It is difficult beyond the power of man to conceive an eternal duration of what we call time; but it is more impossible to conceive a time when there shall be no time.

In like manner of reasoning, everything we behold carries in itself the internal evidence that it did not make itself. Every man is an evidence to himself, that he did not make himself; neither could his father make himself, nor his grandfather, nor any of his race; neither could any tree, plant, or animal make itself; and it is the conviction arising from this evidence, that carries us on, as it were, by necessity, to the belief of a first cause eternally existing, of a nature totally different to any material existence we know of, and by the power of which all things exist; and this first cause, man calls God.

It is only by the exercise of reason, that man can discover God. Take away that reason, and he would be incapable of understanding anything; and in this case it would be just as consistent to read even the book called the Bible to a horse as to a man. How then is it that those people pretend to reject reason?

Almost the only parts in the book called the Bible, that convey to us any idea of God, are some chapters in Job, and the 19th Psalm; I recollect no other. Those parts are true *deistical* compositions; for they treat of the *Deity* through his works. They take the book of Creation as the word of God; they refer to no other book; and all the inferences they make are drawn from that volume.

I insert in this place the 19th Psalm, as paraphrased into English verse by Addison.* I recollect not the prose, and where I write this I have not the opportunity of seeing it:

> The spacious firmament on high,
> With all the blue etherial sky,
> And spangled heavens, a shining frame,
> Their great original proclaim.
> The unwearied sun, from day to day,
> Does his Creator's power display,
> And publishes to every land
> The work of an Almighty hand.
> Soon as the evening shades prevail,
> The moon takes up the wondrous tale,
> And nightly to the list'ning earth
> Repeats the story of her birth;
> Whilst all the stars that round her burn,
> And all the planets, in their turn,
> Confirm the tidings as they roll,
> And spread the truth from pole to pole.
> What though in solemn silence all

---

*Joseph Addison (1672–1719), English poet and essayist.

Move round this dark terrestrial ball;
What though no real voice, nor sound,
Amidst their radiant orbs be found,
In reason's ear they all rejoice,
And utter forth a glorious voice,
Forever singing as they shine,
THE HAND THAT MADE US IS DIVINE.

What more does man want to know, than that the hand or power that made these things is divine, is omnipotent? Let him believe this, with the force it is impossible to repel if he permits his reason to act, and his rule of moral life will follow of course.

The allusions in Job have all of them the same tendency with this Psalm; that of deducing or proving a truth that would be otherwise unknown, from truths already known.

I recollect not enough of the passages in Job to insert them correctly; but there is one that occurs to me that is applicable to the subject I am speaking upon. "Canst thou by searching find out God; canst thou find out the Almighty to perfection?"

I know not how the printers have pointed this passage, for I keep no Bible; but it contains two distinct questions that admit of distinct answers.

First, Canst thou by *searching* find out God? Yes. Because, in the first place, I know I did not make myself, and yet I have existence; and by *searching* into the nature of other things, I find that no other thing could make itself; and yet millions of other things exist; therefore it is, that I know, by positive conclusion resulting from this search, that there is a power superior to all those things, and that power is God.

Secondly, Canst thou find out the Almighty to *perfection*? No. Not only because the power and wisdom He has manifested in the structure of the Creation that I behold is to me incomprehensible; but because even this manifestation, great as it is, is probably but a small display of that immensity of power and wisdom, by which millions of other worlds, to me invisible by their distance, were created and continue to exist.

It is evident that both of these questions were put to the reason of the person to whom they are supposed to have been addressed;

and it is only by admitting the first question to be answered affirmatively, that the second could follow. It would have been unnecessary, and even absurd, to have put a second question, more difficult than the first, if the first question had been answered negatively. The two questions have different objects; the first refers to the existence of God, the second to his attributes. Reason can discover the one, but it falls infinitely short in discovering the whole of the other.

I recollect not a single passage in all the writings ascribed to the men called apostles, that conveys any idea of what God is. Those writings are chiefly controversial; and the gloominess of the subject they dwell upon, that of a man dying in agony on a cross, is better suited to the gloomy genius of a monk in a cell, by whom it is not impossible they were written, than to any man breathing the open air of the Creation. The only passage that occurs to me, that has any reference to the works of God, by which only his power and wisdom can be known, is related to have been spoken by Jesus Christ, as a remedy against distrustful care. "Behold the lilies of the field, they toil not, neither do they spin." This, however, is far inferior to the allusions in Job and in the 19th Psalm; but it is similar in idea, and the modesty of the imagery is correspondent to the modesty of the man.

CHAPTER XI.

Of the Theology of the Christians; and the True Theology.

As to the Christian system of faith, it appears to me as a species of atheism; a sort of religious denial of God. It professes to believe in a man rather than in God. It is a compound made up chiefly of man-ism with but little deism, and is as near to atheism as twilight is to darkness. It introduces between man and his Maker an opaque body, which it calls a redeemer, as the moon introduces her opaque self between the earth and the sun, and it produces by this means a religious or an irreligious eclipse of light. It has put the whole orbit of reason into shade.

The effect of this obscurity has been that of turning everything upside down, and representing it in reverse; and among the revolutions it has thus magically produced, it has made a revolution in Theology.

That which is now called natural philosophy, embracing the whole circle of science, of which astronomy occupies the chief place, is the study of the works of God, and of the power and wisdom of God in his works, and is the true theology.

As to the theology that is now studied in its place, it is the study of human opinions and of human fancies *concerning* God. It is not the study of God himself in the works that he has made, but in the works or writings that man has made; and it is not among the least of the mischiefs that the Christian system has done to the world, that it has abandoned the original and beautiful system of theology, like a beautiful innocent, to distress and reproach, to make room for the hag of superstition.

The Book of Job and the 19th Psalm, which even the church admits to be more ancient than the chronological order in which they stand in the book called the Bible, are theological orations conformable to the original system of theology. The internal evidence of those orations proves to a demonstration that the study and contemplation of the works of creation, and of the power and wisdom of God revealed and manifested in those works, made a great part of the religious devotion of the times in which they were written; and it was this devotional study and contemplation that led to the discovery of the principles upon which what are now called Sciences are established; and it is to the discovery of these principles that almost all the Arts that contribute to the convenience of human life owe their existence. Every principal art has some science for its parent, though the person who mechanically performs the work does not always, and but very seldom, perceive the connection.

It is a fraud of the Christian system to call the sciences *human inventions*; it is only the application of them that is human. Every science has for its basis a system of principles as fixed and unalterable as those by which the universe is regulated and governed. Man cannot make principles, he can only discover them.

For example: Every person who looks at an almanack sees an account when an eclipse will take place, and he sees also that it never fails to take place according to the account there given. This shews that man is acquainted with the laws by which the heavenly bodies move. But it would be something worse than ignorance, were any church on earth to say that those laws are an human invention.

It would also be ignorance, or something worse, to say that the scientific principles, by the aid of which man is enabled to calculate and foreknow when an eclipse will take place, are an human invention. Man cannot invent any thing that is eternal and immutable; and the scientific principles he employs for this purpose must, and are, of necessity, as eternal and immutable as the laws by which the heavenly bodies move, or they could not be used as they are to ascertain the time when, and the manner how, an eclipse will take place.

The scientific principles that man employs to obtain the foreknowledge of an eclipse, or of any thing else relating to the motion of the heavenly bodies, are contained chiefly in that part of science that is called trigonometry, or the properties of a triangle, which, when applied to the study of the heavenly bodies, is called astronomy; when applied to direct the course of a ship on the ocean, it is called navigation; when applied to the construction of figures drawn by a rule and compass, it is called geometry; when applied to the construction of plans of edifices, it is called architecture; when applied to the measurement of any portion of the surface of the earth, it is called land-surveying. In fine, it is the soul of science. It is an eternal truth: it contains the *mathematical demonstration* of which man speaks, and the extent of its uses are unknown.

It may be said, that man can make or draw a triangle, and therefore a triangle is an human invention.

But the triangle, when drawn, is no other than the image of the principle: it is a delineation to the eye, and from thence to the mind, of a principle that would otherwise be imperceptible. The triangle does not make the principle, any more than a candle taken into a room that was dark, makes the chairs and tables that before were invisible. All the properties of a triangle exist independently of the figure, and existed before any triangle was drawn or thought of by man. Man had no more to do in the formation of those properties or principles, than he had to do in making the laws by which the heavenly bodies move; and therefore the one must have the same divine origin as the other.

In the same manner as, it may be said, that man can make a triangle, so also, may it be said, he can make the mechanical instrument called a lever. But the principle by which the lever acts, is a thing distinct from the instrument, and would exist if the instrument did not; it attaches itself to the instrument after it is made; the instrument, therefore, can act no otherwise than it does act; neither can all the efforts of human invention make it act otherwise. That which, in all such cases, man calls the *effect*, is no other than the principle itself rendered perceptible to the senses.

Since, then, man cannot make principles, from whence did he gain a knowledge of them, so as to be able to apply them, not only to things on earth, but to ascertain the motion of bodies so immensely distant from him as all the heavenly bodies are? From whence, I ask, *could* he gain that knowledge, but from the study of the true theology?

It is the structure of the universe that has taught this knowledge to man. That structure is an ever-existing exhibition of every principle upon which every part of mathematical science is founded. The offspring of this science is mechanics; for mechanics is no other than the principles of science applied practically. The man who proportions the several parts of a mill uses the same scientific principles as if he had the power of constructing an universe, but as he cannot give to matter that invisible agency by which all the component parts of the immense machine of the universe have influence upon each other, and act in motional unison together, without any apparent contact, and to which man has given the name of attraction, gravitation, and repulsion, he supplies the place of that agency by the humble imitation of teeth and cogs. All the parts of man's microcosm must visibly touch. But could he gain a knowledge of that agency, so as to be able to apply it in practice, we might then say that another *canonical book* of the word of God had been discovered.

If man could alter the properties of the lever, so also could he alter the properties of the triangle: for a lever (taking that sort of lever which is called a steel-yard, for the sake of explanation) forms, when in motion, a triangle. The line it descends from, (one point of that line being in the fulcrum,) the line it descends to, and the chord of the arc, which the end of the lever describes in the air, are the three sides of a triangle. The other arm of the lever describes also a triangle; and the corresponding sides of those two triangles, calculated scientifically, or measured geometrically,—and also the sines, tangents, and secants generated from the angles, and geometrically measured,—have the same proportions to each other as the different weights have that will balance each other on the lever, leaving the weight of the lever out of the case.

It may also be said, that man can make a wheel and axis; that he can put wheels of different magnitudes together, and produce a mill. Still the case comes back to the same point, which is, that he did not make the principle that gives the wheels those powers. This principle is as unalterable as in the former cases, or rather it is the same principle under a different appearance to the eye.

The power that two wheels of different magnitudes have upon each other is in the same proportion as if the semi-diameter of the two wheels were joined together and made into that kind of lever I have described, suspended at the part where the semi-diameters join; for the two wheels, scientifically considered, are no other than the two circles generated by the motion of the compound lever.

It is from the study of the true theology that all our knowledge of science is derived; and it is from that knowledge that all the arts have originated.

The Almighty lecturer, by displaying the principles of science in the structure of the universe, has invited man to study and to imitation. It is as if he had said to the inhabitants of this globe that we call ours, "I have made an earth for man to dwell upon, and I have rendered the starry heavens visible, to teach him science and the arts. He can now provide for his own comfort, AND LEARN FROM MY MUNIFICENCE TO ALL, TO BE KIND TO EACH OTHER."

Of what use is it, unless it be to teach man something, that his eye is endowed with the power of beholding, to an incomprehensible distance, an immensity of worlds revolving in the ocean of space? Or of what use is it that this immensity of worlds is visible to man? What has man to do with the Pleiades, with Orion, with Sirius, with the star he calls the north star, with the moving orbs he has named Saturn, Jupiter, Mars, Venus, and Mercury, if no uses are to follow from their being visible? A less power of vision would have been sufficient for man, if the immensity he now possesses were given only to waste itself, as it were, on an immense desert of space glittering with shows.

It is only by contemplating what he calls the starry heavens, as the book and school of science, that he discovers any use in their being visible to him, or any advantage resulting from his immensity of vision. But when he contemplates the subject in this light, he sees an additional motive for saying, that *nothing was made in vain*; for in vain would be this power of vision if it taught man nothing. . . .

Any person, who has made observations on the state and progress of the human mind, by observing his own, cannot but have observed, that there are two distinct classes of what are called Thoughts; those that we produce in ourselves by reflection and the act of thinking, and those that bolt into the mind of their own accord. I have always made it a rule to treat those voluntary visitors with civility, taking care to examine, as well as I was able, if they were worth entertaining; and it is from them I have acquired almost all the knowledge that I have. As to the learning that any person gains from school education, it serves only, like a small capital, to put him in the way of beginning learning for himself afterwards. Every person of learning is finally his own teacher; the reason of which is, that principles, being of a distinct quality to circumstances, cannot be impressed upon the memory; their place of mental residence is the understanding, and they are never so lasting as when they begin by conception. Thus much for the introductory part.

From the time I was capable of conceiving an idea, and acting upon it by reflection, I either doubted the truth of the christian system, or thought it to be a strange affair; I scarcely knew which it was: but I well remember, when about seven or eight years of age, hearing a sermon read by a relation of mine, who was a great devotee of the church, upon the subject of what is called *Redemption by the death of the Son of God*. After the sermon was ended, I went into the garden, and as I was going down the garden steps (for I perfectly recollect the spot) I revolted at the recollection of what I had heard, and thought to myself that it was making God Almighty act like a passionate man, that killed his son, when he could not revenge himself any other way; and as I was sure a man would be hanged that did such a thing, I could not see for what purpose they preached such sermons. This was not one of those kind of thoughts that had any thing in it of childish levity; it was to me a serious reflection, arising from the idea I had that God was too good to do such an action, and also too almighty to be under any necessity of doing it. I believe in the same manner to this moment; and I moreover believe, that any system of religion that has any thing in it that shocks the mind of a child, cannot be a true system.

It seems as if parents of the christian profession were ashamed to tell their children any thing about the principles of their religion. They sometimes instruct them in morals, and talk to them of the goodness of what they call Providence; for the Christian mythology has five deities: there is God the Father, God the Son, God the Holy Ghost, the God Providence, and the Goddess Nature. But the christian story of God the Father putting his son to death, or employing people to do it, (for that is the plain language of the story,) cannot be told by a parent to a child; and to tell him that it was done to make mankind happier and better, is making the story still worse; as if mankind could be improved by the example of murder; and to tell him that all this is a mystery, is only making an excuse for the incredibility of it.

How different is this to the pure and simple profession of Deism!* The true deist has but one Deity; and his religion consists in contemplating the power, wisdom, and benignity of the Deity in his works, and in endeavouring to imitate him in every thing moral, scientifical, and mechanical.

The religion that approaches the nearest of all others to true Deism, in the moral and benign part thereof, is that professed by the quakers: but they have contracted themselves too much by leaving the works of God out of their system. Though I reverence their philanthropy, I can not help smiling at the conceit, that if the taste of a quaker could have been consulted at the creation, what a silent and drab-colored creation it would have been! Not a flower would have blossomed its gaieties, nor a bird been permitted to sing.

---

*Popular eighteenth-century faith that emphasized reason and design in creation.

Quitting these reflections, I proceed to other matters. After I had made myself master of the use of the globes, and of the orrery,* and conceived an idea of the infinity of space, and of the eternal divisibility of matter, and obtained, at least, a general knowledge of what was called natural philosophy, I began to compare, or, as I have before said, to confront, the internal evidence those things afford with the christian system of faith.

Though it is not a direct article of the christian system that this world that we inhabit is the whole of the habitable creation, yet it is so worked up therewith, from what is called the Mosaic account of the creation, the story bf Eve and the apple, and the counterpart of that story, the death of the Son of God, that to believe otherwise, that is, to believe that God created a plurality of worlds, at least as numerous as what we call stars, renders the christian system of faith at once little and ridiculous; and scatters it in the wind like feathers in the air. The two beliefs can not be held together in the same mind; and he who thinks that he believes both, has thought but little of either.

Though the belief of a plurality of worlds was familiar to the ancients, it is only within the last three centuries that the extent and dimensions of this globe that we inhabit have been ascertained. Several vessels, following the tract of the ocean, have sailed entirely round the world, as a man may march in a circle, and come round by the contrary side of the circle to the spot he set out from. The circular dimensions of our world, in the widest part, as a man would measure the widest round of an apple, or a ball, is only twenty-five thousand and twenty English miles, reckoning sixty-nine miles and an half to an equatorial degree, and may be sailed round in the space of about three years.†

---

*As this book may fall into the hands of persons who do not know what an orrery is, it is for their information I add this note, as the name gives no idea of the uses of the thing. The orrery has its name from the person who invented it. It is a machinery of clock-work, representing the universe in miniature: and in which the revolution of the earth round itself and round the sun, the revolution of the moon round the earth, the revolution of the planets round the sun, their relative distances from the sun, as the center of the whole system, their relative distances from each other, and their different magnitudes, are represented as they really exist in what we call the heavens [Author's note].

†Allowing a ship to sail, on an average, three miles in an hour, she would sail entirely round the world in less than one year, if she could sail in a direct circle, but she is obliged to follow the course of the ocean [Author's note].

A world of this extent may, at first thought, appear to us to be great; but if we compare it with the immensity of space in which it is suspended, like a bubble or a balloon in the air, it is infinitely less in proportion than the smallest grain of sand is to the size of the world, or the finest particle of dew to the whole ocean, and is therefore but small; and, as will be hereafter shewn, is only one of a system of worlds, of which the universal creation is composed.

It is not difficult to gain some faint idea of the immensity of space in which this and all the other worlds are suspended, if we follow a progression of ideas. When we think of the size or dimensions of a room, our ideas limit themselves to the walls, and there they stop. But when our eye, or our imagination darts into space, that is, when it looks upward into what we call the open air, we cannot conceive any walls or boundaries it can have; and if for the sake of resting our ideas we suppose a boundary, the question immediately renews itself, and asks, what is beyond that boundary? and in the same manner, what beyond the next boundary? and so on till the fatigued imagination returns and says, *there is no end*. Certainly, then, the Creator was not pent for room when he made this world no larger than it is; and we have to seek the reason in something else.

If we take a survey of our own world, or rather of this, of which the Creator has given us the use as our portion in the immense system of creation, we find every part of it, the earth, the waters, and the air that surround it, filled, and as it were crouded with life, down from the largest animals that we know of to the smallest insects the naked eye can behold, and from thence to others still smaller, and totally invisible without the assistance of the microscope. Every tree, every plant, every leaf, serves not only as an habitation, but as a world to some numerous race, till animal existence becomes so exceedingly refined, that the effluvia of a blade of grass would be food for thousands.

Since then no part of our earth is left unoccupied, why is it to be supposed that the immensity of space is a naked void, lying in eternal waste? There is room for millions of worlds as large or larger than ours, and each of them millions of miles apart from each other.

Having now arrived at this point, if we carry our ideas only one thought further, we shall see, perhaps, the true reason, at least a very good reason for our happiness, why the Creator, instead of making one immense world, extending over an immense quantity of space, has preferred dividing that quantity of matter into several distinct and separate worlds, which we call planets, of which our earth is one. But before I explain my ideas upon this subject, it is necessary (not for the sake of those that already know, but for those who do not) to shew what the system of the universe is.

CHAPTER XIV.

System of the Universe.

THAT PART OF THE universe that is called the solar system (meaning the system of worlds to which our earth belongs, and of which Sol, or in English language, the Sun, is the center) consists, besides the Sun, of six distinct orbs, or planets, or worlds, besides the secondary bodies, called the satellites, or moons, of which our earth has one that attends her in her annual revolution round the Sun, in like manner as the other satellites or moons, attend the planets or worlds to which they severally belong, as may be seen by the assistance of the telescope.

The Sun is the center round which those six worlds or planets revolve at different distances therefrom, and in circles concentric to each other. Each world keeps constantly in nearly the same tract round the Sun, and continues at the same time turning round itself, in nearly an upright position, as a top turns round itself when it is spinning on the ground, and leans a little sideways.

It is this leaning of the earth (23½ degrees) that occasions summer and winter, and the different length of days and nights. If the earth turned round itself in a position perpendicular to the plane or level of the circle it moves in round the Sun, as a top turns round when it stands erect on the ground, the days and nights would be always of the same length, twelve hours day and twelve hours night, and the season would be uniformly the same throughout the year.

Every time that a planet (our earth for example) turns round itself, it makes what we call day and night; and every time it goes entirely round the Sun, it makes what we call a year, consequently our world turns three hundred and sixty-five times round itself, in going once round the Sun.*

The names that the ancients gave to those six worlds, and which are still called by the same names, are Mercury, Venus, this world that we call ours, Mars, Jupiter, and Saturn. They appear larger to the eye than the stars, being many million miles nearer to our earth than any of the stars are. The planet Venus is that which is called the evening star, and sometimes the morning star, as she happens to set after, or rise before the Sun, which in either case is never more than three hours.

The Sun as before said being the center, the planet or world nearest the Sun is Mercury; his distance from the Sun is thirty-four million miles, and he moves round in a circle always at that distance from the Sun, as a top may be supposed to spin round in the tract in which a horse goes in a mill. The second world is Venus; she is fifty-seven million miles distant from the Sun, and consequently moves round in a circle much greater than that of Mercury. The third world is this that we inhabit, and which is eighty-eight million miles distant from the Sun, and consequently moves round in a circle greater than that of Venus. The fourth world is Mars; he is distant from the sun one hundred and thirty-four million miles, and consequently moves round in a circle greater than that of our earth. The fifth is Jupiter; he is distant from the Sun five hundred and fifty-seven million miles, and consequently moves round in a circle greater than that of Mars. The sixth world is Saturn; he is distant from the Sun seven hundred and sixty-three million miles, and consequently moves round in a circle that surrounds the circles or orbits of all the other worlds or planets.

The space, therefore, in the air, or in the immensity of space, that our solar system takes up for the several worlds to perform their revolutions in round the Sun, is of the extent in a strait line of the whole diameter of the orbit or circle in which Saturn moves round

---

*Those who supposed that the Sun went round the earth every 24 hours made the same mistake in idea that a cook would do in fact, that should make the fire go round the meat, instead of the meat turning round itself towards the fire [Author's note].

the Sun, which being double his distance from the Sun, is fifteen
hundred and twenty-six million miles; and its circular extent is
nearly five thousand million; and its globical content is almost three
thousand five hundred million times three thousand five hundred
million square miles.*

But this, immense as it is, is only one system of worlds. Beyond
this, at a vast distance into space, far beyond all power of calculation,
are the stars called the fixed stars. They are called fixed, because
they have no revolutionary motion, as the six worlds or planets have
that I have been describing. Those fixed stars continue always at the
same distance from each other, and always in the same place, as the
Sun does in the center of our system. The probability, therefore, is,
that each of those fixed stars is also a Sun, round which another system of worlds or planets, though too remote for us to discover, performs its revolutions, as our system of worlds does round our central
Sun.

By this easy progression of ideas, the immensity of space will appear to us to be filled with systems of worlds; and that no part of
space lies at waste, any more than any part of our globe of earth and
water is left unoccupied.

Having thus endeavoured to convey, in a familiar and easy manner, some idea of the structure of the universe, I return to explain
what I before alluded to, namely, the great benefits arising to man
in consequence of the Creator having made a *plurality* of worlds,

---

*If it should be asked, how can man know these things? I have one plain answer
to give, which is, that man knows how to calculate an eclipse, and also how to calculate to a minute of time when the planet Venus, in making her revolutions
round the Sun, will come in a strait line between our earth and the Sun, and will
appear to us about the size of a large pea passing across the face of the Sun. This
happens but twice in about a hundred years, at the distance of about eight years
from each other, and has happened twice in our time, both of which were fore-
known by calculation. It can also be known when they will happen again for a
thousand years to come, or to any other portion of time. As therefore, man could
not be able to do these things if he did not understand the solar system, and the
manner in which the revolutions of the several planets or worlds are performed,
the fact of calculating an eclipse, or a transit of Venus, is a proof in point that the
knowledge exists; and as to a few thousand, or even a few million miles, more or
less, it makes scarcely any sensible difference in such immense distances [Author's
note].

such as our system is, consisting of a central Sun and six worlds, be-sides satellites, in preference to that of creating one world only of a vast extent.

CHAPTER XV.

Advantages of the Existence of Many Worlds in Each Solar System.

IT IS AN IDEA I have never lost sight of, that all our knowledge of science is derived from the revolutions (exhibited to our eye and from thence to our understanding) which those several planets or worlds of which our system is composed make in their circuit round the Sun.

Had then the quantity of matter which these six worlds contain been blended into one solitary globe, the consequence to us would have been, that either no revolutionary motion would have existed, or not a sufficiency of it to give us the ideas and the knowledge of science we now have; and it is from the sciences that all the mechanical arts that contribute so much to our earthly felicity and comfort are derived.

As therefore the Creator made nothing in vain, so also must it be believed that he organized the structure of the universe in the most advantageous manner for the benefit of man; and as we see, and from experience feel, the benefits we derive from the structure of the universe, formed as it is, which benefits we should not have had the opportunity of enjoying if the structure, so far as relates to our system, had been a solitary globe, we can discover at least one rea-son why a *plurality* of worlds has been made, and that reason calls forth the devotional gratitude of man, as well as his admiration.

But it is not to us, the inhabitants of this globe, only, that the benefits arising from a plurality of worlds are limited. The inhabi-tants of each of the worlds of which our system is composed, enjoy the same opportunities of knowledge as we do. They behold the rev-olutionary motions of our earth, as we behold theirs. All the planets revolve in sight of each other; and, therefore, the same universal school of science presents itself to all.

Neither does the knowledge stop here. The system of worlds next to us exhibits, in its revolutions, the same principles and school of science, to the inhabitants of their system, as our system does to us, and in like manner throughout the immensity of space.

Our ideas, not only of the almightiness of the Creator, but of his wisdom and his beneficence, become enlarged in proportion as we contemplate the extent and the structure of the universe. The solitary idea of a solitary world, rolling or at rest in the immense ocean of space, gives place to the cheerful idea of a society of worlds, so happily contrived as to administer, even by their motion, instruction to man. We see our own earth filled with abundance; but we forget to consider how much of that abundance is owing to the scientific knowledge the vast machinery of the universe has unfolded.

CHAPTER XVI.

Application of the Preceding to the System of the Christians.

BUT, IN THE MIDST of those reflections, what are we to think of the christian system of faith that forms itself upon the idea of only one world, and that of no greater extent, as is before shewn, than twenty-five thousand miles. An extent which a man, walking at the rate of three miles an hour for twelve hours in the day, could he keep on in a circular direction, would walk entirely round in less than two years. Alas! what is this to the mighty ocean of space, and the almighty power of the Creator!

From whence then could arise the solitary and strange conceit that the Almighty, who had millions of worlds equally dependent on his protection, should quit the care of all the rest, and come to die in our world, because, they say, one man and one woman had eaten an apple! And, on the other hand, are we to suppose that every world in the boundless creation had an Eve, an apple, a serpent, and a redeemer? In this case, the person who is irreverently called the Son of God, and sometimes God himself, would have nothing else to do than to travel from world to world, in an endless succession of death, with scarcely a momentary interval of life.

It has been by rejecting the evidence, that the word, or works of God in the creation, affords to our senses, and the action of our reason upon that evidence, that so many wild and whimsical systems of faith, and of religion, have been fabricated and set up. There may be many systems of religion that so far from being morally bad are in many respects morally good: but there can be but ONE that is true; and that one necessarily must, as it ever will, be in all things consistent with the ever existing word of God that we behold in his works. But such is the strange construction of the christian system of faith, that every evidence the heavens affords to man, either directly contradicts it or renders it absurd.

It is possible to believe, and I always feel pleasure in encouraging myself to believe it, that there have been men in the world who persuaded themselves that what is called a *pious fraud*, might, at least under particular circumstances, be productive of some good. But the fraud being once established, could not afterwards be explained; for it is with a pious fraud as with a bad action, it begets a calamitous necessity of going on.

The persons who first preached the christian system of faith, and in some measure combined with it the morality preached by Jesus Christ, might persuade themselves that it was better than the heathen mythology that then prevailed. From the first preachers the fraud went on to the second, and to the third, till the idea of its being a pious fraud became lost in the belief of its being true; and that belief became again encouraged by the interest of those who made a livelihood by preaching it.

But though such a belief might, by such means, be rendered almost general among the laity, it is next to impossible to account for the continual persecution carried on by the church, for several hundred years, against the sciences, and against the professors of science, if the church had not some record or tradition that it was originally no other than a pious fraud, or did not foresee that it could not be maintained against the evidence that the structure of the universe afforded.

CHAPTER XVII.

*Of the Means Employed in All Time, and Almost
Universally, to Deceive the Peoples.*

HAVING THUS SHEWN THE irreconcileable inconsistencies between the real word of God existing in the universe, and that which
is called *the word of God*, as shewn to us in a printed book that any
man might make, I proceed to speak of the three principal means
that have been employed in all ages, and perhaps in all countries, to
impose upon mankind.

Those three means are Mystery, Miracle, and Prophecy. The first
two are incompatible with true religion, and the third ought always
to be suspected.

With respect to Mystery, every thing we behold is, in one sense,
a mystery to us. Our own existence is a mystery: the whole vegetable
world is a mystery. We cannot account how it is that an acorn, when
put into the ground, is made to develop itself and become an oak.
We know not how it is that the seed we sow unfolds and multiplies
itself, and returns to us such an abundant interest for so small a
capital.

The fact however, as distinct from the operating cause, is not a
mystery, because we see it; and we know also the means we are to
use, which is no other than putting the seed in the ground. We
know, therefore, as much as is necessary for us to know; and that
part of the operation that we do not know, and which if we did, we
could not perform, the Creator takes upon himself and performs it
for us. We are, therefore, better off than if we had been let into the
secret, and left to do it for ourselves.

But though every created thing is, in this sense, a mystery, the
word mystery cannot be applied to *moral truth*, any more than obscurity can be applied to light. The God in whom we believe is a
God of moral truth, and not a God of mystery or obscurity. Mystery is the antagonist of truth. It is a fog of human invention that
obscures truth, and represents it in distortion. Truth never invelops
itself in mystery; and the mystery in which it is at any time enveloped, is the work of its antagonist, and never of itself.

Religion, therefore, being the belief of a God, and the practice of moral truth, cannot have connection with mystery. The belief of a God, so far from having any thing of mystery in it, is of all beliefs the most easy, because it arises to us, as is before observed, out of necessity. And the practice of moral truth, or, in other words, a practical imitation of the moral goodness of God, is no other than our acting towards each other as he acts benignly towards all. We cannot *serve* God in the manner we serve those who cannot do without such service; and, therefore, the only idea we can have of serving God, is that of contributing to the happiness of the living creation that God has made. This cannot be done by retiring ourselves from the society of the world, and spending a recluse life in selfish devotion.

The very nature and design of religion, if I may so express it, prove even to demonstration that it must be free from every thing of mystery, and unincumbered with every thing that is mysterious. Religion, considered as a duty, is incumbent upon every living soul alike, and, therefore, must be on a level to the understanding and comprehension of all. Man does not learn religion as he learns the secrets and mysteries of a trade. He learns the theory of religion by reflection. It arises out of the action of his own mind upon the things which he sees, or upon what he may happen to hear or to read, and the practice joins itself thereto.

When men, whether from policy or pious fraud, set up systems of religion incompatible with the word or works of God in the creation, and not only above but repugnant to human comprehension, they were under the necessity of inventing or adopting a word that should serve as a bar to all questions, inquiries and speculations. The word *mystery* answered this purpose, and thus it has happened that religion, which is in itself without mystery, has been corrupted into a fog of mysteries.

As *mystery* answered all general purposes, *miracle* followed as an occasional auxiliary. The former served to bewilder the mind, the latter to puzzle the senses. The one was the lingo, the other the legerdemain.

But before going further into this subject, it will be proper to inquire what is to be understood by a miracle.

In the same sense that every thing may be said to be a mystery, so also may it be said that every thing is a miracle, and that no one thing is a greater miracle than another. The elephant, though larger, is not a greater miracle than a mite: nor a mountain a greater miracle than an atom. To an almighty power it is no more difficult to make the one than the other, and no more difficult to make a million of worlds than to make one. Every thing, therefore, is a miracle, in one sense; whilst, in the other sense, there is no such thing as a miracle. It is a miracle when compared to our power, and to our comprehension. It is not a miracle compared to the power that performs it. But as nothing in this description conveys the idea that is affixed to the word miracle, it is necessary to carry the inquiry further.

Mankind have conceived to themselves certain laws, by which what they call nature is supposed to act; and that a miracle is something contrary to the operation and effect of those laws. But unless we know the whole extent of those laws, and of what are commonly called the powers of nature, we are not able to judge whether any thing that may appear to us wonderful or miraculous, be within, or be beyond, or be contrary to, her natural power of acting.

The ascension of a man several miles high into the air, would have everything in it that constitutes the idea of a miracle, if it were not known that a species of air can be generated several times lighter than the common atmospheric air, and yet possess elasticity enough to prevent the balloon, in which that light air is inclosed, from being compressed into as many times less bulk, by the common air that surrounds it. In like manner, extracting flashes or sparks of fire from the human body, as visibly as from a steel struck with a flint, and causing iron or steel to move without any visible agent, would also give the idea of a miracle, if we were not acquainted with electricity and magnetism; so also would many other experiments in natural philosophy, to those who are not acquainted with the subject. The restoring persons to life who are to appearance dead, as is practised upon drowned persons, would also be a miracle, if it were not known that animation is capable of being suspended without being extinct.

Besides these, there are performances by slight of hand, and by persons acting in concert, that have a miraculous appearance, which, when known, are thought nothing of. And, besides these, there are mechanical and optical deceptions. There is now an exhibition in Paris of ghosts or spectres, which, though it is not imposed upon the spectators as a fact, has an astonishing appearance. As, therefore, we know not the extent to which either nature or art can go, there is no criterion to determine what a miracle is; and mankind, in giving credit to appearances, under the idea of their being miracles, are subject to be continually imposed upon.

Since then appearances are so capable of deceiving, and things not real have a strong resemblance to things that are, nothing can be more inconsistent than to suppose that the Almighty would make use of means, such as are called miracles, that would subject the person who performed them to the suspicion of being an impostor, and the person who related them to be suspected of lying, and the doctrine intended to be supported thereby to be suspected as a fabulous invention.

Of all the modes of evidence that ever were invented to obtain belief to any system or opinion to which the name of religion has been given, that of miracle, however successful the imposition may have been, is the most inconsistent. For, in the first place, whenever recourse is had to show, for the purpose of procuring that belief (for a miracle, under any idea of the word, is a show) it implies a lameness or weakness in the doctrine that is preached. And, in the second place, it is degrading the Almighty into the character of a show-man, playing tricks to amuse and make the people stare and wonder. It is also the most equivocal sort of evidence that can be set up; for the belief is not to depend upon the thing called a miracle, but upon the credit of the reporter, who says that he saw it; and, therefore, the thing, were it true, would have no better chance of being believed than if it were a lie.

Suppose I were to say, that when I sat down to write this book, a hand presented itself in the air, took up the pen and wrote every word that is herein written; would any body believe me? Certainly they would not. Would they believe me a whit the more if the thing had been a fact? Certainly they would not. Since then a real miracle, were it to happen, would be subject to the same fate as the falsehood, the inconsistency becomes the greater of supposing the Almighty would make use of means that would not answer the purpose for which they were intended, even if they were real.

If we are to suppose a miracle to be something so entirely out of the course of what is called nature, that she must go out of that course to accomplish it, and we see an account given of such a miracle by the person who said he saw it, it raises a question in the mind very easily decided, which is,—Is it more probable that nature should go out of her course, or that a man should tell a lie? We have never seen, in our time, nature go out of her course; but we have good reason to believe that millions of lies have been told in the same time; it is, therefore, at least millions to one, that the reporter of a miracle tells a lie.

The story of the whale swallowing Jonah,* though a whale is large enough to do it, borders greatly on the marvellous; but it would have approached nearer to the idea of a miracle, if Jonah had swallowed the whale. In this, which may serve for all cases of miracles, the matter would decide itself as before stated, namely, Is it more probable that a man should have swallowed a whale, or told a lie?

But suppose that Jonah had really swallowed the whale, and gone with it in his belly to Nineveh, and to convince the people that it was true have cast it up in their sight, of the full length and size of a whale, would they not have believed him to have been the devil instead of a prophet? or if the whale had carried Jonah to Nineveh, and cast him up in the same public manner, would they not have believed the whale to have been the devil, and Jonah one of his imps?

The most extraordinary of all the things called miracles, related in the New Testament, is that of the devil flying away with Jesus Christ, and carrying him to the top of a high mountain; and to the top of the highest pinnacle of the temple, and showing him and promising to him *all the kingdoms of the world*. How happened it that he did not discover America? or is it only with *kingdoms* that his sooty highness has any interest.

I have too much respect for the moral character of Christ to believe that he told this whale of a miracle himself: neither is it easy to account for what purpose it could have been fabricated, unless it were to impose upon the connoisseurs of miracles, as is sometimes practised upon the connoisseurs of Queen Anne's farthings, and collectors of relics and antiquities; or to render the belief of miracles

---

*Son of the prophet Amittai, Jonah allegedly was swallowed by a fish; see the Bible, 2 Kings 14:25, and Jonah 1–2.

ridiculous, by outdoing miracle, as Don Quixote* outdid chivalry; or to embarrass the belief of miracles, by making it doubtful by what power, whether of God or of the devil, any thing called a miracle was performed. It requires, however, a great deal of faith in the devil to believe this miracle.

In every point of view in which those things called miracles can be placed and considered, the reality of them is improbable, and their existence unnecessary. They would not, as before observed, answer any useful purpose, even if they were true; for it is more difficult to obtain belief to a miracle, than to a principle evidently moral, without any miracle. Moral principle speaks universally for itself. Miracle could be but a thing of the moment, and seen but by a few; after this it requires a transfer of faith from God to man to believe a miracle upon man's report. Instead, therefore, of admitting the recitals of miracles as evidence of any system of religion being true, they ought to be considered as symptoms of its being fabulous. It is necessary to the full and upright character of truth that it rejects the crutch; and it is consistent with the character of fable to seek the aid that truth rejects. Thus much for Mystery and Miracle.

As Mystery and Miracle took charge of the past and the present, Prophecy took charge of the future, and rounded the tenses of *faith*. It was not sufficient to know what had been done, hut what would be done. The supposed prophet was the supposed historian of times to come; and if he happened, in shooting with a long bow of a thousand years, to strike within a thousand miles of a mark, the ingenuity of posterity could make it point-blank; and if he happened to be directly wrong, it was only to suppose, as in the case of Jonah and Nineveh, that God had repented himself and changed his mind. What a fool do fabulous systems make of man!

It has been shewn, in a former part of this work, that the original meaning of the words *prophet* and *prophesying* has been changed, and that a prophet, in the sense of the word as now used, is a creature of modern invention; and it is owing to this change in the meaning of the words, that the flights and metaphors of the Jewish poets, and phrases and expressions now rendered obscure by our not

---

*Title character in the novel by Miguel de Cervantes (1547–1616).

being acquainted with the local circumstances to which they applied at the time they were used, have been erected into prophecies, and made to bend to explanations at the will and whimsical conceits of sectaries, expounders, and commentators. Every thing unintelligible was prophetical, and every thing insignificant was typical. A blunder would have served for a prophecy; and a dish-clout for a type.

If by a prophet we are to suppose a man to whom the Almighty communicated some event that would take place in future, either there were such men, or there were not. If there were, it is consistent to believe that the event so communicated would be told in terms that could be understood, and not related in such a loose and obscure manner as to be out of the comprehension of those that heard it, and so equivocal as to fit almost any circumstance that might happen afterwards. It is conceiving very irreverently of the Almighty, to suppose he would deal in this jesting manner with mankind; yet all the things called prophecies in the book called the Bible come under this description.

But it is with Prophecy as it is with Miracle. It could not answer the purpose even if it were real. Those to whom a prophecy should be told could not tell whether the man prophesied or lied, or whether it had been revealed to him, or whether he conceited it; and if the thing that he prophesied, or pretended to prophesy, should happen, or some thing like it, among the multitude of things that are daily happening, nobody could again know whether he foreknew it, or guessed at it, or whether it was accidental. A prophet, therefore, is a character useless and unnecessary; and the safe side of the case is to guard against being imposed upon, by not giving credit to such relations.

Upon the whole, Mystery, Miracle, and Prophecy, are appendages that belong to fabulous and not to true religion. They are the means by which so many *Lo heres!* and *Lo theres!* have been spread about the world, and religion been made into a trade. The success of one impostor gave encouragement to another, and the quieting salvo of doing *some good* by keeping up a *pious fraud* protected them from remorse.

RECAPITULATION.

HAVING NOW EXTENDED THE subject to a greater length than I first intended, I shall bring it to a close by abstracting a summary from the whole.

First, That the idea or belief of a word of God existing in print, or in writing, or in speech, is inconsistent in itself for the reasons already assigned. These reasons, among many others, are the want of an universal language; the mutability of language; the errors to which translations are subject; the possibility of totally suppressing such a word; the probability of altering it, or of fabricating the whole, and imposing it upon the world.

Secondly, That the Creation we behold is the real and ever existing word of God, in which we cannot be deceived. It proclaimeth his power, it demonstrates his wisdom, it manifests his goodness and beneficence.

Thirdly, That the moral duty of man consists in imitating the moral goodness and beneficence of God manifested in the creation towards all his creatures. That seeing as we daily do the goodness of God to all men, it is an example calling upon all men to practise the same towards each other; and, consequently, that every thing of persecution and revenge between man and man, and every thing of cruelty to animals, is a violation of moral duty.

I trouble not myself about the manner of future existence. I content myself with believing, even to positive conviction, that the power that gave me existence is able to continue it, in any form and manner he pleases, either with or without this body; and it appears more probable to me that I shall continue to exist hereafter than that I should have had existence, as I now have, before that existence began.

It is certain that, in one point, all nations of the earth and all religions agree. All believe in a God. The things in which they disagree are the redundancies annexed to that belief; and therefore, if ever an universal religion should prevail, it will not be believing any thing new, but in getting rid of redundancies, and believing as man believed at first. Adam, if ever there was such a man, was created a Deist; but in the mean time, let every man follow, as he has a right to do, the religion and worship he prefers.

THE AGE OF REASON.
PART II.

Preface.

I HAVE MENTIONED IN the former part of *The Age of Reason* that it had long been my intention to publish my thoughts upon Religion; but that I had originally reserved it to a later period in life, intending it to be the last work I should undertake. The circumstances, however, which existed in France in the latter end of the year 1793, determined me to delay it no longer. The just and humane principles of the Revolution which Philosophy had first diffused, had been departed from. The Idea, always dangerous to Society as it is derogatory to the Almighty,—that priests could forgive sins,—though it seemed to exist no longer, had blunted the feelings of humanity, and callously prepared men for the commission of all crimes. The intolerant spirit of church persecution had transferred itself into politics; the tribunals, stiled Revolutionary, supplied the place of an Inquisition; and the Guillotine of the Stake. I saw many of my most intimate friends destroyed; others daily carried to prison; and I had reason to believe, and had also intimations given me, that the same danger was approaching myself.

Under these disadvantages, I began the former part of the Age of Reason; I had, besides, neither Bible nor Testament to refer to, though I was writing against both; nor could I procure any; notwithstanding which I have produced a work that no Bible Believer, though writing at his ease, and with a Library of Church Books about him, can refute. Towards the latter end of December of that year, a motion was made and carried, to exclude foreigners from the Convention. There were but two, Anacharsis Cloots* and my-

---

*Jean-Baptiste du Val-de-Grâce, baron de Cloots (1755–1794), Prussian participant in the French Revolution.

self; and I saw I was particularly pointed at by Bourdon de l'Oise,* in his speech on that motion.

Conceiving, after this, that I had but a few days of liberty, I sat down and brought the work to a close as speedily as possible; and I had not finished it more than six hours, in the state it has since appeared, before a guard came there, about three in the morning, with an order signed by the two Committees of Public Safety and Surety General, for putting me in arrestation as a foreigner, and conveying me to the prison of the Luxembourg. I contrived, in my way there, to call on Joel Barlow,† and I put the Manuscript of the work into his hands, as more safe than in my possession in prison; and not knowing what might be the fate in France either of the writer or the work, I addressed it to the protection of the citizens of the United States.

It is justice that I say, that the guard who executed this order, and the interpreter to the Committee of General Surety, who accompanied them to examine my papers, treated me not only with civility, but with respect. The keeper of the Luxembourg, Benoit, a man of good heart, shewed to me every friendship in his power, as did also all his family, while he continued in that station. He was removed from it, put into arrestation, and carried before the tribunal upon a malignant accusation, but acquitted.

After I had been in Luxembourg about three weeks, the Americans then in Paris went in a body to the Convention, to reclaim me as their countryman and friend; but were answered by the President, Vadier, who was also President of the Committee of Surety General, and had signed the order for my arrestation, that I was born in England. I heard no more, after this, from any person out of the walls of the prison, till the fall of Robespierre, on the 9th of Thermidor— July 27, 1794.

About two months before this event, I was seized with a fever that in its progress had every symptom of becoming mortal, and from the effects of which I am not recovered. It was then that I remembered with renewed satisfaction, and congratulated myself most sincerely, on having written the former part of *The Age of Rea-*

---

*François-Louis Bourdon (1758–1798), French Revolutionary leader.
†Barlow (1754–1812) was an American poet and diplomat.

son. I had then but little expectation of surviving, and those about me had less. I know therefore by experience the conscientious trial of my own principles.

I was then with three chamber comrades: Joseph Vanheule of Bruges, Charles Bastini, and Michael Robyns of Louvain. The unceasing and anxious attention of these three friends to me, by night and day, I remember with gratitude and mention with pleasure. It happened that a physician (Dr. Graham) and a surgeon, (Mr. Bond,) part of the suite of General O'Hara, were then in the Luxembourg: I ask not myself whether it be convenient to them, as men under the English Government, that I express to them my thanks; but I should reproach myself if I did not; and also to the physician of the Luxembourg, Dr. Markoski.

I have some reason to believe, because I cannot discover any other, that this illness preserved me in existence. Among the papers of Robespierre* that were examined and reported upon to the Convention by a Committee of Deputies, is a note in the hand writing of Robespierre, in the following words:

"Démander que Thomas Paine soit décrété d'accusation, pour l'intérêt de l'Amérique autant que de la France."	Demand that Thomas Paine be decreed of accusation, for the interest of America, as well as of France.

From what cause it was that the intention was not put in execution, I know not, and cannot inform myself; and therefore I ascribe it to impossibility, on account of that illness.

The Convention, to repair as much as lay in their power the injustice I had sustained, invited me publickly and unanimously to return into the Convention, and which I accepted, to shew I could bear an injury without permitting it to injure my principles or my disposition. It is not because right principles have been violated, that they are to be abandoned.

I have seen, since I have been at liberty, several publications written, some in America, and some in England, as answers to the former

---

*Maximilien François Marie Isidore de Robespierre (1758–1794), leader of the Jacobins in the French Revolution.

part of "The Age of Reason." If the authors of these can amuse themselves by so doing, I shall not interrupt them. They may write against the work, and against me, as much as they please; they do me more service than they intend, and I can have no objection that they write on. They will find, however, by this Second Part, without its being written as an answer to them, that they must return to their work, and spin their cobweb over again. The first is brushed away by accident.

They will now find that I have furnished myself with a Bible and Testament; and I can say also that I have found them to be much worse books than I had conceived. If I have erred in any thing, in the former part of the Age of Reason, it has been by speaking better of some parts than they deserved.

I observe, that all my opponents resort, more or less, to what they call Scripture Evidence and Bible authority, to help them out. They are so little masters of the subject, as to confound a dispute about authenticity with a dispute about doctrines; I will, however, put them right, that if they should be disposed to write any more, they may know how to begin.

THOMAS PAINE.

OCTOBER, 1795.

CHAPTER III.

Conclusion.

IN THE FORMER PART of *The Age of Reason* I have spoken of the three frauds, *mystery, miracle*, and *prophecy*; and as I have seen nothing in any of the answers to that work that in the least affects what I have there said upon those subjects, I shall not encumber this Second Part with additions that are not necessary.

I have spoken also in the same work upon what is called *revelation*, and have shewn the absurd misapplication of that term to the books of the Old Testament and the New; for certainly revelation is out of the question in reciting any thing of which man has been the actor or the witness. That which man has done or seen, needs no revelation to tell him he has done it, or seen it—for he knows it already—nor to enable him to tell it or to write it. It is ignorance, or imposition, to apply the term revelation in such cases; yet the Bible and Testament are classed under this fraudulent description of being all *revelation*.

Revelation then, so far as the term has relation between God and man, can only be applied to something which God reveals of his will to man; but though the power of the Almighty to make such a communication is necessarily admitted, because to that power all things are possible, yet, the thing so revealed (if any thing ever was revealed, and which, by the bye, it is impossible to prove) is revelation to the person *only to whom it is made*. His account of it to another is not revelation; and whoever puts faith in that account, puts it in the man from whom the account comes; and that man may have been deceived, or may have dreamed it; or he may be an impostor and may lie. There is no possible criterion whereby to judge of the truth of what he tells; for even the morality of it would be no proof of revelation. In all such cases, the proper answer should be, "When it is revealed to me, I will believe it to be revelation; but it is not and cannot be incumbent upon me to believe it to be revelation before; neither is it proper that I should take the word of man as the word of God, and put man in the place of God." This is the manner in which I have spoken of revelation in the former part of *The Age of Reason*; and which, whilst it reverentially admits revelation as a possible thing, because, as before said, to the Almighty all things are possible, it prevents the imposition of one man upon another, and precludes the wicked use of pretended revelation.

But though, speaking for myself, I thus admit the possibility of revelation, I totally disbelieve that the Almighty ever did communicate any thing to man, by any mode of speech, in any language, or by any kind of vision, or appearance, or by any means which our senses are capable of receiving, otherwise than by the universal display of himself in the works of the creation, and by that repugnance we feel in ourselves to bad actions, and disposition to good ones.

The most detestable wickedness, the most horrid cruelties, and the greatest miseries, that have afflicted the human race, have had their origin in this thing called revelation, or revealed religion. It has been the most dishonourable belief against the character of the divinity, the most destructive to morality, and the peace and happiness of man, that ever was propagated since man began to exist. It is better, far better, that we admitted, if it were possible, a thousand devils to roam at large, and to preach publicly the doctrine of devils, if there were any such, than that we permitted one such impostor and monster as Moses, Joshua, Samuel, and the Bible prophets, to come with the pretended word of God in his mouth, and have credit among us.

Whence arose all the horrid assassinations of whole nations of men, women, and infants, with which the Bible is filled; and the bloody persecutions, and tortures unto death and religious wars, that since that time have laid Europe in blood and ashes; whence arose they, but from this impious thing called revealed religion, and this monstrous belief that God has spoken to man? The lies of the Bible have been the cause of the one, and the lies of the Testament [of] the other.

Some Christians pretend that Christianity was not established by the sword; but of what period of time do they speak? It was impossible that twelve men could begin with the sword: they had not the power; but no sooner were the professors of Christianity sufficiently powerful to employ the sword than they did so, and the stake and faggot too; and Mahomet could not do it sooner. By the same spirit that Peter cut off the ear of the high priest's servant (if the story be true) he would cut off his head, and the head of his master, had he been able. Besides this, Christianity grounds itself originally upon the [Hebrew] Bible, and the Bible was established altogether by the sword, and that in the worst use of it—not to terrify, but to extirpate. The Jews made no converts: they butchered all. The Bible is the sire of the [New] Testament, and both are called the *word of God*. The Christians read both books; the ministers preach from both books; and this thing called Christianity is made up of both. It is then false to say that Christianity was not established by the sword.

The only sect that has not persecuted are the Quakers; and the only reason that can be given for it is, that they are rather Deists than Christians. They do not believe much about Jesus Christ, and they call the scriptures a dead letter. Had they called them by a worse name, they had been nearer the truth.

It is incumbent on every man who reverences the character of the Creator, and who wishes to lessen the catalogue of artificial miseries, and remove the cause that has sown persecutions thick among mankind, to expel all ideas of a revealed religion as a dangerous heresy, and an impious fraud. What is it that we have learned from this pretended thing called revealed religion? Nothing that is useful to man, and every thing that is dishonourable to his Maker. What is it the Bible teaches us?—rapine, cruelty, and murder. What is it the Testament teaches us?—to believe that the Almighty committed debauchery with a woman engaged to be married; and the belief of this debauchery is called faith.

As to the fragments of morality that are irregularly and thinly scattered in those books, they make no part of this pretended thing, revealed religion. They are the natural dictates of conscience, and the bonds by which society is held together, and without which it cannot exist; and are nearly the same in all religions, and in all societies. The Testament teaches nothing new upon this subject, and where it attempts to exceed, it becomes mean and ridiculous. The doctrine of not retaliating injuries is much better expressed in Proverbs, which is a collection as well from the Gentiles as the Jews, than it is in the Testament. It is there said, (xxv. 21) "*If thine enemy be hungry, give him bread to eat; and if he be thirsty, give him water to drink.*"* but when it is said, as in the Testament, "*If a man smite thee on the right cheek, turn to him the other also,*" it is assassinating the dignity of forbearance, and sinking man into a spaniel.

Loving of enemies is another dogma of feigned morality, and has besides no meaning. It is incumbent on man, as a moralist, that he does not revenge an injury; and it is equally as good in a political sense, for there is no end to retaliation; each retaliates on the other, and calls it justice: but to love in proportion to the injury, if it could

---

*According to what is called Christ's sermon on the mount, in the book of Matthew, where, among some other [and] good things, a great deal of this feigned morality is introduced, it is there expressly said, that the doctrine of forbearance, or of not retaliating injuries, *was not any part of the doctrine of the Jews;* but as this doctrine is found in "Proverbs," it must, according to that statement, have been copied from the Gentiles, from whom Christ had learned it. Those men whom Jewish and Christian idolators have abusively called heathen, had much better and clearer ideas of justice and morality than are to be found in the Old Testament, so far as it is Jewish, or in the New. The answer of Solon on the question, "Which is the most perfect popular government," has never been exceeded by any man since his time, as containing a maxim of political morality. "That," says he, "where the least injury done to the meanest individual, is considered as an insult on the whole constitution." Solon lived about 500 years before Christ [Author's note].

be done, would be to offer a premium for a crime. Besides, the word *enemies* is too vague and general to be used in a moral maxim, which ought always to be clear and defined, like a proverb. If a man be the enemy of another from mistake and prejudice, as in the case of religious opinions, and sometimes in politics, that man is different to an enemy at heart with a criminal intention; and it is incumbent upon us, and it contributes also to our own tranquillity, that we put the best construction upon a thing that it will bear. But even this erroneous motive in him makes no motive for love on the other part; and to say that we can love voluntarily, and without a motive, is morally and physically impossible.

Morality is injured by prescribing to it duties that, in the first place, are impossible to be performed, and if they could be would be productive of evil; or, as before said, be premiums for crime. The maxim *of doing as we would be done unto* does not include this strange doctrine of loving enemies; for no man expects to be loved himself for his crime or for his enmity.

Those who preach this doctrine of loving their enemies, are in general the greatest persecutors, and they act consistently by so doing; for the doctrine is hypocritical, and it is natural that hypocrisy should act the reverse of what it preaches. For my own part, I disown the doctrine, and consider it as a feigned or fabulous morality; yet the man does not exist that can say I have persecuted him, or any man, or any set of men, either in the American Revolution, or in the French Revolution; or that I have, in any case, returned evil for evil. But it is not incumbent on man to reward a bad action with a good one, or to return good for evil; and wherever it is done, it is a voluntary act, and not a duty. It is also absurd to suppose that such doctrine can make any part of a revealed religion. We imitate the moral character of the Creator by forbearing with each other, for he forbears with all; but this doctrine would imply that he loved man, not in proportion as he was good, but as he was bad.

If we consider the nature of our condition here, we must see there is no occasion for such a thing as *revealed religion*. What is it we want to know? Does not the creation, the universe we behold, preach to us the existence of an Almighty power, that governs and regulates the whole? And is not the evidence that this creation holds out to our senses infinitely stronger than any thing we can read in a book, that any imposter might make and call the word of God? As for morality, the knowledge of it exists in every man's conscience.

Here we are. The existence of an Almighty power is sufficiently demonstrated to us, though we cannot conceive, as it is impossible we should, the nature and manner of its existence. We cannot conceive how we came here ourselves, and yet we know for a fact that we are here. We must know also, that the power that called us into being, can if he please, and when he pleases, call us to account for the manner in which we have lived here; and therefore, without seeking any other motive for the belief, it is rational to believe that he will, for we know beforehand that he can. The probability or even possibility of the thing is all that we ought to know; for if we knew it as a fact, we should be the mere slaves of terror; our belief would have no merit, and our best actions no virtue.

Deism then teaches us, without the possibility of being deceived, all that is necessary or proper to be known. The creation is the Bible of the deist. He there reads, in the hand-writing of the Creator himself, the certainty of his existence, and the immutability of his power; and all other Bibles and Testaments are to him forgeries. The probability that we may be called to account hereafter, will, to reflecting minds, have the influence of belief; for it is not our belief or disbelief that can make or unmake the fact. As this is the state we are in, and which it is proper we should be in, as free agents, it is the fool only, and not the philosopher, nor even the prudent man, that will live as if there were no God.

But the belief of a God is so weakened by being mixed with the strange fable of the Christian creed, and with the wild adventures related in the Bible, and the obscurity and obscene nonsense of the Testament, that the mind of man is bewildered as in a fog. Viewing all these things in a confused mass, he confounds fact with fable; and as he cannot believe all, he feels a disposition to reject all. But the belief of a God is a belief distinct from all other things, and ought not to be confounded with any. The notion of a Trinity of Gods has enfeebled the belief of *one* God. A multiplication of beliefs acts as a division of belief; and in proportion as anything is divided, it is weakened.

Religion, by such means, becomes a thing of form instead of fact; of notion instead of principle: morality is banished to make room for an imaginary thing called faith, and this faith has its origin in a supposed debauchery; a man is preached instead of a God; an execution is an object for gratitude; the preachers daub themselves with the blood, like a troop of assassins, and pretend to admire the brilliancy it gives them; they preach a humdrum sermon on the merits of the execution; then praise Jesus Christ for being executed, and condemn the Jews for doing it.

A man, by hearing all this nonsense lumped and preached together, confounds the God of the Creation with the imagined God of the Christians, and lives as if there were none.

Of all the systems of religion that ever were invented, there is none more derogatory to the Almighty, more unedifying to man, more repugnant to reason, and more contradictory in itself, than this thing called Christianity. Too absurd for belief, too impossible to convince, and too inconsistent for practice, it renders the heart torpid, or produces only atheists and fanatics. As an engine of power, it serves the purpose of despotism; and as a means of wealth, the avarice of priests; but so far as respects the good of man in general, it leads to nothing here or hereafter.

The only religion that has not been invented, and that has in it every evidence of divine originality, is pure and simple deism. It must have been the first and will probably be the last that man believes. But pure and simple deism does not answer the purpose of despotic governments. They cannot lay hold of religion as an engine but by mixing it with human inventions, and making their own authority a part; neither does it answer the avarice of priests, but by incorporating themselves and their functions with it, and becoming, like the government, a party in the system. It is this that forms the otherwise mysterious connection of church and state; the church human, and the state tyrannic.

Were a man impressed as fully and strongly as he ought to be with the belief of a God, his moral life would be regulated by the force of belief; he would stand in awe of God, and of himself, and would not do the thing that could not be concealed from either. To give this belief the full opportunity of force, it is necessary that it acts alone. This is deism.

But when, according to the Christian Trinitarian scheme, one part of God is represented by a dying man, and another part, called the Holy Ghost, by a flying pigeon, it is impossible that belief can attach itself to such wild conceits.*

It has been the scheme of the Christian church, and of all the other invented systems of religion, to hold man in ignorance of the Creator, as it is of government to hold him in ignorance of his rights. The systems of the one are as false as those of the other, and are calculated for mutual support. The study of theology as it stands in Christian churches, is the study of nothing; it is founded on nothing; it rests on no principles; it proceeds by no authorities; it has no data; it can demonstrate nothing; and admits of no conclusion. Not any thing can be studied as a science without our being in possession of the principles upon which it is founded; and as this is not the case with Christian theology, it is therefore the study of nothing.

Instead then of studying theology, as is now done, out of the Bible and Testament, the meanings of which books are always controverted, and the authenticity of which is disproved, it is necessary that we refer to the Bible of the creation. The principles we discover there are eternal, and of divine origin: they are the foundation of all the science that exists in the world, and must be the foundation of theology.

We can know God only through his works. We cannot have a conception of any one attribute, but by following some principle that leads to it. We have only a confused idea of his power, if we have not the means of comprehending something of its immensity. We can have no idea of his wisdom, but by knowing the order and manner in which it acts. The principles of science lead to this knowledge; for the Creator of man is the Creator of science, and it is through that medium that man can see God, as it were, face to face.

Could a man be placed in a situation, and endowed with power of vision to behold at one view, and to contemplate deliberately, the structure of the universe, to mark the movements of the several planets, the cause of their varying appearances, the unerring order in which they revolve, even to the remotest comet, their connection

---

*The book called the book of Matthew, says, (iii. 16,) that *the Holy Ghost descended in the shape of a dove.* It might as well have said a goose; the creatures are equally harmless, and the one is as much a nonsensical lie as the other. Acts, ii. 2, 3, says, that it descended in a mighty *rushing wind,* in the shape of *cloven tongues:* perhaps it was cloven feet. Such absurd stuff is fit only for tales of witches and wizards [Author's note].

and dependence on each other, and to know the system of laws established by the Creator, that governs and regulates the whole; he would then conceive, far beyond what any church theology can teach him, the power, the wisdom, the vastness, the munificence of the Creator. He would then see that all the knowledge man has of science, and that all the mechanical arts by which he renders his situation comfortable here, are derived from that source: his mind, exalted by the scene, and convinced by the fact, would increase in gratitude as it increased in knowledge: his religion or his worship would become united with his improvement as a man: any employment he followed that had connection with the principles of the creation,—as everything of agriculture, of science, and of the mechanical arts, has,—would teach him more of God, and of the gratitude he owes to him, than any theological Christian sermon he now hears. Great objects inspire great thoughts; great munificence excites great gratitude; but the grovelling tales and doctrines of the Bible and the Testament are fit only to excite contempt.

Though man cannot arrive, at least in this life, at the actual scene I have described, he can demonstrate it, because he has knowledge of the principles upon which the creation is constructed. We know that the greatest works can be represented in model, and that the universe can be represented by the same means. The same principles by which we measure an inch or an acre of ground will measure to millions in extent. A circle of an inch diameter has the same geometrical properties as a circle that would circumscribe the universe. The same properties of a triangle that will demonstrate upon paper the course of a ship, will do it on the ocean; and, when applied to what are called the heavenly bodies, will ascertain to a minute the time of an eclipse, though those bodies are millions of miles distant from us. This knowledge is of divine origin; and it is from the Bible of the creation that man has learned it, and not from the stupid Bible of the church, that teaches man nothing.*

---

*The Bible-makers have undertaken to give us, in the first chapter of Genesis, an account of the creation; and in doing this they have demonstrated nothing but their ignorance. They make there to have been three days and three nights, evenings and mornings, before there was any sun; when it is the presence or absence of the sun that is the cause of day and night—and what is called his rising and setting, that of

All the knowledge man has of science and of machinery, by the aid of which his existence is rendered comfortable upon earth, and without which he would be scarcely distinguishable in appearance and condition from a common animal, comes from the great machine and structure of the universe. The constant and unwearied observations of our ancestors upon the movements and revolutions of the heavenly bodies, in what are supposed to have been the early ages of the world, have brought this knowledge upon earth. It is not Moses and the prophets, nor Jesus Christ, nor his apostles, that have done it. The Almighty is the great mechanic of the creation, the first philosopher, and original teacher of all science. Let us then learn to reverence our master, and not forget the labours of our ancestors.

Had we, at this day, no knowledge of machinery, and were it possible that man could have a view, as I have before described, of the structure and machinery of the universe, he would soon conceive the idea of constructing some at least of the mechanical works we now have; and the idea so conceived would progressively advance in practice. Or could a model of the universe, such as is called an orrery, be presented before him and put in motion, his mind would arrive at the same idea. Such an object and such a subject would, whilst it improved him in knowledge useful to himself as a man and a member of society, as well as entertaining, afford far better matter for impressing him with a knowledge of, and a belief in the Creator, and of the reverence and gratitude that man owes to him, than the stupid texts of the Bible and the Testament, from which, be the talents of the preacher what they may, only stupid sermons can be preached. If man must preach, let him preach something that is edifying, and from the texts that are known to be true.

---

morning and evening. Besides, it is a puerile and pitiful idea, to suppose the Almighty to say, "Let there be light." It is the imperative manner of speaking that a conjuror uses when he says to his cups and balls, Presto, be gone—and most probably has been taken from it, as Moses and his rod is a conjuror and his wand. Longinus calls this expression the sublime; and by the same rule the conjuror is sublime too; for the manner of speaking is expressively and grammatically the same. When authors and critics talk of the sublime, they see not how nearly it borders on the ridiculous. The sublime of the critics, like some parts of Edmund Burke's sublime and beautiful, is like a windmill just visible in a fog, which imagination might distort into a flying mountain, or an archangel, or a flock of wild geese [Author's note].

The Bible of the creation is inexhaustible in texts. Every part of science, whether connected with the geometry of the universe, with the systems of animal and vegetable life, or with the properties of inanimate matter, is a text as well for devotion as for philosophy— for gratitude, as for human improvement. It will perhaps be said, that if such a revolution in the system of religion takes place, every preacher ought to be a philosopher. *Most certainly*, and every house of devotion a school of science.

It has been by wandering from the immutable laws of science, and the light of reason, and setting up an invented thing called "revealed religion," that so many wild and blasphemous conceits have been formed of the Almighty. The Jews have made him the assassin of the human species, to make room for the religion of the Jews. The Christians have made him the murderer of himself, and the founder of a new religion to supersede and expel the Jewish religion. And to find pretence and admission for these things, they must have supposed his power or his wisdom imperfect, or his will changeable; and the changeableness of the will is the imperfection of the judgement. The philosopher knows that the laws of the Creator have never changed, with respect either to the principles of science, or the properties of matter. Why then is it to be supposed they have changed with respect to man?

I here close the subject. I have shewn in all the foregoing parts of this work that the Bible and Testament are impositions and forgeries; and I leave the evidence I have produced in proof of it to be refuted, if any one can do it; and I leave the ideas that are suggested in the conclusion of the work to rest on the mind of the reader; certain as I am that when opinions are free, either in matters of government or religion, truth will finally and powerfully prevail.

END OF "THE AGE OF REASON."

AGRARIAN JUSTICE

[1795]

AGRARIAN JUSTICE,

OPPOSED TO

AGRARIAN LAW,

AND TO

AGRARIAN MONOPOLY.

BEING A PLAN FOR MELIORATING
THE CONDITION OF MAN,
BY CREATING IN EVERY NATION,
A NATIONAL FUND,

To Pay to every Person, when arrived at the Age of
TWENTY-ONE YEARS, the Sum of FIFTEEN
POUNDS Sterling, to enable HIM or HER to begin
the World!
and also,

Ten Pounds Sterling per Annum during life to every
Person now living of the Age of FIFTY YEARS, and to
all others when they shall arrive at that Age, to enable
them to live in Old Age without Wretchedness, and
go decently out of the World.

AUTHOR'S INSCRIPTION.

*To the Legislature and the Executive Directory
of the French Republic.*

THE PLAN CONTAINED IN this work is not adapted for any particular country alone: the principle on which it is based is general. But as the rights of man are a new study in this world, and one needing protection from priestly imposture, and the insolence of oppressions too long established, I have thought it right to place this little work under your safeguard. When we reflect on the long and dense night which France and all Europe have remained plunged by their governments and their priests, we must feel less surprise than grief at the bewilderment caused by the first burst of light that dispels the darkness. The eye accustomed to darkness can hardly bear at first the broad daylight. It is by usage the eye learns to see, and it is the same in passing from any situation to its opposite.

As we have not at one instant renounced all our errors, we cannot at one stroke acquire knowledge of all our rights. France has had the honour of adding to the word *Liberty* that of *Equality*; and this word signifies essentially a principal that admits of no gradation in the things to which it applies. But equality is often misunderstood, often misapplied, and often violated.

Liberty and *Property* are words expressing all those of our possessions which are not of an intellectual nature. There are two kinds of property. Firstly, natural property, or that which comes to us from the Creator of the universe,—such as the earth, air, water. Secondly, artificial or acquired property,—the invention of men. In the latter equality is impossible; for to distribute it equally it would be necessary that all should have contributed in the same proportion, which can never be the case; and this being the case, every individual would hold on to his own property, as his right share. Equality of natural property is the subject of this little essay. Every individual in the world is born therein with legitimate claims on a certain kind of property, or its equivalent.

The right of voting for persons charged with the execution of the laws that govern society is inherent in the word Liberty, and constitutes the equality of personal rights. But even if that right (of voting) were inherent in property, which I deny, the right of suffrage would still belong to all equally, because, as I have said, all individuals have legitimate birthrights in a certain species of property.

I have always considered the present Constitution of the French Republic the *best organized system* the human mind has yet produced. But I hope my former colleagues will not be offended if I warn them of an error which has slipped into its principle. Equality of the right of suffrage is not maintained. This right is in it connected with a condition on which it ought not to depend; that is, with a proportion of a certain tax called "direct." The dignity of suffrage is thus lowered; and, in placing it in the scale with an inferior thing, the enthusiasm that right is capable of inspiring is diminished. It is impossible to find any equivalent counterpoise for the right of suffrage, because it is alone worthy to be its own basis, and cannot thrive as a graft, or an appendage.

Since the Constitution was established we have seen two conspiracies stranded,—that of Babeuf,* and that of some obscure personages who decorate themselves with the despicable name of "royalists." The defect in principle of the Constitution was the origin of Babeuf's conspiracy. He availed himself of the resentment caused by this flaw, and instead of seeking a remedy by legitimate and constitutional means, or proposing some measure useful to society, the conspirators did their best to renew disorder and confusion, and constituted themselves personally into a Directory, which is formally destructive of election and representation. They were, in fine, extravagant enough to suppose that society, occupied with its domestic affairs, would blindly yield to them a directorship usurped by violence.

The conspiracy of Babeuf was followed in a few months by that of the royalists, who foolishly flattered themselves with the notion

---

*François-Noël Babeuf (also known as Gracchus Babeuf; 1760–1797), radical French Revolutionary leader.

of doing great things by feeble or foul means. They counted on all the discontented, from whatever cause, and tried to rouse, in their turn, the class of people who had been following the others. But these new chiefs acted as if they thought society had nothing more at heart than to maintain courtiers, pensioners, and all their train, under the contemptible title of royalty. My little essay will disabuse them, by showing that society is aiming at a very different end,—maintaining itself.

We all know or should know, that the time during which a revolution is proceeding is not the time when its resulting advantages can be enjoyed. But had Babeuf and his accomplices taken into consideration the condition of France under this constitution, and compared it with what it was under the tragical revolutionary government, and during the execrable reign of Terror, the rapidity of the alteration must have appeared to them very striking and astonishing. Famine has been replaced by abundance, and by the well-founded hope of a near and increasing prosperity.

As for the defect in the Constitution, I am fully convinced that it will be rectified constitutionally, and that this step is indispensable; for so long as it continues it will inspire the hopes and furnish the means of conspirators; and for the rest, it is regrettable that a Constitution so wisely organized should err so much in its principle. This fault exposes it to other dangers which will make themselves felt. Intriguing candidates will go about among those who have not the means to pay the direct tax and pay it for them, on condition of receiving their votes. Let us maintain inviolably equality in the sacred right of suffrage: public security can never have a basis more solid. Salut et Fraternité.

Your former colleague,

THOMAS PAINE.

PREFACE.

THE FOLLOWING LITTLE PIECE was written in the winter of 1795 and 96; and, as I had not determined whether to publish it during the present war, or to wait till the commencement of a peace, it has lain by me, without alteration or addition, from the time it was written.

What has determined me to publish it now is, a sermon preached by Watson, *Bishop of Llandaff*. Some of my Readers will recollect, that this Bishop wrote a Book entitled *An Apology for the Bible*, in answer to my *Second Part of the Age of Reason*. I procured a copy of his Book, and he may depend upon hearing from me on that subject.

At the end of the Bishop's Book is a List of the Works he has written. Among which is the sermon alluded to; it is entitled: "The Wisdom and Goodness of God, in having made both Rich and Poor; with an Appendix, containing Reflections on the Present State of England and France."

The error contained in this sermon determined me to publish my AGRARIAN JUSTICE. It is wrong to say God made *rich* and *poor;* he made only *male* and *female;* and he gave them the earth for their inheritance. . . .

Instead of preaching to encourage one part of mankind in insolence . . . it would be better that Priests employed their time to render the general condition of man less miserable than it is. Practical religion consists in doing good: and the only way of serving God is, that of endeavouring to make his creation happy. All preaching that has not this for its object is nonsense and hypocracy.

THOMAS PAINE.

AGRARIAN JUSTICE.

To PRESERVE THE BENEFITS of what is called civilized life, and remedy at the same time the evil which it has produced, ought to be considered as one of the first objects of reformed legislation.

Whether that state that is proudly, perhaps erroneously, called civilization, has most promoted or most injured the general happiness of man, is a question that may be strongly contested. On one side, the spectator is dazzled by splendid appearances; on the other, he is shocked by extremes of wretchedness; both of which it has erected. The most affluent and the most miserable of the human race are to be found in the countries that are called civilized.

To understand what the state of society ought to be, it is necessary to have some idea of the natural and primitive state of man; such as it is at this day among the Indians of North America. There is not, in that state, any of those spectacles of human misery which poverty and want present to our eyes in all the towns and streets in Europe. Poverty, therefore, is a thing created by that which is called civilized life. It exists not in the natural state. On the other hand, the natural state is without those advantages which flow from agriculture, arts, science, and manufactures.

The life of an Indian is a continual holiday, compared with the poor of Europe; and, on the other hand it appears to be abject when compared to the rich. Civilization, therefore, or that which is so called, has operated two ways: to make one part of society more affluent, and the other more wretched, than would have been the lot of either in a natural state.

It is always possible to go from the natural to the civilized state, but it is never possible to go from the civilized to the natural state. The reason is, that man in a natural state, subsisting by hunting, requires ten times the quantity of land to range over to procure himself sustenance, than would support him in a civilized state, where the earth is cultivated. When, therefore, a country becomes populous by the additional aids of cultivation, art, and science, there is a necessity of preserving things in that state; because without it there cannot be sustenance for more, perhaps, than a tenth part of its inhabitants. The thing, therefore, now to be done is to remedy the evils and preserve the benefits that have arisen to society by passing from the natural to that which is called the civilized state.

In taking the matter upon this ground, the first principle of civilization ought to have been, and ought still to be, that the condition of every person born into the world, after a state of civilization commences, ought not to be worse than if he had been born before that period. But the fact is, that the condition of millions, in every country in Europe, is far worse than if they had been born before civilization began, or had been born among the Indians of North-America at the present day. I will shew how this fact has happened.

It is a position not to be controverted that the earth, in its natural uncultivated state was, and ever would have continued to be, *the common property of the human race.* In that state every man would have been born to property. He would have been a joint life proprietor with the rest in the property of the soil, and in all its natural productions, vegetable and animal.

But the earth in its natural state, as before said, is capable of supporting but a small number of inhabitants compared with what it is capable of doing in a cultivated state. And as it is impossible to separate the improvement made by cultivation from the earth itself, upon which that improvement is made, the idea of landed property arose from that inseparable connection; but it is nevertheless true, that it is the value of the improvement only, and not the earth itself, that is individual property. Every proprietor, therefore, of cultivated land, owes to the community a *ground-rent* (for I know of no better term to express the idea) for the land which he holds; and it is from this ground-rent that the fund proposed in this plan is to issue.

It is deducible, as well from the nature of the thing as from all the histories transmitted to us, that the idea of landed property commenced with cultivation, and that there was no such thing as landed property before that time. It could not exist in the first state of man, that of hunters. It did not exist in the second state, that of shepherds: neither Abraham, Isaac, Jacob, nor Job, so far as the history of the Bible may be credited in probable things, were owners of land. Their property consisted, as is always enumerated, in flocks and herds, and they travelled with them from place to place. The frequent contentions at that time, about the use of a well in the dry country of Arabia, where those people lived, also shew that there was no landed property. It was not admitted that land could be claimed as property.

There could be no such thing as landed property originally. Man did not make the earth, and, though he had a natural right to *occupy* it, he had no right to *locate as his property* in perpetuity any part of it; neither did the creator of the earth open a land-office, from whence the first title-deeds should issue. Whence then, arose the idea of landed property? I answer as before, that when cultivation began the idea of landed property began with it, from the impossibility of separating the improvement made by cultivation from the earth itself, upon which that improvement was made. The value of the improvement so far exceeded the value of the natural earth, at that time, as to absorb it; till, in the end, the common right of all became confounded into the cultivated right of the individual. But there are, nevertheless, distinct species of rights, and will continue to be so long as the earth endures.

It is only by tracing things to their origin that we can gain rightful ideas of them, and it is by gaining such ideas that we discover the boundary that divides right from wrong, and teaches every man to know his own. I have entitled this tract Agrarian Justice, to distinguish it from Agrarian Law. Nothing could be more unjust than Agrarian Law in a country improved by cultivation; for though every man, as an inhabitant of the earth, is a joint proprietor of it in its natural state, it does not follow that he is a joint proprietor of cultivated earth. The additional value made by cultivation, after the system was admitted, became the property of those who did it, or who inherited it from them, or who purchased it. It had originally no owner. Whilst, therefore, I advocate the right, and interest myself in the hard case of all those who have been thrown out of their natural inheritance by the introduction of the system of landed property, I equally defend the right of the possessor to the part which is his.

Cultivation is at least one of the greatest natural improvements ever made by human invention. It has given to created earth a tenfold value. But the landed monopoly that began with it has produced the greatest evil. It has dispossessed more than half the inhabitants of every nation of their natural inheritance, without providing for them, as ought to have been done, an indemnification for that loss, and has thereby created a species of poverty and wretchedness that did not exist before.

In advocating the case of the persons thus dispossessed, it is a right, and not a charity, that I am pleading for. But it is that kind of right which, being neglected at first, could not be brought forward afterwards till heaven had opened the way by a revolution in the system of government. Let us then do honour to revolutions by justice, and give currency to their principles by blessings.

Having thus in a few words, opened the merits of the case, I shall now proceed to the plan I have to propose, which is,

To create a National Fund, out of which there shall be paid to every person, when arrived at the age of twenty-one years, the sum of fifteen pounds sterling, as a compensation in part, for the loss of his or her natural inheritance, by the introduction of the system of landed property:

And also, the sum of ten pounds per annum, during life, to every person now living, of the age of fifty years, and to all others as they shall arrive at that age.

Means by Which the Fund Is to be Created.

I have already established the principle, namely, that the earth, in its natural uncultivated state was, and ever would have continued to be, the *common property of the human race;* that in that state, every person would have been born to property; and that the system of landed property, by its inseparable connection with cultivation, and with what is called civilized life, has absorbed the property of all those whom it dispossessed, without providing, as ought to have been done, an indemnification for that loss.

The fault, however, is not in the present possessors. No complaint is intended, or ought to be alleged against them, unless they adopt the crime by opposing justice. The fault is in the system, and it has stolen imperceptibly upon the world, aided afterwards by the agrarian law of the sword. But the fault can be made to reform itself by successive generations; and without diminishing or deranging the property of any of the present possessors, the operation of the fund can yet commence, and be in full activity, the first year of its establishment, or soon after, as I shall shew.

It is proposed that the payments, as already stated, be made to every person, rich or poor. It is best to make it so, to prevent invidious distinctions. It is also right it should be so, because it is in lieu of the natural inheritance, which, as a right, belongs to every man, over and above the property he may have created, or inherited from those who did. Such persons as do not choose to receive it can throw it into the common fund.

Taking it then for granted that no person ought to be in a worse condition when born under what is called a state of civilization, than he would have been had he been born in a state of nature, and that civilization ought to have made, and ought still to make, provision for that purpose, it can only be done by subtracting from property a portion equal in value to the natural inheritance it has absorbed.

Various methods may be proposed for this purpose, but that which appears to be the best (not only because it will operate without deranging any present possessors, or without interfering with the collection of taxes or *emprunts* necessary for the purposes of government and the revolution, but because it will be the least troublesome and the most effectual, and also because the subtraction will be made at a time that best admits it) is at the moment that property is passing by the death of one person to the possession of another. In this case, the bequeather gives nothing: the receiver pays nothing. The only matter to him is, that the monopoly of natural inheritance, to which there never was a right, begins to cease in his person. A generous man would not wish it to continue, and a just man will rejoice to see it abolished.

My state of health prevents my making sufficient inquiries with respect to the doctrine of probabilities, whereon to found calculations with such degrees of certainty as they are capable of. What, therefore, I offer on this head is more the result of observation and reflection than of received information; but I believe it will be found to agree sufficiently with fact.

In the first place, taking twenty-one years as the epoch of maturity, all the property of a nation, real and personal, is always in the possession of persons above that age. It is then necessary to know, as a datum of calculation, the average of years which persons above that age will live. I take this average to be about thirty years, for though many persons will live forty, fifty, or sixty years after the age of twenty-one years, others will die much sooner, and some in every year of that time.

Taking, then, thirty years as the average of time, it will give, without any material variation one way or other, the average of time in which the whole property or capital of a nation, or a sum equal thereto, will have passed through one entire revolution in descent, that is, will have gone by deaths to new possessors; for though, in many instances, some parts of this capital will remain forty, fifty, or sixty years in the possession of one person, other parts will have revolved two or three times before those thirty years expire, which will bring it to that average; for were one half the capital of a nation to revolve twice in thirty years, it would produce the same fund as if the whole revolved once.

Taking, then, thirty years as the average of time in which the whole capital of a nation, or a sum equal thereto, will revolve once, the thirtieth part thereof will be the sum that will revolve every year, that is, will go by deaths to new possessors; and this last sum being thus known, and the ratio per cent. to be subtracted from it determined, it will give the annual amount or income of the proposed fund, to be applied as already mentioned.

In looking over the discourse of the English minister, Pitt,* in his opening of what is called in England the budget, (the scheme of finance for the year 1796,) I find an estimate of the national capital of that country. As this estimate of a national capital is prepared ready to my hand, I take it as a datum to act upon. When a calculation is made upon the known capital of any nation, combined with its population, it will serve as a scale for any other nation, in proportion as its capital and population be more or less. I am the more disposed to take this estimate of Mr. Pitt, for the purpose of showing to that minister, upon his own calculation, how much better money may be employed than in wasting it, as he has done, on the wild project of setting up Bourbon kings. What, in the name of heaven, are Bourbon kings to the people of England? It is better that the people have bread.

---

*William Pitt, first earl of Chatham (1708–1778), a great British parliamentary leader.

Mr. Pitt states the national capital of England, real and personal, to be one thousand three hundred millions sterling, which is about one-fourth part of the national capital of France, including Belgia. The event of the last harvest in each country proves that the soil of France is more productive than that of England, and that it can better support twenty-four or twenty-five millions of inhabitants than that of England can seven or seven and a half millions.

The thirtieth part of this capital of 1,300,000,000*l.* is 43,333,333*l.* which is the part that will revolve every year by deaths in that country to new possessors; and the sum that will annually revolve in France in the proportion of four to one, will be about one hundred and seventy-three millions sterling. From this sum of 43,333,333*l.* annually revolving, is to be subtracted the value of the natural inheritance absorbed in it, which, perhaps, in fair justice, cannot be taken at less, and ought not to be taken for more, than a tenth part.

It will always happen, that of the property thus revolving by deaths every year a part will descend in a direct line to sons and daughters, and the other part collaterally, and the proportion will be found to be about three to one; that is, about thirty millions of the above sum will descend to direct heirs, and the remaining sum of 13,333,333*l.* to more distant relations, and in part to strangers.

Considering, then, that man is always related to society, that relationship will become comparatively greater in proportion as the next of kin is more distant, it is therefore consistent with civilization to say that where there are no direct heirs society shall be heir to a part over and above the tenth part *due* to society. If this additional part be from five to ten or twelve per cent., in proportion as the next of kin be nearer or more remote, so as to average with the escheats that may fall, which ought always to go to society and not to the government (an addition of ten per cent. more), the produce from the annual sum of 43,333,333*l.* will be:

From 30,000,000*l.* at ten per cent .... 3,000,000*l.*
From 13,333,333*l.* at ten per cent. with the ⎫
                addition of ten ⎬ 2,666,666
                per cent. more. ⎭

    43,333,333*l.*   5,666,666*l.*

Having thus arrived at the annual amount of the proposed fund, I come, in the next place, to speak of the population proportioned to this fund, and to compare it with the uses to which the fund is to be applied.

The population (I mean that of England) does not exceed seven millions and a half, and the number of persons above the age of fifty will in that case be about four hundred thousand. There would not, however, be more than that number that would accept the proposed ten pounds sterling per annum, though they would be entitled to it. I have no idea it would be accepted by many persons who had a yearly income of two or three hundred pounds sterling. But as we often see instances of rich people falling into sudden poverty, even at the age of sixty, they would always have the right of drawing all the arrears due to them. Four millions, therefore, of the above annual sum of 5,666,666*l*. will be required for four hundred thousand aged persons, at ten pounds sterling each.

I come now to speak of the persons annually arriving at twenty-one years of age. If all the persons who died were above the age of twenty-one years, the number of persons annually arriving at that age, must be equal to the annual number of deaths, to keep the population stationary. But the greater part die under the age of twenty-one, and therefore the number of persons annually arriving at twenty-one will be less than half the number of deaths. The whole number of deaths upon a population of seven millions and an half will be about 220,000 annually. The number arriving at twenty-one years of age will be about 100,000. The whole number of these will not receive the proposed fifteen pounds, for the reasons already mentioned, though, as in the former case, they would be entitled to it. Admitting then that a tenth part declined receiving it, the amount would stand thus:

Fund annually . . . . .5,666,666*l*.
To 400,000 aged persons at 10*l*.
       each . . . . 4,000,000*l*.
To 90,000 persons of 21 years, 15*l*.
       ster. each 1,350,000

                                      5,350,000
                      Remains 316,666*l*.

There are, in every country, a number of blind and lame persons, totally incapable of earning a livelihood. But as it will always happen that the greater number of blind persons will be among those who are above the age of fifty years, they will be provided for in that class. The remaining sum of 316,666*l*. will provide for the lame and blind under that age, at the same rate of 10*l*. annually for each person.

Having now gone through all the necessary calculations, and stated the particulars of the plan, I shall conclude with some observations.

It is not charity but a right, not bounty but justice, that I am pleading for. The present state of civilization is as odious as it is unjust. It is absolutely the opposite of what it should be, and it is necessary that a revolution should be made in it. The contrast of affluence and wretchedness continually meeting and offending the eye, is like dead and living bodies chained together. Though I care as little about riches, as any man, I am a friend to riches because they are capable of good. I care not how affluent some may be, provided that none be miserable in consequence of it. But it is impossible to enjoy affluence with the felicity it is capable of being enjoyed, whilst so much misery is mingled in the scene. The sight of the misery, and the unpleasant sensations it suggests, which, though they may be suffocated cannot be extinguished, are a greater drawback upon the felicity of affluence than the proposed 10 per cent. upon property is worth. He that would not give the one to get rid of the other has no charity, even for himself.

There are, in every country, some magnificent charities established by individuals. It is, however, but little that any individual can do, when the whole extent of the misery to be relieved is considered. He may satisfy his conscience, but not his heart. He may give all that he has, and that all will relieve but little. It is only by organizing civilization upon such principles as to act like a system of pullies, that the whole weight of misery can be removed.

The plan here proposed will reach the whole. It will immediately relieve and take out of view three classes of wretchedness—the blind, the lame, and the aged poor; and it will furnish the rising generation with means to prevent their becoming poor; and it will do this without deranging or interfering with any national measures. To

shew that this will be the case, it is sufficient to observe that the operation and effect of the plan will, in all cases, be the same as if every
individual were *voluntarily* to make his will and dispose of his property in the manner here proposed.

But it is justice, and not charity, that is the principle of the plan.
In all great cases it is necessary to have a principle more universally
active than charity; and, with respect to justice, it ought not to be
left to the choice of detached individuals whether they will do justice or not. Considering then, the plan on the ground of justice, it
ought to be the act of the whole, growing spontaneously out of the
principles of the revolution, and the reputation of it ought to be national and not individual.

A plan upon this principle would benefit the revolution by the
energy that springs from the consciousness of justice. It would multiply also the national resources; for property, like vegetation, increases by offsets. When a young couple begin the world, the
difference is exceedingly great whether they begin with nothing or
with fifteen pounds a piece. With this aid they could buy a cow, and
implements to cultivate a few acres of land; and instead of becoming burdens upon society, which is always the case where children
are produced faster than they can be fed, would be put in the way of
becoming useful and profitable citizens. The national domains also
would sell the better if pecuniary aids were provided to cultivate
them in small lots.

It is the practice of what has unjustly obtained the name of civilization (and the practice merits not to be called either charity or
policy) to make some provision for persons becoming poor and
wretched only at the time they become so. Would it not, even as a
matter of economy, be far better to adopt means to prevent their becoming poor? This can best be done by making every person when
arrived at the age of twenty-one years an inheritor of something to
begin with. The rugged face of society, chequered with the extremes
of affluence and want, proves that some extraordinary violence has
been committed upon it, and calls on justice for redress. The great
mass of the poor in all countries are become an hereditary race, and
it is next to impossible for them to get out of that state of themselves. It ought also to be observed that this mass increases in all

countries that are called civilized. More persons fall annually into it than get out of it.

Though in a plan of which justice and humanity are the foundation-principles, interest ought not to be admitted into the calculation, yet it is always of advantage to the establishment of any plan to shew that it is beneficial as a matter of interest. The success of any proposed plan submitted to public consideration must finally depend on the numbers interested in supporting it, united with the justice of its principles.

The plan here proposed will benefit all, without injuring any. It will consolidate the interest of the Republic with that of the individual. To the numerous class dispossessed of their natural inheritance by the system of landed property it will be an act of national justice. To persons dying possessed of moderate fortunes it will operate as a tontine to their children, more beneficial than the sum of money paid into the fund: and it will give to the accumulation of riches a degree of security that none of the old governments of Europe, now tottering on their foundations, can give.

I do not suppose that more than one family in ten, in any of the countries of Europe, has, when the head of the family dies, a clear property left of five hundred pounds sterling. To all such the plan is advantageous. That property would pay fifty pounds into the fund, and if there were only two children under age they would receive fifteen pounds each, (thirty pounds,) on coming of age, and be entitled to ten pounds a-year after fifty. It is from the overgrown acquisition of property that the fund will support itself; and I know that the possessors of such property in England, though they would eventually be benefited by the protection of nine-tenths of it, will exclaim against the plan. But without entering into any inquiry how they came by that property, let them recollect that they have been the advocates of this war, and that Mr. Pitt has already laid on more new taxes to be raised annually upon the people of England, and that for supporting the despotism of Austria and the Bourbons against the liberties of France, than would pay annually all the sums proposed in this plan.

I have made the calculations stated in this plan, upon what is called personal, as well as upon landed property. The reason for making it upon land is already explained; and the reason for taking personal property into the calculation is equally well founded though on a different principle. Land, as before said, is the free gift of the Creator in common to the human race. Personal property is the *effect of society;* and it is as impossible for an individual to acquire personal property without the aid of society, as it is for him to make land originally. Separate an individual from society, and give him an island or a continent to possess, and he cannot acquire personal property. He cannot be rich. So inseparably are the means connected with the end, in all cases, that where the former do not exist the latter cannot be obtained. All accumulation, therefore, of personal property, beyond what a man's own hands produce, is derived to him by living in society; and he owes on every principle of justice, of gratitude, and of civilization, a part of that accumulation back again to society from whence the whole came. This is putting the matter on a general principle, and perhaps it is best to do so; for if we examine the case minutely it will be found that the accumulation of personal property is, in many instances, the effect of paying too little for the labour that produced it; the consequence of which is, that the working band perishes in old age, and the employer abounds in affluence. It is, perhaps, impossible to proportion exactly the price of labour to the profits it produces; and it will also be said, as an apology for the injustice, that were a workman to receive an increase of wages daily he would not save it against old age, nor be much better for it in the interim. Make, then, society the treasurer to guard it for him in a common fund; for it is no reason, that because he might not make a good use of it for himself, another should take it.

The state of civilization that has prevailed throughout Europe, is as unjust in its principle, as it is horrid in its effects; and it is the consciousness of this, and the apprehension that such a state cannot continue when once investigation begins in any country, that makes the possessors of property dread every idea of a revolution. It is the hazard and not the principle of revolutions that retards their progress. This being the case, it is necessary as well for the protection of property, as for the sake of justice and humanity, to form a system that, whilst it preserves one part of society from wretchedness, shall secure the other from depredation.

The superstitious awe, the enslaving reverence, that formerly surrounded affluence, is passing away in all countries, and leaving the possessor of property to the convulsion of accidents. When wealth and splendour, instead of fascinating the multitude, excite emotions of disgust; when, instead of drawing forth admiration, it is beheld as an insult upon wretchedness; when the ostentatious appearance it makes serves to call the right of it in question, the case of property becomes critical, and it is only in a system of justice that the possessor can contemplate security.

To remove the danger, it is necessary to remove the antipathies, and this can only be done by making property productive of a national blessing, extending to every individual. When the riches of one man above another shall increase the national fund in the same proportion; when it shall be seen that the prosperity of that fund depends on the prosperity of individuals; when the more riches a man acquires, the better it shall be for the general mass; it is then that antipathies will cease, and property be placed on the permanent basis of national interest and protection.

I have no property in France to become subject to the plan I propose. What I have, which is not much, is in the United States of America. But I will pay one hundred pounds sterling towards this fund in France, the instant it shall be established; and I will pay the same sum in England, whenever a similar establishment shall take place in that country.

A revolution in the state of civilization is the necessary companion of revolutions in the system of government. If a revolution in any country be from bad to good, or from good to bad, the state of what is called civilization in that country, must be made conformable thereto, to give that revolution effect. Despotic government supports itself by abject civilization, in which debasement of the human mind, and wretchedness in the mass of the people, are the chief criterions. Such governments consider man merely as an animal; that the exercise of intellectual faculty is not his privilege; *that he has nothing to do with the laws but to obey them;** and they politically depend more upon breaking the spirit of the people by poverty, than they fear enraging it by desperation.

---

*Expression of Horsley, an English bishop, in the English parliament [Author's note].

It is a revolution in the state of civilization that will give perfection to the revolution of France. Already the conviction that government by representation is the true system of government is spreading itself fast in the world. The reasonableness of it can be seen by all. The justness of it makes itself felt even by its opposers. But when a system of civilization, growing out of that system of government, shall be so organized that not a man or woman born in the Republic but shall inherit some means of beginning the world, and see before them the certainty of escaping the miseries that under other governments accompany old age, the revolution of France will have an advocate and an ally in the heart of all nations.

An army of principles will penetrate where an army of soldiers cannot; it will succeed where diplomatic management would fail: it is neither the Rhine, the Channel, nor the Ocean that can arrest its progress: it will march on the horizon of the world, and it will conquer.

Means for Carrying the Proposed Plan into Execution, and to Render It at the Same Time Conductive to the Public Interest.

I. Each canton shall elect in its primary assemblies, three persons, as commissioners for that canton, who shall take cognizance, and keep a register of all matters happening in that canton, conformable to the charter that shall be established by law for carrying this plan into execution.

II. The law shall fix the manner in which the property of deceased persons shall be ascertained.

III. When the amount of the property of any deceased person shall be ascertained, the principal heir to that property, or the eldest of the co-heirs, if of lawful age, or if under age the person authorized by the will of the deceased to represent him or them, shall give bond to the commissioners of the canton to pay the said tenth part thereof in four equal quarterly payments, within the space of one year or sooner, at the choice of the payers. One half of the whole property shall remain as a security until the bond be paid off.

IV. The bond shall be registered in the office of the commissioners of the canton, and the original bonds shall be deposited in the national bank at Paris. The bank shall publish every quarter of a year the amount of the bonds in its possession, and also the bonds that shall have been paid off, or what parts thereof, since the last quarterly publication.

V. The national bank shall issue bank notes upon the security of the bonds in its possession. The notes so issued, shall be applied to pay the pensions of aged persons, and the compensations to persons arriving at twenty-one years of age. It is both reasonable and generous to suppose, that persons not under immediate necessity, will suspend their right of drawing on the fund, until it acquire, as it will do, a greater degree of ability. In this case, it is proposed, that an honorary register be kept, in each canton, of the names of the persons thus suspending that right, at least during the present war.

VI. As the inheritors of property must always take up their bonds in four quarterly payments, or sooner if they choose, there will always be *numéraire* [cash] arriving at the bank after the expiration of the first quarter, to exchange for the bank notes that shall be brought in.

VII. The bank notes being thus put in circulation, upon the best of all possible security, that of actual property, to more than four times the amount of the bonds upon which the notes are issued, and with *numéraire* continually arriving at the bank to exchange or pay them off whenever they shall be presented for that purpose, they will acquire a permanent value in all parts of the Republic. They can therefore be received in payment of taxes, or *emprunts* equal to *numéraire*, because the government can always receive *numéraire* for them at the bank.

VIII. It will be necessary that the payments of the ten per cent. be made in *numéraire* for the first year from the establishment of the plan. But after the expiration of the first year, the inheritors of property may pay ten per cent. either in bank notes issued upon the fund, or in *numéraire*. If the payments be in *numéraire*, it will lie as a deposit at the bank, to be exchanged for a quantity of notes equal to that amount; and if in notes issued upon the fund, it will cause a demand upon the fund, equal thereto; and thus the operation of the plan will create means to carry itself into execution.

THOMAS PAINE.

LETTERS TO THE CITIZENS
OF THE UNITED STATES

---

*And particularly to the Leaders of the
Federal Faction.*

*Nos. One–Five [1802]
No. Six [1803]*

LETTER NO. ONE

AFTER AN ABSENCE OF almost fifteen years, I am again returned to the country in whose dangers I bore my share, and to whose greatness I contributed my part.

When I sailed for Europe, in the spring of 1787, it was my intention to return to America the next year, and enjoy in retirement the esteem of my friends, and the repose I was entitled to. I had stood out the storm of one revolution, and had no wish to embark in another. But other scenes and other circumstances than those of contemplated ease were allotted to me. The French revolution was beginning to germinate when I arrived in France. The principles of it were good, they were copied from America, and the men who conducted it were honest. But the fury of faction soon extinguished the one, and sent the other to the scaffold. Of those who began that revolution, I am almost the only survivor, and that through a thousand dangers. I owe this not to the prayers of priests, nor to the piety of hypocrites, but to the continued protection of Providence.

But while I beheld with pleasure the dawn of liberty rising in Europe, I saw with regret the lustre of it fading in America. In less than two years from the time of my departure some distant symptoms painfully suggested the idea that the principles of the revolution were expiring on the soil that produced them. I received at that time a letter from a female literary correspondent, and in my answer to her, I expressed my fears on that head.

I now know from the information I obtain upon the spot, that the impressions that then distressed me, for I was proud of America, were but too well founded. She was turning her back on her own glory, and making hasty strides in the retrograde path of oblivion. But a spark from the altar of *Seventy-six*, unextinguished and unextinguishable through the long night of error, is again lighting up, in every part of the Union, the genuine name of rational liberty.

As the French revolution advanced, it fixed the attention of the world, and drew from the pensioned pen of Edmund Burke a furious attack. This brought me once more on the public theatre of politics, and occasioned the pamphlet *Rights of Man*. It had the greatest run of any work ever published in the English language. The number of copies circulated in England, Scotland, and Ireland, besides translations into foreign languages, was between four and five hundred thousand. The principles of that work were the same as those in *Common Sense*, and the effects would have been the same in England as that had produced in America, could the vote of the nation been quietly taken, or had equal opportunities of consulting or acting existed. The only difference between the two works was, that the one was adapted to the local circumstances of England, and the other to those of America. As to myself, I acted in both cases alike; I relinquished to the people of England, as I had done to those of America, all profits from the work. My reward existed in the ambition to do good, and the independent happiness of my own mind.

But a faction, acting in disguise, was rising in America; they had lost sight of first principles. They were beginning to contemplate government as a profitable monopoly, and the people as hereditary property. It is, therefore, no wonder that the *Rights of Man* was attacked by that faction, and its author continually abused. But let them go on; give them rope enough and they will put an end to their own insignificance. There is too much common sense and independence in America to be long the dupe of any faction, foreign or domestic.

But, in the midst of the freedom we enjoy, the licentiousness of the papers called Federal, (and I know not why they are called so, for they are in their principles anti-federal and despotic,) is a dishonour to the character of the country, and an injury to its reputation and importance abroad. They represent the whole people of America as destitute of public principle and private manners. As to any injury they can do at home to those whom they abuse, or service they can render to those who employ them, it is to be set down to the account of noisy nothingness. It is on themselves the disgrace recoils, for the reflection easily presents itself to every thinking mind, that *those who abuse liberty when they possess it would abuse power could they obtain it*; and, therefore, they may as well take as a general motto, for all such papers, *We and our patrons are not fit to be trusted with power*.

There is in America, more than in any other country, a large body of people who attend quietly to their farms, or follow their several occupations; who pay no regard to the clamours of anonymous scribblers, who think for themselves, and judge of government, not by the fury of newspaper writers, but by the prudent frugality of its measures, and the encouragement it gives to the improvement and prosperity of the country; and who, acting on their own judgment, never come forward in an election but on some important occasion. When this body moves, all the little barkings of scribbling and witless curs pass for nothing. To say to this independent description of men, "You must turn out such and such persons at the next election, for they have taken off a great many taxes, and lessened the expenses of government, they have dismissed my son, or my brother, or myself, from a lucrative office, in which there was nothing to do"—is to show the cloven foot of faction, and preach the language of ill-disguised mortification. In every part of the Union, this faction is in the agonies of death, and in proportion as its fate approaches, gnashes its teeth and struggles. My arrival has struck it as with an hydrophobia, it is like the sight of water to canine madness.

As this letter is intended to announce my arrival to my friends, and to my enemies if I have any, for I ought to have none in America, and as introductory to others that will occasionally follow, I shall close it by detailing the line of conduct I shall pursue.

I have no occasion to ask, and do not intend to accept, any place or office in the government. There is none it could give me that would be any ways equal to the profits I could make as an author, for I have an established fame in the literary world, could I reconcile it to my principles to make money by my politics or religion. I must be in every thing what I have ever been, a disinterested volunteer; my proper sphere of action is on the common floor of citizenship, and to honest men I give my hand and my heart freely.

I have some manuscript works to publish, of which I shall give proper notice, and some mechanical affairs to bring forward, that will employ all my leisure time. I shall continue these letters as I see occasion, and as to the low party prints that choose to abuse me, they are welcome; I shall not descend to answer them. I have been too much used to such common stuff to take any notice of it. The government of England honoured me with a thousand martyrdoms, by burning me in effigy in every town in that country, and their hirelings in America may do the same.

THOMAS PAINE.

CITY OF WASHINGTON.

LETTER NO. TWO

As THE AFFAIRS OF the country to which I am returned are of more importance to the world, and to me, than of that I have lately left, (for it is through the new world the old must be regenerated, if regenerated at all,) I shall not take up the time of the reader with an account of scenes that have passed in France, many of which are painful to remember and horrid to relate, but come at once to the circumstances in which I find America on my arrival.

Fourteen years, and something more, have produced a change, at least among a part of the people, and I ask myself what it is? I meet or hear of thousands of my former connexions, who are men of the same principles and friendships as when I left them. But a non-descript race, and of equivocal generation, assuming the name of *Federalist*,—a name that describes no character of principle good or bad, and may equally be applied to either,—has since started up with the rapidity of a mushroom, and like a mushroom is withering on its rootless stalk. Are those men *federalized* to support the liberties of their country or to overturn them? To add to its fair fame or riot on its spoils? The name contains no defined idea. It is like John Adams's definition of a Republic, in his letter to Mr. Wythe of Virginia.* *It is,* says he, *an empire of laws and not of men.* But as laws may be bad as well as good, an empire of laws may be the best of all governments or the worst of all tyrannies. But John Adams is a man of paradoxical heresies, and consequently of a bewildered mind. He wrote a book entitled, "*A Defence of the American Constitutions,*" and the principles of it are an attack upon them. But the book is de-

---

*George Wythe (1726–1806), American Revolutionary leader and Virginia jurist.

scended to the tomb of forgetfulness, and the best fortune that can attend its author is quietly to follow its fate. John was not born for immortality. But, to return to Federalism.

In the history of parties and the names they assume, it often happens that they finish by the direct contrary principles with which they profess to begin, and thus it has happened with Federalism.

During the time of the old Congress, and prior to the establishment of the federal government, the continental belt was too loosely buckled. The several states were united in name but not in fact, and that nominal union had neither centre nor circle. The laws of one state frequently interferred with, and sometimes opposed, those of another. Commerce between state and state was without protection, and confidence without a point to rest on. The condition the country was then in, was aptly described by Pelatiah Webster,* when he said, "*thirteen staves and ne'er a hoop will not make a barrel.*"

If, then, by *Federalist* is to be understood one who was for cementing the Union by a general government operating equally over all the States, in all matters that embraced the common interest, and to which the authority of the States severally was not adequate, for no one State can make laws to bind another; if, I say, by a *Federalist* is meant a person of this description, (and this is the origin of the name,) *I ought to stand first on the list of Federalists*, for the proposition for establishing a general government over the Union, came originally from me in 1783, in a written Memorial to Chancellor Livingston, then Secretary for Foreign Affairs to Congress, Robert Morris, Minister of Finance, and his associate, Gouverneur Morris,† all of whom are now living; and we had a dinner and conference at Robert Morris's on the subject. The occasion was as follows:

Congress had proposed a duty of five per cent. on imported articles, the money to be applied as a fund towards paying the interest of loans to be borrowed in Holland. The resolve was sent to the several States to be enacted into a law. Rhode Island absolutely refused. I was at the trouble of a journey to Rhode Island to reason with them on the subject. Some other of the States enacted it with

---

*Congregational minister and author of economic pamphlets (1726–1795).
†American Revolutionary leader and prominent Federalist (1752–1816).

alterations, each one as it pleased. Virginia adopted it, and afterwards repealed it, and the affair came to nothing.

It was then visible, at least to me, that either Congress must frame the laws necessary for the Union, and send them to the several States to be enregistered without any alteration, which would in itself appear like usurpation on one part and passive obedience on the other, or some method must be devised to accomplish the same end by constitutional principles; and the proposition I made in the memorial was, to *add a continental legislature to Congress, to be elected by the several States.* The proposition met the full approbation of the gentlemen to whom it was addressed, and the conversation turned on the manner of bringing it forward. Gouverneur Morris, in walking with me after dinner, wished me to throw out the idea in the newspaper; I replied, that I did not like to be always the proposer of new things, that it would have too assuming an appearance; and besides, that *I did not think the country was quite wrong enough to be put right.* I remember giving the same reason to Dr. Rush* at Philadelphia, and to General Gates,[†] at whose quarters I spent a day on my return from Rhode Island; and I suppose they will remember it, because the observation seemed to strike them.

But the embarrassments increasing, as they necessarily must from the want of a better cemented union, the State of Virginia proposed holding a commercial convention, and that Convention, which was not sufficiently numerous, proposed that another convention, with more extensive and better defined powers, should be held at Philadelphia, May 10, 1787.

When the plan of the Federal Government, formed by this Convention, was proposed and submitted to the consideration of the several States, it was strongly objected to in each of them. But the objections were not on anti-federal grounds, but on constitutional points. Many were shocked at the idea of placing what is called Executive Power in the hands of a single individual. To them it had too much the form and appearance of a military government, or a

---

*Benjamin Rush (1745–1813), physician, essayist, and leader in American Revolution.
†Horatio Gates (1728–1806), British officer who became an American in the Revolutionary War.

despotic one. Others objected that the powers given to a president were too great, and that in the hands of an ambitious and designing man it might grow into tyranny, as it did in England under Oliver Cromwell,* and as it has since done in France. A Republic must not only be so in its principles, but in its forms. The Executive part of the Federal government was made for a man, and those who consented, against their judgment, to place Executive Power in the hands of a single individual, reposed more on the supposed moderation of the person they had in view, than on the wisdom of the measure itself.

Two considerations, however, overcame all objections. The one was, the absolute necessity of a Federal Government. The other, the rational reflection, that as government in America is founded on the representative system any error in the first essay could be reformed by the same quiet and rational process by which the Constitution was formed, and that either by the generation then living, or by those who were to succeed. If ever America lose sight of this principle, she will no longer be the *land of liberty*. The father will become the assassin of the rights of the son, and his descendants be a race of slaves.

As many thousands who were minors are grown up to manhood since the name of *Federalist* began, it became necessary, for their information, to go back and show the origin of the name, which is now no longer what it originally was; but it was the more necessary to do this, in order to bring forward, in the open face of day, the apostacy of those who first called themselves Federalists.

To them it served as a cloak for treason, a mask for tyranny. Scarcely were they placed in the seat of power and office, than Federalism was to be destroyed, and the representative system of government, the pride and glory of America, and the palladium of her liberties, was to be overthrown and abolished. The next generation was not to be free. The son was to bend his neck beneath the father's foot, and live, deprived of his rights, under hereditary control. Among the men of this apostate description, is to be ranked the ex-president *John Adams*. It has been the political career of this man to

---

*Cromwell (1599–1658) was a parliamentary general in the English Civil War (1642–1648) who became lord protector of England.

begin with hypocrisy, proceed with arrogance, and finish in contempt. May such be the fate of all such characters.

I have had doubts of John Adams ever since the year 1776. In a conversation with me at that time, concerning the pamphlet *Common Sense*, he censured it because it attacked the English form of government. John was for independence because he expected to be made great by it; but it was not difficult to perceive, for the surliness of his temper makes him an awkward hypocrite, that his head was as full of kings, queens, and knaves, as a pack of cards. But John has lost deal.

When a man has a concealed project in his brain that he wants to bring forward, and fears will not succeed, he begins with it as physicians do by suspected poison, try it first on an animal; if it agree with the stomach of the animal, he makes further experiments, and this was the way John took. His brain was teeming with projects to overturn the liberties of America, and the representative system of government, and he began by hinting it in little companies. The secretary of John Jay, an excellent painter and a poor politician, told me, in presence of another American, Daniel Parker, that in a company where himself was present, John Adams talked of making the government hereditary, and that as Mr. Washington had no children, it should be made hereditary in the family of Lund Washington. John had not impudence enough to propose himself in the first instance, as the old French Normandy baron did, who offered to come over to be king of America, and if Congress did not accept his offer, that they would give him thirty thousand pounds for the generosity of it; but John, like a mole, was grubbing his way to it under ground. He knew that Lund Washington was unknown, for nobody had heard of him, and that as the president had no children to succeed him, the vice-president had, and if the treason had succeeded, and the hint with it, the goldsmith might be sent for to take measure of the head of John or of his son for a golden wig. In this case, the good people of Boston might have for a king the man they have rejected as a delegate. The representative system is fatal to ambition.

Knowing, as I do, the consummate vanity of John Adams, and the shallowness of his judgment, I can easily picture to myself that when he arrived at the Federal City he was strutting in the pomp of his imagination before the presidential house, or in the audience hall, and exulting in the language of Nebuchadnezzar,* "Is not this great Babylon, that I have built for the honour of my Majesty!" But in that unfortunate hour, or soon after, John, like Nebuchadnezzar, was driven from among men, and fled with the speed of a post-horse.

Some of John Adams's loyal subjects, I see, have been to present him with an address on his birthday; but the language they use is too tame for the occasion. Birthday addresses, like birthday odes, should not creep along like mildrops down a cabbage leaf, but roll in a torrent of poetical metaphor. I will give them a specimen for the next year. Here it is—

When an Ant, in travelling over the globe, lift up its foot, and put it again on the ground, it shakes the earth to its centre: but when YOU, the mighty Ant of the East, was born, &c. &c. &c., the centre jumped upon the surface.

This, gentlemen, is the proper style of addresses from *well-bred* ants to the monarch of the ant hills; and as I never take pay for preaching, praying, politics, or poetry, I make you a present of it. Some people talk of impeaching John Adams; but I am for softer measures. I would keep him to make fun of. He will then answer one of the ends for which he was born, and he ought to be thankful that I am arrived to take his part. I voted in earnest to save the life of one unfortunate king, and I now vote in jest to save another. It is my fate to be always plagued with fools. But to return to Federalism and apostacy.

The plan of the leaders of the faction was to overthrow the liberties of the new world, and place government on the corrupt system of the old. They wanted to hold their power by a more lasting tenure than the choice of their constituents. It is impossible to account for their conduct and the measures they adopted on any other ground. But to accomplish that object, a standing army and a prodigal revenue must be raised; and to obtain these, pretences must be invented to deceive. Alarms of dangers that did not exist even in imagination, but in the direct spirit of lying, were spread abroad. Apostacy stalked through the land in the garb of patriotism, and the torch of treason blinded for a while the flame of liberty.

---

*King of Babylonia (ruled c.605–562 B.C.; died 562 B.C.) who destroyed Jerusalem in 586 B.C. He is mentioned in numerous books of the Old Testament.

For what purpose could an army of twenty-five thousand men be wanted? A single reflection might have taught the most credulous that while the war raged between France and England, neither could spare a man to invade America. For what purpose, then, could it be wanted? The case carries its own explanation. It was wanted for the purpose of destroying the representative system, for it could be employed for no other. Are these men Federalists? If they are, they are federalized to deceive and to destroy.

The rage against Dr. Logan's* patriotic and voluntary mission to France was excited by the shame they felt at the detection of the false alarms they had circulated. As to the opposition given by the remnant of the faction to the repeal of the taxes laid on during the former administration, it is easily accounted for. The repeal of those taxes was a sentence of condemnation on those who laid them on, and in the opposition they gave in that repeal, they are to be considered in the light of criminals standing on their defence, and the country has passed judgment upon them.

THOMAS PAINE.

CITY OF WASHINGTON, LOVETT'S HOTEL,
NOV. 19, 1802.

LETTER NO. THREE

TO ELECT, AND TO reject, is the prerogative of a free people.

Since the establishment of Independence, no period has arrived that so decidedly proves the excellence of the representative system of government, and its superiority over every other, as the time we now live in. Had America been cursed with John Adams's *hereditary Monarchy*, or Alexander Hamilton's *Senate for life*, she must have sought, in the doubtful contest of civil war, what she now obtains by

---

*George Logan (1753–1821), Quaker physician who initiated a personal diplomatic mission to France in 1798.

the expression of public will. An appeal to elections decides better than an appeal to the sword.

The Reign of Terror that raged in America during the latter end of the Washington administration, and the whole of that of Adams, is enveloped in mystery to me. That there were men in the government hostile to the representative system, was once their boast, though it is now their overthrow, and therefore the fact is established against them. But that so large a mass of the people should become the dupes of those who were loading them with taxes in order to load them with chains, and deprive them of the right of election, can be ascribed only to that species of wildfire rage, lighted up by falsehood, that not only acts without reflection, but is too impetuous to make any.

There is a general and striking difference between the genuine effects of truth itself, and the effects of falsehood believed to be truth. Truth is naturally benign; but falsehood believed to be truth is always furious. The former delights in serenity, is mild and persuasive, and seeks not the auxiliary aid of invention. The latter sticks at nothing. It has naturally no morals. Every lie is welcome that suits its purpose. It is the innate character of the thing to act in this manner, and the criterion by which it may be known, whether in politics or religion. When any thing is attempted to be supported by lying, it is presumptive evidence that the thing so supported is a lie also. The stock on which a lie can be grafted must be of the same species as the graft.

What is become of the mighty clamour of French invasion, and the cry that our country is in danger, and taxes and armies must be raised to defend it? The danger is fled with the faction that created it, and what is worst of all, the money is fled too. It is I only that have committed the hostility of invasion, and all the artillery of popguns are prepared for action. Poor fellows, how they foam! They set half their own partisans in laughter; for among ridiculous things nothing is more ridiculous than ridiculous rage. But I hope they will not leave off. I shall lose half my greatness when they cease to lie.

So far as respects myself, I have reason to believe, and a right to say, that the leaders of the Reign of Terror in America and the leaders of the Reign of Terror in France, during the time of Robespierre, were in character the same sort of men; or how is it to be accounted for, that I was persecuted by both at the same time? When I was voted out of the French Convention, the reason assigned for it was, that I was a foreigner. When Robespierre had me seized in the night, and imprisoned in the Luxembourg, (where I remained eleven months,) he assigned no reason for it. But when he proposed bringing me to the tribunal, which was like sending me at once to the scaffold, he then assigned a reason, and the reason was, *for the interests of America as well as of France. "Pour les interests de l' Amérique autant que de la France."* The words are in his own hand-writing, and reported to the Convention by the committee appointed to examine his papers, and are printed in their report, with this reflection added to them, *"Why Thomas Paine more than another? Because he contributed to the liberty of both worlds."*

There must have been a coalition in sentiment, if not in fact, between the Terrorists of America and the Terrorists of France, and Robespierre must have known it, or he could not have had the idea of putting America into the bill of accusation against me. Yet these men, these Terrorists of the new world, who were waiting in the devotion of their hearts for the joyful news of my destruction, are the same banditti who are now bellowing in all the hacknied language of hacknied hypocrisy, about humanity, and piety, and often about something they call infidelity, and they finish with the chorus of *Crucify him, crucify him.* I am become so famous among them, they cannot eat or drink without me. I serve them as a standing dish, and they cannot make up a bill of fare if I am not in it.

But there is one dish, and that the choicest of all, that they have not presented on the table, and it is time they should. They have not yet *accused Providence of Infidelity.* Yet according to their outrageous piety, she must be as bad as Thomas Paine; she has protected him in all his dangers, patronized him in all his undertakings, encouraged him in all his ways, and rewarded him at last by bringing him in safety and in health to the Promised Land. This is more than she did by the Jews, the chosen people, that they tell us she brought out of the land of Egypt, and out of the house of bondage; for they all died in the wilderness, and Moses too.

I was one of the nine members that composed the first Committee of Constitution. Six of them have been destroyed. Sieyès*

---

*Emmanuel Joseph Sieyès (1748–1836), French Revolutionary leader and radical pamphleteer; see *Rights of Man*, p. 194.

and myself have survived—he by bending with the times, and I by not bending. The other survivor joined Robespierre, he was seized and imprisoned in his turn, and sentenced to transportation. He has since apologized to me for having signed the warrant, by saying he felt himself in danger and was obliged to do it.

Herault Sechelles, an acquaintance of Mr. Jefferson, and a good patriot, was my *suppléant* as member of the Committee of Constitution, that is, he was to supply my place, if I had not accepted or had resigned, being next in number of votes to me. He was imprisoned in the Luxembourg with me, was taken to the tribunal and the guillotine, and I, his principal, was left.

There were two foreigners in the Convention, Anarcharsis Clootz* and myself. We were both put out of the Convention by the same vote, arrested by the same order, and carried to prison together the same night. He was taken to the guillotine, and I was again left. Joel Barlow[†] was with us when we went to prison.

Joseph Lebon, one of the vilest characters that ever existed, and who made the streets of Arras run with blood, was my *suppléant*, as member of the Convention for the department of the Pas de Calais. When I was put out of the Convention he came and took my place. When I was liberated from prison and voted again into the Convention, he was sent to the same prison and took my place there, and he was sent to the guillotine instead of me. He supplied my place all the way through.

One hundred and sixty-eight persons were taken out of the Luxembourg in one night, and a hundred and sixty of them guillotined next day, of which I now know I was to have been one; and the manner I escaped that fate is curious, and has all the appearance of accident.

The room in which I was lodged was on the ground floor, and one of a long range of rooms under a gallery, and the door of it opened outward and flat against the wall; so that when it was open

---

*That is, Anacharsis Cloots: Jean-Baptiste du Val-de-Grâce, baron de Cloots (1755–1794), Prussian participant in the French Revolution; see *The Age of Reason*, p. 307.
[†]Barlow (1754–1812) was an American poet and diplomat; see *The Age of Reason*, p. 308.

the inside of the door appeared outward, and the contrary when it was shut. I had three comrades, fellow prisoners with me, Joseph Vanhuele, of Bruges, since President of the Municipality of that town, Michael Rubyns, and Charles Bastini of Louvain.

When persons by scores and by hundreds were to be taken out of the prison for the guillotine it was always done in the night, and those who performed that office had a private mark or signal, by which they knew what rooms to go to, and what number to take. We, as I have stated, were four, and the door of our room was marked, unobserved by us, with that number in chalk; but it happened, if happening is a proper word, that the mark was put on when the door was open, and flat against the wall, and thereby came on the inside when we shut it at night, and the destroying angel passed by it. A few days after this, Robespierre fell, and Mr. Monroe* arrived and reclaimed me, and invited me to his house.

During the whole of my imprisonment, prior to the fall of Robespierre, there was no time when I could think my life worth twenty-four hours, and my mind was made up to meet its fate. The Americans in Paris went in a body to the Convention to reclaim me, but without success. There was no party among them with respect to me. My only hope then rested on the government of America, that it would *remember me*. But the icy heart of ingratitude, in whatever man it be placed, has neither feeling nor sense of honour. The letter of Mr. Jefferson has served to wipe away the reproach, and done justice to the mass of the people of America.

When a party was forming, in the latter end of 1777, and beginning of 1778, of which John Adams was one, to remove Mr. Washington from the command of the army on the complaint that *he did nothing*, I wrote the fifth number of the Crisis, and published it at Lancaster, (Congress then being at Yorktown, in Pennsylvania,) to ward off that meditated blow; for though I well knew that the black times of '76 were the natural consequence of his want of military judgment in the choice of positions into which the army was put about New York and New Jersey, I could see no possible advantage, and nothing but mis-

---

*James Monroe (1758–1831), fifth president of the United States, who, while he was the American minister to France in 1794, befriended Paine.

chief, that could arise by distracting the army into parties, which would have been the case had the motion gone on.

General [Charles] Lee, who with a sarcastic genius joined a great fund of military knowledge, was perfectly right when he said "*We have no business on islands, and in the bottom of bogs, where the enemy, by the aid of its ships, can bring its whole force against a part of ours and shut it up.*" This had like to have been the case at New York, and it was the case at Fort Washington, and would have been the case at Fort Lee if General [Nathaniel] Greene had not moved instantly off on the first news of the enemy's approach. I was with Greene through the whole of that affair, and know it perfectly.

But though I came forward in defence of Mr. Washington when he was attacked, and made the best that could be made of a series of blunders that had nearly ruined the country, he left me to perish when I was in prison. But as I told him of it in his life-time, I should not now bring it up if the ignorant impertinence of some of the Federal papers, who are pushing Mr. Washington forward as their stalking horse, did not make it necessary.

That gentleman did not perform his part in the Revolution better, nor with more honour, than I did mine, and the one part was as necessary as the other. He accepted as a present, (though he was already rich,) a hundred thousand acres of land in America, and left me to occupy six foot of earth in France. I wish, for his own reputation, he had acted with more justice. But it was always known of Mr. Washington, by those who best knew him, that he was of such an icy and death-like constitution, that he neither loved his friends nor hated his enemies. But, be this as it may, I see no reason that a difference between Mr. Washington and me should be made a theme of discord with other people. There are those who may see merit in both, without making themselves partisans of either, and with this reflection I close the subject.

As to the hypocritical abuse thrown out by the Federalists on other subjects, I recommend to them the observance of a commandment that existed before either Christian or Jew existed:

> Thou shalt make a covenant with thy senses:
> With thine eye, that it behold no evil,
> With thine ear, that it hear no evil,

> With thy tongue, that it speak no evil,
> With thy hands, that they commit no evil.

If the Federalists will follow this commandment, they will leave off lying.

THOMAS PAINE.

FEDERAL CITY, LOVETT'S HOTEL,
NOV. 26, 1802.

LETTER NO. FOUR

AS CONGRESS IS ON the point of meeting, the public papers will necessarily be occupied with the debates of the ensuing session, and as, in consequence of my long absence from America, my private affairs require my attendance, (for it is necessary I do this, or I could not preserve, as I do, my independence,) I shall close my address to the public with this letter.

I congratulate them on the success of the late elections, and *that* with the additional confidence, that while honest men are chosen and wise measures pursued, neither the treason of apostasy, masked under the name of Federalism, of which I have spoken in my second letter, nor the intrigues of foreign emissaries, acting in concert with that mask, can prevail.

As to the licentiousness of the papers calling themselves *Federal*, a name that apostasy has taken, it can hurt nobody but the party or the persons who support such papers. There is naturally a wholesome pride in the public mind that revolts at open vulgarity. It feels itself dishonoured even by hearing it, as a chaste woman feels dishonour by hearing obscenity she cannot avoid. It can smile at wit, or be diverted with strokes of satirical humour, but it detests the *blackguard*. The same sense of propriety that governs in private companies, governs in public life. If a man in company runs his wit upon another, it may draw a smile from some persons present, but as soon as he turns a blackguard in his language the company gives him up;

and it is the same in public life. The event of the late election shows this to be true; for in proportion as those papers have become more and more vulgar and abusive, the elections have gone more and more against the party they support, or that supports them. Their predecessor, *Porcupine* [Cobbett*] had wit—these scribblers have none. But as soon as his *blackguardism* (for it is the proper name of it) outran his wit, he was abandoned by every body but the English Minister who protected him.

The Spanish proverb says, "*there never was a cover large enough to hide itself*"; and the proverb applies to the case of those papers and the shattered remnant of the faction that supports them. The falsehoods they fabricate, and the abuse they circulate, is a cover to hide something from being seen, but it is not large enough to hide itself. It is as a tub thrown out to the whale to prevent its attacking and sinking the vessel. They want to draw the attention of the public from thinking about, or inquiring into, the measures of the late administration, and the reason why so much public money was raised and expended; and so far as a lie today, and a new one tomorrow, will answer this purpose, it answers theirs. It is nothing to them whether they be believed or not, for if the negative purpose be answered the main point is answered, to them.

He that picks your pocket always tries to make you look another way. "Look," says he, "at yon man t'other side the street—what a nose he has got? Lord, yonder is a chimney on fire!—Do you see yon man going along in the salamander great coat? That is the very man that stole one of Jupiter's satellites, and sold it to a countryman for a gold watch, and it set his breeches on fire!" Now the man that has his hand in your pocket, does not care a farthing whether you believe what he says or not. All his aim is to prevent your looking at *him;* and this is the case with the remnant of the Federal faction. The leaders of it have imposed upon the country, and they want to turn the attention of it from the subject.

In taking up any public matter, I have never made it a consideration, and never will, whether it be popular or unpopular; but whether it be *right* or *wrong*. The right will always become the popular, if it

---

*Reference to "Peter Porcupine," the English wit and political essayist William Cobbett (1763–1835).

has courage to show itself, and the shortest way is always a straight line. I despise expedients, they are the gutter-hole of politics, and the sink where reputation dies. In the present case, as in every other, I cannot be accused of using any; and I have no doubt but thousands will hereafter be ready to say, as Gouverneur Morris said to me, after having abused me pretty handsomely in Congress for the opposition I gave the fraudulent demand of Silas Deane* of two thousand pounds sterling: "*Well, we were all duped, and I among the rest!*"

Were the late administration to be called upon to give reasons for the expence it put the country to, it can give none. The danger of an invasion was a bubble that served as a cover to raise taxes and armies to be employed on some other purpose. But if the people of America believed it true, the cheerfulness with which they supported those measures and paid those taxes is an evidence of their patriotism; and if they supposed me their enemy, though in that supposition they did me injustice, it was not injustice in them. He that acts as he believes, though he may act wrong, is not conscious of wrong.

But though there was no danger, no thanks are due to the late administration for it. They sought to blow up a flame between the two countries; and so intent were they upon this, that they went out of their way to accomplish it. In a letter which the Secretary of State, Timothy Pickering, wrote to Mr. Skipwith, the American Consul at Paris, be broke off from the official subject of his letter, to *thank God* in very exulting language, *that the Russians had cut the French army to pieces.* Mr. Skipwith, after showing me the letter, very prudently concealed it.

It was the injudicious and wicked acrimony of this letter, and some other like conduct of the then Secretary of State, that occasioned me, in a letter to a friend in the government, to say, that if there was any official business to be done in France, till a regular Minister could be appointed, it could not be trusted to a more proper person than Mr. Skipwith. "*He is,*" said I, "*an honest man, and will do business, and that with good manners to the government he is commis-*

---

*Deane (1737–1789) was a Continental Congressman and diplomat involved in controversial foreign loans.

sioned to act with. A faculty which that BEAR, *Timothy Pickering, wanted, and which the* BEAR *of that* BEAR, *John Adams, never possessed."*

In another letter to the same friend, in 1797, and which was put unsealed under cover to Colonel Burr* I expressed a satisfaction that Mr. Jefferson, since he was not president, had accepted the vice presidency; *"for,"* said I, *"John Adams has such a talent for blundering and offending, it will be necessary to keep an eye over him."* He has now sufficiently proved, that though I have not the spirit of prophecy, I have the gift of *judging right*. And all the world knows, for it cannot help knowing, that to judge *rightly* and to write *clearly*, and that upon all sorts of subjects, to be able to command thought and as it were to play with it at pleasure, and be always master of one's temper in writing, is the faculty only of a serene mind, and the attribute of a happy and philosophical temperament. The scribblers, who know me not, and who fill their papers with paragraphs about me, besides their want of talents, drink too many slings and drains in a morning to have any chance with me. But, poor fellows, they must do something for the little pittance they get from their employers. This is my apology for them.

My anxiety to get back to America was great for many years. It is the country of my heart, and the place of my political and literary birth. It was the American revolution that made me an author, and forced into action the mind that had been dormant, and had no wish for public life, nor has it now. By the accounts I received, she appeared to me to be going wrong, and that some meditated treason against her liberties lurked at the bottom of her government. I heard that my friends were oppressed, and I longed to take my stand among them, and if other times to *try men's souls* were to arrive, that I might bear my share. But my efforts to return were ineffectual.

As soon as Mr. Monroe had made a good standing with the French government, for the conduct of his predecessor [Morris] had made his reception as Minister difficult, he wanted to send despatches to his own government by a person to whom he could confide a verbal communication, and he fixed his choice on me. He

---

*Aaron Burr (1756–1836); U.S. vice president (1801–1805), famous for shooting Alexander Hamilton in a duel.

then applied to the Committee of Public Safety for a passport; but as I had been voted again into the Convention, it was only the Convention that could give the passport; and as an application to them for that purpose, would have made my going publicly known, I was obliged to sustain the disappointment, and Mr. Monroe to lose the opportunity.

When that gentleman left France to return to America, I was to have gone with him. It was fortunate I did not. The vessel he sailed in was visited by a British frigate, that searched every part of it, and down to the hold, for Thomas Paine. I then went, the same year, to embark at Havre. But several British frigates were cruizing in sight of the port who knew I was there, and I had to return again to Paris. Seeing myself thus cut off from every opportunity that was in my power to command, I wrote to Mr. Jefferson, that, if the fate of the election should put him in the chair of the presidency, and he should have occasion to send a frigate to France, he would give me the opportunity of returning by it, which he did. But I declined coming by the *Maryland*, the vessel that was offered me, and waited for the frigate that was to bring the new Minister, Mr. Chancellor Livingston, to France. But that frigate was ordered round to the Mediterranean; and as at that time the war was over, and the British cruisers called in, I could come any way. I then agreed to come with Commodore Barney in a vessel be had engaged. It was again fortunate I did not, for the vessel sank at sea, and the people were preserved in the boat.

Had half the number of evils befallen me that the number of dangers amount to through which I have been preserved, there are those who would ascribe it to the wrath of heaven; why then do they not ascribe my preservation to the protecting favour of heaven? Even in my worldly concerns I have been blessed. The little property I left in America, and which I cared nothing about, not even to receive the rent of it, has been increasing in the value of its capital more than eight hundred dollars every year, for the fourteen years and more that I have been absent from it. I am now in my circumstances independent; and my economy makes me rich. As to my health, it is perfectly good, and I leave the world to judge of the stature of my mind. I am in every instance a living contradiction to the mortified Federalists.

In my publications, I follow the rule I began with in *Common Sense*, that is, to consult nobody, nor to let any body see what I write till it appears publicly. Were I to do otherwise, the case would be, that between the timidity of some, who are so afraid of doing wrong that they never do right, the puny judgment of others, and the despicable craft of preferring *expedient to right*, as if the world was a world of babies in leading strings, I should get forward with nothing. My path is a right line, as straight and clear to me as a ray of light. The boldness (if they will have it to be so) with which I speak on any subject, is a compliment to the judgment of the reader. It is like saying to him, *I treat you as a man and not as a child.* With respect to any worldly object, as it is impossible to discover any in me, therefore what I do, and my manner of doing it, ought to be ascribed to a good motive.

In a great affair, where the happiness of man is at stake, I love to work for nothing; and so fully am I under the influence of this principle, that I should lose the spirit, the pleasure, and the pride of it, were I conscious that I looked for reward; and with this declaration, I take my leave for the present.

THOMAS PAINE.

FEDERAL CITY, LOVETT'S HOTEL,
DEC. 3, 1802.

LETTER NO. FIVE

IT IS ALWAYS THE interest of a far greater part of the nation to have a thing right than to have it wrong; and therefore, in a country whose government is founded on the system of election and representation, the fate of every party is decided by its principles.

As this system is the only form and principle of government by which liberty can be preserved, and the only one that can embrace all the varieties of a great extent of country, it necessarily follows, that to have the representation real, the election must be real; and that where the election is a fiction, the representation is a fiction also. *Like will always produce like.*

A great deal has been said and written concerning the conduct of Mr. Burr, during the late contest, in the federal legislature, whether Mr. Jefferson or Mr. Burr should be declared President of the United States. Mr. Burr has been accused of intriguing to obtain the Presidency. Whether this charge be substantiated or not makes little or no part of the purport of this letter. There is a point of much higher importance to attend to than any thing that relates to the individual Mr. Burr: for the great point is not whether Mr. Burr has intrigued, but whether the legislature has intrigued with *him.*

Mr. Ogden, a relation of one of the senators of New Jersey of the same name, and of the party assuming the style of Federalists, has written a letter published in the New York papers, signed with his name, the purport of which is to exculpate Mr. Burr from the charges brought against him. In this letter he says:

"When about to return from Washington, two or three *members of Congress* of the federal party spoke to me of *their views*, as to the election of a president, desiring me to converse with Colonel Burr on the subject, and to ascertain *whether he would enter into terms.* On my return to New York I called on Colonel Burr, and communicated the above to him. He explicitly declined the explanation, and did neither propose nor agree to any terms."

How nearly is human cunning allied to folly! The animals to whom nature has given the faculty we call *cunning*, know always when to use it, and use it wisely; but when man descends to cunning, he blunders and betrays.

Mr. Ogden's letter is intended to exculpate Mr. Burr from the charge of intriguing to obtain the presidency; and the letter that he (Ogden) writes for this purpose is direct evidence against his party in Congress, that they intrigued with Burr to obtain him for President, and employed him (Ogden) for the purpose. To save *Aaron*, he betrays *Moses*, and then turns informer against the *Golden Calf.**

It is but of little importance to the world to know if Mr. Burr *listened* to an intriguing proposal, but it is of great importance to the

---

*See the Bible, Exodus 32.

constituents to know if their representatives in Congress made one. The ear can commit no crime, but the tongue may; and therefore the right policy is to drop Mr. Burr, as being only the hearer, and direct the whole charge against the Federal faction in Congress as the active original culprit, or, if the priests will have scripture for it, as the serpent that beguiled Eve.

The plot of the intrigue was to make Mr. Burr President, on the private condition of his agreeing to, and entering into, terms with them, that is, with the proposers. Had then the election been made, the country, knowing nothing of this private and illegal transaction, would have supposed, for who could have supposed otherwise, that it had a President according to the forms, principles, and intention of the constitution. No such thing. Every form, principle, and intention of the constitution would have been violated; and instead of a President, it would have had a mute, a sort of image, hand-bound and tongue-tied, the dupe and slave of a party, placed on the theatre of the United States, and acting the farce of President.

It is of little importance, in a constitutional sense, to know what the terms to be proposed might be, because any terms other than those which the constitution prescribes to a President are criminal. Neither do I see how Mr. Burr, or any other person put in the same condition, could have taken the oath prescribed by the constitution to a President, which is, "*I do solemnly swear* (or affirm,) *that I will faithfully execute the office of President of the United States, and will to the best of my ability preserve, protect, and defend the Constitution of the United States.*"

How, I ask, could such a person have taken such an oath, knowing at the same time that he had entered into the Presidency on terms unknown in the Constitution, and private, and which would deprive him of the freedom and power of acting as President of the United States, agreeably to his constitutional oath?

Mr. Burr, by not agreeing to terms, has escaped the danger to which they exposed him, and the perjury that would have followed, and also the punishment annexed thereto. Had he accepted the Presidency on terms unknown in the constitution, and private, and had the transaction afterwards transpired, (which it most probably would, for roguery is a thing difficult to conceal,) it would have produced a sensation in the country too violent to be quieted, and too just to be resisted; and in any case the election must have been void.

But what are we to think of those members of Congress, who having taken an oath of the same constitutional import as the oath of the President, violate that oath by tampering to obtain a President on private conditions. If this is not sedition against the constitution and the country, it is difficult to define what sedition in a representative can be.

Say not that this statement of the case is the effect of personal or party resentment. No. It is the effect of *sincere concern* that such corruption, of which this is but a sample, should, in the space of a few years, have crept into a country that had the fairest opportunity that Providence ever gave, within the knowledge of history, of making itself an illustrious example to the world.

What the terms were, or were to be, it is probable we never shall know; or what is more probable, that feigned ones, if any, will be given. But from the conduct of the party since that time we may conclude, that no taxes would have been taken off, that the clamour for war would have been kept up, new expences incurred, and taxes and offices increased in consequence; and, among the articles of a private nature, that the leaders in this seditious traffic were to stipulate with the mock President for lucrative appointments for themselves.

But if the plotters against the Constitution understood their business; and they had been plotting long enough to be masters of it, a single article would have comprehended every thing, which is, *That the President (thus made) should be governed in all cases whatsoever by a private junto appointed by themselves.* They could then, through the medium of a mock President, have negatived all bills which their party in Congress could not have opposed with success, and reduced representation to a nullity.

The country has been imposed upon, and the real culprits are but few; and as it is necessary for the peace, harmony, and honour of the Union, to separate the deceiver from the deceived, the betrayer from the betrayed, that men who once were friends, and that in the worst of times, should be friends again, it is necessary, as a beginning, that this dark business be brought to full investigation. Ogden's letter is direct evidence of the fact of tampering to obtain a conditional President. He knows the two or three members of Congress that commissioned him, and they know who commissioned them.

THOMAS PAINE.

FEDERAL CITY, LOVETT'S HOTEL,
JAN. 29TH, 1803.

LETTER NO. SIX

RELIGION AND WAR IS the cry of the Federalists; Morality and Peace the voice of Republicans. The union of Morality and Peace is congenial; but that of Religion and War is a paradox, and the solution of it is hypocrisy.

The leaders of the Federalists have no judgment; their plans no consistency of parts; and want of consistency is the natural consequence of want of principle.

They exhibit to the world the curious spectacle of an *Opposition* without a *cause*, and conduct without system. Were they, as doctors, to prescribe medicine as they practise politics, they would poison their patients with destructive compounds.

There are not two things more opposed to each other than War and Religion; and yet, in the double game those leaders have to play, the one is necessarily the theme of their politics, and the other the text of their sermons. The week-day orator of Mars, and the Sunday preacher of Federal Grace, play like gamblers into each other's hands, and this they call Religion.

Though hypocrisy can counterfeit every virtue, and become the associate of every vice, it requires a great dexterity of craft to give it the power of deceiving. A painted sun may glisten, but it cannot warm. For hypocrisy to personate virtue successfully it must know and feel what virtue is, and as it cannot long do this, it cannot long deceive. When an orator foaming for War breathes forth in another sentence a *plaintive piety of words*, he may as well write HYPOCRISY on his front.

The late attempt of the Federal leaders in Congress (for they acted without the knowledge of their constituents) to plunge the country into War, merits not only reproach but indignation. It was madness, conceived in ignorance and acted in wickedness. The head and the heart went partners in the crime.

A neglect of punctuality in the performance of a treaty is made a *cause* of war by the *Barbary powers*, and of remonstrance and explanation by *civilized powers*. The Mahometans of Barbary negociate by the sword—they seize first, and expostulate afterwards; and the federal leaders have been labouring to *barbarize* the United States by adopting the practice of the Barbary States, and this they call honnour. Let their honour and their hypocrisy go weep together, for both are defeated. Their present Administration is too moral for hypocrites, and too economical for public spendthrifts.

A man the least acquainted with diplomatic affairs must know that a neglect in punctuality is not one of the legal causes of war, unless that neglect be confirmed by a refusal to perform; and even then it depends upon circumstances connected with it. The world would be in continual quarrels and war, and commerce be annihilated, if Algerine policy was the law of nations. And were America, instead of becoming an example to the old world of good and moral government and civil manners, or, if they like it better, of gentlemanly conduct towards other nations, to set up the character of ruffian, that of *word and blow, and the blow first*, and thereby give the example of pulling down the little that civilization has gained upon barbarism, her Independence, instead of being an honour and a blessing, would become a curse upon the world and upon herself.

The conduct of the Barbary powers, though unjust in principle, is suited to their prejudices, situation, and circumstances. The crusades of the church to exterminate them fixed in their minds the unobliterated belief that every Christian power was their mortal enemy. Their religious prejudices, therefore, suggest the policy, which their situation and circumstances protect them in. As a people, they are neither commercial nor agricultural, they neither import nor export, have no property floating on the seas, nor ships and cargoes in the ports of foreign nations. No retaliation, therefore, can be acted upon them, and they sin secure from punishment.

But this is not the case with the United States. If she sins as a Barbary power, she must answer for it as a Civilized one. Her commerce is continually passing on the seas exposed to capture, and her ships and cargoes in foreign ports to detention and reprisal. An act of War committed by her in the Mississippi would produce a War against the commerce of the Atlantic States, and the latter would have to curse the policy that provoked the former. In every point, therefore, in which the character and interest of the United States be considered, it would ill become her to set an example contrary to the policy and custom of Civilized powers, and practised only by the Barbary powers, that of striking before she expostulates.

But can any man, calling himself a Legislator, and supposed by his constituents to know something of his duty, be so ignorant as to imagine that seizing on New Orleans would finish the affair or even contribute towards it? On the contrary it would have made it worse. The treaty right of deposite at New Orleans, and the right of the navigation of the Mississippi into the Gulph of Mexico, are distant things. New Orleans is more than an hundred miles in the country from the mouth of the river, and, as a place of deposite, is of no value if the mouth of the river be shut, which either France or Spain could do, and which our possession of New Orleans could neither prevent or remove. New Orleans in our possession, by an act of hostility, would have become a blockaded port, and consequently of no value to the western people as a place of deposite. Since, therefore, an interruption had arisen to the commerce of the western states, and until the matter could be brought to a fair explanation, it was of less injury to have the port shut and the river open, than to have the river shut and the port in our possession.

That New Orleans could be taken required no stretch of policy to plan, nor spirit of enterprize to effect. It was like marching behind a man to knock him down: and the dastardly slyness of such an attack would have stained the fame of the United States. Where there is no danger cowards are bold, and Captain Bobadils* are to be found in the Senate as well as on the stage. Even *Gouverneur*, on such a march, dare have shown a leg.

---

*Spanish soldier Francisco de Bobadilla (died 1502) sent to Santo Domingo by Ferdinand and Isabella of Spain on reports of dissension between Christopher Columbus and other Spaniards; Bobadilla returned Columbus to Spain in chains but he was later freed to make his fourth and final voyage for the Spanish monarchs.

The people of the western country to whom the Mississippi serves as an inland sea to their commerce, must be supposed to understand the circumstances of that commerce better than a man who is a stranger to it; and as they have shown no approbation of the war-whoop measures of the Federal senators, it becomes presumptive evidence they disapprove them. This is a new mortification for those war-whoop politicians; for the case is, that finding themselves losing ground and withering away in the Atlantic States, they laid hold of the affair of New Orleans in the vain hope of rooting and reinforcing themselves in the western States; and they did this without perceiving that it was one of those ill judged hypocritical expedients in politics, that whether it succeeded or failed the event would be the same. Had their motion [that of Ross and Morris] succeeded, it would have endangered the commerce of the Atlantic States and ruined their reputation there; and on the other hand the attempt to make a tool of the western people was so badly concealed as to extinguish all credit with them.

But hypocrisy is a vice of sanguine constitution. It flatters and promises itself every thing; and it has yet to learn, with respect to moral and political reputation, it is less dangerous to offend than to deceive.

To the measures of administration, supported by the firmness and integrity of the majority in Congress, the United States owe, as far as human means are concerned, the preservation of peace, and of national honour. The confidence which the western people reposed in the government and their representatives is rewarded with success. They are reinstated in their rights with the least possible loss of time; and their harmony with the people of New Orleans, so necessary to the prosperity of the United States, which would have been broken, and the seeds of discord sown in its place, had hostilities been preferred to accommodation, remains unimpaired. Have the Federal ministers of the church meditated on these matters? and laying aside, as they ought to do, their electioneering and vindictive prayers and sermons, returned thanks that peace is preserved, and commerce, without the stain of blood?

In the pleasing contemplation of this state of things the mind, by comparison, carries itself back to those days of uproar and extravagance that marked the career of the former administration, and decides, by the unstudied impulse of its own feelings, that something must then have been wrong. Why was it, that America, formed for happiness, and remote by situation and circumstances from the troubles and tumults of the European world, became plunged into its vortex and contaminated with its crimes? The answer is easy. Those who were then at the head of affairs were apostates from the principles of the revolution. Raised to an elevation they had not a right to expect, nor judgment to conduct, they became like feathers in the air, and blown about by every puff of passion or conceit.

Candour would find some apology for their conduct if want of judgment was their only defect. But error and crime, though often alike in their features, are distant in their characters and in their origin. The one has its source in the weakness of the head, the other in the hardness of the heart, and the coalition of the two, describes the former Administration.*

Had no injurious consequences arisen from the conduct of that Administration, it might have passed for error or imbecility, and been permitted to die and be forgotten. The grave is kind to innocent offence. But even innocence, when it is a cause of injury, ought to undergo an enquiry.

The country, during the time of the former Administration, was kept in continual agitation and alarm; and that no investigation might be made into its conduct, it entrenched itself within a magic circle of terror, and called it a SEDITION LAW. Violent and mysterious in its measures and arrogant in its manners, it affected to disdain information, and insulted the principles that raised it from obscurity. John Adams and Timothy Pickering were men whom nothing but the accidents of the times rendered visible on the political horizon. Elevation turned their heads, and public indignation hath cast them to the ground. But an inquiry into the conduct and measures of that Administration is nevertheless necessary.

The country was put to great expense. Loans, taxes, and standing armies became the standing order of the day. The militia, said Secretary Pickering, are not to be depended upon, and fifty thousand men must be raised. For what? No cause to justify such measures has yet appeared. No discovery of such a cause has yet been made. The

---

*Reference to the administration of John Adams (1735–1826), who served as second U.S. president from 1797 to 1801.

pretended Sedition Law shut up the sources of investigation, and the precipitate flight of John Adams closed the scene. But the matter ought not to sleep here.

It is not to gratify resentment, or encourage it in others, that I enter upon this subject. It is not in the power of man to accuse me of a persecuting spirit. But some explanation ought to be had. The motives and objects respecting the extraordinary and expensive measures of the former Administration ought to be known. The Sedition Law, that shield of the moment, prevented it then, and justice demands it now. If the public have been imposed upon, it is proper they should know it; for where judgment is to act, or a choice is to be made, knowledge is first necessary. The conciliation of parties, if it does not grow out of explanation, partakes of the character of collusion or indifference.

There has been guilt somewhere; and it is better to fix it where it belongs, and separate the deceiver from the deceived, than that suspicion, the bane of society, should range at large, and sour the public mind. The military measures that were proposed and carrying on during the former administration, could not have for their object the defence of the country against invasion. This is a case that decides itself; for it is self evident, that while the war raged in Europe, neither France nor England could spare a man to send to America. The object, therefore, must be something at home, and that something was the overthrow of the representative system of government, for it could be nothing else. But the plotters got into confusion and became enemies to each other. Adams hated and was jealous of Hamilton, and Hamilton hated and despised both Adams and Washington. Surly Timothy stood aloof, as he did at the affair of Lexington, and the part that fell to the public was to pay the expense.

But ought a people who, but a few years ago, were fighting the battles of the world, for liberty had no home but here, ought such a people to stand quietly by and see that liberty undermined by apostacy and overthrown by intrigue? Let the tombs of the slain recall their recollection, and the forethought of what their children are to be revive and fix in their hearts the love of liberty.

If the former administration can justify its conduct, give it the opportunity. The manner in which John Adams disappeared from the government renders an inquiry the more necessary. He gave some account of himself, lame and confused as it was, to certain *eastern wise men* who came to pay homage to him on his birthday. But if he thought it necessary to do this, ought he not to have rendered an account to the public. They had a right to expect it of him. In that *tête-à-tête* account, he says, "Some measures were the effect of imperious necessity, much against my inclination." What measures does Mr. Adams mean, and what is the imperious necessity to which he alludes? "Others (says he) were measures of the Legislature, which, although approved when passed, were never previously proposed or recommended by me." What measures, it may be asked, were those, for the public have a right to know the conduct of their representatives? "Some (says he) left to my discretion were never executed, because no necessity for them, in my judgment, ever occurred."

What does this dark apology, mixed with accusation, amount to, but to increase and confirm the suspicion that something was wrong? Administration only was possessed of foreign official information, and it was only upon that in formation communicated by him publicly or privately, or to Congress, that Congress could act; and it is not in the power of Mr. Adams to show, from the condition of the belligerent powers, that any imperious necessity called for the warlike and expensive measures of his Administration.

What the correspondence between Administration and Rufus King* in London, or Quincy Adams in Holland, or Berlin,† might be, is but little known. The public papers have told us that the former became cup-bearer from the London underwriters to Captain Truxtun,‡ or which, as Minister from a neutral nation, he ought to have been censured. It is, however, a feature that marks the politics of the Minister, and hints at the character of the correspondence.

I know that it is the opinion of several members of both houses of Congress, that an enquiry, with respect to the conduct of the late Administration, ought to be gone into. The convulsed state into which the country has been thrown will be best settled by a full and fair exposition of the conduct of that Administration, and the causes

---

*King (1755–1827) was American minister to Great Britain from 1796 to 1803.
†John Quincy Adams (1767–1848), the sixth U.S. president, was appointed minister to the Netherlands in 1794 and later promoted to the Berlin Legation.
‡Thomas Truxtun (1755–1822), American naval officer.

and object of that conduct. To be deceived, or to remain deceived, can be the interest of no man who seeks the public good; and it is the deceiver only, or one interested in the deception, that can wish to preclude enquiry.

The suspicion against the late Administration is, that it was plotting to overturn the representative system of government, and that it spread alarms of invasions that had no foundation, as a pretence for raising and establishing a military force as the means of accomplishing that object.

The law, called the Sedition Law, enacted, that if any person should write, or publish, or cause to be written or published, any libel [without defining what a libel is] against the Government of the United States, or either house of congress, or against the President, he should be punished by a fine not exceeding two thousand dollars, and by imprisonment not exceeding two years.

But it is a much greater crime for a president to plot against a Constitution and the liberties of the people, than for an individual to plot against a President; and consequently, John Adams is accountable to the public for his conduct, as the individuals under his administration were to the sedition law.

The object, however, of an enquiry, in this case, is not to punish, but to satisfy; and to shew, by example, to future administrations, that an abuse of power and trust, however disguised by appearances, or rendered plausible by pretence, is one time or other to be accounted for.

THOMAS PAINE.

BORDENTOWN, ON THE DELAWARE,
NEW JERSEY, MARCH 12, 1803.

INSPIRED BY THOMAS PAINE
AND HIS WRITINGS

History is to ascribe the American Revolution to Thomas Paine.
                                                    —*John Adams*

Thomas Paine had a galvanizing impact on pre-Revolutionary America. Before *Common Sense* was published, many residents of the colonies were unsure whether independence from Britain was in their best interests. The clarity and energy of Paine's landmark tract, one of the best-selling texts of the eighteenth century, turned the tide of public opinion toward revolution. The impact of *Common Sense*, coupled with Paine's intellectual relationship with many of America's founding fathers, led John Adams, who wrote bitterly about Paine at times, to deliver the oft-quoted epigram that history would ascribe the Revolution to this incendiary pamphleteer. Thomas Edison elaborated on this sentiment in 1925, remarking that Paine "was the equal of Washington in making American liberty possible. Where Washington performed Paine devised and wrote. The deeds of one in the Weld were matched by the deeds of the other with his pen" (from "The Philosophy of Paine"). Where General Washington was the hero of the sword, Thomas Paine was the originator of ideas.

Paine's work has several other distinctions. His "African Slavery in America" (1775) was among the earliest abolitionist writings in the colonies, while his series of essays collectively called *The American Crisis* (1776–1783) frequently receives credit for introducing the name "the United States of America." And the U.S. Social Security Administration praises *Agrarian Justice* (1797) for including the first proposal for benefits to the elderly in the United States.

Nonetheless, the great radical's legacy has been troubled at best. This is in great part due to the anticlerical opinions expressed in *The*

Age of Reason (1794), which Paine wrote after a lifetime of witnessing religion's abuse at the hands of politics and the church. The treatise earned the author countless enemies beyond those who disagreed with his political views. For numerous people, *The Age of Reason* overshadowed Paine's valuable service on behalf of American liberty. Many of his ideological opponents stooped to the lowest forms of slander in their attempts to discredit Paine and his notions of freedom: Hostile newspaper articles and vicious, so-called biographies by George Chalmers (writing in 1791 as Francis Oldys) and James Cheetham (published 1809) were widely circulated.

Partially because of these spurious biographies, the public for whom Paine had striven to advocate believed him to be a drunk, philanderer, tyrant, and thief, and he was dismissed during his later years, and after his death. The author, who retained none of the profits from his publications—he donated the proceeds to the American Revolution and other causes—died penniless and alone in New York City in 1809. Memories of Paine were not fond. A popular nursery rhyme appeared:

> Poor Tom Paine! There he lies:
> Nobody laughs and nobody cries.
> Where he has gone or how he fares
> Nobody knows and nobody cares.

And English poet Lord Byron, referring to a fervent Paine admirer who wished to transfer the author's remains to England, wrote in 1820:

> In digging up your bones, Tom Paine,
> Will Cobbett has done well;
> You visit him on earth again,
> He'll visit you in hell.

Most famously, Theodore Roosevelt, largely ignorant of Paine's contributions, dismissed the author as a "filthy little atheist" in his 1891 biography of Gouverneur Morris. This invidious tag sticks to Paine even today. The mid-nineteenth century, however, also saw some of the first balanced assessments of Paine to appear after his death. But it was the next century that would embrace Thomas Paine and his nuanced history, in the form of new scholarship, renewed publication of Paine's writing, and, most interestingly, original plays written in the hopes of humanizing "Poor Tom Paine."

Twentieth-Century Accounts of Thomas Paine

In the twentieth century, many writers presented more historically accurate estimations of Paine, including several interesting dramas based on the author's life. The best-selling novel *Citizen Tom Paine* (1943), by Howard Fast, a prominent American communist who was jailed for three months during the dark days of McCarthyism, presents Paine as a hothead idealist who has trouble getting along in society due to his brashness and refusal to accept the status quo. Eschewing the elaborate attention to setting that can bog down a historical novel, Fast's energetic work successfully imparts the vitality and urgency of Paine's life and message. The book also sensitively describes the inner torments that shaped Paine's irascible character. Where some ultimately positive portrayals of Paine shy away from the dark elements of the patriot's life—his drinking, his repellent personal hygiene—Fast's book portrays the ugly side of the *Common Sense* author. Featuring the founding fathers as supporting characters, *Citizen Tom Paine* deftly portrays both the American and the French Revolutions through Paine's unique point of view.

Fast took up the topic of Paine again for his 1986 play bearing the same title. But Fast's stage adaptation of *Citizen Tom Paine* benefits from wisdom garnered from more than four decades of experience. "I didn't write it from the book at all," Fast told the *Washington Post* in 1985. "There's almost half a century between then and now. When I was writing the novel I was 23 and a revolutionary. Now I'm 71 and someone who's been a revolutionary. The play is about how a revolution destroys its makers."

Other plays inspired by Paine include Joseph Lewis's *The Tragic Patriot* (1954), a production in five acts that follows the author's adventures in France. Using direct quotations from Paine's writings for some of its dialogue, the play traces Paine's arrival in France, his imprisonment, and his rescue by James Monroe. The play ends as Paine returns to America, but not before he denounces Napoleon for betraying the ideals of the French Revolution. *The Tragic Patriot* packs in as much historical detail as possible, featuring many very long monologues, real letters quoted verbatim, and a final script totaling more than 200 pages.

A more experimental play, Paul Foster's *Tom Paine* (1967) introduces a character known as "Tom Paine's Reputation" in addition to the real Tom Paine. The innovative production calls for audience participation, extended improvisation on the part of the actors, and surreal set pieces such as turtles with candles on their backs. Paine at thirty-seven appears on stage alongside Paine at sixteen and Paine on his deathbed. The author's entire life takes shape through the aggregation of these animated selves.

Jack Shepherd's *In Lambeth* (1989) speculates about the relationship between Paine and another great eighteenth-century thinker, the poet William Blake. Set in Blake's garden in Lambeth (near London), the play features the dramatic counterpoints between the practicality of Paine and the divine visions of Blake as they discuss the French Revolution. Shepherd's preface states that he based the play on Blake's idea that "opposition is true friendship." In a dramatic highlight of the play, the poet asks Paine, in regard to revolution, "How can you be sure you have not torn down one form of tyranny only to replace it with another?" Paine replies, "You *can't* be sure. . . . You have to *dedicate* yourself to the idea, to the *hope* that society can be changed for the better." The play ends with Blake urging his friend to flee England to save his life.

COMMENTS & QUESTIONS

In this section, we aim to provide the reader with an array of perspectives on the text, as well as questions that challenge those perspectives. The commentary has been culled from sources as diverse as reviews contemporaneous with the work, letters written by the author, literary criticism of later generations, and appreciations written throughout the work's history. Following the commentary, a series of questions seeks to filter Thomas Paine's Common Sense and Other Writings *through a variety of points of view and bring about a richer understanding of these enduring works.*

Comments

GEORGE WASHINGTON

A few more of such flaming arguments, as were exhibited at Falmouth and Norfolk, added to the sound doctrine and unanswerable reasoning contained in the pamphlet *Common Sense*, will not leave numbers at a loss to decide upon the propriety of a separation.

—from a letter to Joseph Reed (January 31, 1776)

ABIGAIL ADAMS

I am charmed by the Sentiments of *Common Sense*; and wonder how an honest Heart, one who wishes the welfare of their country, and the happiness of posterity can hesitate one moment at adopting them; I want to know how those Sentiments are received in Congress? I dare say there would be no difficulty in procuring a vote and instructions from all the Assemblies in New England for independency. I most sincerely wish that now in the Lucky Minuet it might be done.

—from a letter to John Adams (March 2, 1776)

GEORGE WASHINGTON

Can nothing be done in our Assembly for poor Paine? Must the merits, and Services of *Common Sense* continue to glide down the stream of time, unrewarded by this Country? His writings certainly have had a powerful effect on the public mind; ought they not then to meet an adequate return? He is poor! he is chagrined! and almost, if not altogether, in despair of relief. New York it is true, not the least distressed, nor best able State in the Union, has done something for him. This kind of provision he prefers to an allowance from Congress; he has reasons for it, which to him are conclusive, and such I think as would have weight on others. His views are moderate; a decent independency is, I believe, all he aims at. Should he not obtain this? If you think so, I am sure you will not only move the matter, but give it your support.

—from a letter to James Madison (June 12, 1784)

JAMES MADISON

Should exertions of genius which have been everywhere admired, and in America unanimously acknowledged, not save the author from indigence & distress, the loss of national character will hardly be balanced by the savings at the Treasury.

—from a letter to George Washington (August 12, 1784)

BENJAMIN FRANKLIN

Be assured, my dear friend, that instead of repenting that I was your introducer into America, I value myself on the share I had in procuring for it the acquisition of so useful and valuable a citizen.

—from a letter to Thomas Paine (September 27, 1785)

THOMAS JEFFERSON

Mr. Paine's answer to Burke will be a refreshing shower to their minds. It would bring England itself to reason and revolution if it was permitted to be read there.

—from a letter to Benjamin Vaughan (May 11, 1791)

THOMAS PAINE

And as to you, Sir, treacherous in private friendship (for so you have been to me, and that in the day of danger) and a hypocrite in public life, the world will be puzzled to decide whether you are an apostate or an impostor; whether you have abandoned good principles, or whether you ever had any.

—from a letter to George Washington (July 30, 1796)

JAMES MONROE

The citizens of the United States can never look back to the æra of their own revolution, without remembering, with those of other distinguished Patriots, the name of Thomas Paine. The services which he rendered them in their struggle for liberty have made an impression of gratitude which will never be erased, whilst they continue to merit the character of a just and generous people. He is now in prison, languishing under a disease, and which must be increased by his confinement. Permit me then, to call your attention to his situation, and to require that you will hasten his trial in case there be any charge against him, and if there be none, that you will cause him to be set at liberty.

—from *Letter to the Committee of General Surety* (November 1, 1794)

SAMUEL ADAMS

I have frequently with pleasure reflected on your services to *my* native and *your* adopted country. Your *Common Sense*, and your *Crisis*, unquestionably awakened the public mind, and led the people loudly to call for a declaration of our national independence. I therefore esteemed you as a warm friend to the liberty and lasting welfare of the human race. But when I heard you had turned your mind to a defence of infidelity, I felt myself much astonished and more grieved, that you had attempted a measure so injurious to the feelings and so repugnant to the true interest of so great a part of the citizens of the United States. The people of New England, if you will allow me to use a Scripture phrase, are fast returning to their first love. Will you excite among them the spirit of angry controversy at a time when they are hastening to amity and peace? I am told that some of our newspapers have announced your intention to publish an additional pamphlet upon the principles of your *Age of Reason*. Do you think that your pen, or the pen of any other man, can unchristianize the mass of our citizens, or have you hopes of converting a few of them to assist you in so bad a cause? We ought to think ourselves happy in the enjoyment of opinion, without the danger of persecution by civil or ecclesiastical law. Our friend, the President of the United States, has been calumniated for his liberal sentiments by men who have attributed that liberality to a latent design to promote the cause of infidelity. This, and all other slanders, have been made without the least shadow of proof. Neither religion nor liberty can long subsist in the tumult of altercation, and amidst the noise and violence of faction. *Felix qui cautus.* Adieu.

—from a letter to Thomas Paine (November 30, 1802)

JAMES CHEETHAM

As a literary work, *Common Sense*, energetically as it promoted the cause of independence, has no merit. Defective in arrangement, inelegant in diction, here and there a sentence excepted; with no profundity of argument, no felicity of remark, no extent of research, no classical allusion, nor comprehension of thought, it is fugitive in nature, and cannot be appealed to as authority on the subject of government. Its distinguishing characteristics are boldness and zeal; low sarcasm and deep-rooted malevolence. It owed its unprecedented popularity, on the one hand, to the British cabinet, which sought to triumph by bare-faced force instead of generous measures; and, on the other, to the manly spirit of the colonists, which, though often depressed, could not be conquered.

—from *The Life of Thomas Paine* (1809)

THOMAS CLIO RICKMAN

The *Life* by Cheetham is so palpably written to distort, disfigure, mislead, and vilify, and does this so bunglingly, that it defeats its own purposes, and becomes entertaining from the excess of its laboured and studied defamation. . . .

It is true that on his return [to America] in 1802, he received great attention from many of those who remembered the mighty influence of his writings in the gloomy period of the Revolution; and from others who had since embraced his principles; but these attentions were not, by many, long continued.

Thousands, who had formerly looked up to Mr. Paine as the principal founder of the Republic, had imbibed a strong dislike to him on account of his religious principles; and thousands more, who were opposed to his political principles, seized hold of the mean and dastardly expedient of attacking those principles through religious feelings and prejudices of the people. The vilest calumnies were constantly veiled against him in the public papers, and the weak minded were afraid to encounter the popular prejudice.

The letter he wrote to General Washington also estranged him from many of his old friends, and has been to his adversaries a fruitful theme of virulent accusation, and a foundation on which to erect a charge of ingratitude and intemperance. It must certainly be confessed that his naturally warm feelings, which could ill brook any slight, particularly where he was conscious he so little deserved it, appear to have led him to form a somewhat precipitated judgment of the conduct of the American president, with regard to his (Mr. Paine's) imprisonment in France, and to attribute to design and wilful neglect what was probably only the result of inattention or perhaps misinformation; and under the influence of this incorrect impression he seems to have indulged, rather too hastily, suspicions of Washington's political conduct with respect to England. But surely some little allowance should be made for the circumstances under which he wrote; just escaped from the horrors of a prison where he had been for several months confined under the sanguinary reign of Robespierre, when death strode incessantly through its cells, and the guillotine floated in the blood of its wretched inhabitants; and if, with the recollection of these scenes of terror fresh in his memory, and impressed with the idea that it was by Washington's neglect that his life had been thus endangered, he may have been betrayed into a style of severity which was perhaps not quite warranted, we can only lament, without attaching blame to either, that any thing jarring should have occurred between two men who were both staunch supporters of the cause of freedom, and thus have given the enemies of liberty occasion to triumph because its advocates were not more than mortal. . . .

Paine was not one of the great men who live amid great events, and forward and share their splendour; he created them; and, in this point of view, he was a very superior character to Washington. . . .

Mr. Paine having ever in his mind the services he had rendered the United States, of whose independence he was the principal author and means, it cannot be matter of wonder that he was deeply hurt and affected at not being recognized and treated by the Americans as he deserved, and as his labours for their benefit merited.

—from *The Life of Thomas Paine* (1819)

RALPH WALDO EMERSON

Each man too is a tyrant in tendency, because he would impose his idea on others; and their trick is their natural defence. Jesus would absorb the race; but Tom Paine or the coarsest blasphemer helps humanity by resisting this exuberance of power.

—from *Essays, Second Series* (1844)

ELKANAH WATSON

In '75 or '76, I was present, at Providence, Rhode Island, in a social assembly of most of the prominent leaders of the State. I recollect, that the subject of independence was cautiously introduced by an ardent Whig; and the thought seemed to excite the abhorrence of the whole circle.

A few weeks after, Paine's *Common Sense* appeared, and passed through the continent, like an electric spark. It everywhere flashed conviction; and aroused a determined spirit, which resulted in the Declaration of Independence, upon the 4th of July ensuing. The name of Paine was precious to every Whig heart, and had resounded throughout Europe.

—from *Men and Times of the Revolution; or, Memoirs of Elkanah Watson, Including His Journals of Travels in Europe and America, from the Year 1777 to 1842, and His Correspondence with Public Men, and Reminiscences and Incidents of the American Revolution* (1856)

ROBERT G. INGERSOLL

In my judgment, Thomas Paine was the best political writer that ever lived. "What he wrote was pure nature, and his soul and his pen ever went together." Ceremony, pageantry, and all the paraphernalia of power, had no effect upon him. He examined into the why and wherefore of things. He was perfectly radical in his mode of thought. Nothing short of the bed-rock satisfied him. His enthusiasm for what he believed to be right knew no bounds. During all the dark scenes of the Revolution, never for one moment did he despair. Year after year his brave words were ringing through the land, and by the bivouac fires the weary soldiers read the inspiring words of *Common Sense*, filled with ideas sharper than their swords, and consecrated themselves anew to the cause of Freedom.

—from *Gods and Other Lectures* (1874)

Questions

1. Is Paine's opposition to institutional religion of a piece with his other ideas? Or does it seem to you a quirk, an irrational prejudice, or something personal?

2. What in these writings by Paine—which ideas, which arguments—should be brought to bear on the current American political scene? Do you see anything in Paine's approach to liberty, government, and rights that we can learn from today?

3. "Its disgusting characteristics are boldness and zeal; low sarcasm and deep-rooted malevolence," said James Cheetham of *Common Sense*. Does anything in *Common Sense*'s ideas or the way it's written disgust you? Where do you think Cheetham was coming from?

4. "Reason" was an important word to Paine. To endorse Reason in Paine's time implied a belief that a national government should be formed by reason and observation—that Reason should rule, rather than tradition, habit, heredity, religious faith, or wealth. Do you see any flaws or negative consequences in such faith in Reason? In the broad area of governance, are there any limits to Reason's positive effects?

FOR FURTHER READING

Writings of Thomas Paine

Foner, Philip S., ed. *The Complete Writings of Thomas Paine.* 2 vols. New York: Citadel Press, 1945.

Biographies

Aldridge, A. Owen. *Man of Reason: The Life of Thomas Paine.* London: Cresset Press, 1960.

Conway, Moncure. *The Life of Thomas Paine.* London: Watts, 1909.

Gimbel, Richard. *Thomas Paine: A Bibliographical Check List of Common Sense, with an Account of Its Publication.* New Haven, CT: Yale University Press, 1956.

Hawke, David Freeman. *Paine.* New York: Harper and Row, 1974.

Philp, Mark. *Paine.* Oxford and New York: Oxford University Press, 1989.

Powell, David. *Tom Paine: The Greatest Exile.* London: Croom Helm, 1985.

Critical Works

Claeys, Gregory. *Thomas Paine: Social and Political Thought.* London and Boston: Unwin Hyman, 1989.

Fennessy, R. R. *Burke, Paine, and the Rights of Man.* The Hague: Martinus Nijhoff, 1963.

Foner, Eric. *Tom Paine and Revolutionary America.* New York: Oxford University Press, 1976.

Fruchtman, Jack, Jr. *Thomas Paine and the Religion of Nature.* Baltimore, MD: Johns Hopkins University Press, 1993.

Books about Revolution

Bailyn, Bernard. *The Ideological Origins of the American Revolution.* Cambridge, MA: Belknap Press of Harvard University Press, 1967.
———. *Faces of Revolution: Personalities and Themes in the Struggle for American Independence.* New York: Alfred A. Knopf, 1990.

Bonwick, Colin. *English Radicals and the American Revolution.* Chapel Hill: University of North Carolina Press, 1977.

Butler, Marilyn, ed. *Burke, Paine, Godwin, and the Revolution Controversy.* Cambridge and New York: Cambridge University Press, 1984.

Elliott, Emory. *Revolutionary Writers: Literature and Authority in the New Republic, 1725–1810.* New York: Oxford University Press, 1982.

Goodwin, Albert. *The Friends of Liberty: The English Democratic Movement in the Age of the French Revolution.* London: Hutchinson, 1979.

Ishay, Micheline. *The History of Human Rights: From Ancient Times to the Globalization Era.* Berkeley: University of California Press, 2004.

Kramnick, Isaac. *Republicanism and Bourgeois Radicalism: Political Ideology in Late Eighteenth-Century England and America.* Ithaca, NY: Cornell University Press, 1990.

Lucas, Stephen E. *Portents of Rebellion: Rhetoric and Revolution in Philadelphia, 1765–1776.* Philadelphia: Temple University Press, 1976.

White, Morton. *The Philosophy of the American Revolution.* New York: Oxford University Press, 1978.